Joan Hessayon was born in Louisville, Kentucky but grew up in Missouri. In 1949 she went to Paris where she met her husband, Dr David Hessayon, the creator of the bestselling *Expert* series of gardening books. They married in 1951 and share a love of history, plants and writing. Joan Hessayon's first novel was published in 1983, *Capel Bells* is her tenth novel. She lives in Hertfordshire and has two daughters and four grandchildren.

CAPEL BELLS

Joan Hessayon

CORGI BOOKS

CAPEL BELLS
A CORGI BOOK: 0 552 14220 4

First publication in Great Britain

PRINTING HISTORY
Corgi edition published 1995

Copyright © Joan Hessayon 1995

The right of Joan Hessayon to be identified as the author
of this work has been asserted in accordance with the
Copyright Designs and Patents Act 1988.

Set in 10/11pt Linotron Bembo by
Falcon Graphic Art Ltd

Corgi Books are published by Transworld Publishers Ltd,
61–63 Uxbridge Road, London W5 5SA,
in Australia by Transworld Publishers (Australia) Pty Ltd,
15–25 Helles Avenue, Moorebank, NSW 2170,
and in New Zealand by Transworld Publishers (NZ) Ltd,
3 William Pickering Drive, Albany, Auckland.

Reproduced, printed and bound in Great Britain by
Cox & Wyman Ltd, Reading, Berks.

This book is for my daughters
Angelina Gibbs and Jacqueline Norris

Foreword

What better place to set a totally fictional story of 1912 than at the actual estate of Capel Manor? After all, the house now known as Capel Manor is, in fact, Capel House. No-one knows for sure where on the property the manor was sited. It was owned for many years by the Warren family, and later by Colonel Medcalf.

The present gardens have been designed for dreaming, since for almost twenty years the property has been the home of the Capel Manor Horticultural College. There are nearly thirty acres of grounds, mainly divided into small plots set out as imaginary back gardens for terraced houses, or for those who are wheel-chair bound or visually impaired. There are gardens for those who don't like gardening and ideas for those who live for their hobby.

So I make no apology for usurping the beautiful old house for my story of floral decorating and gardening folk, nor for creating a totally fictitious garden surrounding it. The idea of writing about Capel Manor was first put to me by the present Principal and Chief Executive, Dr Steve Dowbiggen, although he had something more factual in mind. I am indebted to Steve and his staff for their support.

The neighbourhood is rich in horticultural associations. The great gardening writer, Frances Perry, lived most of her life just a few hundred yards from the estate. It was her idea to turn the empty property into a horticultural college.

Her mentor was Mr E. A. Bowles, the writer, plant hunter and Royal Horticultural Society stalwart. His home, Myddleton House, is about a mile from Capel's front gate. Mr Bowles plays a small part in my story. There is no doubt that he visited Capel Manor on occasion, but I have given him dialogue of my own devising. However, in the scene where he shows guests around his own property, I felt I could not do better than to let him describe it in his own words. My thanks to Brigadier Parker Bowles for permission to quote from *My Garden in Summer*.

Miss Gertrude Jekyll certainly knew Gussie Bowles and visited his home. It is doubtful if she ever saw Capel Manor. I chose to imagine her making a brief visit. Readers who feel I may have misrepresented her views should dip into her book, *Wood and Garden*. She was a product of her time and station.

My thanks to Jack Wilson, fuchsia breeder and creator of 'Capel Bells'.

The Pulhamite grotto that features in the story is actually on the front lawn of the Bath Spa Hotel, where it is insufficiently appreciated by the guests.

I am indebted to the RHS Lindley library staff and in particular to its librarian, Brent Elliot, for the generous use of his remarkable memory and encyclopedic knowledge of gardening history.

Michael Goulding's floral decorating reminiscences were of a later period, needless to say, but I enjoyed them and they gave me a clearer picture of what my Charlotte's business would have been like.

My old friend, Robin Harcourt-Williams, archivist at Hatfield House, was also generous with his time. At the turn of the century, Hatfield had forty-five gardeners, among them Squabby Horn and Dangler Stritch. I have no idea how these men acquired their nicknames, but I couldn't let such wonderful sobriquets fade into obscurity, so I named two of my characters after them.

In order to create the mood of the times, I gave

Charlotte floral decorating ideas which had been recorded over a twenty year period around the turn of the century. My imagination played a very small part in the designs included here, until the final chapter.

The first mention of a house named Theobalds was in 1441. Bought by William Cecil, Lord Burghley, it was completely rebuilt in 1585. In 1607, King James the First exchanged Hatfield House for Theobalds, but during the Commonwealth period, the house was razed for the value of the materials.

In 1762, a new house was built on the estate, and it is this one which can be so clearly seen coming south towards the M25 at Junction 25. Sir Henry Meux came to the house in 1820 and made many changes. The family continued to live in the house until the death of Valerie Susie, Lady Meux in 1910. Her heir, Admiral Sir Hedworth Lambton, who changed his name to Meux, lived there until 1929. Following his death, the house had a varied career as a hotel and school, among other things. Later, it was owned by Enfield Council and was magnificently restored by the Property Services Agency. I am indebted to Rob Tate for taking me on a guided tour as it has recently been sold.

My thanks go to Peggy Holt, and to Constance Barry for her researches on telephones of the period.

Finally, I must thank my husband, Dave Hessayon, not only for his technical advice, but also for his enthusiasm and support. Thanks, too, to my daughter, Angelina Gibbs, for her eagle eyes: much appreciated. And last, but far from least, thank you to my Editor of the Year, Diane Pearson.

Chapter One

'Good afternoon. I am Miss Blair. Have you come to take me to Capel Manor?' The words came out in a whisper; she would have to try again.

It was the stillness that struck her most forcibly. She had been the only passenger to disembark at Cheshunt station on the southern border of Hertfordshire, brushing specks of soot from her costume as she heard the heavy bang of the carriage door, the shout of the station-master and the shrilling of his whistle. By the time she had passed through the gloomy waiting-room, the train was gone. She stood alone on the forecourt, the absence of sound enveloping her like a swansdown cloak. Such tranquillity as this was unnerving to a London-bred girl.

As promised, he was there with the fly, the only person in sight, standing by the horse's head. She noticed the green gardener's apron, the dusty bowler hat, the buttoned waistcoat and loop of watch chain. She supposed there would be a razor-sharp pruning knife in his apron pocket and probably a length of twine, and in his head a lifetime's knowledge of the eccentricities of every garden plant.

'I say! Good afternoon! I am Miss Charlotte Blair. Have you come to take me to Capel Manor?'

He started, turned his head and waved her to the fly. 'Yes, ma'am. Mrs Gryce sent me.'

There was a door at the rear and two wooden seats running the length of it. Lifting her skirt to expose her black patent leather bottines with two buttons missing, she took a seat, drawing in her knees so that he could squeeze in opposite her. He sat down and looked straight ahead.

The straw boater sat lightly on her gleaming blond hair, offering no shade to her fair skin. Blue eyes beneath arched eyebrows gave her a deceptive look of fragility, but nervousness had stiffened her pretty mouth into an uncompromising slit.

Almost as unaccustomed to speaking to servants as she was to their masters, she didn't know how to pitch her conversation with the gardener. 'I saw a great many glasshouses from the train,' she said as they left the small sweep drive of the railway station.

'Rochford's houses are in Cheshunt, but you wouldn't have seen them from the train.'

'Fine growers, the Rochfords. Their palms and orchids are famous.'

How do you do, Mrs Gryce, she thought, practising the vital first moments of her meeting. *I am . . .*

'Stuart Low in Enfield.'

'Yes?'

'Rose grower, not far from here.'

'I see,' said Charlotte. 'And you are?'

'John Green, head gardener of Capel Manor.'

She studied him as he held the reins. The bowler sat low on his head, resting on his thick eyebrows, extending the tips of his ears outward. The skin around his eyes was creased from years of squinting against the sun. She couldn't tell what sort of mouth he had since it was hidden entirely by a huge, straggly moustache which was urgently in need of trimming. His nails were grimy and bitten below the pad of his fingers, and his cheeks were ruddy and wind-whipped. Nevertheless, she wasn't fooled into misjudging his age. John Green, head gardener of Capel Manor, was very young to hold such an important position. He could not be much older than she was.

They turned down a narrow road with red brick

houses on either side, sitting smugly behind their clipped hedges. There was no-one about, not so much as a nurse wheeling a pram. Half an hour earlier, Charlotte had boarded the train at Liverpool Street station in the sooty air of the City, deafened by the cries of unhappy children, the whine of beggars, the scolding of irritated mothers and the bellows of station staff. Fifteen miles north of this cacophony, the outer reaches of Enfield were a paradise of leafy trees and empty roads. She had not seen a single motor car. Judging by the state of the roads, there weren't even many horses in the vicinity. Not long now.

How do you do, Mrs Gryce. I am Miss Blair and . . . Charlotte moistened her lips and ran a smoothing hand over the blue serge skirt. Her mother, an elegant woman even during the times when they were reduced to bread and milk for supper, had often lectured Charlotte on her style of dress, or rather her lack of style. 'Why can't you show some flair?' she used to say. 'You put on the first thing that comes to hand, mix old with new, pin what you can't be bothered to sew, and top off the entire ensemble with a dozen cheap necklaces.'

So on this day, Charlotte had left her tawdry but much-loved collection of necklaces in their box, and was wearing a navy costume and yellowing high-collared shirt that had been laid away carefully in mothballs the day after her mother died, nearly two years ago. Maud Blair had been larger around the waist than her daughter, so Charlotte had been forced to cinch the skirt with safety pins and an old belt. She felt most uncomfortable in such alien attire, like an actress playing a part.

How do you do, Mrs Gryce. I . . .

The gardener cleared his throat and pointed with his whip. 'Blue hydrangeas. I suppose you have heard of hydrangeas.'

'Mr Green, have I offended you in some way?'

'Offended me? Good Lord, no! Just because Mrs Gryce sent for you when I've been doing the flowers for the house for months, why should I be offended? The old lady used to like the way I arranged the flowers. I could make an arrangement with a star in the middle and rows of different flowers in circles around the star, and every flower was so neatly lying against its neighbour, you couldn't see the sand they was set in. I've kept that house supplied with aspidistras and ferns and palms for the last eighteen months. One time I had the dinner table looking like an oasis. Big palms and little palms – two dozen of them. You've never seen the like. But I'm not offended she sent for you. Oh, no!'

Charlotte had grown up among the porters, street sellers and hauliers of Covent Garden; no amount of male anger frightened her, and she could give as good as she got if the situation warranted it. But this was different. She would need the gardener's co-operation, would depend on his contribution of plants and foliage and his good strong back to keep down her costs.

'I'm sure you do splendid work. Mr and Mrs Gryce must be fortunate to have you. Many head gardeners have no flair for floral decoration. It's just this one occasion, you know. I was invited by Mrs Gryce to do the flowers for their sixtieth wedding anniversary celebrations, and I was recommended by Lady Smythe. A busy man like you wouldn't have the time for so much extra work, nor would you be able to obtain the foreign flowers and all the foliage necessary. I work in King Street, a stone's throw from Covent Garden market. I can get exotic blooms at keen prices. I'm sorry if you are offended, but just this once Mr and Mrs Gryce want to make a splash.'

His lower lip protruded, giving him the look of a sulky schoolboy. 'I warn you, I'm not letting this go without a fight. I've got staff what could turn to and help me. What's more, don't think you're going to get any help from me and my men. All that money going to waste.'

'Look, Mr Green!' snapped Charlotte, and her carefully correct vowel sounds, so painstakingly learned, were completely forgotten. 'It's not for you to say who's to do things. You mind your pea sticks and potting sheds. I'll attend to the flowers, and I'll do it for a fair price. Not the way the great Mr Felton charges, of course; he's very expensive. He once used eighteen tons of ivy at the Mansion House for a ball, and just last week there was a grand affair in Aberdeen where the floral decorator charged fourteen hundred pounds, no less.'

He lapsed into a furious silence. *Oh, dear,* she thought. *Why am I always my own worst enemy? I wish I could just keep control of my temper now and again!*

She tried to compose herself for her meeting with Mrs Gryce. This was her most important commission since opening her own florist shop. In September of 1911, she reckoned there couldn't be more than a few thousand women who had their own businesses. She was proud of her achievement, in spite of the fact that her shop had made only a little more than one hundred pounds profit in twelve months of trading. She was independent, mistress of her own fortunes and answerable to no man. Less interested in having the vote than in being able to support herself, she worked fourteen hours a day, which left no time at all for a rewarding social life, and she knew that she worked her sixteen-year-old assistant, Molly, far too hard. The commission at Capel Manor was to be the turning point for her business, the turning point of her life. Wealth, recognition and success were just around the corner. And she had just endangered the whole thing by quarrelling with the head gardener, who could damage the entire enterprise if he chose.

They turned onto a broad, tree-lined road. 'Bullsmoor Lane,' he said. 'Them's the gates of Capel Manor.'

She scarcely had time to notice the poor condition of the stone coping on the gateposts, the paint peeling from the wrought-iron gates, before the horse was trotting down the broad drive, and the stables and outbuildings were in sight. The drive swept to the left between empty paddocks. They passed a few yards of walling about six feet high, and there before them stood a handsome country house basking in the September sunshine, a perfect gem that had never been tampered with by unsympathetic owners.

Yet it was not the grand mansion – not a Hatfield House or Syon Park – that she had been expecting. There was no attempt to impress, no pomposity about the Manor. It had been built with care, lovingly tended through several centuries, a house for living in comfortably, not for making the reputation of a young floral decorator.

'That's Capel Manor? I thought it was a huge estate of two hundred acres, thirty-five bedrooms, a menagerie and an Egyptian museum. I heard they even brought out one of the old gates of the City of London to use as an entrance.'

It was John Green's moment of triumph. 'The old gate is called Temple Bar and was removed to be the entrance gate of the estate, Theobalds Park, over that way. The present house is on the site of what used to be called Tibbalds, the home of James the First. It has a common border with ours, but there ain't much else that's the same. We've got thirty acres here. Lady Meux – you know, Meux beer – used to own it, but she passed away. Admiral Sir Hedworth Meux owns it now. I reckon if he wanted a floral decorator to do up his place, he'd get Mr Feltham—'

'Felton.'

'One of them fancy types like Mr Felton,' he corrected himself. 'Why they might be something special, might be worth sending for. I daresay Mr Felton's got his own nursery, too. But you! Who's ever heard of you, when all's said and done? You ain't nobody. So I could do the flowers for the anniversary party. Why should an old couple like Mr and Mrs Gryce want to be fashionable? Lady Smythe recommended you? She's been to Capel a few times. On the fringes of society, she is. Not top quality at all. The Admiral wouldn't choose some scrap of a girl like you.'

'Capel Manor is charming. It must be all of two hundred years old. I was misinformed, that's all. I'm not the least disappointed, I assure you.'

This was a lie and he knew it. 'Mrs Gryce told me the party is to be on the south lawn, here in front of the house,' he said, helping her out of the dog cart. 'You can be sure that on the great day I'll have that lawn mown and rolled just perfect. You won't find no rabbit holes to go falling into. I just hope that when the party's over, there's something of my lawn left.'

'There is bound to be some damage done,' she said. 'I'm to hire a large marquee to hold a hundred people for afternoon tea. Then I must obtain a bandstand. The bandsmen will be trampling on your lawn with their big feet. I'll have pots of cinerarias and geraniums at the entrance to the marquee. Some trellis work, of course. Swags across the front of the top table and up the tent posts, arrangements on the tables. It would be far too much work for you. My assistant and I will be working on nothing else for ten days or more before the big event.'

Without waiting for his reaction to her plans, she entered the small porch with its white wooden classical columns, and rapped the knocker against the brass plate. The palms of her hands were wet inside the brown cloth gloves. She wished her heart was not beating quite so frantically as she straightened her tie. The late summer air was warm and still. To her left, a pair of copper beeches stretched into the clear sky, their dark red leaves brilliant against the uncluttered blue. Ivy clung to the walls of the house, a lovely contrast between the green of the leaves and the rich redness of the old, imperfect bricks.

The elderly woman who opened the door had thin white hair drawn loosely into a bun on the crown of her head. Her black gown was silky and fussy with tucks and frills – a dress that had been the height of fashion twenty years earlier.

'Mrs Gryce? I am—'

'Certainly not! I am Mrs Snodsby, the housekeeper. I presume you are the young person who is to do the floral decorating. You are to study the dining-room and the drawing-room carefully, visit the glasshouses and speak to the head gardener. You are to make a plan of the south lawn and calculate the approximate cost. Then, when you are quite prepared, Mrs Gryce will speak to you briefly. Mr Gryce is not at all well and Mrs Gryce is sitting with him.' Having seen Charlotte into the lobby, and looking her most carefully up and down, she indicated the direction of the two rooms and left her alone.

The front door led directly into a handsome hallway lit by two tall sash windows. Charlotte drew in her breath with pleasure. Oak panelling, polished floorboards, a brilliantly patterned round rug with a fringed edge and an old-fashioned gate-legged table were the main furnishings. There was a pungent smell of beeswax. An orange, yellow and brown vase of simple design stood on the table, and there were a few portraits hung from the picture rail. Capel Manor was lived in and loved, a real home, not a statement of wealth and position. She looked forward to decorating it for such a happy occasion. How remarkable that two people had been married for sixty years.

The front door led into the far right-hand corner of the entrance hall, and the dining-room was immediately to the right of the front door. Apparently, the staircase was directly ahead, but hidden behind a door. Nothing dramatic could be made of a staircase so placed, so there was no need to waste time and money on swags of greenery.

Like the hall, the dining-room faced due south and was lit by a row of sash windows. The room was rich yet bright with its oak-panelled walls and long refectory table. The fireplace was at the far end. Only ten people were to have lunch in the dining-room; a cold collation, she had been told. Charlotte decided that an Ellen Terry stand would be perfect for the middle of the table. This new type of flower container consisted of a bowl at the base with ample space for arranging flowers around the central post, which then rose a full twenty-four inches and was topped by another bowl to take a really spectacular arrangement of flowers. The stand was the invention of the great decorator, Mr Felton of Hanover Square, and had cost Charlotte more than she wished to pay, but it was perfect for professional work. By filling the top bowl with moss, well wired in, she could insert several dozen carnations on eighteen-inch stems and let them arch over the diners' heads. She would need seven or nine specimen vases (never an even number) which could be placed on the cloth. They might hold a few sprays of orchids or other exceptional blooms, the only rule being that the vases must not be arranged in straight lines. Finally, trails of asparagus fern would snake directly across the cloth in a graceful manner.

The drawing-room was at the other end of the house, and faced north. A William Morris paper of autumn leaves, a rather gloomy choice for a north-facing room, had been laid above the chair rail, and the fireplace sat in an inglenook at the far end. She decided she could make festoons of box and French myrtle, and crisscross them from the picture rail over the entire room – an expensive and time-consuming decoration, but very effective.

After walking over the south lawn and deciding where to have the marquee erected, Charlotte walked around to the side of the house and entered the walled garden with its fruit trees neatly fanned against the walls and its ground marked out in geometric patterns, each segment containing a vegetable or salading. Several glasshouses sweated in the heat, their ventilators wide open. A lean-to glasshouse, forty or fifty feet long, rested against the ten-foot-high south wall. Charlotte found John Green at the far end of it. The house had a narrow path tiled in an intricate pattern of black, white and terracotta, which had just been watered down. The air was hot and damp, catching at the throat.

'Mr Green, what a splendid house!' She ignored his sulky shrug of the shoulders and approached him with a smile, waiting until he finally lifted a hand in a sign of submission to show their quarrel was over. 'I forgot to say that I will, of course, need your expert help in making the day a special one for Mr and Mrs Gryce. I need hardly tell you that I expect to pay for your services. Will half a crown be satisfactory?'

He stared at his feet, probably wishing he could bear to pass up so much money. 'That'll do. You'll want to see what I have that could be used, I suppose. I've got plenty of asparagus fern, smilax, that sort of thing. A few pots of montbretia, but I don't suppose you'll want yellows and oranges.'

'No, I think not. Palms? Ferns?'

He nodded and led her into another house where she made notes of numbers and types of plants, noticing that there were a few dozen palms of a suitable size. She had been mistaken in supposing that the head gardener had insufficient material at his disposal. The kitchen garden had a large bed devoted to flowers for cutting. Smilax and asparagus fern grew in profusion in the houses, and the grounds were probably overflowing with laurel, huge fern fronds and miles of ivy just waiting to be cut. John Green could very well have produced an acceptable display, therefore she must rack her brains to find a scheme so new and so daringly beautiful that the Gryces would feel justified in paying her.

She was not certain exactly what scheme to use. Indecision was not one of Charlotte's faults, but this commission was so important that she was almost incapable of a coherent thought. And Mrs Gryce expected to be given some rough sketches and a price within the next half hour!

'I've a lot of fuchsias. I love fuchsias. Breed my own. I've got something special coming along. Want to see them?'

Fuchsias were not good for cutting, their stems being

too short for tall arrangements, and she hadn't thought of including them in pots. However, John Green sounded considerably more friendly when talking about his favourite flower, so she said she would love to see them.

The fuchsia house was empty at this time of year, as all the plants had been put into their summer homes, be they baskets, stone pots or formal beds. Those that had not been needed stood in pots outside the house, their blooms dazzling in the late summer sunshine. She recognized 'Amy Lye' with its greenish-white tube and sepals and coral corolla, and the new 'Alice Hoffman' with the colouring in reverse: pink tube and sepals and white corolla. The others were unknown to her. There was never enough time to learn about every flower. Charlotte memorized the names of the best varieties of those flowers she needed in her work and had never bothered to learn about the rest. She spoke enthusiastically about fuchsias and praised the skill of the grower. John Green, a simple man, began to warm to her.

After a few minutes, they were joined by Jacko Boon who was introduced as foreman of the leisure gardens. It would be Mr Boon and his staff who would prepare the lawn, cut whatever she needed and move the heavy pots into place. Charlotte studied the man carefully. He was small, around thirty years old, with a very quiet way of speaking and a shock of bright yellow hair that was neatly greased into submission before being parted in the middle and half hidden by a cloth cap.

As Mr Green leaned against the staging, Jacko Boon made several suggestions about where she might hire extra plants locally, how she might purchase roses from Stuart Low Nurseries (thus cutting out the salesmen at the market), and he even suggested that he should help her in her work by fetching what was needed on the day and seeing to it that his improver journeyman and a boy were on hand to help.

'Your assistant is a girl, you say? Well, Miss Blair,

you won't want to be struggling with the heavy work, will you? I'll take care of all that.'

She nodded to him solemnly, indicating that he, too, would be rewarded, although she had no intention of giving him half a crown!

'And do you like fuchsias, Mr Boon?' Charlotte asked. 'This is certainly a fine display.'

'No, ma'am. Mr Green tends to all the fuchsias himself. He's the master here. I don't care for them. A bit old-fashioned. The old queen probably liked them, and you used to find them as standards in every garden in the country at one time. Well, we've got them here, but Mrs Gryce won't have them in the house. She don't like them.'

Charlotte wondered if Mrs Gryce knew how much space under glass was being taken up by a flower she didn't like, and changed her mind about having a display of fuchsias leading to the front door.

Her notebook was full, and she had swallowed a mug of strong sweet tea brewed by Jacko Boon's improver journeyman, a cheerful fellow in his late forties mysteriously named Squabby Horn, when a maid came in search of her to say that Madam would like to see her.

They entered through the kitchen door on the side of the house. The housekeeper was waiting for her in the hall. 'If you will go into the morning-room, that door directly opposite the front door, Mrs Gryce will join you in a moment.'

Entering the morning-room, which faced north, was like stepping back to Queen Victoria's youth. All the walls were hung with pictures, every surface was covered with ornaments. The chairs were comfortable but had seen better days, and the muslin summer curtains still hung limply by the open windows. Photographs of several generations of Gryces were crowded together on every table top.

Charlotte moved restlessly about the room, picking up a miniature china teapot with the words 'souvenir of

Margate' and setting it down beside a Toby jug with the face of a tinker. She read the religious sayings which were neatly printed on thick card and hung from every spare hook on the walls. She studied the two watercolours of lotuses, done in the snaky Art Nouveau tradition, that were prominently signed by one Matthew Warrender.

'Thinks well of himself,' she murmured. 'More conceit than talent.' And suddenly everything came together in her mind. She knew what sort of decorations Mrs Gryce would prefer. Deepest purple, through the delicate shades of lavender and mauve to brilliant white. Heliotrope, lavender, violets, orchids by the score. What a perfect colour scheme for an elderly couple! *Auratum* lilies were five shillings a bunch at this time of year, and must certainly be a part of her scheme. *Cattleya* orchids were twelve shillings a dozen, but *Odontoglossums* were just three to four shillings. All orchids looked expensive, even if they weren't. Charlotte scribbled in her notebook, made a few calculations in the margins. She would use the cheaper ones, yet achieve the desired sense of richness: lavender silk runners on every table, an orchid tucked into each napkin. The sketches she had prepared did not indicate varieties or colours; there was no need to draw completely new plans. But how she would sell her ideas to the old lady! Two hundred and fifty pounds was a nice round figure. The lilies and orchids would cost about seventy pounds. She could save on smilax, twopence a trail at the market, but free by courtesy of Mr Green. Several gross of lily of the valley would scent the air, while she could keep the cost down by using as much from Capel's garden and glasshouses as possible.

Mr Felton would certainly charge more than two hundred and fifty pounds, but she didn't dare to add on too much for profit. She had decided early in her career to calculate the cost of the flowers and charge three times as much. A certain person might tell her that this was too simple a way to calculate her charges. She was, for instance, ignoring labour, rent, rates and heating charges in her calculations. She thought she was doing well enough and need not change her methods.

She looked at the decaying bulrushes plunged into a tankard like rusting spears and a vase of once-fluffy dried grasses now covered in dust, and thought of the colour and freshness and originality she would bring to Capel Manor. The old house would not be the same after she had left her mark. No longer would Mrs Gryce be satisfied with a *Weddeliana* palm in the corner. She would want high style. Her friends would be so dazzled that everyone would demand Charlotte's address. Now, a certain person would recognize how daring and foresighted she had been in having a telephone installed! The telephone line would sing with orders and—

There was a scream from somewhere, most likely on the staircase. Charlotte clutched her notebook and handbag and hurried into the hall. There was no-one in sight, but the wailing continued, louder still. She opened the door leading to the staircase and was in time to see the maid running up the stairs two at a time.

'Hurry!' cried the housekeeper from somewhere above.

Another maid appeared and nearly knocked Charlotte to the ground in her eagerness to get up the stairs. There was no mistaking the sound: it was the desperate cry of an elderly woman counterpointed by the soothing tones of the housekeeper. A moment's hush, then more high-pitched jabbering. The second maid came down the stairs, glaring at Charlotte.

'The master's passed away! I must send for the doctor. There will be no anniversary celebrations now. Mrs Snodsby says you are to go away immediately.'

The maid went on towards the kitchen door as Charlotte stood perfectly still at the foot of the stairs. She could scarcely comprehend what had happened.

The death of an unseen old man reminded her of the loss of her mother. The pain was still raw, the sound of Mrs Gryce's agony an echo of her own. Charlotte pitied her, but couldn't enter fully into the tragedy. Her thoughts were for herself. In the space of a minute or two, all her hopes for the future were dashed. She couldn't feel deeply about the passing of the man, only about the death of her dream. Nor could she expect Lady Smythe to recommend her work to anyone else. 'Good fortune', her mother used to say, 'happens rarely; chances must be seized or lost for ever.' Capel Manor, which she had come to love in less than an hour, would never welcome her again. It was over.

Grieving for her lost hopes, she let herself out of the front door and, finding no-one about, walked quickly to the railway station. Her greatest opportunity for advancement had come and gone within twenty-four hours.

Chapter Two

When Charlotte returned to London, she told Molly that the Capel Manor commission had been cancelled, and Molly's disappointment was all that she could have wished. There was no-one else who would have cared one way or another, so she kept her grief to herself.

For many years she had been a poorly paid employee of Ingamells, Forster and Robins, who were commission salesmen with large premises in the Flower Market on Tavistock Street. The work was hard, requiring much lifting and a deaf ear to the rough teasing of the male employees. It grieved her that the firm would never allow her to have her own book, to take orders in her own name.

When she was twenty, she had a stroke of luck, one of those moments her mother warned her must be taken with both hands. Mr Goodenough, who rented the shop below the rooms she shared with her mother, offered her eight shillings a week to help him in his florist shop and learn the business. He was in his late sixties, a shy bachelor who didn't know how to speak a word of encouraging praise. She was, nevertheless, quick to learn and loved her work. When he died in the autumn of 1910, he left her his 'goods and chattels' in his will. She was a woman of substance.

With great daring, she approached an old friend and borrowed fifty pounds. A new lease had to be negotiated from the agent of the Duke of Bedford. A new sign needed to be painted: C. A. BLAIR, FLORIST. The sight of it always gave her a tingle of pride.

Mr Goodenough had been happy to do just enough business to feed and clothe himself, but Charlotte had more ambitious ideas. A visit to the great florists of London taught her much. Every one of them had a telephone. Moyses Stevens had two telephone lines. Edward Goodyear was court florist by special appointment to H M the King. Taviners had been established in 1868. Mr Felton had written a book about floral decorating, and had arranged the flowers for visiting Japanese royalty.

Most of them had photographs or drawings of the funeral wreaths, crosses and floral open Bibles which they shipped all over the country, and could provide photographic proof of their many commissions in palaces, churches and public occasions abroad.

Charlotte Blair, established in 1911, had no telephone, was by appointment to no-one and had an unfashionable address. Pretending to be interested in commissioning some work from these gods of the floral decorating fraternity, she readily collected a selection of photographs and drawings, with notations about prices. Yet something more was needed, so she bought a gallon of paint, and with her own hands painted the framework of the shop's bow window in a bright pink. Or rather, she nearly managed to paint the whole frame pink, before the Duke's agent discovered what she was up to and threatened eviction if she didn't paint it over. Another gallon of paint, this time sober green, soothed his sensibilities, but she knew she had tested his patience to the full. He had not been keen to lease the property to a young woman in the first place.

Thwarted of her colourful approach, she gathered up her courage and spent the last of her loan in having a telephone installed by the National Telephone Company. Her banker did not hesitate to call her a fool. On most days, she was certain she had been right to invest in one. The number was printed on her business cards: 3111 City. Lady Smythe, having taken a card from her at the flower show where they met, had telephoned her commission. Mrs Gryce's French maid had telephoned, having obtained the number from Lady Smythe. Charlotte knew that the instrument had not recovered its cost, but its occasional ring never failed to impress the customers in the shop as they chose their shilling bunches of flowers to take home.

The most painful lesson she had learned was that no supplier would extend credit, not even those firms with which Mr Goodenough had done business for decades. She was burdened by the fifty pound loan which she had promised to repay within twelve months. Although she had to pay for everything at the time of purchase, she was often not paid by her customers until the end of the month, or even the end of the quarter. Having committed herself in several directions, she was able to save money only on food and fuel. In the first six months, she lost twelve pounds in weight, while repaying twenty-five pounds of her loan.

Fortunately, business looked up. When old Mr Robins died suddenly, Charlotte sold seven half-crown wreaths, two lily of the valley crosses. When Mrs Robins ordered a Gates of Heaven, Charlotte supplied it free of charge as a mark of respect for a man who had helped her greatly. Such large funerals naturally drew attention to her work.

During the second six months she had the help of Molly. First, of course, she had to train the girl. Molly was neat and quick-fingered, but she had no flair. She quickly learned to make up the gum arabic that had to be dabbed with precision into the centre of a flower to keep it open, or used to touch up the calyx so that the bloom didn't part company with the stem before the customer had paid for the arrangement. This quick, willing help freed Charlotte to create interesting table designs with which she entered numerous flower competitions. It was at a north London flower show, just after she had won first prize for a design employing only orchids, that she first met Lady Smythe.

Molly was Charlotte's greatest admirer. How she had gasped when Charlotte sketched her plan for a little girl's fifth birthday party!

Fanny Walgrave lived in a mid-Victorian semi-detached house off the Strand, the spoiled daughter of a stock jobber who had five older sons. Charlotte constructed a wire frame to be set over and behind the dining chair of the birthday girl. One Sunday, she scoured the deserted acres of Epping Forest and carried home a huge bundle of ivy to cover the frame. This bower was then interlaced with three dozen pink carnations to make a throne for Fanny, bringing exclamations of delight from her mother.

Charlotte later heard that little Fanny and her thirty guests fought lustily for the privilege of sitting in the bower, and that they soon had it torn to shreds. Mrs Walgrave, however, had been very pleased with the flowers and now made all her flower purchases from C. A. Blair. The success of the floral bower fired her ambition. No longer satisfied with funeral work and the occasional birthday party, Charlotte longed for grand commissions where her growing skills and creative imagination could be fully stretched.

But that was months ago. There had been no opportunity to show what she was capable of since then. One day, several weeks after the visit to Capel Manor, she happened to pick up a discarded copy of *The Times* in a coffee shop. Reports about the continuing trouble in the Balkans, and Mr Churchill's appointment as First Lord of the Admiralty, didn't interest her, but the obituary column did. Mrs Gryce, probably heart-broken by the death of her dear husband, had followed him to the grave.

Perhaps the new owner would ask her to arrange

flowers at Capel Manor. Molly was serving a customer when Charlotte returned to the shop, but she pushed past him without a greeting, and reached for the telephone that hung on the wall. Mrs Snodsby answered on the third ring. She was reluctant to speak to Charlotte, but in the face of relentless questioning finally said that the house had been inherited by Mr Matthew Warrender, the son of the Gryce's only daughter. Charlotte needn't think she would get any business from him, because Mr Warrender lived abroad and was not expected home in the near future. Furthermore, he had ordered the house to be put up for rent, but there were no takers. Shortly before Christmas, Mrs Snodsby would be off to a cottage bought for her by Mr Gryce. The French maid had already taken up a new appointment. No-one knew what was to happen to the remainder of the staff, but they most definitely did not need a floral decorator.

Undaunted by the housekeeper's rudeness, Charlotte hung up and leant her head against the telephone box. The house was empty! Those lofty rooms, the stillness, the scents of late summer flowers mingling with beeswax, and no-one to appreciate them. The house was empty. As she stood in the shop with her eyes closed, breathing in the icy perfume of violets, heliotrope and lily of the valley, a plan began to form in her head – dangerous, wild and irresistible.

'I'm going upstairs,' she said to Molly.

Ten steep steps brought her to the door of the little flat. Her father had painted the door blue six weeks before he died. In the last fifteen years, no-one had considered giving it a fresh coat. Gathered gingham curtains, crisp and clean but skimpy, hung on a cord in front of the only window. Pushed against the wall were a small kitchen table covered in oil cloth, and two rickety chairs. The easy chair by the fire had wooden arms and frayed upholstery. In the bedroom, which was scarcely bigger than a cupboard, her bed sagged. Worst of all, on a hot summer's day, she could smell the privy in the yard from her bedroom window. This was the only home Charlotte had ever known; the rent was cheap, but it was time to move.

She looked up at the sitting-room ceiling where the faint signs of wheel marks still travelled for a short distance across the yellowing paint work. Those wheel marks embodied her philosophy of life.

She had been five years old. Her father had made a crude tricycle for her from scavenged materials. Normally, she rode it along the pavement in front of the building, but on this day Mum and Dad had a visitor, Vic Tavern, a young neighbour.

'I want to ride on the ceiling, Dada,' she had said, pulling at her parent's coat. 'Hold me up so's I can ride on the ceiling.'

Her father, a wiry man in his late fifties, glared down at her in surprise. 'Stop it, stupid girl. You can't ride on the ceiling. Nobody can. It ain't possible. Besides, I wouldn't have the strength, nor I'm not tall enough to reach.'

Charlotte continued to nag, her most unfortunate trait as a child. 'Here,' said Vic Tavern, standing up and knocking the glowing ash from the end of his cigarette. He placed the cigarette behind his ear and somehow managed for a few seconds to hold both child and tricycle to the ceiling.

'Look at them marks!' her mother had cried. 'For God's sake, put her down, Vic. Haven't you any sense?'

Vic did put her down. His face was red from the effort and he was breathing hard, but he wore a triumphant look. 'I've got sense, Maud. You bet I've got sense. There ain't nothing a person can't do but what they makes up their minds to do it. Charlotte rode on the ceiling. Nobody else has ever done it. She's special. You keep aiming to do the impossible, my girl. You may grow up to achieve something worth doing.'

Charlotte had been given a lesson in life she had

never forgotten. There was no shame in aiming for the impossible. And yet she hadn't enjoyed having her dream fulfilled. It had been uncomfortable and a little frightening. Therefore, the child had often wondered, should one aim for the impossible, even though reaching one's goal was strange and worrying?

A flick through her accounts book, a few moments of careful thought, and she negotiated the dark steps once more to reach the telephone. She spent a frustrating few minutes on the instrument, making several trunk calls at threepence each, but the result was the telephone number of a lawyer in Enfield who was known to be handling the leasing of Capel Manor.

Charlotte wanted six months to attempt to reach her impossible goal, to live in splendour, to experience luxury and enviable standards of beauty and cleanliness while taking her business to new heights. Even if she had to go hungry again, she would live in Capel Manor.

Upstairs, she had decided that she could afford her dream, but she soon discovered that there were three huge obstacles to overcome. The agent would not rent for less than eighteen months, he wanted all the money paid in advance, and the sum was four hundred and twenty pounds. This was three times the amount that she had imagined it would be for a year and a half. Capel Manor was beyond her grasp, after all.

Or perhaps not. She would have her dream. Taking pencil and paper, she sat down at the old kitchen table and began making calculations. She could only guess at future difficulties, since her business experience was limited. Yet she must try to anticipate every difficulty. Some surprises could be fatal for a business. That night she went to bed feeling very depressed, but awoke in the morning, having found the one ingredient necessary for success: faith in herself. Copying her notations in ink on clean paper in a neat hand, she gathered them together in order of importance, rehearsing her opening speech like a barrister going into court.

The next step was to visit her banker, Vic Tavern, pawnbroker of King Street, Covent Garden. When she was a child, she had happily received gifts of a substantial nature from Vic. Yet, as an adult, she had found him unpredictable. He had readily advanced her that first fifty pounds, refusing to take any interest. He had laughed at the pink paint, which in truth had been a piece of folly, but had roared like a bull when he saw the telephone.

He had no time for telephones, he said, they were an unnecessary expense. For the price of a telephone call, you could pay a boy to deliver your message. Better to put twenty quid on a hopeless nag, because that way there would be just a chance of getting one's money back. The telephone company was manned by rogues. You paid to have the instrument installed, then you paid again when you made a call. As if that weren't bad enough, most likely the person you urgently wished to contact didn't have one. Vic, who many times had lost twenty pounds on a horse, never let her forget the foolishness of installing a telephone in a florist's shop.

The story of his life was a fascinating one, and she had heard it often as a child. He had been born forty-odd years before in one of the nastier back alleys in Whitechapel, and never knew his father. By the time he was old enough to take notice of such things, his mother was addled from the gin. Her drunkenness had offended Vic's memory of her more than the fact that she neglected her three children by three different fathers, none of whom had stayed around long enough to help financially. He was the eldest, old far beyond his years at eight, when he first took charge of the family. He began to regulate his mother's drinking as best he could, managed the few coppers she got from begging and within a year began to make a real difference to their income by running errands for people and making deliveries; but mostly – and here Vic would pause for dramatic effect – by stealing. He was quick and bold, but at the great age of twelve his nerve failed him as he began to understand the penalties for being caught.

'Neither of me sisters appreciated what I done for them. They stood around on street corners with me mum, looking all pathetic and hungry, and they got a few coppers that way. Real money came from me, though.'

Charlotte could remember visiting Vic as a child, sitting in the small room at the back of his shop, her nostrils filled with the sour smell of dirty clothing, some of which he hung outside on hooks to tempt the customers. His window was filled with unclaimed items from top to bottom, and you could buy a pair of boots with holes in both soles for a penny.

He was tall, dark and rather handsome despite his impressive nose, which had been broken a few times, a man who dressed splendidly in the evenings when he went out on the town. Most of the time, however, he shuffled around in old clothes so that the customers wouldn't guess he was getting rich on their misery. She used to love hearing about his early days before he came to Covent Garden.

He assured her (and she believed him) that he was exceptional in his family because he could read and because he found sums easy. At thirteen, he went to work for a nearby pawnbroker. The work had been simple enough, sweeping the floor, stacking the pawned items in the warehouse at the back and sleeping as best he could under the counter at night.

Soon he was accepting the pawned items, listing them in the big ledger, making out the two tickets, one for the customer, one to be attached to the pawned object, taking the unclaimed goods, and those which the pawnbroker had bought outright, to the auction house. He received one and sixpence a week and gave tenpence to his family. At fifteen, he left home for good.

'You don't know you're born,' he used to say to

her, an expression that left her rather confused. 'Things are tough for really poor people. On Monday morning, the women come in with the children's Sunday best clothes, their husband's best suit, perhaps the whole of the week's washing, neatly ironed and stacked. In return, they receive a few shillings to buy food and fuel for the week. On Saturday night, everything is redeemed for use during the weekend. You see, the way pawnshops work is, the interest is calculated by the month. The folks my gaffer dealt with redeemed their possessions every week, but they still had to pay the monthly interest rate. When I got smart enough to think things through, I calculated that it works out at an annual rate of six-hundred and fifty per cent.'

Charlotte's family had been poor. Her father was a porter in the market. Her mother, who was an actress and a trifle grander, had occasionally been called for small parts in the nearby theatres, getting more work in her late fifties than she had when she was younger. But the family had never been reduced to pawning their clothing. They were almost always reasonably warm and adequately fed, even after her father died. For a time, when she was very young, Charlotte had also trodden the boards. The theatre had saved her and her mother from the worst sort of poverty, but she had no hankering for the glamour of the stage, nor for the uncertainty of the work.

She stepped over the rotting doorstep and entered the large shop, waved a hand at Billy Tavern, Vic's natural son, and headed for the back room. She found her oldest friend seated by a small fire, holding a Woodbine between thumb and first finger, as if to keep it from being discovered. His upstairs rooms held ranks of paper-wrapped parcels, waiting for their owners to redeem them. There was no kipping down above the shop for Vic and Billy. They lived in a decent, if small, terraced house off the Strand.

'Sit yourself down, Charlotte. You're looking very

pretty today, but I hate to see a lovely thing like you wearing them blue serge two-piece things. And a tie! You look like a bleeding suffragette. You ought never to have left the theatre. You could've been another Marie Lloyd. Better legs, too.'

'I can't carry a tune, Vic. Never mind that.' She sat down opposite him. 'I was never any good, and didn't get enough work to keep a flea alive. I'm doing pretty well with my business. So well, in fact, that I'm thinking of moving to a country estate. Thirty acres, and greenhouses to supply my needs. It's in Enfield, right north on the Hertfordshire border.'

'Oh, yes.' He squeezed out the lit end of his cigarette with calloused fingers and stood up, the better to glare at her. 'And who, might I ask, is setting you up?'

'You are.' She gave him her cheekiest grin, but he frowned at her so fiercely that the smile froze on her face. 'Come on, Vic. I can rent it for eighteen months for four hundred and twenty pounds.'

'*What?* You could buy a neat semi for that *and* have enough left over to furnish the place.'

'I don't want a neat semi. I want my time in the manor house. You can lend me that, can't you? My business is doing really well. I have five pounds under my mattress.'

'Four hundred and twenty pounds! I suppose the first thing you'd do is install a telephone in every room.'

'It already has a telephone.'

'Any brats out that way wanting ivy cages? Think you'd do a roaring trade, do you?'

'If I lived at Capel Manor,' she said, 'I could put that on my business cards. Think how impressive that would be.'

'Huh!'

'The place has about an acre under glass. I would be able to make use of what they grow for my business. Lilies, roses, greenery—'

'Huh!'

'I've thought it out very carefully, Vic. Here are my calculations. It's a good business investment. As well as all the money I can save on flowers – and that alone will be a huge sum – I'll be able to supply the shop as well as my floral decorations. But, in addition, there's all the toffs living nearby; it would be a new market for me! I'll get to know them and they'll ask me to do the flowers for them. I'll have cards printed and push them through the letter boxes of every home in the neighbourhood.'

'Why not use the damned telephone? That would impress them.'

She looked at him, her eyes filling with tears. He was going to refuse. Ever since her visit to Capel Manor, her need to produce magnificent decorations for grand homes had obsessed her. Arranging flowers, which she had begun as a very pleasing way of supporting herself, had become her ruling passion. She craved more and bigger challenges to perfect her skills.

Strangely, for a young woman known for her down-to-earth attitudes, she felt an almost mystical affinity with Capel Manor. If she could just sleep beneath its roof and walk through its warm and pleasant rooms, the nagging sense of being unfulfilled in some way might cease to torment her. Ever since her mother's death, she had longed for something dramatic to happen to her. She had no idea what exactly she craved, but felt certain that a few months living in the old house in Enfield would solve the mystery and give her peace.

'Charge me any interest you think fair.'

He could never meet her eyes when she was deeply distressed, being very tender hearted where she was concerned. Nevertheless, he spoke harshly. 'Oh yes? What do you know about interest? You couldn't calculate interest if your life depended on it. Right, then. I'll make it easy for you. Cent per cent. I lend you four hundred and twenty pounds. You pay me eight hundred and forty.'

'Vic, you don't mean it.'

They argued for a few minutes. Vic was so opposed

to the idea that Charlotte thought there was no hope, when suddenly his attitude changed.

He snapped his fingers, looking sly. 'Oh, God, how can I refuse you? When you speak, it's like pearls coming out of your mouth, my girl. I daresay Queen Mary don't speak better than what you do. I can't resist you when you talk fancy.'

Charlotte looked at him carefully, trying to see beyond the beaming smile. Mention of the quality of her speech was Vic's way of reminding her that she had taken elocution lessons for six months when she was eleven, and that Vic had paid for them. Unfortunately, her mother had been altogether too willing to take gifts from Vic. Charlotte was indebted to the man in a thousand ways that she could never repay.

'I thank you, kind sir, for the pretty compliment. But I really do want to borrow the money from you. Please set a reasonable interest. The sort you would charge other people.'

'You aren't other people, Charlotte. You're my own dear friend what looks the spitting image of her ma. Tell you what I'll do: I'll come with you to give the place a looking over. If I think it's all right and tight, I'll give you the bloody money, so you can live like a toff for a while and get the urge out of your system. You wasn't meant for country living, old girl. You'll go barmy, what with the neighbours turning up their noses at you and the birds croaking and the cows mooing and nary a boozer in sight.'

She paid scant attention to anything he said after the magic words about giving her the money. She should not take such a large gift from Vic, but he had always seemed like a rich man to her, known to have large amounts of cash hidden in his home, since he didn't trust banks. Her conscience didn't trouble her too much, because she was sure she could increase her income so dramatically by living in the country that the money would soon be available to repay Vic, whether he wished to be repaid or not. Who could say how much work might be the result of living in such a grand place?

Wills and Segar (by appointment to Royalty) were among London's finest decorators, together with R. Forester Felton and Sons, who had splendid premises in Hanover Square. Both these firms made a great deal of money by catering for the better families. A girl needed flowers for her christening party, again when she was presented at Court, then again when she married and had her own children to be christened, presented and married, and finally flowers were needed for all the family funerals. If Charlotte could just get a few rich families onto her books, she figured she could live off them for years. The words 'Capel Manor' printed boldly on the stationery would surely help to attract such a clientele. Therefore, there was no need to worry about accepting so much money from Vic. It was a temporary arrangement. Nor need she wonder why her friend should give her such a valuable gift. Vic was an impulsive man, given to surprising acts of generosity.

The next day was Wednesday, a slow one for pawnbrokers, so they travelled out to Enfield in Vic's motor car. Charlotte had to walk round to the Strand to get in, for Vic would not be seen in the vicinity of his shop riding in such a splendid vehicle. He and Billy were sitting in it when she arrived. As usual, they were arguing.

'Charlotte! Get into the back. I have decided to allow Billy to drive after all. The boy works hard.'

Billy turned to grin at her, quite accustomed to being referred to as if he weren't there. 'The boy thinks his father won't know how to handle this car. It's a thirty horsepower, Coventry-built Humber with four forward gears. Dad doesn't know how to change gears. Just three years old. Got it cheap: a hundred pounds.'

'Think how many cars I could buy if I wasn't renting you a house, Charlotte,' said Vic pleasantly, and Charlotte wondered how long she would have to listen to these pleas for gratitude. Probably for the rest of her life.

Billy Tavern had straight black eyebrows and high cheekbones. His mouth was thin, but his broad jaw and muscled neck gave him a look of manly strength that had the local girls intrigued. They flirted with him whenever the chance arose and quivered with delight when he suggested a stroll round to the nearest pub for half a pint. Molly was not immune to his charms; Charlotte had been forced to forbid him to enter her shop when Molly was working alone. His conversation was almost non-existent, and he disappeared from time to time, staying away for several days. He was a great worry to Vic.

For this important visit to Capel Manor, she wore her fawn costume with a high lace under-blouse, which showed off her long neck, and a great hat with ostrich feathers on it that had been worn by her mother in an Oscar Wilde play. She thought she looked like the sort of woman who could afford to rent Capel Manor. Billy looked unusually smart in a fine wool suit with a belt in the back and a matching waistcoat. He wore his well-brushed bowler at a rakish angle and seemed perfectly at home in his fine clothes. Vic, on the other hand, was dressed in a frock coat, striped trousers, top hat and spats.

They must have made an impressive trio, for the lawyer, Mr Sloper, smiled broadly and said he would be delighted to accompany them in their motor car to Capel Manor.

'S'truth!' said Vic when he first saw the house. 'What a fine residence! Yes, sir, almost worth the money you're asking.'

'Furnished,' Mr Sloper reminded him. 'I don't think you could expect a home of this quality for less.'

'You know,' Charlotte said grandly to the lawyer, who was surely calculating his commission, 'I am a floral decorator of some renown, and these premises are just what I am looking for. I shall keep my London accommodation, of course. But here I can grow the plants most useful to my work.'

Mrs Snodsby could barely bring herself to be civil when she was told that Charlotte proposed to rent the manor. If the housekeeper was unhappy about Charlotte's imminent arrival, John Green was thunderstruck. 'You?' he said. 'You're going to live here?'

'And keep a roof over your head and money in your pocket, Mr Green. Not such a bad thing after all. Mr Boon, step forward. I want you to meet Mr Victor Tavern, a business associate of mine, and his son, Mr William Tavern.'

Jacko Boon slid forward and wisely spoke to the men with great respect, having undoubtedly sniffed out the source of the money. The entire staff would draw its own conclusions about her relationship with Vic, but it couldn't be helped.

They stayed for three-quarters of an hour. Vic was obviously impressed by the size and grandeur of the house, and spoke loudly to the agent to disguise his awe, commenting on the furnishings, which he said were a little old-fashioned for his taste. He approved of the echoing stables, and patted the head of the only occupant, an elderly horse which was no doubt used for pulling the mowing machine, as well as for collecting visitors from the nearby railway station.

Upstairs, the house had two bathrooms, all brass pipes and gleaming porcelain, and five large bedrooms, the largest being at the corner of the house, overlooking both the front drive and the walled kitchen garden. Charlotte felt the ghostly presence of the elderly couple who had made this house their home for so long, but their disapproving spirits could do nothing to dampen her enthusiasm. Although the agent was stunned to be paid in cash, she let out her breath in a long sigh when Vic handed over the money so that she could sign the lease.

Back in Enfield Town, they shook hands with Mr Sloper and drove off, with Billy once more behind the wheel. Charlotte felt weak with joy, too full of precious dreams to talk to anyone. Vic was unusually silent.

Billy had much to say on the subject of the grand house, in which, he said, Charlotte would rattle around like a shrivelled pea in a pod. 'You'll be working night and day just to pay for the coal, Charlotte. I reckon ten tons a year for the house and as much again for the glass-houses. Those things eat fuel. I won't even mention the telephone and the servants' wages.'

These practical words had the effect of bursting the bubble of her absurd dreams. She would need to pay the servants, buy food, travel to London. Unless something extraordinary happened she would starve, while running so deeply into debt that she would never get out. In all her calculations, she had forgotten the need for cash to tide her over until the money started coming in. There was nothing for it but to approach a bank to see if they would lend her a comparatively small sum, and wondered what collateral she could offer a wing-collared stranger who was probably accustomed to dealing in thousands.

She had a good view of Vic's neck from her seat in the back, but no idea of his expression. He was a deep one, a canny man to whom financial calculations were second nature. Why on earth had he let her walk into such a situation?

'You'll be needing operating capital,' he said, without turning round. 'I'll lend you another hundred and fifty quid. I'm not giving you another penny. You've got to learn your lesson.'

'Thank you,' she said humbly. Her hands were shaking; she clasped them tightly. She had been right to try for success at Capel Manor. Vic wouldn't let her fail miserably, although she might have to listen to a life-time of scolding if the business didn't go as she planned. But that was an attitude of defeat. She would win! She would triumph! Vic would be amazed and proud of her.

Holding to these optimistic thoughts, she pulled the lap rug around her knees and dreamed of the grand life.

When the London party had driven off, John Green returned to his favourite house where some of his fuchsias were being allowed to rest for the winter. He had three hundred plants in the house, many of which would be overwintered. 'Soon go to sleep, my babies,' he said, and heaved a large pot of 'Amy Lye' onto a two-wheeled trolley. 'Next year you're going to be a beauty. You'll be the best bloody pillar fuchsia that young woman has ever seen. Anybody can grow standards, but she probably ain't never seen a pillar!'

Growing a fuchsia into a pillar was a tricky business. Jacko Boon couldn't do it, no sir. He might talk big and make a good impression on people, but nobody could grow fuchsias like John did. The only trouble was, not everyone wanted fuchsias these days. A few standards for the formal gardens in the summer, maybe a hanging basket or two, but the great days of fuchsia cultivation had been over before John's father was out of short trousers. It was the very contempt with which the flower was held by the better class of person that attracted John to them. 'We're two of a kind,' he used to say. 'Old-fashioned. But I've got a few surprises up my sleeve.'

'I thought I'd find you in here, Mr Green,' said Jacko, entering the house. 'You'll be putting your babies to sleep in a week or two, eh?'

'I'm just going through the stock, throwing out what I don't plan to overwinter. It's overcrowding that lets in the grey mould.'

Jacko nodded. The mould was death to resting plants and could take hold between one inspection and the next. All those plants which were to be dormant during the winter needed to have their foliage cut back by a half. John Green would be careful to trim them to a neat shape, after which they would be stored beneath the staging. Being a fine fuchsia grower, he would keep them very dry at the roots for a few weeks, while making sure that they didn't become too dry. And he would make sure that the temperature in the house never fell below freezing. He would inspect them for grey mould regularly, giving them a little water, and watch for the right moment to start them into growth again.

'Floral decorators can't get enough orchids,' murmured Jacko maliciously. 'You don't suppose Miss Blair will demand that you heat this house up to grow orchids, do you?'

John turned to him in alarm. 'No! She wouldn't!'

Greenhouse management was an art, and different types of plants required different treatment. Orchids liked heat, the sort of temperatures that would force the fuchsias into growth. In this fuchsia house, the roof ventilators would be opened a few inches on the side away from the wind whenever the weather was dry and above the minimum temperature of the house. Where fuchsias were concerned, air humidity had to be reduced. Cold, damp air was an invitation to grey mould and other diseases. On the other hand, orchids loved heat and damp air. The two plants could not be successfully grown in the same house.

'I'll bet Mr Warrender would be furious if he knew what was happening here at his home. She'll be stripping Capel for her own business.'

'I don't want you to worry, Mr Green.' Jacko touched his governor's jacket briefly in a sympathetic gesture. 'I'll keep her away from you. Meantime, I'll see to it that I grow everything she wants. Supply her needs, sort of thing. Keep her happy, sort of thing. No need for you to take the raw end of her tongue.'

'She can be a tartar. Rounded on me in the dog cart like a wildcat. I'd hand in my notice if I didn't have responsibilities. Mabel and all that.'

'Oh, you wouldn't want to do that,' said Jacko, shaking his head slowly. 'The lodge is a fine house.

You would have to go far to find a better one. I do envy you. I can't think of getting married until I get me a post with that sort of accommodation.'

John sucked on his teeth for a moment as he studied his leisure garden foreman. 'Don't you go thinking of leaving, Jacko. I'm going to need you.'

Chapter Three

Charlotte's possessions made a very small pile, but included some old costumes of her mother's. There was nothing in her rooms that she wished to see displayed at Capel Manor, except photographs of her parents taken when she was a baby. The costumes would go with her for practical reasons, since the cloth was still good in most of them. They could be made into gowns to be worn at her new home. Proper ladies, she had read, changed their clothing all day long, for mornings, luncheons, afternoon teas and dinners. There was no end to it.

Before leaving, she gave Molly numerous instructions about managing the shop in her absence, cautioned her not to skimp on flowers when preparing the three-guinea wreaths, then told her she could sleep in the rooms upstairs when Charlotte was away.

'You'll have to go home on the nights I want to be here, mind. I'm not sharing my bed with anyone.'

The girl was pathetically grateful for this small favour. The eldest of ten children, she was always eager to slip away from her child-minding duties.

The first day at Capel was traumatic for everyone, especially for the housekeeper, Mrs Snodsby. She followed Charlotte into the morning-room, wiping the tears from her eyes as she gathered all the photographs of the Gryce family to be put away in the attic. Charlotte had ordered their removal, because Capel was hers now.

'The family's gone,' moaned Mrs Snodsby, 'and him not even here to sort through his own things.' She picked up a heavily chased silver frame and handed it to Charlotte. 'Young Mister Matthew Warrender. That's him. Their only grandson. The Gryces didn't breed well. If he doesn't marry, the family will die out. Well, the Gryce family name has already died out. I don't know if there are any more Warrenders. Mister Matthew's parents drowned at sea when he was sixteen, and he came here to live with his grandparents. He was a solemn boy who didn't have much to say for himself and didn't have anything in common with Mr and Mrs Gryce. Mister Matthew's father was something of a Bohemian. Mr Gryce put the boy in the Colonial Service to knock that sort of thing out of him, I expect.'

Charlotte looked at the photograph, finding no hint of the Bohemian in the son, certainly not a velvet-suited Oscar Wilde sort of man with a green carnation in his buttonhole. What, she wondered, was Mrs Snodsby's definition of a Bohemian?

In the picture, Matthew Warrender, who was apparently in his early thirties, was seated on the edge of a table, glaring at the camera through dark eyes deeply set beneath straight brows, apparently daring the camera to record his likeness. His dark hair was parted slightly to one side and cut short, the moustache was centre-parted and swept to either side, military fashion, lending distinction to a handsome face.

A panama hat with a wide band was crushed under his left upper arm, while his right hand rested on a silver-topped cane. There was arrogance in the pose. A stiff, turned-down collar and a tightly knotted tie looked surprisingly comfortable on him. His lounge jacket and matching high-cut, double-breasted waistcoat were well cut, but his pale trousers needed pressing.

Poor Mr and Mrs Gryce had probably found it unsettling to have a sixteen-year-old boy thrust among them, but it was foolish to think that the sobering influence of the Colonial Service was just what the orphaned boy needed. The Gryces had not waited for their grandson to go through a rebellious phase. They had sent him away.

'Since Mr Warrender is the owner of Capel Manor, perhaps it would be proper to leave his photograph here in the morning-room,' she said politely. 'Is this a recent likeness?'

'Taken about a year ago and sent to Mr and Mrs Gryce from Hong Kong. Have you seen the flower paintings he did? Not to my taste, nor I may say, to Mrs Gryce's. They don't really look like flowers, do they? All those winding lines. They're not real flowers at all.'

'In the Art Nouveau tradition, plants are drawn in a stylized way. Some Liberty prints are like that, but—'

'Painted them ten years ago when he was twenty-two. Mr Gryce said he must not have much understanding of the botany of plants to draw like that, and after all that expensive schooling.'

Having said her piece about the grandson, Mrs Snodsby suggested that she introduce Charlotte to the indoor staff. This was quickly done. Two sisters, Rachel and Sarah Duck, were horsey-faced women in their early thirties. Sarah was the cook, Rachel the parlour maid. Cora Bent came in once a week to do some heavy cleaning.

After a brief discussion about the house and a further reminder from Mrs Snodsby that she would soon be leaving, Charlotte went into the library where she had been told the household accounts had been laid out for her inspection.

Like the dining-room, the library was wood-panelled from floor to ceiling. A leather-topped desk sat in the bay window. By sitting in the intimidating desk chair and swivelling round, she could see Jacko Boon mowing the south lawn. The pony was wearing leather boots on his hooves to protect the lawn and was pulling a thirty-inch mower, the largest one the old horse could be expected to haul. Surely, she thought, the feed for such a small creature would not cost more than one and sixpence a week.

Mrs Snodsby had kept the accounts for forty years, and had grown old and frail in the service of the Gryces. The books she had written up for 1911 were in a decidedly shaky hand, and there were a few mistakes in the additions and subtractions.

To her horror, Charlotte discovered that she was responsible for a large outdoor staff. Under John Green was Jacko Boon, as leisure garden foreman in charge of the grounds and flowering plants. Squabby Horn was improver journeyman under him. Dangler Stritch was the foreman of the kitchen garden and vines, and Bertie Cox was his improver journeyman. Nobbie Clark was the crock boy. Mrs Squabby Horn ran the bothy where the unmarried gardeners lived and had their meals, and Nat Horn, a small boy, did occasional weeding. Five men and two boys: six pounds, ten shillings a week for garden staff alone.

As if this expense was not bad enough, as lady of the manor she had to provide Mr Green and his wife with a handsome three-bedroom lodge which was larger than anything Charlotte had ever occupied, and all of these people were eating, sleeping and keeping warm at her expense. Mr Green's annual wage came to more than Charlotte had earned the previous year. Thank heavens Vic had lent her a hundred and fifty pounds for operating expenses!

It was necessary to stay in London when she had commissions in Town, because the train service couldn't get her to market at three o'clock in the morning on Tuesdays, Thursdays and Saturdays. She usually remembered to telephone the shop and warn Molly to vacate her rooms, but on one occasion in late November, she forgot to ring. Arriving late, she struggled with thirty trails of smilax and the same quantity of myrtle and ivy (a saving of ten shillings on market prices) and walked from

Liverpool Street to Covent Garden. The church bells had just tolled eleven o'clock when she put the key into the lock of the outside door. She closed it behind her, put her right hand against the cold wall, feeling her way in the pitch dark, and began to ascend the stairs.

'Don't get a fright, Molly!' she called. 'I forgot to tell you I'd be coming home tonight.'

There was a squeal of dismay from Molly, then the desperate growl of a masculine voice. The door at the top of the stairs opened, sending out a faint light. Charlotte had a split second's vision of a man's form, his large flat cap held up to shield his features. Then he began to run down the stairs.

She realized he couldn't see her and flattened herself against the wall. No use. The staircase was too narrow for the two of them to pass without touching. He knocked the breath from her, tripped over the plants she had been forced to release and swore bitterly as he clattered and clumped the rest of the way down the stairs. He was out of the door while she was still gasping for breath.

Molly, all tearful apologies, held a flickering candle to light the way. It took Charlotte a few moments to limp up the stairs, but she was still sufficiently angry to tell Molly what she thought of her.

'You fool! Does your ma know what you get up to? I didn't give you permission to bring men in here.'

Molly ran clawed fingers through her dishevelled hair. 'Don't tell me mum! Oh, please don't tell her.'

'You could get yourself in trouble.' Charlotte found a chair and sat down. 'You're sixteen. Do you want to start breeding at your age? Think about your career. You've got a little independence these days. You could work your way up to something special. I've raised your pay to fifteen shillings a week. I believe that's more than your dad gets. Have some sense, Molly, and don't go with all sorts.'

'He's not all sorts. He's fine and I love him. Anyway, we didn't do nothing wrong, just kisses, that's all.'

Charlotte shrugged. 'I can't say I'm all that interested in your affairs, Molly. Take the candle and help me to recover my cut foliage. It's worth ten shillings. I can't afford to have those trails lost, especially when we have the table for Mrs Clark's dinner party to do. If you don't want to go home at this late hour, fix yourself a bed by the fire. That old settee should be comfortable enough for what's left of the night.'

The next morning, Molly rose early and prepared a hearty breakfast for her employer. Charlotte never carried a grudge or remembered a quarrel and was surprised that the girl was in what she called a snivelling mood.

'Please don't tell me mum, Miss Blair. I couldn't bear it. She'd kick me out of the house.'

'Of course I won't tell your mother! What sort of person do you take me for? I was just tired and cross last night. I think you are unwise, but you are sixteen now. You must make your own decisions. Just don't use my rooms to entertain men late at night, that's all.'

The late autumn days passed unsatisfactorily, with Charlotte discontented wherever she stayed. Covent Garden was dirty, noisy and crowded. Capel Manor was inhabited by strangers, a lonely and chilly place which impressed upon her that she was not wanted. As the weather got colder, she would wrap up warmly, put on overshoes and stroll through the grounds of her rented home alone, searching for suitable material to cut. At this time of year, the pines and cedars looked gloomy in their dark greenery against a pewter sky, while the naked branches of the rare Zelcova and the two copper beeches sang in the wind. The beeches were said to have been planted in 1770, but there were yews in the grounds which were probably older.

Now that the leaves had fallen and been swept into hidden places to be rotted for mulch, it was possible to get a good view of Theobalds Park from the northern boundary of Capel. A red brick mansion dressed with white stone, it dominated the landscape for miles around with its tower and flagpole rising high above the trees. Over the quiet meadows of Capel, she stared at the fairy-tale palace and wondered how her life would have turned out if her commission had been to provide flowers for Theobalds Park. She would probably have failed to satisfy her employer. For the present, Theobalds Park was beyond her capacity to decorate. Her reputation would have suffered and, worst of all, she would never have seen Capel.

Her lively imagination, which had enabled her to envisage living in her beloved manor house, would not stretch to placing her in Theobalds. It was too large for dreams. How on earth had Lady Meux found the strength to march from the vast dining-room to the enormous drawing-room, and from there to the frozen wastes of her bedroom? The upper classes had great reserves of stamina. No wonder they didn't work for their daily bread: they must surely be exhausted from moving round their ancient homes and changing their clothes five times a day!

One afternoon, on returning from her solitary walk, she heard a drawling voice speaking to John Green. Instead of letting herself in by the kitchen door as she had intended, she walked round to the front of the house, to see an elegant man leaning on a cane and discussing with great seriousness the proper management of beech trees. That is, he was laying down the law and the head gardener was making mewling sounds of agreement. The man caught sight of Charlotte and smiled as he quickly removed his right glove to shake her hand. She recognized those patrician features, but for a split second could not think where she had seen the man before.

'This is Mr Edward Augustus Bowles, come to see you, Miss Blair,' said the head gardener deferentially.

Of course, Mr 'Gussie' Bowles, one of the most distinguished men in the Royal Horticultural Society! She had seen him at a few exhibitions, had him pointed out to her, had even admired the perfection of his clean-shaven face. He was forty something and had the features of a West End leading man. Plant hunter, noted gardener, author of books about his garden, he was the most famous person she had ever stood close to. And he had come to visit her!

'I thought I really must call round, Miss Blair. We're near neighbours. My home, Myddleton House, is just a short distance away.'

In spite of her desire to appear sophisticated, Charlotte spluttered out phrases of humble adoration, and then invited him indoors.

With considerable presence of mind, John Green had raced towards the kitchen door as soon as he had introduced Charlotte. As a result, the front door flew open as if by magic, and Mrs Snodsby was even more effusive than Charlotte had been. Mr Bowles responded without surprise. Charlotte supposed that he was quite accustomed to this sort of fawning.

They took tea in the morning-room: seed cake and small ham sandwiches. Charlotte felt desperately ill-equipped to lead the conversation, but fortunately this wasn't necessary. Mr Bowles talked about himself. She learned that his brother lived in the magnificent Forty Hall, that his own garden was 'just a few acres', that he would soon be off on another plant-hunting expedition, that he was very excited about the International Flower Exhibition that was to be held for the first time in the grounds of the Chelsea Hospital, in May. The RHS was not organizing it, but several members of the Society had been asked to take part in planning it. It had been more than twenty years since the last international exhibition, and it was going to be magnificent.

For fully fifteen minutes he spoke about the plants at Capel Manor, at Myddleton House, at Forty Hall. She heard about his hay fever and how it forced him to leave the country during the early part of the summer, and discovered that Capel Manor was situated in a very interesting part of the country, horticulturally speaking. She must know that Pulhamite, the artificial stone, was made a few miles north in Broxbourne. But did she know that the first tea rose was sent from China and grown in a garden in nearby Wormley? Of course, she knew that those splendid growers, Rochfords, were just a mile or two away, and that there were many flower, fruit and vegetable growers in the area. Lea Valley glasshouses were famous all over the country.

The teapot was empty, the sandwiches and seed cake eaten. The great man rose to go, then paused.

'I understand from Mr Green that you are a floral decorator. Where did you train? Felton's? Wills and Segar?'

'No, I'm afraid not. I was taken on by a great friend of my parents who owned a small florist shop in King Street, Covent Garden. The owner took an interest in me, because I loved flowers. My father used to grow auriculas in the back yard.'

'Ah.'

Charlotte paused, realizing at once she had made a terrible mistake. She should not have mentioned the auriculas. Mechanics, poor people, the working classes grew auriculas in pots wherever they could find a spot of sun. They grew them to extremely high standards and travelled considerable distances to exhibit them. The middle and upper classes did not participate in such pastimes. By mentioning her father's hobby, she had not only explained her own early interest in plants, she had placed herself unequivocally among the lower orders. She and her father might have been butterflies, pinned to cork and properly labelled '*Working class* var. Covent Garden'.

'I worked for the florist for several years, learning all he could teach me. When he died, he left the shop to me in his will.'

'Such a short apprenticeship,' he murmured, failing to comment about the auriculas as if they were shameful.

He bent to study the simple bowl of gleanings from the Capel wild garden: a few trails of Virginia creeper, some berried branches and half a dozen bracken fronds that she had pressed several months earlier. It was not one of her better arrangements, so she was apprehensive as he delicately touched a leaf. 'Charming. Yes, charming. Very restrained. Have you read Miss Gertrude Jekyll's book on flower arranging?'

'No, I—'

'She has such refinement of taste that she must be of value to even the most humble lover of plants in the home. I suppose you do know dear Mr Felton?'

'No, I—'

'Brilliant man. Few people could have handled the decorations at Claridge's for the visit of the Japanese Crown Prince a few years back. He has the capacity to think on a grand scale.'

She was glad when he left, better able to put herself wholeheartedly into saying goodbye than she had been in asking how he liked his tea. She saw him to the door, noticing that he laid a calling card in the tray that rested on the hall table. It had been immensely exciting to receive a proper caller, but she felt the visit had gone wrong, and it had been a strain. But at least, she recalled, he had said she must visit his garden in the warmer weather.

At the door he paused to shake her hand once more, before putting on his gloves. He had a passion for the unusual, he said; she really must see his oddities on one of his open days. Not a private visit then. She would not be invited to his home; she must not expect him to call again. She had been tested and found wanting in some way. Yet another dream about Capel had been dashed. No work whatsoever would come her way by virtue of her splendid new address. She was not to be embraced by the good families. On one point only was she successful. The gardens and houses of Capel had saved her a considerable amount of money, pounds, shillings and pence which were immediately swallowed up by her greater expenses.

December was unusually cold, with a bitter north wind. She ordered her meals to be served on a tray in the morning-room, so the dining-room was opened only for Rachel or Cora to clean it. The mahogany table that could seat sixteen continued to glow in the brief winter sunshine, for it was polished every week, but the room began to smell musty and damp.

Three days before Christmas, she was bent over her account book in the morning-room while a gale blew around the old walls and wailed in the trees. By dint of working very hard, she was managing to keep out of debt. All her profits went on maintaining the house and the staff, with just forty pounds of Vic's loan kept under her mattress for occasions when she needed to make cash purchases. It might seem pointless to work so hard merely to maintain others, but she reminded herself that she was indulging a dream.

Strangely, she had not thought how lonely she would be. She had placed herself in limbo, loving every brick and blade of grass of her temporary home, yet unable to speak to anyone in a free and relaxed manner. She had left the stage, knowing she was an abysmal actress, only to spend every waking moment attempting to play the part of a refined lady. Her hands were calloused and permanently grimy from her work with rusting stub wires, while her speech was of necessity a strained imitation of Mr Bowles's effortless drawl.

She heard the telephone ring in the hall and started up from the table, but Rachel reached it first.

'Hello, hello!' she screamed. 'Who is it? Speak up.'

'I'll take the call,' said Charlotte, coming into the entrance lobby and holding out her hand for the ear piece.

'Hello, old girl, this is Vic. I'm calling from your shop. Don't see why I should have the expense of a trunk call. Are you keeping well?'

'Very well, Vic. It's good to hear your voice. I've been so busy lately, I haven't had time to visit you.'

'Don't worry about it, my dear. Billy and me is coming for Christmas. Keep you company. Got a few friends. Remember Arthur? Arthur Brock? Wait till you hear what's happened to him! He'll be coming. And you don't know Popple Douse, but he was a solicitor. Posh type what got into a spot of bother. He'll be bringing his daughter, Florence. So there'll be two of you pretty young girls to keep us on our toes, eh?'

'Vic, what are you saying? Five people for Christmas? I can't afford it. Anyway, I've promised the servants the day off.'

Vic spoke over her words, never a great one for listening to others. 'Just you buy yourself a twenty pound turkey and tell those females to bake up some cakes and the like. I'll bring the bevy. You tell them skivvies to get the beds ready. I'll share with Billy. Otherwise, everybody is going to need a room to hisself, to be proper like.'

She gave in. Without Vic and his generosity she could not have had this chance to experience life at Capel Manor. Miss Sarah Duck, whom she had learned to address as Mrs Duck, a courtesy title due to her being the cook, and Rachel might sneer at her guests, feeling themselves too superior to wait on such people. The outdoor staff would only need to catch a glimpse of these town types to put Charlotte firmly in her proper place in the social order. Let them. The dream that was life at Capel was about to collide with the reality of her background.

Chapter Four

The reaction of the small indoor staff to the imminent arrival of five guests was one of loud complaint as they were short-handed, Mrs Snodsby having left for her cottage in Devon and Cora being laid low with the grippe. Rachel and Mrs Duck felt they could not adequately prepare a house of Capel's size for so many visitors in three days. In the face of such reasonable complaints, Charlotte then scandalized them by insisting that she would help to make up the beds and polish the silver. Nothing, she told them, would interfere with their having Christmas day with their family.

With the exception of the one in which she slept, all the Capel beds sagged with age. The Gryces had not entertained weekend guests. Only Matthew Warrender had slept there during the previous five years. The bedrooms smelled of damp, so that fires had to be built in all the small grates, and bowls of potpourri placed nearby to sweeten the air.

Rachel worried about providing hot shaving water for so many men, since carrying great copper cans of water up the stairs was no easy task. Capel had an intriguing system whereby the horse could be used to draw water from the well outside the kitchen door and was mechanically pumped to storage tanks in the attic. The taps in the bathrooms gushed cold water, which was some help, but there were no geysers in the bathrooms. Mr and Mrs Gryce had lived their long lives without such luxuries and saw no reason to make radical changes in their old age.

There was very little time to prepare the food for the unexpected party. Sarah suggested that the Bride – as she called John Green's new wife – should be told to come up to the house to help out on the following two days.

The next day when Charlotte went to the kitchen to discuss what was to be done, she met Mabel Green and, not for the first time, had serious doubts about John's good sense. Surely only a fool would choose such a bride. Mabel wasn't exactly fat, merely shapeless. Her light brown hair was so thin that her scalp was clearly visible and, to make matters worse, she scraped it into such a tight bun that it dragged her eyebrows upwards at the corners.

Mabel had come unwillingly to help in the kitchen, and refused to acknowledge Charlotte who had greeted her pleasantly. Annoyed, Charlotte put her hands on her hips and stood over the young girl who was seated with a bowl of water in her lap as she peeled potatoes. 'I shall be paying you for your work. Nearly two shillings a day. Isn't that enough?'

'Yes, ma'am, but I get tired so easy. My mum says I ought not to do anything heavy, as I'm not strong.'

'You look well enough to me. I'm only asking you to do a little washing up for Mrs Duck when she's baking, after all. Just you help out here so that Cook isn't worn to the bone.'

'Couldn't Cora—'

'Cora's poorly!'

Mabel put her hands over her ears and hunched her shoulders as if expecting a blow. 'Don't shout at me! I'll faint! I'm not used to being shouted at. My mum says—'

Charlotte threw up her hands, gave Mrs Duck a speaking glance and left the kitchen. She was so angry as she walked away that she gave the baize door a push with her arm held stiffly in front of her. It crashed against the wall and swung back with great force, hitting Rachel who was following behind.

Rachel laughed off Charlotte's contrite apology. 'It was a treat to see your face, ma'am, when she started to cry. Why ever did John marry her? We've known that Mabel was a lazy cow ever since he brought her here. He turns up at the kitchen door most days with some excuse about Mabel being tired and begs some dinner off us. And wait till you meet his mother-in-law! What a tartar. John's scared to death of her. My sister won't get much work out of the Bride, but she's better than no help at all.'

Charlotte liked the sisters. They knew their jobs and took pride in their work. They deserved to have a happy Christmas. The plan was for them to serve breakfast on Christmas morning, put the turkey on to roast, leave the prepared vegetables where she could find them and then head for their own celebrations at their parents' home. They hadn't far to travel, just to Enfield Town, and would return to Capel late on Christmas night.

She could not let the festivities pass without making an effort to decorate the house with plants, greenery and flowers, so palms and ferns were brought indoors. Every mantelpiece was covered with berried holly and boughs of cone-heavy conifers. It was not until she began to plan the table for the first meal on Christmas Eve that she faced up to a major difficulty about her guests.

Vic and Billy would certainly never have seen a table laid for the sort of meals that were commonplace in a manor house. The Duck sisters had been trained to set the table with nine pieces of cutlery and three glasses at every place. They knew that the salt cruets were invariably flanked by two salt spoons and laid at the corners of the table, that each intricately folded napkin held a bread roll which was to be transferred immediately to the side plate. Water carafes had their appointed places on the table and water glasses were different from champagne and claret glasses, which were in turn different from the sherry and port. Coffee could be taken at the table or in the drawing-room. Even if everyone else behaved well,

Vic would be sure to make some humorous comment that would shame his hostess.

By virtue of keeping her mouth shut and her eyes open, Charlotte had become accustomed to this style of eating. Besides, although she had scarcely given a thought to the arrangement of tables as she decorated them, she had at least seen the way in which the upper sorts dined. Had Vic ever sat down to such an array? She thought not. He could afford to eat at the better hotels and restaurants, but he had often told her that he would be uncomfortable in such places. About Billy and Arthur, Charlotte had no doubts. They were happy in the roughest of company. The Douses, father and daughter, were an unknown quantity. For all she knew, they might have exquisite manners. But then, what were they doing in Vic's company?

'Just a small family dinner on Christmas Eve, Mrs Duck,' she said casually at the first opportunity.

'Oh, nothing fancy, I'm sure,' replied the cook. 'Brown soup, followed by whitings because they're your favourite, a saddle of lamb and vegetables, or if anyone prefers, some curried rabbit, and all followed by a lemon pudding, blancmanges and apple charlotte, and fruit and cheese. Will that do?'

It had to do. She could not criticize such industry. The guests would have to follow her lead. The servants, for their part, would have to look the other way.

The guests arrived at four o'clock, coming in with a rush of cold air and hearty greetings. Vic lifted Charlotte right off her feet in a bear hug. As he twirled her round, she caught a glimpse of Rachel's horrified face. It was going to be an interesting holiday.

'Here's Arthur Brock!' bellowed Vic in her ear as he set her down. 'You'll never guess what's happened to him.'

'Lost a leg,' she said promptly, and earned herself a peal of laughter out of all proportion to her little joke.

'Came into a bit of money from some cousin or other,' volunteered Arthur. 'Damned if a second cousin of mine didn't up and die, and I'm his heir.'

'We'll spare his blushes and not ask how much he got, eh?' said Vic. He whipped off his hat, put his muffler and gloves in it and began to unbutton his great coat, handing the lot to Rachel with a leer.

Arthur Brock was about the same age as Vic, another figure from her childhood, and with a fund of stories about the upper classes. They fascinated him as he went about his business beside the nation's race tracks. He described his work as helping the toffs to place their bets. Charlotte had no idea what this entailed. His features were slightly more refined than Vic's, making it just possible for her to believe he had a rich relative. Of no more than medium height, his large head looked strange, set as it was on a narrow-shouldered body. He had always attempted to dress in a dashing manner, although his clothes tended to be threadbare. His bowler hat was a size too small for him and sat ludicrously high on his thick brown hair. For a change, on this Christmas Eve, he looked less raffish than usual in his new tweeds and creaking brown shoes.

Mr Popplewell Douse and his daughter were more restrained than the others. Mr Douse was in his late forties, and had a fringe of white hair around his pink bald head. A huge moustache grew with the curve of his cheeks to meet the hair above his ears. Upper eyelids like crêpe paper half hid his bloodshot eyes. Charlotte, a careful observer, marked him down as a drinker and, when he bent to kiss her hand with a flourish, as a practised charmer.

Florence was so beautiful and delicately built that she came close to spoiling the entire day for Charlotte. The girl had very thick black hair which she combed into a quite extravagant pompadour. Straight black eyebrows emphasized the calculating nature of her eyes. An exquisite complexion and tight lacing that gave her a Gibson girl figure were apparently mesmerizing to Billy. Charlotte felt a stab of pity for little Molly who still adored Billy. Who could compete with this gorgeous woman?

Her voice was girlish and high, and she spoke with the merest hint of a lisp. 'It's ever so kind of you to invite Popple and me to spend Christmas with you, Charlotte. May I call you Charlotte? I'm Florence and everyone calls my father Popple. Even me. It's sort of like Poppa, so I call him what everybody else does. He says it's fast. Do you think it's fast? I've never stayed in such an elegant establishment before. I understand country houses are always cold, so I've brought my woollen drawers.' She giggled, then turned to survey the room. 'Are those paintings of ancestors? I wish I had ancestors, but Popple says we did have ancestors, it's just that we wouldn't want anybody to know what they got up to. Popple is very droll. You'll like him. He was a solicitor, but everyone was horrible to him, so now he's retired and I don't mind a bit, except that we have less money which is a terrible bore because, let me tell you, I have very expensive tastes. My mother was a great beauty. I've a reputation to keep up, haven't I, Popple?'

She turned to her father for confirmation, but he was with Vic and Arthur, warming his hands before the fire at the far end of the hall. This nineteen-year-old girl, thought Charlotte, was much less mature than poor Molly.

The situation was unreal; something dramatic was called for. Charlotte spoke a line she had heard a hundred times in a disastrous play called *Lady Beatrice Triumphs*. 'How absolutely charming to meet you. I say, shall we retire to the drawing-room? Tea will be served directly.'

They showed their appreciation of everything, commenting, touching, asking questions. Who had carved the fancy work over the doors? How big was the lounge? Who had papered the walls? How much did the electric light cost? Of them all, Vic was the most trying, for he would exclaim over everything. 'Who'd have thought we'd be sitting here like the upper classes sipping tea?' and 'Look at that garden! You could put a couple of rows of houses down that lawn and have room left over for a knocking shop.' And when shown to his room, 'Look at them two narrow beds, Billy. Wouldn't do for a Romeo like you, would they?'

The party reassembled in the drawing-room at half past six, everyone wearing evening dress. Florence wore a gown of pale blue silk that had a hobble skirt so tight that she could hardly walk.

Charlotte, thinking her guests would not be able to dress for dinner, had chosen a mauve high-waisted gown with a skirt that allowed her to walk naturally. As a result, she felt dowdy and old and very annoyed with Florence. If the holidays were to be a time of fashion rivalry, she couldn't compete. Keeping up with the latest fashions had never been very important to her, so she was surprised at her irrational jealousy of a foolish young girl. Nevertheless, she would wear her most striking gown on Christmas night. Even a floral decorator should be allowed to look attractive occasionally.

Despite this unpromising beginning, the evening was a magnificent success. The dining-room was lit entirely by candles, twenty of them. The fire added to the welcome, and the silver and crystal on the table reflected the light. There were gasps of pleasure from the guests and extravagant compliments about the floral decorations.

Charlotte felt a wave of gratitude towards these warm-hearted people – at last somebody was praising her. Nor did they let her down over the cutlery. Vic was suddenly silent, straightening the knives and forks on either side of his plate, dropping his chin and glancing up slyly to check on the actions of others. Far from making crude comments in a loud voice, he carried off the entire meal with dignity and quiet good humour. They toasted one another in half a dozen bottles of claret and champagne, and rose from the table in good humour as the grandfather clock in the hall chimed nine o'clock.

The cold air of the entrance hall was in marked contrast to the warmth of the dining-room. With flirtatious cries of distress, Florence announced that she would freeze to death if Billy didn't run upstairs that minute and fetch her woollen shawl from the back of her dressing-table chair. He hurried away to do her bidding while everyone else made their way into the drawing-room.

This room lacked the charm of others in the house. Charlotte loved the library and felt comfortable in the morning-room, but tended to avoid the drawing-room for reasons she couldn't identify. Nevertheless, she urged her guests to the far end where they sat down on over-stuffed chairs close to the fire and the single electric light that stood near the inglenook.

After a minute or two, Rachel entered, wheeling a trolley on which were set the coffee things.

'Cor, it's cold in here,' said Billy, returning with Florence's shawl. 'You've got more fires going than I've ever seen. Why don't we all sit in the morning-room? That's cosy and the fire's blazing away.' Billy rubbed his hands together. 'Didn't I warn you, Charlotte? A fire in the hall, one in here, one in the dining-room and another in the morning-room. All the bedrooms have fires, and I daresay they're keeping warm in the servants' quarters. Then there's the lodge and the bothy. All that money and it's perishing in here.'

'Go into the morning-room, then,' said Vic irritably. 'Take Florence with you. She looks cold.'

With surprising speed, Florence obediently rose from her seat and started towards the door. 'Are you coming, Billy?'

Charlotte watched them go in some surprise, and turned to Vic in an effort to find out what was afoot. None of the remaining men seemed to be at all uncom-fortable in the drawing-room. As the door closed behind Billy, the genial, rather drunken smile fell from Vic's face, while Arthur and Popple Douse developed a sudden interest in their fingernails and shoe tops.

'What's going on, Vic?' she asked. 'Is there something I should know?'

'I'm really glad I put up the readies for you to live in this place, old girl. It was a large investment, but—'

'Investment?' She felt her heart lurch. Apparently, she had made a bargain with the devil. Now here was Vic to claim her soul. 'I'm grateful. You know that. Why, I've loved every minute of my time here, but if you want me to leave, I expect you can get your money back.'

'I've paid up front, Charlotte. Nobody's going to give me my money back. Nor I'm not asking you to leave your magnificent castle in the air. A small favour, nothing much, that's all I ask in return. Why, cheer up, old girl, we want you to come into business with us.'

'What sort of business?' she croaked.

'Gold mining. We three men here are setting up a company to prospect for gold in Australia.'

'I haven't got any money to invest.'

Hearty masculine laughter greeted this remark. Of course she would not be expected to put up any money, they said. Perish the thought. They all wanted her to be a company director, however. Wouldn't that be dandy? Not many young women could claim to be directors of legitimate companies. Vic stressed the word legitimate. Of course, the nature of the business being what it was, she mustn't tell anyone she was a director. Men (investors) liked to feel that other men (the trio of tycoons seated before her) were in charge. Women were not considered to be either wise or bringers of good luck in business. However, Vic, Popple and Arthur were very anxious for her to participate. She had a quick mind and would no doubt make a considerable contribution to the board meetings. She would be registered as a director under the name of C. A. Blair.

She wanted to say, no, I won't. Thoughts of Capel Manor and the money Vic had paid out constrained her. 'I see. Yes, I think I understand. What do I have to do?'

The pleasant Popple Douse turned suddenly into a

dynamic, rather unpleasant man of business. With a flourish, he drew some papers from an inside jacket pocket, while Arthur swiftly pulled some chairs round into a tight circle. They gathered, knees almost touching, and bent forward the better to hear Vic's quiet words.

'A business has a better chance of getting going if it has an impressive list of directors. We could really do with a peer of the realm on the board, but Arthur didn't reckon he knew any of the racing fraternity well enough to invite them. Popple here, being a former solicitor, can rattle off the jargon and keep the books. Arthur knows ever so many men of substance who may wish to buy shares in our private company. We're not quoted on the stock exchange nor nothing like that. Now as for me, I am, I fancy, a leader of men. All contributing something, you see.'

Charlotte saw her chance of escape. 'You won't want me. I can't do anything. I really don't know about anything at all, except flowers. So—'

'Hold your horses,' said Vic. 'You're C. A. Blair of Capel Manor. That's who you are. Looks good, you see. Capel Manor would be just the place to register as our head office. This fine address has worked for you, now it can do the same for us. I'm sure you won't object.'

'You mean all the correspondence will come here?' she asked faintly. That meant frequent visits from this trio to collect their letters. 'I don't know if the lease allows—'

'Allows a business to be run from here? You're running your business from here, don't forget. Anyways, I checked the lease before I handed over the money. I look after your interests, my girl.'

'I appreciate it, Vic. I do, really.'

'Australia', said Popple, 'is a land of opportunity. There really is gold there, you know. However, it takes money to hire surveyors and travel all that way in search of it. We will sell shares in our little business to raise the capital to go gold hunting. Quite simple, really.'

Charlotte shifted in her chair. 'But what if you don't find any?'

'We are raising money in order to explore. No share-holder will be left in doubt of the purpose to which we will be putting our money,' replied Popple. 'All legal and above board.'

'I see no reason why we can't have our first board meeting here and now,' said Arthur, trying to sound as if he had just thought of it. 'This could be your great opportunity, Charlotte. Within the next twelve months, our little venture could make you enough money to buy Capel Manor.'

'I keep telling you, I haven't any money to buy shares!'

'Keep your hair on,' said Vic. 'I will lend you the money.' He patted her on the knee, smiling. 'Don't forget the director's fees. During the next year, I'd say they would come to about a hundred pounds. In fact, what the hell. We'll vote them to you in advance.'

She was silenced. In return for her compliance, she was to have enough money to maintain the home Vic had rented for her. What could she do but smile and say how happy she was to co-operate?

Popple Douse left his seat to fetch a briefcase he had earlier put beside a writing desk. He dropped a sheaf of papers onto her lap. 'Here is a copy of the Articles of Association. Glance through them and give them back to me. No need to read them carefully. A pretty young lady like you doesn't want to soil her hands in the murkier, well not murkier but mundane – yes, that's the word – more mundane aspects of business. We'll talk about your shares in a moment.'

Charlotte flipped the pages and read down an alarming catalogue of powers. The company's name was to be Goldseekers Limited. Its registered office was to be Capel Manor, Middlesex, England, its purpose to prospect for gold. These were the least alarming sections. There were phrases like 'to purchase or by any other means acquire and take options over any property whatever', and 'to invest and deal with the moneys of the Company not immediately required in such manner as may from time to time be determined'.

The Company would have the power to lend and advance money or give credit, and to borrow and raise money in any manner. They could draw, make, accept, endorse, discount, negotiate, execute and issue cheques, bills of exchange, promissory notes, bills of lading, warrants, debentures and other negotiable or transferable instruments.

Before she had finished reading the Memorandum, Popple snatched it from her fingers, took up an official document and began to read in a curious drone. 'Minutes of the first meeting of the directors held at Capel Manor on 24 December, 1911. Present, da de da de da. We know who's here. Mr Popplewell Douse reported the incorporation da de da de da. Let's see here. What's next? I shall be Company Secretary. Additional directors. That's you, Charlotte. It was resolved that—' he looked up briefly, 'Mr Victor Tavern be elected Chairman of the Board. It was reported that notice had been given to the Register of Companies that the registered office was situated at Capel Manor. It was resolved that Messrs (we'll fill that in later) be appointed auditors. Da de da de da Companies Act of 1908. Subscriber shares. Let's see, we can fill that in later. I've put you down for ten thousand shares, Charlotte.'

'Ten thousand!'

'At two shillings a share. The money will be paid on your behalf and the shares will be delivered to you as soon as they have been printed, stamped and all the legal business completed,' said Popple. He nodded to Vic.

'Any other business?' No-one answered Vic's question. The board meeting was declared over.

They were seated in the drawing-room of Capel Manor, so Charlotte wondered why she felt as if she was drowning. 'Are all of you buying a thousand pounds worth of shares?'

'We've already done so,' said Vic. 'It's the law. Companies Act 1908.'

She clutched her hands together to prevent her fellow directors from seeing how they trembled. These three men, a pawnbroker, a disgraced solicitor and a race-course tipster, apparently had enough money to buy a thousand pounds worth of shares each. And Vic, who lived quite modestly, was seemingly also rich enough to put in a thousand pounds on her account. What if they all went bankrupt?

'Excuse me.' The return of her customary spirited way of speaking caused the men to pause. 'This all seems to have been got up in a bit of a rush. What if the company goes bankrupt? Will I be an undischarged bankrupt for the rest of my life?'

'Limited companies don't go bankrupt,' said Popple. 'They go into liquidation. Your liability will be only so much as you invested. Or has been invested on your behalf. You, personally, will not be bankrupt.'

At that moment, Florence came into the drawing-room. 'Have you lot finished your business? Billy has won a shilling from me playing pontoon, and I'm tired of playing. I think I'll go to bed. Are you coming up, Charlotte?'

Grateful for the interruption, Charlotte said she felt extremely tired and would have to be up early the next morning. She said good night to her guests and quickly left the room with Florence, before anything more could be said about Goldseekers Limited.

They were silent as they made their way to the room Florence was using, which was next door to Charlotte's.

'I'll just come in to make sure you have everything you want,' she said, and closed the door behind them. 'Ah, yes, a nice fire. The room is cosy, isn't it?'

'It's beautiful,' said Florence, 'but I would hardly call it cosy. I prefer our house in Bayswater. It's a terraced house, but quite comfortable and easy to run. This place must be a nightmare.'

'Perhaps you are right. Are you sweet on Billy?'

'Why, the things you say, Charlotte. Of course I'm not sweet on him. He's a strange boy. Besides Popple doesn't have any money. I've got to look for a husband with a good position and a house.'

'Really?' asked Charlotte in surprise. 'I was under the impression your father was very well off. I must have misunderstood.'

In the drawing-room, Popple gathered up his papers and put them back in the brown leather briefcase. Billy wandered about the room, looking at the pictures on the wall, and paused to pick up from a side table the silver-framed photograph of a handsome man with a panama hat crushed under one arm.

'Can't you settle, lad?' asked Vic. 'If you're bored, why don't you go to bed? We might find some excitement tomorrow morning.'

Billy turned. 'Are you going to give me an orange and some Brazil nuts? I'd rather have shares in your new business.'

'Hush. That matter is well in hand. Charlotte is a director. I don't want you on the board. One of us in the family is enough.'

Billy looked at the three men, all of whom seemed to be a trifle worried. 'Did she cut up rough? She's a clever girl. I think you made a mistake there.'

'Billy's right, Vic,' said Arthur. 'We could have done without her.'

'She lives here, dammit. We had to have her in on it. C. A. Blair of Capel Manor. You process those share certificates smartly, Popple. We want to get them signed.'

'I hope', said Arthur, 'that you don't expect me to actually *buy* a thousand pounds worth of shares. That's twice what my cousin left me. And what's more I wouldn't give it to you if I had it.'

Popple tucked the briefcase under his arm, as if he couldn't trust the handle. 'Calm yourself, my friend. I don't have a thousand pounds or even half that amount, although I suspect Vic could find it if he had to. It will be all right. I'll put the money in for our shares as soon as we receive the readies from share sales.'

'You can't have one pound in two places, Mr Douse,' murmured Billy.

'That, young sir, is just where you're wrong. It's called accounting, and I know a fair bit about it.'

Vic grinned. 'Is that how you came to leave the legal profession?'

'It is,' said Popple with a nod. 'By the way, just so that we all understand one another, this is, as I said to Charlotte, a limited liability company. However, if we should be found guilty of fraud then there is no limit to our liability.'

'Hold on!' cried Brock. 'I don't like the sound of that.'

Popple Douse smiled slightly. 'Will you excuse me? I shall go to my room and work on these papers.'

Vic, badly shaken, hid his surprise in gruffness. 'Don't snivel, Arthur.' He found a seat and stretched out his legs in a casual gesture that cost him much. 'Just don't you forget who it is you want to outsmart, Douse. It's the great British investor, not me.'

Chapter Five

The next morning was cold and misty. Eighteen hours after arriving, the Londoners were already bored, yet no-one wanted to adopt extreme measures to dispel the lethargy by taking a walk in the grounds. Charlotte, who never missed an opportunity to walk, put the turkey on to roast, the pudding on to boil, wrapped up warmly and set out to tour the pleasure gardens, intending to end with an inspection of the houses.

A strong northerly breeze stung her cheeks and cleared away the fuzziness that was the result of a poor night's sleep. She reached the pond's edge, out of sight of the windows of the house, and stood quietly watching a pair of ducks leave the water in hopes of a crust of bread from her pocket. Surely, she reasoned, Vic would not embroil her in a crooked business. She refused to think of him as a thief. He might have turned a blind eye occasionally when presented with stolen property, but he was basically an honest man. She was almost sure of it, although the police visited his shop often enough.

What if Goldseekers happened to be both honest *and* successful? She would be able to buy Capel Manor and live in the country, alone and sad, for the rest of her life: hardly the glorious future she had once dreamed of. She almost wished that she had never moved into the house, since experiencing a more refined style of life had made her discontented. She had lost something valuable, which was the ability to be happy in the company of Vic and his friends, while nothing had occurred to take the place of the old shoulder-rubbing, mutually supporting community life. Ambition had turned out to be a poor companion.

The wind rose. Before she could decide whether to go back to the house or press on, it began to rain hard. It was too far to run back to the house, much simpler to take shelter in the grotto. In its depths it was so dark that she stumbled over artful arrangements of Pulhamite stone, designed to hold the overflow from a cascade long since out of action, and had to feel about for somewhere reasonably dry to sit. Rain pounded on the glass above, inevitably found the broken pane, and soon began to form a puddle at her feet.

The four entrances to the grotto each had their own chamber which led into the central one. She heard no sound except the rain, until Jacko suddenly appeared in the gloom, standing in the archway of the north chamber like a pantomime villain.

Charlotte gasped. 'You gave me a fright! I didn't expect anyone to be around on Christmas morning.'

'I'm sorry, miss. I was down by the reeds.' He walked to the middle of the central chamber and was struck on the head by dripping rain. Looking up, he got several more raindrops full in the face.

'You ought to take better care of this place.'

'I will, now that there's somebody to appreciate it, sort of thing. I've been wanting to talk to you, Miss Blair. You'll be needing me to grow flowers for your business. Stands to reason, what with you having to buy everything in the market up to now. What I'm getting round to is, you'll need another glasshouse here at Capel. Orchids. That's what I should grow for you. I mean, who wants fuchsias these days? Our grandparents thought they was fine and dandy, but they're old-fashioned. I could buy two hundred young orchids for a tenner and grow them on. There used to be another house here at Capel. The frames and some of the glass is put away in a shed. The thing is, I'd need some casual labour.'

Remembering her guaranteed director's shares, she felt she could afford this comparatively small expense. 'In that case, get on with it, Mr Boon.' She peered out of the nearest passageway. 'The rain has turned to snow, but it doesn't seem to be sticking. I'll be on my way.'

Her guests had assembled in the morning-room. No-one had visited the library to find a suitable book, but Florence was thumbing through one of Charlotte's magazines. Popple had been reading an old newspaper, but it now covered his face as he slept. Arthur Brock, Billy and Vic were playing cards.

'Florence,' she said quietly, 'I'm going to need some help in the kitchen.'

Florence looked up from the magazine. 'What sort of help? Not cooking, I hope. I don't cook. Aren't there any servants?'

'It's Christmas day. They've gone to see their family. The turkey is in the oven, the pudding is simmering. I just need you to watch the sprouts and chestnuts, and to make some bread sauce. Mrs Duck left everything to hand. You can do that, can't you?'

'What will you be doing?'

Charlotte sighed. 'I will be setting the table and doing the table decoration. Please, Florence. I'll give you a nice big apron to protect your gown. I want the table to look special today.'

'I suppose you will be asking me to wash dishes, too.' The girl reluctantly laid her magazine aside and stood up. 'Well, I refuse to ruin my hands. Those two women can do it when they come back.'

Despite her grumblings, Florence seemed quite at home in the kitchen. She denied ever having to set foot in her father's. 'We are well staffed, I assure you,' she said haughtily, but Charlotte suspected this was not entirely true. She left her in order to set the table and assemble the decorations.

Given that she had very short notice, she had planned quite elaborate decorations for the Christmas table. First the stiff white damask cloth, and down the centre a drift of red and silver gauze. On either side she placed trails of smilax which darted in and out of small wire arches covered in mistletoe. In the centre of the table she placed a small ivy tree which she found among John Green's treasured possessions. He feared for the tree's safety in the heat of the dining-room, but she assured him it would be returned on Boxing Day. From her collection of ornaments, she placed a dozen tiny bells on the tree. Capel Manor possessed two magnificent candelabra which she placed either side. Smilax was stretched several inches above the cloth from one candelabrum to the other and was also used to link the four silver vases at the corners of the table filled with red carnations. A dainty buttonhole of maidenhair fern and a red carnation placed in the elaborately folded napkins completed the table.

The room was not decorated to her satisfaction until she brought in a three-foot-tall, narrow-waisted basket with a huge handle and put it on the sideboard. Filled with expensive blooms of poinsettia, its handle wrapped with scarlet ribbon, it dominated the room and glowed against the rich panelling.

When, at one o'clock, the dinner was served, she was amply rewarded for her pains. Everyone exclaimed at the beauty of the room and talked of nothing else until the turkey was brought in. Dinner was a huge success. Charlotte forgot her morose reflections of earlier in the day and enjoyed the company of her friends.

After they had eaten their fill of turkey and were still attempting to demolish the Christmas pudding, Vic passed round cigars for the men, but Charlotte would not allow them to light up. 'I've no right to fill Capel's dining-room curtains with cigar smoke. It will have to be the library, Vic.'

'Oh, ho! It will be a cold smoke, lads,' he said jovially, but she knew he was annoyed.

Eventually, everyone decided on an afternoon sleep.

They parted, and didn't reassemble until four o'clock. Afternoon tea was a haphazard affair, served in the morning-room. No-one wanted an early evening meal, so it was decided that they would eat their cold turkey, roast ham and left-over fried Christmas pudding at half past nine.

The women were not to be denied a chance to wear their best frocks, however, so everyone had to put on evening dress. They were to meet in the morning-room at seven o'clock.

For the occasion, Charlotte had saved her new gown: a peach velvet creation cut very low in the front, with a high waist defined by a broad band of brocade. The short sleeves were of matching peach gauze. The outstanding feature, and the one that revealed the origins of the gown, was the surcoat of peach brocade which reached nearly to her knees. This had no sleeves, but two long loops of enormous paste diamonds that were attached to the shoulders and hung below her waist at each side. The surcoat was part of an old costume which had belonged to her mother, the sleeves of which had been removed due to their untreatable grubbiness. With a peach feather on a bandeau circling her forehead, she looked grand, and as she said herself, ready for the part of an ugly sister in Cinderella. She loved the flamboyance of theatrical costumes and saw no reason to be a slave to current fashions. Personal adornment was an expression of oneself. Why shouldn't she wear whatever she chose, so long as it was decent? Because people will laugh at you, her mother had once explained. Don't give anyone a chance to laugh.

Florence was most definitely not wearing a made-over stage costume. She had chosen a pale green crêpe gown with a hobble skirt slit to the knee and topped by a fur-trimmed peplum that stood out all round. At first glance, the gown seemed modest enough, but managed to show off a fair amount of cleavage, and her matching turban gave the girl a sultry look.

The men were profuse in their praise but more interested in dipping into the port. Charlotte had ordered two bottles of champagne to be iced, and this was also served. Alcohol gave the guests that extra exuberance that had been previously lacking. A game of charades quickly got out of hand. No-one would obey the rules and there was much adolescent giggling in corners.

'This won't do,' said Vic finally. 'We men have got a surprise for you. You two just sit there, looking pretty, and wait for us.' On his signal, they all left the room, shouting and swearing and punching each other playfully, like a crowd of ten-year-old boys.

'Whooee!' said Florence. 'Isn't it nice to be quiet for a minute or two? I never saw such rowdiness.'

'They're having a good time. Your gown is very beautiful. Is it a couture gown?'

The girl smiled, appreciating the compliment. 'No, of course not. It was quite expensive, however. You mustn't tell Popple. He'd kill me, he really would. Sometimes, I visit the better hotels and take tea all by myself. I've met some really interesting men that way.'

'Good God, Florence! You've chosen a dangerous pastime. Wouldn't you do better with some safer hobby? How about knitting? That should keep you out of trouble.'

Florence rolled her eyes. 'I'll say! This one time, I met the most charming older man and he suggested that we return to his home so that he could change his jacket and collect some money before going out to dinner. Well! I went inside to wait for him in his lobby and was nearly ravaged. I promised to inform the police. That frightened him! He gave me twenty pounds for the indignity I had suffered, and I didn't have supper with him, after all. For weeks I was too afraid to have tea anywhere on my own.'

Charlotte made no comment. The girl had confirmed all her earlier suspicions. She was a dangerous young lady to know, apt to contaminate by association. Floral decorators needed to consort with the best people in order to get lucrative contracts. She would make sure that Florence was never present when she was attempting to impress a future client.

The morning-room door burst open and the four men entered with a loud hurrah. Billy was playing some unidentifiable tune on a comb and tissue paper.

'It's topsy-turvy!' cried Vic. 'Like we used to do in the old days. When I was a lad, we all went out in the streets for a knees up. The authorities didn't like it, of course. You can't get drunk in the streets these days and expect to be left alone to enjoy yourself. How do we look?'

They looked perfect fools. Vic must have brought their clothing with him, for they had rolled up their trousers (or taken them off) and put on drawstring skirts. Each man had a calico scarf tied under his chin and, of course, they all clutched shawls over their shirts and preened in the manner they imagined to be authentic of the vainer sex. Vic had apparently come by some theatrical make-up, as they had rosy cheeks and even rosier lips. They had even attempted to blacken their eyelashes, but this was a skilled business. Black greasepaint had to be heated in a spoon over a lit candle and dropped onto the lashes with a hairpin. Charlotte was adept at it, but only wore it on stage. The men had settled for smearing black greasepaint all over their eyelids which made them look more like drunken owls than women.

They danced and sang and pranced about. It was crude and unprofessional, but it was funny. The central table had to be moved so that they could link arms like a row of Tiller girls and attempt to kick their legs. They told jokes in the manner of the minstrel shows, some of them very near the knuckle, and in general imitated every performance of every sort of show they had ever seen.

Charlotte was well aware of the old tradition of topsy-turvey. Her father, a man twenty-five years Vic's senior, had often spoken of it with affection. Everything was upside down for one day. Drunks played at arresting policemen. Schoolboys locked their masters out of the schoolrooms and men dressed as women. Her father had mourned the passing of street entertainment by 'the people', as he used to call them, claiming that 'they' were trying to destroy the old ways.

Capel Manor rang to the old traditions for almost an hour, helped along by copious quantities of alcohol. By nine o'clock the performers were tired and hoarse. They sprawled on occasional chairs and roared good-naturedly for their supper.

'Florence,' said Charlotte, getting to her feet, 'I think we had better lay out the supper.'

Florence lay back in her chair and complained that she was exhausted. She didn't think she could get up even to eat her supper, so Charlotte went into the kitchen alone and had just transferred all the dishes from the larder to the sideboard when the Duck sisters returned and said they would serve the meal.

As she crossed the hall to call her visitors to supper, the doorbell clanged loudly. It never occurred to her to wait until Rachel could reach the hall. She stepped forward, opened the front door and had a heavy suitcase thrust into her hand.

'There you are, my girl. Please take that inside. I must pay off the cabby. A shilling, old chap? Put the trunk in the hall, there's a good fellow.'

Dumbly, she carried the suitcase into the hall and set it down. A gentleman in an expensive Chesterfield coat and bowler hat entered. Pale electric light from the chandelier fell on his face, and she blinked in surprise. Matthew Warrender had returned from abroad.

'Where is Mrs Snodsby? You received my cablegram, didn't you?'

'There's been no cable.'

At this moment, her appearance registered with him and he realized that he was not addressing a servant. He looked her up and down, taking in the string of blatantly artificial diamonds, the feather and the glossy blond pompadour hairstyle, so different from anything a servant would be allowed to wear.

'Who the devil are you?'

'I am Miss Charlotte Blair. I gather you are Mr Warrender. I rented Capel Manor for eighteen months. The agent is Mr Sloper. Surely you knew I was living here. I presume you instructed him to rent out your home. It's all paid for. Mrs Snodsby has retired to Devon.'

'Good Lord! I do beg your pardon. I thought no-one would move in until March.' He took off his hat. 'I have just returned from Hong Kong, a long and tedious journey, I assure you. I believe I did fire off a cable to Sloper when I heard that both my grandparents had died. I didn't know then that I would . . . but never mind that. I must leave at once. However, the cabby has gone. Will you have a servant telephone for another cab?'

A thousand thoughts crossed her mind. If he stayed for supper, he would see the table decorations and know how clever she was. But if he stayed any longer he might see that she kept his photograph prominently displayed in the drawing-room. If he stayed for supper, he might begin to experience some of the romantic attraction that his photograph had aroused in her. Yet if he stayed for supper, he would discover what sort of friends she was entertaining. Most importantly, if he left immediately, she might never see him again.

'Won't you stay for—'

Florence opened the morning-room door as Vic's voice rang out. 'That's all bleeding horse manure, if you ask me, Arthur. What are you thinking of?'

'Oh, I do beg your pardon,' giggled the girl. 'What must you think of us? Mr Tavern has celebrated a trifle too much and—'

'Obviously!' Despite the steel in his voice, Charlotte noticed that his expression softened at the sight of Florence.

She looked at the girl in surprise. Was she pretty enough to have such a dramatic effect on a well-bred gentleman? It was all very galling. Mr Warrender, the object of Charlotte's intense speculation for the past few months, was intrigued by the vulgar Miss Douse. Then, to complete the destruction of her day, the four men in women's dress emerged from the morning-room.

'Oh, ho!' said Vic heartily. 'You see before you, sir, four men intent on the revels of their ancestors. Topsy-turvey as in the old days. I have some more clothing upstairs. Care to join us?'

Mr Warrender looked in surprise at the drawstring skirts, the rouge on sweating faces and said firmly that he would not be in need of anything. If someone could just call a cab, please, he would return to London.

'This is Mr Warrender who owns Capel Manor, Vic,' said Charlotte. 'He has returned from Hong Kong, having completely forgotten that Capel is rented to me.'

Vic blinked, his mind working slowly. Suddenly, he smiled. 'Welcome to Capel Manor. I am Victor Tavern. Your tenant is Miss Charlotte Blair, a . . . business associate of mine. This is my son, Billy. Mr Arthur Brock and Mr Douse. And last, but far from least, Miss Florence Douse. We're a bit crowded, but we can double up to make room for you. You must stay the night. Christmas night and all. Celebrations. Spirit of goodwill. Arthur, you and Popple can bunk together.'

To her surprise, Mr Warrender accepted this drunken invitation to his own home and decided that he would, after all, spend the night. For a few minutes, there was considerable excitement and confusion. Rachel appeared, silent and watchful. Warrender removed his handsome coat to reveal a tweed jacket and a waistcoat of impeccable cut, neatly pressed trousers and gleaming shoes. He was not as tall as Charlotte had imagined he would be, but not so slightly built as she had thought from a careful study of the photograph.

'I don't believe I've ever heard of topsy-turvey,' he said politely. He spoke to Vic as if addressing a rather bright monkey.

'It's your working class custom, Mr Warrender,' said Billy. 'I'm not surprised you've never heard of it. In olden times, the common people had one day in which to turn the tables on their betters, get their own back. All in the best of spirits, of course. Topsy-turveys were street revelries, before the spoil-sports drove people off the streets into their homes. Our sort of people used to get a lot of pleasure from street revels. It didn't matter to us if there was a little drunkenness, a little pocket dipping, a few fights.'

'Indeed.'

Charlotte thought that this one word, uttered so effectively, showed the difference between the well bred and the rest. No longer in doubt about where her loyalties lay, she wished Vic and his friends had never come to spend Christmas with her. She would have been alone when Mr Warrender arrived, could have made sure that his first impression of her was a favourable one. She didn't belong in Covent Garden, and had grown out of her past. She belonged at Capel Manor, among people who could put great meaning into a single word like 'indeed'.

'Isn't he handsome?' asked Florence, as the men left the room to sort out the sleeping arrangements. 'I think he admired . . . my gown, don't you?'

'Oh, he admired *you*, Florence. That was obvious from the first. He admired you very much. Will you excuse me? I must see that an extra place is laid at the table.'

At ten o'clock, they sat down to supper. The men had cleaned their faces, rolled down their trousers, put on their jackets and their best behaviour; all except Vic, who was determined to be offensive. Charlotte couldn't understand what he hoped to gain by his rudeness. He affected not to know which knife and fork to use, slurped

83

wine from his glass and made crude references to people whom Matthew Warrender could not possibly care about.

Mr Warrender, seated on her right, seemed at ease. With casual grace he turned to engage her in conversation. Charlotte gripped her spoon, but dared not dip it into the soup, for fear of splashing it on her lap.

'So,' he said, 'Amundsen has beaten Scott to the Pole.'

'Yes.'

'Rather worrying, don't you think, that no-one has heard from Captain Scott since November?'

'If he's dead, it's his own fault,' said Charlotte, sounding so callous she scarcely recognized her own voice. 'He shouldn't have gone to the North Pole.'

He paused, his soup-spoon halfway to his lips. She had said something ridiculous! What could it be?

'The South Pole, wasn't it? I'm afraid one doesn't get much news in Hong—'

'Yes, the South Pole.'

'I was amazed to read that Madame Curie has been given the Nobel Prize.'

Charlotte replaced the soup-spoon in her soup and leaned back so that Rachel could remove her plate. She had not heard of Madame Curie, and was not entirely sure what the Nobel Prize was. Her wine glass was inches away; its contents might steady her failing nerves, but she daren't reach for it, lest he see the violent shake of her hand.

With a barely audible sigh he turned to Florence on his other side and enquired what she thought of Capel Manor. The girl chattered on amusingly for several minutes about the shock a country house could give a town-bred girl. Three or four times, Mr Warrender laughed out loud.

Down the table, Vic and Arthur were holding forth about a horse they had lost a good deal of money on. Mr Warrender ignored them, turning from the charming Florence to Charlotte, whose growing sense of inadequacy was robbing her of even the most trite phrases. She could not even offer him the salt, for fear that her voice would fail her. And when he helped himself to the salt, he placed it all on the side of his plate! Glimpses of his long, sensitive hands, the crisp line of his jaw, unnerved her completely. He was the man around whom she had woven sentimental, foolish dreams. She was not prepared to risk her heart to anything more substantial than a photograph, for a photograph could not interfere with her plans for a successful career. A photograph could never remind one of one's own inadequacies. To clutch an image in a silver frame to one's bosom in a moment of loneliness and undefined longing, was quite different from sitting next to the original and having to speak sensibly to it. Florence's success served to highlight her failure.

Paralysed by a fear of revealing her tender interest in this demigod from across the world, she couldn't help but show her worst side: distrustful, humourless and boring. Charlotte knew that her attitudes had been learned at a very early age from her mother. Maud Blair's bitter experiences had formed a philosophy of life that she was eager to pass on to her only living child. How often had the older woman said to her growing daughter: If a person is not for you, he's against you? How many times had she repeated: Every woman is your enemy, every man doubly so? Or: Smile when you are hurt. Never let the enemy know he has wounded you?

With such a training, it was no wonder that mother and daughter clung to one another, shunning all others. Nor was it any wonder that, when Maud Blair died, Charlotte felt herself to be alone in a terrifying world. She had to succeed. She had to make a lot of money. How else was she to fend off the alien hoard who would crush her? Vic was her only true link with ordinary people. He had a wide circle of friends, whom she did not trust. It was imperative that she trust Vic, that Vic should not fail her.

Otherwise, she would know that no human being could be counted on to offer succour, love or companionship. And tonight a stranger had come among them whom she had wanted to impress. Instead, he saw qualities in Florence that Charlotte had not known existed within the girl's empty head.

As they were about to rise from the table, Vic asked for words of appreciation for the modest flowers on the table. 'Miss Blair is a professional floral decorator, you know,' he said. 'She runs her business from Capel Manor. A fine address is necessary to do business, I always say.'

Childishly, Charlotte crossed her fingers. Please God, let him be impressed by the flowers!

Matthew Warrender was startled, frowned as he studied the decorations on the table. 'Very seasonal,' was his cool reply, and left the dining-room.

Matthew had been awake since five o'clock and finally climbed out of his sagging bed at half past seven. It was not only the bed that had kept him awake. His tenant and her friends had seriously interfered with his peace of mind. What a damnable business! He would inform Sloper that in future he could not be trusted with Warrender affairs unless he showed more discrimination. Thanks to Sloper's eagerness to rent, Matthew found himself without a decent home in England. Fortunately, Grandfather Gryce had owned a *pied à terre* in London, a very small flat on a top floor in Hanover Square, with a twenty-year lease.

He had left an intolerable situation in Hong Kong, only to find himself tied by a legal document to a woman who might do almost anything to his home. Not that he had any particular love for the place, far from it. He had been staying at Capel Manor when news arrived that his parents had died at sea in their flimsy yacht.

'That damnable father of yours has got himself killed,'

was the way Grandfather had worded it. 'And he's killed my only child along with himself.'

Before the sixteen-year-old boy had properly assimilated this devastating fact, Grandfather had gone on to tell him that, from now on, things would be very different.

'I'm too old to beat sense into you, and you are perhaps too old to learn from such a method, but by God, sir, you will become a gentleman. You will be worthy of the Gryce family, though you don't bear our name. I'm told your French is tolerable and your German as well. So be it. When you finish your studies at Haileybury, you shall try for a cadetship in Hong Kong. Brigg's boy, Pelham, can keep an eye on you there.'

A defence had to be discovered against such grandfatherly spite, and Matthew quickly learned to distance himself from all emotions and treat the world as a huge joke. He prided himself on his sense of humour, on his ability to see the funny side of everything. An inexhaustible fund of boyish wisecracks and a keen eye for the absurdities of life made him good company. He occasionally turned his wit on others, but Pelham Briggs, several years his senior, was not afraid of Matthew's tongue, only of Matthew's superior intelligence.

He hated the idea of going to Hong Kong, mostly because it was what Grandfather wanted. There was a brief rebellion that came to nothing, then Matthew accepted his fate. There was never any doubt that he would pass the entrance examination with high grades. What Pelham had managed, Matthew could certainly achieve. The system was that bright young men were chosen, sent to Hong Kong and there subjected to intensive study in the two necessary Chinese dialects: Mandarin and Cantonese. After this, they began work in one of the many government departments as interpreters. Few were chosen, but for those the opportunities were great.

Matthew had been reasonably content in Hong Kong,

being about as far away as he could get from Grandfather Gryce. The difficult languages came easily to him; Pelham, with a slight edge to his teasing, referred often to the fact that Matthew spoke the languages as well as any yellow devil. A friendly rivalry, which only occasionally became vicious, developed between them, the great difference being that Pelham was the son of a titled surgeon, while Matthew's father was generally considered to have been an eccentric wastrel. There were those in Hong Kong who had met Aubrey Warrender, and these people spoke of his charm, his unreliability and his incredible courage. But Aubrey Warrender was not the sort of parent to own up to if one wanted to succeed in the stratified, narrow, vicious society that was the white colony in Hong Kong.

Susie Yin, the beautiful daughter of a purveyor of Chinese medicines, had accepted his protection, comforted his nights, listened to his musings and laughed with him. Her veneer of refinement, the delicacy of her small body, concealed a tough spirit, which was just as well. The white lords had no time for the native Chinese. By taking her into his quarters, Matthew condemned himself to life at the bottom of the hill, down among the sweating throng, instead of high in the beautiful hills. A cable car separated him – and Susie – from all that was desirable in that closed society. Only Pelham, an enigma, had braved the disapproval of his friends to champion Matthew. Meanwhile, Matthew set about alternately outraging and courting the society he despised, but occasionally longed to join.

So it came as a dreadful shock to him when Susie one day announced that she had found another protector and was moving from his home. When he asked her why, she had said simply, 'I must look after myself. Your grandparents have died. You are a rich man now and will go home to lead the life of a gentleman, marry well and father many children. There will be no place for Susie Yin.'

In fact, he had not planned to return home, being quite content to lead an undemanding life in the Far East. He had no ambition, no desire to progress to a higher position, which would bring with it greater responsibility.

It transpired that Pelham Briggs had lured her away. Matthew's famed sense of detachment, his vaunted ability to laugh at himself, had deserted him entirely. He did not see the humour of the situation. Dammit! He had been fond of Susie. Within days, he resigned his post, sorted out his affairs and sailed for England, only to find a party of lunatics living in his house. There was Brock, the tout, confident that he and Matthew had mutual friends; Miss Douse, as consummate a flirt as he had ever met, and her father, a pompous bore whom she addressed by his first name. As for the Taverns, *père et fils*, the son was a smirking lout, while the father seemed determined to prove beyond doubt that he was a coarse man who was out of his depth at Capel.

Matthew's tenant, Miss Charlotte Blair, was a woman of contradictions: well spoken yet wearing a garish gown. Silent and rather grave, she attacked her supper as if it were her mortal enemy. She had no conversation whatsoever! He marked her down as an ignorant upstart, but had to admit that the house seemed well run.

He had partially unpacked his bags the night before, having refused the tentative offer of help from the parlour maid. He could not remember when he had last packed and unpacked his own belongings and found the experience very frustrating.

Rather than summon a servant, he shaved in cold water and dressed himself in the badly crushed tweeds he had failed to lay out carefully the night before. There followed a search for a clean handkerchief which was then used to rub up his brown shoes. His hair brushes were discovered under a stack of shirts, but it took him five minutes to find a pair of cuff-links. Muttering to himself that he would have to employ a valet, no matter what the state of his inheritance, he chanced to look out of the bedroom window onto the north lawn. A small figure in a mackintosh with a broad hat pulled low on her forehead was ambling across the lawn. Seeing the perfect opportunity to discover the true nature of the dour Miss Blair, he left his room and raced down the stairs and out the back door.

'Good morning, Miss Blair! Do you mind if I walk with you? I haven't seen the garden in years.'

She turned. 'Good morning.'

'I had been hoping to have a private conversation with you. Do you mind if I ask you a few questions as we walk along?'

'I was sure you would wish to.'

'How did you happen to rent Capel Manor? Are you from these parts?'

She threw a suspicious glance at him. 'You must know I'm not. Like my friends, I'm London-bred. I was born just half a mile from Covent Garden market, and we moved to a few rooms on King Street when I was quite small.'

'Oh, I thought—'

'That my speech is different from theirs? I may as well tell you, for Mr Tavern certainly will. When I was eleven he paid for me to have elocution lessons. I'm a good mimic, don't you think?'

'*Pax*,' he said, raising his hands in submission. 'I pay no attention to accents, which are an unreliable guide to a person's worth. I'm not a snob, I assure you.'

'No? You surprise me. I could have sworn you were turning up your nose at us last night.'

He took a deep breath. 'Look here. Any man returning from foreign parts who finds four men dressed as women and his tenant wearing a gown best suited to the circus must be a trifle surprised. You can't blame me for wondering what was going on.'

'Dressed for the circus? Some parts of it were . . . but I took the design from a fashion magazine. That style is perfectly acceptable in the best circles, sir. You've been away too long. Probably gone native.'

He started to reply in kind, but realized he had unwittingly wounded her deeply. While he prided himself on the well honed put-down, he hated to insult people unintentionally. 'My favourite place in this garden was the grotto, because my grandparents never entered it. Is it still there?'

'Yes, but in need of repairs.'

'I shall have to have a word with Buller.'

'If you mean the previous head gardener, he's dead. The present man is John Green. I'll introduce him to you. The foreman of the leisure gardens is Jacko Boon, a sharp type, cocksure but capable.'

'Once again, how did you happen to rent Capel Manor, Miss Blair?'

They strode down the garden towards the grotto. 'I was employed to do the floral decorations for your grandparents' sixtieth wedding celebrations. I was here, having just worked out my plans, when your grandfather died. I'm sorry for your loss, by the way. I suppose you are alone in the world now. No relatives? Neither have I.'

He studied her carefully: the full lips, the distrustful eyes, the way she hunched her shoulders in her coat as if she expected to be hurt and was bracing herself against his next words. 'And you paid the rate Sloper demanded?'

'Fully.'

'Does the lease permit you to run a business from Capel Manor?' They ducked their heads and walked into the dank interior of the grotto.

'It does. However, say the word and I will pack my things and get out. You can return Vic's money for what is left of the lease. He paid in full in advance. Not many people would do that.'

'May I ask what your relationship is to Victor Tavern?'

'I've known him all my life. He is a friend, nothing more. He is not connected with my business, and with the exception of the money he put up for the lease on my behalf, I owe him nothing. Whatever certain people may think, there is nothing improper in our friendship.'

He was aware of an impatient temperament being kept in check. He knew he was being offensive. Why didn't she tell him so?

'I will honour the lease, of course. I have a place in London which will suit me very well for the next few months.' He placed a hand against a clammy, uneven wall, searched one of the planting pockets, then inspected his hand. 'Amazing stuff, Pulhamite. Brickbats and concrete, I believe. The company is said to be able to concoct a passable imitation of any sort of stone you care to mention. This place is a good example. It looks like a cave that has been partially melted by intense heat, or so I used to feel. Now that I have seen the grotto, I believe I had better meet the new head gardener. What was his name, again?'

'John Green. He'll be in his beloved fuchsia house. I don't think he does much else.'

They left the grotto and crunched across the crisp, frosted grass to enter the walled garden from the north end. John Green's fuchsia house was directly to the left, hugging the south-facing wall. He was there, of course, his notebook lying open on the bench as he gathered empty pots to be scrubbed by the pot boy.

'Mr Warrender, may I introduce you to your head gardener, Mr Green?' said Charlotte. 'This is Mr Matthew Warrender, the owner of Capel Manor.'

Green removed his cap. 'How do you do, sir? Does this mean you will be leaving Capel Manor, Miss Blair?'

'No,' she said grimly. 'I will be here for the full term of my lease. Will you show Mr Warrender your fuchsias?'

John's lower lip came out half an inch. 'Certainly, Mr Warrender. I'm sure you will appreciate them. Miss Blair has gone and fixed up to have another greenhouse erected here in the kitchen garden. Arranged it all with

Jacko Boon. Not a word to me. Anyone would think I don't matter.'

Charlotte seemed taken aback, unaware that she had committed any sort of error of management. It had taken Matthew no more than ten seconds to sum up the new head gardener as a man totally unsuited to his position. How Buller would have snorted with disgust!

'I'm sure Miss Blair had every intention of discussing the matter with you in due course. Which fuchsias are you bringing into bloom for the manor during the winter?' asked Matthew, who could see that there was not a single plant in active growth.

'Nobody appreciates my fuchsias, so I give them a rest during the winter. Mrs Gryce wouldn't have them in the house.'

'If no-one wants fuchsias, why is so much space given to them?' pursued Matthew. 'Have you not a great many other duties? Capel Manor does not exist to support your hobby.'

'No, I reckon not. But nobody's complained up to now.'

'May I see your daily records?'

The head gardener glanced away, biting his lower lip. He seemed incapable of acting like a grown man. 'Jacko keeps his records, and Dangler Stritch keeps his records of the vegetables and vines – only the vines died. I only keeps a note of the poisons when we use 'em.'

'Let us leave him to get on with his work.' Suddenly anxious to get away, Charlotte took Matthew by the arm and practically dragged him from the glasshouse, leading him along the path to the west wall door, as if he didn't know the way.

He smiled as he allowed himself to be led. She was vulnerable, poor thing. The similarity between her and dear Susie was very real. When in doubt, glower, that was this young woman's motto. 'Miss Blair, I gather you have never lived on an estate like Capel. Obviously, you can't appreciate how exalted a position is that of head gardener. Some of the most knowledgeable growers in the country are head gardeners on private estates. That man is a disgrace to his profession. He clearly doesn't know what is going on in this garden, and I very much doubt that he has any control over the men. As for the fuchsias, I daresay he sells them on the sly. I would not be at all surprised if he isn't denuding the garden, while charging you for materials he never actually purchases. He should be dismissed.'

'He is probably as bad as you say. You can sack him ten times over when Capel reverts to you. I intend to keep him. You obviously can't appreciate how hard life is for people like John Green and his wife. They live in the lodge. If I dismissed him, he might find it very difficult to get another job. They could be homeless. That's a terrible thing, let me tell you. When my lease runs out, you can do as you please.'

'How generous of you. Does the lease permit you to erect glasshouses whenever and wherever you choose?'

She stopped, gave a short embarrassed laugh and said, 'I don't know. We must have a word with Vic.'

They found Victor Tavern alone in the dining-room, about to tackle a plate of scrambled eggs, bacon and sausage. Graciously, he invited them both to take a seat. 'What can I do for you?'

Matthew breathed deeply of the warm air and headed for a chair close to the fire, then suddenly remembered his manners and held out a chair for Charlotte. Her cheeks were glowing from the morning walk, her nose only slightly pink. She was the perfect picture of a healthy young woman. He, on the other hand, was chilled to the marrow, being unaccustomed, after so many years in Hong Kong, to cold weather.

'Vic, can I put up a glasshouse if I wish?' she asked. 'What does it say in the lease?'

'You can build an extension to the house if you so choose,' said Vic. 'It says so, but don't look so black,

Mr Warrender. She ain't got the wherewithal to do it, and I've not got the inclination.'

'I'm relieved to hear it.' Matthew smiled encouragingly at the young woman who served his coffee, and was told that Rachel and her sister, the cook, had served his grandparents for three years. Victor Tavern's eggs appeared to be perfectly cooked, the toast was presented as Matthew liked it. Apparently, the Duck sisters were content to work for Charlotte, which spoke well for his tenant. Rachel insisted on filling his plate from the sideboard for him. He suspected that he looked as cold as he felt.

'You know,' said Vic, leaning back in his chair and almost overbalancing, 'this pretty young thing used to be on the stage. Could have been a star. What do you think of that? Threw it all up to get dirt under her fingernails. What a disappointment to her mother.'

Charlotte grimaced. 'Don't listen to him. Let me tell you what the theatre is all about. Vic put it into my mother's head that I could help out with the household expenses by going into pantomime when I was ten years old. The season always starts on Boxing Night, but we had to rehearse for six weeks before that, getting paid only for the last week of rehearsals. As opening night approached and we children failed to learn what we were supposed to do, so rehearsals got longer and longer. The year I was twelve, we were summoned on Christmas Eve and kept working for twelve hours. For this I received the handsome sum of twelve shillings a week. I gave my mother five, tipped the call boy and laundress, bought myself the bare minimum of food and worked for eight months of the year. And all so that men could stare at my legs. The year I was thirteen, I was told I was too old and too tall to be a child performer, and there was nothing for me as an adult.'

'But isn't there a law to protect children from exploitation?'

'Easily ignored, I assure you.'

Victor Tavern's expression was grim. He had been making snorting noises throughout Charlotte's explanation, but could contain himself no longer. 'I started work much younger than you did, and so did your poor mother. And after your dad died, there was no money.'

'I don't begrudge the hours I spent, nor the schooling I missed. But I prefer to be a floral decorator. My father was a super, Mr Warrender. That's how he met my mother.' Seeing Matthew's look of incomprehension, she explained. 'A supernumerary. He was recruited by a super-master who would find non-speaking bit parts for him. The work was badly paid, there was no chance for advancement and no opportunity to learn proper acting. He did this for years, going on the stage whenever he could and portering in the market when there was no work. The theatre is cruel, it eats up lives. Unfortunately, portering is even worse. My father loved plants and in his spare time grew auriculas – to a very high standard. He used to win prizes. It is from him that I get my love of flowers.'

'Huh!' said Vic.

'And I could trust him,' she added, remembering some past grievance. 'He was a plain-spoken man who held nothing back. There was never any da de das with my father, like there was when Popple Douse was talking to me the other night. My father spoke straight from the heart. Nothing concealed.'

Matthew was confused, but Vic seemed to understand her perfectly well. 'You don't trust the da de das? Why the devil didn't you say so at the time? There's nothing suspicious about the da de das. Just a way of getting through the business quickly. You could have said "hold your horses" or something. You could have asked. Since when have you played the meek little miss? Don't give me that pathetic young thing routine. Anyway, I've never let you down before. You know you can trust me.'

'You've never before pushed me into something like

this . . .' she glanced at Matthew, 'like this da de da business. I warn you, Vic: I'm grateful to you, but there is a limit.'

'Thank you for your plain speaking, Miss Blair!' Vic stood up, slammed his crumpled napkin onto the table and walked from the room, very much on his dignity.

What on earth could these two eccentrics have been discussing, wondered Matthew. Whatever the full story was, Vic Tavern and the very serious Miss Blair, with her no-nonsense attitude to life, had dispelled his gloom. His sense of the ridiculous had returned and he was able, once more, to distance himself from others and laugh at them. In a strange way, Charlotte Blair reminded him of Susie Yin. There was the same surface grace and sophistication masking the same sort of determination and skill for surviving against the odds. What a principal boy she would have made!

'Miss Blair, I wonder if I may take advantage of your hospitality for one more night? My lawyer is in Enfield Town. It would be convenient if I could visit him the first thing tomorrow.'

'Are you going to dismiss him because he didn't draw up a better lease?'

'Of course not,' he said and laughed. After a second or two, her solemn expression faded and she allowed herself a cautious smile. Yes, he thought. She's like Susie Yin, but infinitely prettier and far more intelligent.

Chapter Six

On the morning after Boxing Day, everyone was up by half past nine, except Vic. Boxing Day evening had been one of riotous celebration, at least Vic and Brock had celebrated it riotously. Popple didn't know what had got into the two men. Mr Matthew Warrender had sat in the drawing-room with the entire party, wearing a slight smile and a distant manner as if watching a stage play. Meanwhile, Vic had done his best to disgust the man with a display of crude drunkenness that Popple had never seen before. Vic was not normally a drinking man! Brock, on the other hand, usually followed the lead of others. Poor Charlotte had not known what to do for the best, and had taken Florence up to her room at nine o'clock. 'To discuss clothes,' she had said, but Popple knew better. He had seen the tears in the young woman's eyes. She was ashamed of her friends, of their manner of speech and behaviour in the presence of a gentleman.

Popple, having brushed and clipped his whiskers carefully, put on his new Norfolk jacket and plus fours, and came downstairs for breakfast with Florence. He suggested to his daughter that she might care to take a brisk pre-breakfast walk in the grounds with him. He gave her no reason, but there were a number of things he wished to say to her, private matters that required a quiet place away from eavesdroppers, for he was afraid she would raise a rumpus.

Florence would have none of it. It was too cold; there were black clouds in the sky; she was hungry. Hurrying away from him, as if she knew he was displeased with her, she joined Matthew Warrender as he was about to enter the dining-room, caught him by the arm and demanded playfully that he escort her to breakfast. This bold order brought a look of pure delight to Warrender's face, as he readily agreed.

That is when Popple had a sudden, highly satisfactory idea. The visit to Capel Manor had not gone entirely the way Popple had hoped and expected. First of all, Charlotte Blair's dignity and common sense threw into relief his daughter's flighty, flirtatious nature. Charlotte was the sort of girl Popple would have liked to call daughter. Florence was altogether too much like her late mother.

Then there was the matter of Goldseekers Limited. Vic was a forceful character, a man determined to get his own way and totally incapable of listening to good advice. Popple had suggested, and later begged, that Charlotte should be asked to act merely as a post box for the company, and that she be told nothing whatsoever of the scheme. Vic insisted on making her a director. What folly! Charlotte, who had been quite lively before the meeting of the board of directors, now scowled at everyone.

Presented with two young ladies of opposite colouring and disposition, Popple would have had no hesitation in choosing Charlotte. Amazingly, Matthew Warrender seemed to prefer the livelier girl. What better way to ensure that Florence was well looked after and protected from the consequences of her own foolishness than to get her married to a rich man like Warrender?

Billy Tavern, already seated at the table with Brock and Charlotte, frowned as Florence and Matthew entered arm-in-arm. Better and better, thought Popple. It would be a catastrophe to have Vic's boy as a son-in-law. The lad was very strange, an odd mixture of sullen reserve and madcap adventurer. Too much like Florence, in fact.

'I understand you're going into Enfield Town this

morning, Warrender,' said Billy. 'I could take you in me dad's car, if you like.'

'Splendid! I certainly don't fancy such a long walk on a cold day.' Everyone laughed at the idea of a gentleman like Matthew walking to Enfield Town.

'Florence, my dear,' murmured Popple, 'wouldn't you like to visit the shops in Enfield? I might be persuaded to donate a guinea to the cause of your happiness. You wouldn't mind sharing a ride with my daughter, would you, Warrender?'

Matthew smiled broadly. 'I should be charmed.'

Florence was very pleased, but first she must have a cup of coffee and a piece of toast. Could she beg Charlotte to lend her a thick cardigan to put under her coat? She had a dust coat to wear in the motor, of course. She and Popple and Uncle Arthur Brock had travelled to Capel in the motor car, but oh, it had been so cold.

Charlotte grimly laid her knife and fork across her plate and stood up. 'I'll find something suitable, Florence. Don't, whatever you do, get up. Have your coffee.'

Vic came into the dining-room before Charlotte had a chance to leave it. She looked him up and down, made a disapproving noise in her throat and left the room without a word to her oldest friend. He scratched his head, then examined his nails, as if looking for nits. 'What a night, eh?'

Popple didn't bother to reply. Billy, he noticed, was attending to his breakfast, careful to avoid his father's eye.

'You certainly enjoyed it,' said Warrender with amusement. 'I didn't know one man could drink so much and remain standing. Although, now that I think of it, you didn't remain standing all evening, did you?'

'Cheap wine,' mumbled Vic.

'Must have been,' added Arthur, who was holding his coffee cup with both hands to steady it. 'I don't normally succumb, but last night I was really blotto.'

'You were both quite disgusting,' said Florence, cheerfully, then turned to Warrender. 'What must you think of us?'

'What, indeed?' he said, enigmatically.

Dressed in borrowed dustcoat and goggles, Matthew was somewhat dismayed to find that the motor car was open-topped. It had not occurred to him that he would be riding several miles on a bitterly cold day, exposed to the elements. He listened without interest as Billy Tavern gave the motor car's pedigree, nodded as if impressed by the number of its cylinders, and refused to join Florence in the back seat.

To his relief, he soon realized that Billy was an excellent driver, a young man perfectly capable of talking non-stop while keeping his eyes on the road. 'My old man can usually hold his liquor. Don't know what got into him last night.'

'He seemed to take exception to Brock's paying so much attention to Miss Blair,' suggested Matthew.

'My father is very fond of Charlotte. He's known her all her life, you see. Brock's not a suitable husband for her.'

'I believe Brock only said how attractive she looked,' said Matthew mildly. 'Your father spoke of little else for the next three hours. Extraordinary.'

'I don't want you to go thinking things about my old man and Charlotte. There's nothing untoward between them, mark my words. I know he seems to prefer her to his own son, but I don't mind a jot, I promise you.'

Matthew smiled. 'Of course you don't. He has been very generous to her, wanting to promote her business.'

Billy said nothing for a moment or two, busy manoeuvring his way past a beer wagon. 'Yes, Charlotte's business is the be-all and end-all, ain't it? I could lie down and die, and he wouldn't notice so long as Charlotte was looked after. It's time I branched out on me own. Had my own business. The old boy won't cough up for me, though. Keeps me working my tail off in his business.'

'Which is?'

'He's a pawnbroker, isn't he?'

When Matthew failed to say anything at all in reply to this information, Florence said, 'It's good money, you know. My father says it's respectable, too. A pawnbroker was mayor of Bristol. They've got an association and everything. They have banquets.'

'How delightful. You know, I don't believe I've ever met a pawnbroker before.'

'Don't your sort ever get into debt?' asked Billy.

Matthew's 'sort' most definitely did get into debt, as Mr Sloper later pointed out to him, referring to Grandfather Gryce. 'I know you didn't want me to rent out Capel Manor until the spring, Mr Warrender,' he said twenty minutes later when Matthew was warming his hands in front of the gas fire in the agent's office. 'But Mr Gryce owed me a good deal of money. Now, you owe it me. Two hundred pounds. If you've your cheque book with you, you can pay me right now. Or better still, I'll pay you what's left of Miss Blair's rent money after taking out for all debts. That will give you . . .' he scribbled in his chequebook, 'a clear one hundred and fifty pounds.'

'Is that all?'

'I'm afraid so, sir. Mr Gryce made some strange purchases in the last five years of his life. There was no stopping him. I think his mind was . . . well, he was getting old, wasn't he?'

Matthew took the cheque for one hundred and fifty pounds and studied it carefully. 'What sort of purchases?'

'One motor car after another. Bought and sold, always at a loss. He couldn't drive any of them. I think he paid over the odds, as well. It is most fortunate for you, Mr Warrender, that Miss Blair came along. Her protector paid in advance and—'

'You didn't think I might object to having a man like Victor Tavern anywhere near Capel?'

'Beggars can't be—'

'He is not her protector, by the way. He is a business associate, only. However, he is an unsavoury man, as is his son, his friends and the very common daughter of one of them. I have nothing against Miss Blair. She seems to be a hard-working, decent woman, but she should choose her associates more carefully. Unfortunately, she is an orphan and has no-one to advise her.'

'She won't be living at Capel Manor for many more months, Mr Warrender,' said Sloper, apparently regretting his previous harsh tone. 'I wish to act in your best interests. I thought they would be gone before you returned to England. Otherwise, I would not have allowed them to rent, but, well, it's only for a few months. You'll have the income from Home Farm and the Spotted Cow next year, and as you know, your grandfather had a tidy little set of rooms in Hanover Square. You'll be snug there, I've no doubt. I think he rented garage space nearby for a motor car. You may find yourself owner of one.'

'Do I understand that my grandfather went regularly to London and stayed in Hanover Square?'

Sloper, a small man in his late fifties, had about him the crumpled air of an unsuccessful country lawyer, but Matthew knew he had a handsome house on the Ridgeway. 'He did, sir, but I paid off the lady. Here's the key. You know the address, I believe. What a grand old man he was.'

'Yes,' said Matthew. 'A grand old man.'

Florence left Billy and went straight into Pearson Brothers' store to see what was on offer so far from the smart shops in Town. She looked at some gloves and tried on a few hats, and was about to go upstairs when it occurred to her that she was being followed. Stopping by a handkerchief counter, she turned her head slightly and met the piercing eyes belonging to a strikingly attractive man of about thirty years. Unblinking, he returned her stare with a slight smile, showing no embarrassment at having been caught out.

'Like the whistle, do you?' he said softly.

'I don't care what you wear, sir.'

The man grinned broadly. 'But you understood me. Whistle and flute, suit. You knew what I meant. Now, how is it that a grand lady like you understands Cockney rhyming slang?'

Florence drew in her breath sharply. She had that delicious breathless feeling she always got during an encounter with a strange man. It was so exciting! He might be any type, a dangerous man who would swoop on her, carry her away . . .

'I may know a few words of Cockney. Just for amusement, but I am not accustomed to hearing such cant in my own home. I'm a respectable girl, so don't you go getting ideas. I could send for the police to arrest a masher.'

'I'm no masher, miss, just a man as appreciates a beautiful face.'

'You're wicked.' Her smile took the sting from her words.

'What do you think of our town?'

'Provincial. I'm used to having the best of everything in London.'

'You're used to *seeing* the best of everything, maybe,' he corrected her. 'Oh, don't frown at me. I admire you, I really do. But your sort don't belong at Capel Manor. All them toffs, sort of thing. I'd like to see you in your own home, among your own sort.'

This was going too far. No other man had ever spoken to her in such a frank way. They played the game, treating her like an innocent lady, at least until they invited her to go out with them in the evening. 'I'll have you know my father is a solicitor, a man of the law. Now, kindly leave me alone. I'm not accustomed to having conversations with strange men.'

He didn't challenge the statement, but the smile broadened, exposing good teeth, while his eyes almost disappeared into their deep sockets. His suit was cheap, ready-made. He was definitely not worth her consideration. Billy Tavern wore better suits. Yet this stranger had the power to make her blush, while Billy had no power over her at all. She permitted herself the hint of a smile, then moved gracefully away. He made no attempt to follow her or speak again. Filled with disappointment and the familiar sense of anti-climax, she left Pearson's and walked up the street. The shops were inferior and there were none that interested her. Unfortunately, Mr Warrender wouldn't be finished with his business for another quarter of an hour. She sighed, deciding that she might as well join Billy in the Nag's Head.

She had hardly finished asking Billy to get her a lemonade when the mysterious man came in and sat down in the far corner. He had taken off his large flat cap, allowing her to discover that his hair was a pale blond. She hadn't noticed before. Eventually, the man got up and ordered half a pint of beer at the bar, slurping the foam off the top as he returned to his seat. Never once did their eyes meet, and he left before Florence and Billy did, but she considered her day a most fantastic success. It was not until she was back at Capel Manor that she wondered how the stranger knew she was a visitor there.

'May I have a word with you, Vic?' asked Charlotte, leading the way to the library without waiting for an answer.

'Well?' he said, closing the door behind them. 'It's perishing in here. What do you want?'

'I want to know why you behaved so badly last night. Anyone would think you had been brought up in a . . . anyone would think you didn't know how to act properly indoors.'

'Brought up in a pig sty? Oh, aye, I was. I've been a very naughty boy, but I'm not the prize fool in this house. It's you what's the fool. The likes of Matthew Warrender ain't for you, Charlotte. He's out of your class. You can't fight up to his weight. Don't break your heart.'

'What nonsense you talk,' she said vehemently to conceal her shock. Had she been so transparent? Perhaps Matthew Warrender also realized she had a tenderness for him, a thought too embarrassing to dwell on. 'He much prefers Florence's type to mine.'

'No, he don't. You've pretty manners and he ain't got nothing against you. Like he ain't got nothing against the Duck girls. But Florence! Why, he's laughing his head off at her. Every mistake she makes, every crude or innocent remark makes him laugh inside. Believe me. I've lived a long time and I know what I'm talking about. I don't want to see you hurt and I don't want him laughing at us. If I give him plenty of reasons to despise us, he'll stay away.'

Now that she was forced to think about it, she knew Vic was right. Of course he didn't admire Florence. How could he? A day or two ago, Charlotte had suggested to him that he was laughing at her friends, but he had shrugged off the accusation. Her embarrassing infatuation had blinded her to the meaning of his actions, the way he talked to Florence, drawing her out, getting her to tell him about herself.

'He owns Capel Manor,' she said. 'I can hardly tell him to stay away.'

'No, nor me. But I can make him want to keep his distance. You'll have your time here. Enjoy what's left. We're going to be rich one day, you and me.'

This last remark was a mistake, reminding Charlotte of her other grievance. 'It's crooked, isn't it? Goldseekers Limited. We're going to be found out and we'll all go to jail.'

'Nonsense. Would I do a thing like that to you? Trust me. We're two of a kind, old girl. I'll always see you right.'

Arthur Brock went into the drawing-room in search of some hair of the dog, and had just located the whisky decanter when the door opened and Popple came to join him.

'Care for a snifter?'

'Isn't the tantalus locked?' asked Popple.

'What's that?'

Popple lifted the mahogany box, containing three cut crystal decanters, by its handle. 'This thing. It's kept locked so that servants won't be tempted to help themselves. You see how the handle prevents me from removing a decanter? You need a key to . . . oh, it's unlocked. In that case, I'll have a small whisky. Are there any glasses?'

Arthur knew exactly where the glasses were and removed two from the cupboard. He poured a generous measure for both of them. 'Good chap, Warrender, don't you think? I'm sure he and I have a few mutual acquaintances, but he's very discreet, you know. I've asked him if he's a gambling man, and he said his whole life is one long gamble. I think I may make a few valuable contacts through him.'

'I wouldn't be surprised,' replied Popple. 'I've found him exceptionally down to earth. Appreciates a pretty face. Has no hesitation in showing his feelings.'

'Oh, aye,' agreed Brock, pouring a second measure. 'No side to him. No turning up the old aristocratic nose. I don't mind telling you . . .' Brock suddenly realized that he was about to reveal too much of his calculations and took a deep swig of the whisky to give himself time to think. No point in telling Popple Douse of his plans to woo a wealthy widow, somebody a little older than himself, beyond child-bearing age, because he didn't want a pack of whelps yapping round his knees. Ideally, she would have married an older man for his money, then seen him into the grave, and should now be on the prowl for the companion of her old age. That was the best way.

He had worked it all out. All, that is, except for the means of carrying out his scheme. Matthew Warrender's approachable nature encouraged Brock to think that here lay his best chance to meet a suitable widow.

'He's the sort of man', pursued Popple, 'who might well think nothing of marrying out of his class, if he should find the right woman.'

'It wouldn't surprise me.' The whisky was taking the edge off Brock's headache. He smiled at his fellow director. Very astute of Popple to have noticed the romantic tension between Warrender and Charlotte. Brock intended to make the most of that little affair.

Rachel entered with a letter on a small silver tray. 'A note for Mr Warrender,' she said, when Charlotte reached out for it.

Matthew Warrender tore it open quickly, wondering aloud who could possibly know he was living at Capel. 'It's from Mr Bowles. He lives—'

'At Myddleton House,' said Charlotte. 'He called here one day, but I haven't been invited to his home.'

'Bachelor establishment,' he murmured in embarrassment. 'I hope you will excuse me if I walk over there this afternoon. I have been invited to take tea with him. I've known Mr Bowles for years. He heard I was visiting Capel and took the opportunity to have a word with me. Do you mind?'

'Of course I don't mind! It's none of my business.' She was determined to hide her hurt. Mr Bowles had been given ample opportunity to invite her to tea, but had managed not to send any communication, dashing her naïve hopes of gaining business through the local gentry. Two days after the socially acceptable Matthew Warrender crossed the threshold, there was a very nice invitation on its way. 'However, Vic and Billy are planning to drive back to Town at two o'clock this afternoon. Billy has no wish to drive so far in the dark. I assumed you would be going with them.'

He took a step nearer to say quietly, 'Between the two of us, Miss Blair, I would far rather take the train. I have spent so long in the steaming heat of Hong Kong that I'm finding it rather difficult to adjust to the rigours of England in the winter. An open car is agony for me. Needless to say, I will be leaving for London this afternoon as soon as I return from Myddleton House. I have a small flat in Hanover Square and wish to get settled in as soon as possible. I'll take the train and have my trunk sent by carrier.'

In the event, the party for London didn't manage to leave until well after three o'clock. They and their luggage were squeezed so tightly into the motor car that there would have been no room for another passenger.

Jacko Boon, who had been waiting for this moment, came round to the front of the house to help store the cases and settle the travellers. It was a moment or two before Miss Florence Douse recognized him. She looked at him in surprise when he took her elbow to steady her as she climbed into the back seat. She smiled politely, then registered dismay, embarrassment and finally anger. He grinned at her throughout.

'It's been a pleasure to meet you, Miss Douse.'

'I could have you sacked,' she hissed.

'Oh, ma'am, what a cruel thing to say! I've wanted to speak to you ever since I was in the storeroom, unloading some stores for Mrs Duck, the cook, when I heard you and Mr Billy . . . er . . . talking on the servants' staircase.'

'I'm not what you think,' she whispered, stricken.

'I think you are the most beautiful woman I ever seen, with a lively spirit. You want to be taken care of by a strong-minded man, that's all, and Mr Billy Tavern ain't the man for the job. I am.'

There was no time to say more. He had to step back to make way for the travellers. Everyone was talking at once. No-one noticed that Miss Douse had gone suddenly quiet. Jacko fancied he could see tears in the young woman's eyes, but reminded himself that it was almost dark on a cold winter's afternoon. He could be mistaken. He almost felt like crying himself. She was beautiful. The trouble was, she wasn't destined for the likes of him. He took off his cap as the car started to move. She turned and met his eyes for a long moment, then waved her hand slightly. Jacko watched the car until it turned onto Bullsmoor Lane.

Matthew had almost reached the fine old bow-windowed Myddleton House before he remembered a most important foible of Mr Bowles. No fires were built at Myddleton until four o'clock in the afternoon, no matter how cold it was out of doors. There was no gas and no electricity. The man who climbed mountains and endured considerable discomfort on his plant-hunting expeditions was not inclined to coddle himself at home.

When they settled into chairs on either side of a handsome fireplace, Matthew noticed that the crumpled newspapers and kindling had received the match, but the coals sat on top of this expert construction in their pristine state, glossy and black. He calculated that the fire might begin to throw out heat just as he was due to leave.

'So you've leased your home,' began Gussie Bowles. 'No-one expected you to return from Hong Kong so soon.'

'Yes, there has been a bit of a mix up. I expected to stay in the colony for some time, but changed my mind. I was under the impression that my lawyer wouldn't lease the estate until the spring, and arrived to find Miss Blair installed. She is a pleasant woman.'

'Yes, she is,' agreed Bowles, 'but I should keep an eye on Capel, if I were you. I fear the lady may have a fancy for carpet bedding!'

'Good Lord!' said Matthew in mock dismay.

'The neighbourhood is ringing with tales about her friends. You have my sympathy.'

'No, no. I don't object to the lady at all. Her friends have returned to London. All will be quiet from now on. I, of course, will also leave today. I'm so glad I had this opportunity to speak to you. Do tell me all the gossip. It's been so long since I was last here.'

'Let me see,' mused Bowles, as a servant entered with the tea trolley. 'You know, of course, that Valerie, Lady Meux has died.'

'No, I didn't! Who lives at Theobalds now?'

Gussie Bowles sat back in his chair, smiling to himself as he took a small sandwich. 'Lady Meux had a friend, Admiral Sir Hedworth Lambton. Shortly before she died last year, she willed her entire estate to Lambton provided he changed his name to Meux. In April of this year, he married Lady Chelsea, a widow who had been living in the Dower House with her five daughters. There was next to nothing in Lady Valerie Meux's will for the late Sir Henry's family, due, the will said, to the omission on their part to receive her as the wife of her late husband. But then, no-one received her, poor dear.'

Matthew listened in amazement to the tale of Lady Meux's final years. Val Meux was a grand lady who was said to have met her husband in a public house, and was believed to have invented a suitable family background for herself. 'Did anyone ever find out how old she was?'

'Never,' said Bowles. 'You never dined there, did you?'

'No,' said Matthew without hesitation. He was aware of the older man's eyes boring into him, but he had given his grandfather his word never to reveal that he had been one of her 'young men', and saw no reason to break that promise now.

The better families in the neighbourhood had snubbed her during all the years she lived at Theobalds. She was inclined to give splendid dinners at which only local tradesmen and young bloods sat down to dine. On a chilly spring day, he had been out riding and had come across the lady just in front of the Temple Bar entrance to the estate. Thrilled by the chance to talk to the dashing Lady Meux, he had no hesitation in accepting an invitation to dine on the following night. He was eighteen years old and had just completed his studies at Haileybury public school.

It had been no mean feat to sneak from his bedroom and escape from Capel Manor in full evening dress, but well worth the risk in order to take part in a revelry that his grandfather had expressly forbidden.

The evening had gone extremely well. Dinner was magnificent. He even had the privilege of seeing three liveried footmen enter the dining-room with three silver dog dishes in order to feed the lady's pets! After coffee, Lady Meux invited them all to walk down the drive to visit the indoor swimming pool. Matthew had drunk a great deal of wine, and was, in any case, drunk on the excitement of the evening.

The pool was magnificent and probably unique in Cheshunt. Its walls were clothed in white tiles with a narrow blue border at head height, and although the water was not heated, the pool house had some form of heat. All the windows were wet with condensation. 'Do you see those ropes hanging down from the ceiling above the pool?' asked Lady Meux. 'They are tethered here at this end of the pool. Now then, I dare three dashing, brave, handsome men to swing from one end of the pool to the other. Who will volunteer?'

In his innocence, Matthew had assumed that every red-blooded man present would be eager to meet this simple challenge. In the event, there was some difficulty in finding two volunteers to attempt the feat with him. They held their ropes as high up as possible, stood back from the pool edge, took a running leap and sailed out across the water. He was aware of whoops of laughter and a few encouraging cries, but there was little time to take in anything very much before he reached the centre of the pool when his rope inexplicably broke, sending him plunging into the deep water in full evening dress.

Even at the moment his feet hit the tiles at the bottom, he thought only that he had been uncommonly unfortunate. But when he heaved himself up from the side of the pool with water gushing from the pockets of his rapidly shrinking jacket, the knowing laughter of the other young men soon alerted him to the fact that he was the victim of a practical joke. Worse was to come, for he lost both shoes in the dive and no-one would volunteer to get them. To loud laughter, Matthew was forced to re-enter the water and dive repeatedly until he rescued his patent leather pumps. Lady Meux, of unknown age and parentage, had a cruel sense of humour. Matthew wondered if the cruel streak had been present before she married Sir Henry, or if she had developed a love of ridicule to ease the pain of being ostracized by her husband's family and friends.

'And now,' said Bowles, 'there is a young lady living at Capel Manor who will also never be received into our homes. The British are a snobbish race, I fear.'

As these words were uttered with all the emphasis of a dire prediction, Matthew had no difficulty in guessing that the older man was warning him not to fall in love with Miss Blair. Otherwise, Bowles seemed to be saying, Matthew would lead the lonely life of a man who had married unacceptably far beneath him.

'Poor Miss Blair,' he said. 'However, I daresay she won't notice any snubs. She has her work which absorbs her, and she will soon be living in London once more. No doubt she has many friends of her own kind there.'

Seemingly satisfied that his warning had been noted, Bowles then launched into an enthusiastic description of the first International Flower Exhibition since 1866, which was to take place in May of 1912. The grounds of Chelsea Hospital were to be the new venue. There was so much work to be done, but what a rewarding occupation! Crowned heads would attend the opening. Rare plants of every description would be displayed for eight days. The gardening world awaited this first international exhibition for forty-six years with great anticipation.

'But, my dear fellow,' exclaimed Bowles suddenly, 'here I am rambling on while you sit there shivering! Malaria, is it?'

'No, it's just—'

'I remember you had wanted to enter the services – the Navy? – but you weren't fit.'

'Consumption. But I am completely cured, I assure you. I was very lucky.'

Arriving home from Theobalds in his wet clothing all those years ago, Matthew had been unable to avoid a confrontation with his grandfather. He had been forced to listen to a homily on the subject of how he had inherited his father's rackety ways, before being told he needed the discipline of a few years abroad. Matthew was as anxious to go abroad as his grandfather was to send him, but was determined not to acquiesce meekly to his fate in Hong Kong. A month later, he tried to enlist in the Navy.

It was due to his attempt to enter the Navy that he discovered he had a touch of consumption. Grandfather Gryce always insisted the illness had been brought on by his plunge into the pool. There followed a year in an isolation hospital, before Matthew easily passed the examinations that led to his being recruited into the Colonial Service. The weakness had never left him, however. Matthew knew he ought to leave Myddleton House, which was extremely cold, and return to the warmth of Capel Manor. He dreaded a return of his illness.

'And I was about to invite you to ice skate at my brother's home, Forty Hall,' Bowles was saying. 'It looks like being a grand winter for skating.'

'Thank you, sir, but I'm not yet accustomed to cold weather. I shall give skating a miss this year.'

Charlotte was looking out of the window of the library as he walked up the drive. He felt a sudden warmth towards this quiet woman. She didn't have Lady Meux's wealth to cushion her from snubs. Matthew's father had been passionate in his hatred of the class system, yet there were times when he craved acceptance by the very people he usually despised. He particularly wanted a measure of respect from his father-in-law. Matthew hoped Miss Charlotte Blair didn't harbour any social ambitions. Surely she was content with her floral decorating business. But was she lonely? Perhaps she was as lonely as he was.

Unbidden, there came into his mind the very pleasant idea that she would make the ideal replacement for Susie Yin. In the space of the few seconds it took him to reach the front door, he had imagined the two of them dining and dancing together, laughing and making love.

Then, she opened the door for him. Her clear gaze and dignified bearing warned him that she would not consent to any such irregular arrangement. They talked in a stilted fashion for fifteen minutes before Rachel came into the hall to say that the pot boy had driven the fly to the front door, waiting to take him to Cheshunt railway station.

They shook hands. He found it impossible to raise her hand to his lips as he had briefly imagined himself doing. This Miss Blair lived in a different world from his own. Now that he was to settle permanently in England, he must look for companionship and eventual marriage among his own sort. Any other course was unthinkable.

Chapter Seven

They had gathered in the estate offices which were built onto the north wall of the vegetable garden for shelter. It was eight o'clock on a very cold and foggy morning, and every man had his hands wrapped around a mug of tea. John looked at his staff: all were present except for Nat Horn, who was in school, and the crock boy, Nobbie Clark, who had been given several dozen terracotta pots to scour.

John was always nervous when the men gathered for a discussion. Before coming to Capel, he had been a labourer at Rochford's nurseries, having progressed very little from his own pot-scrubbing days. His duties had included tasks that required no thought at all, like preparing pots for the sowing of fern spores and, as the little ferns grew, removing the panes of glass from pots of seedlings each day, wiping the condensation from the underside, then turning the glass over and replacing it. He had worked on the clinkering of pathways on the Rochford site, raked the huge furnaces and helped to pack the palms for shipment to the United States, since Rochford's had a healthy trade across the Atlantic.

Mr Buller was a friend of John's father, and had taken the young man on at Capel at a time when the garden was badly under-staffed. His position was officially that of decorator and supplier of plants for the house, because Mr Buller thought John could not get into much trouble in that position. A month before his death, Mr Buller had also taken on Jacko and Dangler as foreman of the leisure gardens and foreman of the vegetables and vineries respectively. However, when the head gardener had suddenly dropped dead, John's was the only face Mr Gryce recognized. Not wanting to trouble himself by advertising for a new head gardener, the old man had appointed John, who had been attempting to live up to his position ever since.

'It's the start of a new year, just about,' said John. 'Dangler, what are you planning for the next few weeks?'

Dangler Stritch, a lanky man in his early twenties, removed his buttocks from the edge of the desk, stood up straight and cleared his throat. 'Planting out Early York cabbages as soon as the weather gets better. Manuring the sparergrass bed. Looking after the hot beds. Sowing some peas, Sangster's No 1 and Tom Thumb. Planting out Ash-leaved Kidney potatoes. I'm giving them a try this year. Pruning the fruit. All the beds is dug. I like to plant the really early varieties to kick off the new year.'

John gave a nod of approval. Dangler was also supposed to be responsible for the vines, but the vines had died. Viticulture was a delicate business. Mr Buller had excelled at it, but Dangler was not so clever. Improper ventilation had allowed rust, then botrytis, to finish off the ageing vines. John had been unable to suggest a remedy, and the vines had eventually been dug out. As no employer had actually given permission for new vines to be purchased, and as John couldn't make up his mind to give the order, there was a lean-to house standing empty. Bertie Cox, the improver journeyman, had suggested the house should be used for figs.

'Jacko, what about you?'

'Everything is in hand, sort of thing. The drive and the sweep need weeding, but there are some repairs needed first. Tyre ruts are bad on the sweep, and Mr Tavern took his car over the drive onto the grass once or twice when the ground was soft and wet. Squabby and I will repair the road, then we'll tackle the weeds. I don't favour sulphuric acid. I'll pickle them with a couple of bagfuls of salt. Then, I'll be wanting to get the new glasshouse put up and—'

'I've been wanting to talk to you about that,' interrupted John, feeling breathless as he always did when about to challenge Jacko. 'You don't need to go putting up a new house.'

'Miss Blair said—'

'I know what Miss Blair said, but she only rents this place. I'm the head gardener as has to take the responsibility. The old vine house will do for your orchids. How many can she need when all's said and done?'

Everyone fell silent. John's display of spirit was the most interesting thing that had happened to them in many months. All eyes were on Jacko, to see how he would react. Jacko, apparently as stunned as the others, carefully finished his tea, put the mug on the mantelpiece and dug his hands into his pockets, but didn't seem inclined to speak. John was determined about this. Today, when all the men were gathered, he wanted to be seen to win a battle. He admitted his debt to Jacko who took a lot of work off his shoulders, but if he was to live in peace at Capel, he had to feel that his position was secure.

As luck would have it, Jacko didn't have to declare himself one way or the other. There was a brief knock on the door, followed immediately by Miss Charlotte Blair, dressed for travel. She smiled at the men as they whipped the caps from their heads. She was charming them with her womanly ways, making it harder for him to control them. He sensed that he was about to lose the argument about the grape house, because Miss Blair liked Jacko.

'I'm pleased that all you men are gathered here, as it makes it easier for me to speak to you. Naturally, I won't interfere with the running of the estate. I'm sure that's well in hand. But I need certain flowers. I want a long succession and I want to be able to pick up what I need at Capel. First of all, orchids: *Cattleyas* and *Odontoglossum crispum*. I also want carnations, long-stemmed, of course. My customers always say "long-stemmed" when ordering flowers, no matter what they are. Long-stemmed blooms are essential. Now, I need a good white variety. In fact, I deal mainly with white flowers, but I will also want some pinks, reds and salmons. Then ferns in pots, fuchsias in pots, Mr Green, and monbretias. And palms. I cannot get enough of palms, mostly *Cocos weddeliana*. What about the new glasshouse?'

Jacko took a step to the middle of the room, grinning at his employer in a knowing way. 'Mr Green feels that the new house shouldn't be built, ma'am. He wants me to use the old vine house.'

'Unless you'd be wanting to replace the vines,' added Dangler eagerly.

'Think about it, Miss Blair,' urged John. He was so nervous he could feel the sweat prickling his armpits. 'We've got the glass and the frames, most of them in decent condition, I grant you. A little rotted wood, maybe, but not too much. But it's the boiler. We ain't got a boiler. And where will the house be situated? There's no more room in the walled garden. And what about all the pipes to run off it? Orchids need heat. You won't want vines. I doubt you care enough about grapes to take up an entire house just to feed one person. Why, you'd be up to your knees in grapes if the vinery was to start fruiting properly, and it would probably take years.'

Charlotte dropped her chin, biting on her thumb-nail as she considered his argument. 'You're right!' she said suddenly. 'Use the vinery. This is Mr Warrender's house. I'm not in the mood to spend too much of my own money improving his property. Now, if the rest of you will excuse us, I would like a word with Mr Green and Jacko.'

With murmurs about the work they had waiting for them, Dangler, Bertie and Squabby left the office, but not before each one had said an ingratiating word or two to the mistress. Squabby, whose wife cleaned the estate office, was moved to apologize for the filth they had brought in on their boots.

'I want to see your records, Mr Green,' said Miss Blair.

'Records?'

'Records! Where are your records of purchases? Where are your records of payment to the men?'

Jacko rested an elbow against the mantel and watched, wearing his customary arrogant smile, as John scratched through a sheaf of papers, hunting for the notebook in which he kept records in a most casual form. Eventually, the book was found and opened for Charlotte as she sat at the desk. For ten minutes no-one spoke.

Finally, she turned round to face the men. 'A penny out in your calculations. Very good. I'm going back to London this morning. I trust you to get on with things. Remember, Jacko, *Cattleyas* and *Odontoglossum crispum*. The flowers that decorators use.'

'There's going to be some expenditure, Miss Blair,' said John, annoyed that she made him feel breathless with nerves. 'Salt to pickle the weeds on the drive. Orchid plants for the new house. When it gets started, we'll need more coal.'

She looked puzzled and seemed to be wondering if he was taking advantage of her. With a leap of the spirits, he realized that she didn't know much about gardening. Nor had she noticed that he had credited his wife with twice as many hours as she could possibly have worked, and had paid her accordingly. Madam was not as sharp as she liked to pretend.

'Do whatever is necessary.' She smiled at the two men and left the office.

'Phew!' said John. 'She don't half make me nervous. I wondered what she was on about when she asked for my records.'

'Probably Mr Warrender put her up to it. We mustn't forget that he knows how an estate should be run.'

John glared at Jacko. 'You didn't help me much. You could've spoke up. You could've said something in my defence, or helped me to look for the bleeding records.

I know you're narked about the new glasshouse, but I done what's best.'

'I just stood back hoping to hear her cussing you out,' laughed Jacko. 'I wanted to find out if she's good at it. No, the truth is, I've got money worries. My mind just won't seem to concentrate on anything else. I sure could do with a few quid.'

'I'm skint. Got nothing to lend you.'

'Oh, good Lord, Mr Green, I'd never ask for money from a married man.'

With a sudden rush of friendliness, John patted Jacko on the shoulder. 'I don't like to refuse you. You're a good man. That's why I let you bugger off the other day to go into Enfield Town. You said you had business to do. Now you say you've got money worries. I just hope there's nothing seriously wrong, Jacko.'

Jacko dropped his head and nudged clods of mud across the floor with the toe of his right boot. 'Look, sir, supposing I was to order two bagfuls of salt and you was to put down in your book that we ordered three? She'd never know and she can afford it. To tell you the truth, I think she deserves to be taken down a peg or two, the way she talks to you. No respect for your position. She's checked the books once and probably won't ever check them again.'

'Well . . .'

'I'll only ever ask you this once, and it would be safe. She didn't ask to see receipts, you noticed.'

'All right. But in future, you back me up in what I say to her. I'll be glad when Mr Warrender is living here. He's a gentleman. He knows how to deal with a head gardener. That is the scratchiest woman I ever did see. Barring my mother-in-law, of course.'

It was after one o'clock when John eventually stepped through his own kitchen door for dinner. He was not surprised that there were no cooking smells of meat or anything substantial enough to satisfy the hunger of a labouring man. He was surprised, however, to find his mother-in-law seated at the kitchen table, glaring at him. Mabel was sitting in the only other chair, crying as she usually did when her mother and husband were in the same room.

'She deserves it,' said Mrs Wheems.

'What?'

'All that work. You ought to be ashamed of yourself, my lad. I didn't bring up my daughter to be a kitchen dab in some rich bitch's house! How dare you? You don't know what you've got here. A jewel is Mabel, but you keep mistreating her. I told her, "You deserve it, girl. Have it." '

'What?' asked John with gathering suspicion. 'What does she deserve?'

Mabel gave a loud sniff and blew her nose, as Mrs Wheems looked significantly at the floor. 'New lino, that's what. With a nice pattern printed on it. Brightens up the place. She deserved to have something new after all the work she done. You ought to keep your wife better, that's what I told Dad only the other night. "Our daughter ought to be kept better, Dad," I said.'

John looked at the lino, just laid, as he tried to formulate a suitable phrase or two of gratitude. The pattern was geometrical in brown, cream and green, and it did brighten the kitchen somewhat. 'That's very kind and generous of you, Mrs Wheems. We—'

'I didn't buy it, you dozy fool! Mabel bought it with her earnings from that Blair bitch, and just a little bit of the housekeeping money. She deserved to spend the money on whatever she wanted.'

'I didn't know you wanted new lino for the kitchen,' said John, watching his wife carefully. 'You never told me you wanted new lino. I thought you wanted a hearth rug. If you had to spend the money, why didn't you buy the hearth rug?'

'Mum said—'

'She can get the hearth rug some other time. This

room wanted brightening up. It was gloomy. Needed something to sort of lift it. I told her. She can buy the hearth rug another time. After what you done to her, you ain't got no business criticizing.'

'What have I done?'

'Oh, nothing much,' said Mrs Wheems, heavily sarcastic. 'Only cost yourself a son, that's all. Only killed your own child, that's what.'

'Mabel! I didn't know—' began John.

'It was you making her work in the big house. Made her start bleeding, and her two days late.'

John was beginning to lose his temper. 'You don't know she was expecting. You don't know that at all. You're just trying to make me feel bad. Well, it wasn't my idea Mabel should work in the kitchen. They were short-handed and there was no time to get anybody else. Miss Blair was determined. She said—'

'Bitch,' said Mrs Wheems. 'You know what you are, don't you, John? A toady. Creeping round, trying to stay on the good side of that woman. Hoping for the leavings from her table. You better go down the pub and get yourself something to eat. Give this poor girl a rest from heavy cooking. I won't have her worked into the grave.'

John balled his fists at his side. 'I'll do that, before I say something we'll all be sorry for. You ought to stay out of our marriage, Mrs Wheems. Let Mabel and me work out our own problems and decide together when we can afford to buy something new for the house.'

'Typical,' said his mother-in-law. 'Didn't I tell you, Mabel, that he was heartless? Here he stands, showing no respect for grey hairs, him with his dad lying on his death bed.'

'What about my dad?'

'He's poorly. Don't you never go round to see your folks? They ain't but half a mile away. Lazy sod.' She patted Mabel's hand. 'It's all right, chuckie. I'll stay with you until five o'clock. I've been up since dawn, doing my housework and I'm tired half to death, but I'll stay with you. Your dad don't need me. He's messing about in the vegetable garden.'

John's family home was on Bull's Cross Ride, past the Spotted Cow. He began to jog along, his mind awash with unspoken ripostes, insults and obscenities that he would like to have fired off, if only he had thought of them. Just when he was convinced he had really told her off, she came back at him with a low blow about his father.

Mabel was the only daughter of Sybil and Ernest Wheems, born to them when they were both forty-three and already had five sons. If John had heard the tale once, he had heard it a dozen times. How Mabel was born a month early and nearly died. How Mrs Wheems hadn't given up hope, but nursed the frail baby night and day.

It never seemed to occur to her that she had destroyed Mabel by her coddling, her spoiling, never letting the growing girl do the things other girls did, never making Mabel buckle down to the chores the way other girls had to. Mabel was spoiled rotten, and fearful that any activity would kill her.

'What's the matter with you, you silly boy?' said his mother at the door. 'Your dad's got a cold, that's all. I suppose that wife of yours wanted you out of the house. Come on in. Dinner's on the table. If you hadn't been such a fool about that girl, you could have married Marie and been looked after properly.'

'Didn't fancy Marie,' he muttered. 'What's for dinner? I'm starved.'

Jacko walked slowly towards the stables where he knew Squabby Horn would be waiting for him. He was about to see his dream fulfilled, a house set aside for the growing of orchids, to be entirely his responsibility. Yet, he felt a fierce resentment. Damn the bitch! Only *Odontoglossum* and *Cattleyas*! Didn't she know there were other orchids?

He had been breaking his back for others since he

was ten years old. A big boy for his age, he had joined a gang of road builders and had begun to swing a pick-axe at fourteen, four years after his parents had done a moonlight flit, leaving the bewildered child to fend for himself on the streets. Miraculously, they had managed to give him a few years of schooling before falling into disastrous debt. He had learned to read and write and to manage numbers well enough to count his money. Although he considered himself fortunate to have had a little learning and to be in excellent health, years of extreme poverty had bred in him a distrust of everyone, and a total reliance on what he believed to be his skills: cunning, ruthlessness and a whole heart. He cared for no-one.

It had been his great good fortune to be taken on the gardening staff at a country house in Surrey when he was fifteen. Five years later, he moved to a larger establish-ment. In this way, he moved steadily up the gardening hierarchy, until he managed to get a post as improver journeyman working in the leisure gardens at Hatfield House. This was by far the largest, most important gar-den he had ever set foot in, but there were drawbacks. The standard of work was so high that he began to feel imprisoned. Everything he did was subject to criticism, discussion and, eventually, complaint. Acutely aware of his shortcomings, he took refuge in a surly attitude, until he was sacked without a reference.

For six months he did whatever odd jobs he could find and slept rough. Then he heard about Capel Manor and Mr Buller, and applied for the job of foreman. His experience was in his favour. The head gardener was a sick man who waived the usual requirement of a good reference. Mr Buller reckoned that any man who had been trained at Hatfield House must be worth his wages. Delighted to have a steady income and a warm bed, Jacko had moved into the bothy and begun to plot his next step. He had a dream more ambitious than being allowed to grow orchids at Capel Manor. He wanted to own an acre of glass and grow orchids for the market.

The major drawback was lack of money. He had saved nearly half his wages, but it would take years to accumulate the forty pounds necessary for every acre of land, to say nothing of the expense of putting up the glasshouse and heating it. That he knew nothing about growing orchids was a minor point. He would learn. What was more, he would learn at Miss Blair's expense. In all his years, he had never worked for a person of his own class, nor had he been answerable to a woman. He felt diminished on both counts and would happily cheat his employer any way he could.

She had committed the unforgivable crime; she had forced him to examine his daydreams and to realize that the greatest obstacle to fulfilment was his own ignorance.

Since he had only his dreams to sustain him, he carried with him at all times an old, out-dated orchid catalogue. *Odontoglossum crispum* presented him with no problems. He would order five dozen plants for a start. As for the *Cattleyas*, the varieties were too numerous to count. Which ones should he buy? A selection? Ask for advice? That would be the answer. He would ask for the nursery to make a selection of five varieties, to send a dozen of each and to enclose a few hints on their proper cultivation. One thing he knew for certain was that these two types of orchids did not require extreme heat. They would be comparatively cheap to grow.

Plant hunters no longer travelled to far-off places in order to dig out and ship out every single plant they found in the wild. There had been such an outcry when millions of orchids came to Britain from every corner of the world, that well before the turn of the century the rape of the wild places had stopped. For some years, breeders had been able to hybridize orchids, although getting them to grow from seeds was a hit-and-miss affair. They were propagated from offshoots very successfully, however.

Recently, the value of cut blooms had dropped. When

Jacko had first hinted at his interest in orchids, John told him that Rochford's had cut back drastically on their orchid growing, and had sold off most of their stock. This was hardly encouraging news for someone who hoped one day to make a living from them, but when a man is merely dreaming, he does not have to consider the market. In the imagination, all things are possible.

With the exception of funeral work, business was extremely slow following Christmas and the New Year. The weather was cold and foggy, trapping the smoke from coal fires and damaging the lungs of young and old. An unusual number of deaths in the city meant that Charlotte and Molly spent many hours arranging the popular tributes for decorating graves. Most people asked for a traditional shape. Cushions and hearts could be done almost in one's sleep. The Empty Chair and the Opened Book took more skill, of course, but the really difficult orders were for the unusual shapes that had to be formed from wire then bound with sphagnum moss before they could be covered with flowers. Charlotte failed several times to calculate the proper number of flowers required when quoting a price to a customer. The result was the loss of money on an arrangement that had perhaps taken several hours to prepare.

In February, the weather improved briefly, and Charlotte's funeral orders went down correspondingly. Funeral work and the sale of cut flowers so close to the market itself could not provide her with the turnover she needed to maintain Capel Manor. To live comfortably while maintaining two homes and a shop, Charlotte needed a few commissions for floral decorating, when the money charged was for her skills and creative imagination more than for materials.

The month was drawing to a close when she received an order for a customer's silver-plated epergne and two silver bowls to be filled with camellias. At this time of year, glasshouse camellias were two shillings for a box of twenty-four. She ordered two boxes for the day they were required and stayed in town, the better to guard the silver and to choose the flowers herself from the market.

As camellias came with little or no stem, due to the fact that cutting them with longer stems would interfere with the next year's blooms, artificial stems had to be made with 25-gauge camellia wires. They were delicate flowers, prone to collapse, so before wiring each bloom had to be gummed with white shellac dissolved in spirits of wine, a drop or two inside the flower and a few more on the outside to prevent it from falling apart.

After every bloom had been gummed, she put a piece of cotton wool in the palm of her left hand, turned a bloom upside down on the cotton and began passing wires horizontally through the heart of the flower, then bent them down and bound them with binding wire to make a stem. Four wires were needed in each of the forty-eight flowers. The first two blossoms shattered in her hand, and she began to doubt if she would get enough of them wired to make an arrangement. However, she managed to control her impatience and complete the last forty-six. It took her an hour, but arranging them in the bowls was done much more quickly. The flowers cost four shillings, with nearly as much again for the greenery, the moss, the wires and the small lead strips with which she would hold the stems in the desired positions. She intended to charge twelve shillings for the three bowls.

'You've spent ages on them camellias, Miss Blair,' said Molly, who was working on a laurel wreath. 'You should have charged more. Them bowls look lovely.'

Charlotte took up a cloth to wipe the silver clean. 'I daren't. We're doing well enough, Molly. Not everyone lives as well as we do, and at least we are doing work that we love. I have to remind myself of that sometimes. I was thinking only the other day about my head gardener's wife. I needed her indoors. She spent two whole days peeling vegetables and washing dishes. I would have hated it. And she only made eight shillings.'

'But that's good money!' exclaimed Molly. 'That would be a pound a week.'

Charlotte laid down her cloth. 'No, I must have made a mistake. Let's see, I paid her one and tenpence a day and she worked . . . oh, forget what I said. I'm getting mixed up.'

She turned away so that Molly couldn't see her confusion. She distinctly remembered hiring the Bride for two days, yet Mr Green had written down that she received eight shillings, more than twice what she should have earned. Charlotte had been cheated. Worse, she had seen with her own eyes that Mr Green was cheating her, but had failed to take in what she read. She had even praised him for his record keeping!

The temptation to tell Molly about the trick must be resisted, no matter how great her need to unburden herself. It would not be wise to tell one employee how another had successfully cheated her. She couldn't talk about it, but she must check on it at Capel.

'Molly, I will get these flowers delivered before I do the other orders. However, when the work is finished this afternoon, I'm going to Capel Manor. You can manage on Saturday, can't you?'

'I suppose so,' said Molly, 'if business is as slow this week as last. I don't know what I'll do if I get any decent orders. Do you have to go?'

Charlotte began packing the silver bowls carefully into a wicker basket. 'Believe me, there is no time to be lost.'

The train arrived at Cheshunt station after dark, but she had telephoned ahead and Squabby Horn met her with the dog cart. 'How are the orchids coming along?' she asked him.

'I don't work with the orchids, Miss Blair. That's Mr Boon's special responsibility, entirely his responsibility.'

Squabby was a serious-looking young man with a neat moustache, a slight limp and a wife who worked hard to keep their three children clean. Normally he spoke very little in Charlotte's presence, and never with such vehemence. His determination to distance himself from the orchid growing was out of character. She therefore demanded to be taken straight to the orchid house where, by the light of a pressure lamp, she found only a dozen pots on the staging of the forty-five feet of the lean-to glasshouse. Half the labels said *Cattleya trianae*, while the remainder were *Odontoglossum crispum*. Not one of the plants had any blooms. Some attempt had been made to fill the house with ferns, which were thriving.

'Miss Blair!' cried Jacko, coming into the house and flinging his cap onto an empty bench. 'I didn't expect you so soon! I thought you would want your tea, maybe come out to the house tomorrow to see them in daylight. Otherwise, I would have been waiting, of course.'

'Is this all the orchids you have? When will I have some blooms? Surely these twelve plants can't provide all the flowers I will need.'

'Orchids are very delicate plants, ma'am. It takes a while to learn their ways, to get into the swing of it, sort of thing. I don't deny we've had a few teething problems. For one thing, I thought they needed to be kept at about eighty degrees, but there I was a little mistaken. Your *Cattleya* likes to be at sixty to sixty-five during the winter, whereas your *Odontoglossum*—'

'All the other plants have died, is that it? How many?'

'I made the mistake of starting off with young plants. Well, they wouldn't have been no good. Orchids take years to get going. So, when they died – I blame the nursery, not myself – when they died, I bought mature plants. We're getting somewhere now. You can't expect them to bloom now, not on these short days. Later—'

'Jacko,' she said wearily. 'Yesterday, in the market, I could buy *Cattleyas* for twelve shillings a dozen and the second quality *Odontoglossums* for four shillings.

Somebody is growing them. Why can't you?'

'Twelve shillings a dozen?' he asked, diverted. 'You get a good orchid nursery going, there must be money in it.'

'How many plants died, Jacko? Give me a figure.'

He sighed, resigned to his fate. 'Five dozen of each.'

She was too shocked to speak. After a moment during which she almost forgot to take a breath, she indicated that she would like to see her head gardener. 'How much?' she croaked as they left the house. 'How much of my money have you wasted?'

'I'm truly sorry, Miss Blair, but an owner has to expect reverses. What with the extra money for heat, the swines cost me fifty pounds, but I'll—'

'No, they cost *me* fifty pounds. Where is Mr Green? I want to see the books.'

Charlotte saw by the records that some mature plants had also died. Jacko plainly knew nothing at all about growing orchids, and she could not afford for him to learn, so there would be no orchids from Capel Manor to cut her costs.

She confirmed her suspicions about the hours credited to Mrs Green and told the husband that he was a stupid little man who had stooped to thieving. She would be within her rights to call the police, but she was tired and couldn't be bothered. If he tried such a trick with her again, he would be out on his backside, and what would his dear wife say then? As for Jacko Boon, he was a conceited idiot.

Neither man made any attempt to excuse his actions, but stood silently waiting to be dismissed. However, Charlotte did not feel able to sack them, knowing the hardship it would cause. Besides, she had no idea how to go about finding replacements. Near to tears, she left them abruptly. Fifty pounds was a debt she would be hard pressed to meet.

'Common slut,' muttered Jacko, when his employer was safely out of earshot. 'A gentleman like Mr Warrender would have taken the loss on the chin, would have acted with dignity. She's dead common, no better than us, for all she puts on airs.'

'I've never liked her,' added John. 'You should hear my mother-in-law on the subject of madam. Did you ever see a temper like that on a woman? She really chewed us out like a man. I've a mind to give in my notice, except I've Mabel to think of. She's happy in the lodge, living close to her old lady. I don't want to move her.' He reached into a drawer of the roll-top desk and removed a small bottle of gin. 'Anyway, she's not so clever. She never noticed about the extra four quid we added to the cost of the orchids.'

'Not clever at all, Mr Green. And why shouldn't we put on a bit extra? We've had a very trying time with them orchids. To tell you the truth, I've gone off them flowers altogether. She'd do better to let me grow roses. I'll put that point to her when she calms down.'

'I feel kind of shaky inside,' said John, unscrewing the top of the gin bottle. 'What with her calling me names and all. I need something to steady my nerves. Want some?'

Chapter Eight

It was by chance that Billy saw Charlotte walking towards the railway station with a small overnight bag in her hands. Going to Capel Manor on Friday afternoon? He couldn't believe his luck. Business was brisk, but he had two men working in the shop, and his father had gone home at noon, complaining of a bad chest. It was Billy's lucky day. Telling Fred that he would be out for the remainder of the day, he snatched his muffler and hat from the stand and almost ran up King Street to the flower shop.

Molly saw him through the window and waved. She was seeing a customer off the premises, having just taken a few pence from him for a small posy of violets. Billy entered the shop and straight away began removing the large water cans with their floral burden to the cool cellar. Molly, having checked the clock on the wall, saw that it was five minutes past six, and decided the remaining three hours on a Friday evening would bring in very little business. She pulled down the blind on the front window, emptied the cash drawer and counted the money.

When all the chores connected with closing up shop had been completed, he held her coat and then playfully arranged the brown tam o'shanter on her black curls. Since the blind had been pulled right to the very bottom of the window, no-one could see into the shop, but he resisted the temptation to kiss her. He never kissed her in the shop, preferring to torment himself by waiting until they were snug in the rooms above.

'Fish and chips?' he asked, watching as she locked the door from the street side and pocketed the key.

'I fancy a pie, but first a beer. I'm really thirsty, Billy.'

'We'll go to the chop house and—'

'No! Miss Blair goes there when she's in town. Let's go somewhere exciting, love. I do like to see the lights and all. Can we? Can we, please?'

He smiled at her affectionately and took her arm. The market had been closed for hours, but Covent Garden was always busy, drawing its crowds from all walks of life to the theatre, to the inns and restaurants, and to the less respectable places of business. Personally, he found the area exciting, but he didn't like to see his Molly working long hours among rough trade. She had many times reminded him that her parents lived not a quarter of a mile east, and that she had never lived in a posh area, but he worried about her just the same.

On one memorable day when Charlotte was busy tarting up some rich woman's house, Molly had been robbed by a man with a knife. In broad daylight! In the shop that anyone might enter! Charlotte, after assuring herself that Molly had been unhurt, had grimly assessed her losses. Three pounds was a great deal of money. Or had been, Billy reminded himself, before Charlotte got grand ideas and took to living part of the time in a manor house.

'And how is our friend?' he asked Molly now. 'Why didn't she stay in the shop and help you? Is she not going to be in town on Saturday?'

Molly looked up at him and smiled. She had a full set of tiny freckles on her pale skin and eyes of such a light blue, he fancied he could see right into her head. His Irish lass, he called her, but his dad had warned him away from the girl, saying she wasn't good enough for Vic Tavern's son.

Matching her steps to his, Molly took his arm with both hands. 'She suddenly decided to go to Capel Manor. I don't know why. Frankly, I think she isn't happy about the staff out there. I daresay they cheat her. How could it be otherwise when she ain't there to keep an eye on them?'

'I wish you didn't work for her. She pushes you too hard.'

'Oh, Billy.' This was an old argument. 'I love my work. It's ever so much better than staying home with my family. You being an only child, you don't know what it's like living in two rooms with ten kids. She's taught me a trade, and I earn good money. I daren't tell my folks what I get. They take two shillings a week off me, and that's all I'm going to give. The twins are bringing in some money these days. I don't know what they're doing for it, though. I wish you could meet my family. Why don't you want to?'

'I've heard enough about Liam and Rory to make me want to run the other way. They're only fifteen, for God's sake. At the rate they're going, they'll be on the gallows before they're twenty-one. As for your dad, he might not think much of me taking you out at your age.'

'I'll be seventeen next month. Will you marry me then?'

Billy squeezed her hand, but he didn't reply. Any answer he might make could be used against him, and he wasn't sure he was ready for the responsibilities of family life.

She looked away. 'Now I've made you angry. Don't be cross, Billy. It was only a joke. I love you so much, I just couldn't help myself saying it.'

'If my old man was as good to me as he is to Charlotte, I could think about a lot of things. She never asks but what she gets. A bleeding manor house, for God's sake! But let me just ask him to set me up in another shop and he goes all red in the face and says I'm ungrateful. "Ungrateful for what?" I say to him. "You've never given me anything but a chance to work my tail off for you." Then he goes to saying as how I'm wild and don't know how to settle down and all. When he starts to compare me to Charlotte, I walk out. Once, I nearly clocked him one. He hit me across the face, because I said Charlotte was a greedy slut. It was a near thing, I'll tell you.'

'You mustn't hit your father, Billy. That'd be wicked. Promise me you won't never hit your father. One day he'll appreciate you. One day he'll see that what he owes his own flesh and blood is greater than what he owes Miss Charlotte. I don't want you to get into any trouble.'

Her sweetness was too much for him. He stopped to kiss her right there on the Strand, ignoring the catcalls from a group of young men. 'I love you,' he whispered in her ear, committing himself, but not caring. 'You are the sweetest woman in the whole world. My dad don't understand you at all.'

She had been snuggling up to him, but now pushed herself away, ever sensitive to his words. 'Your dad knows about us? He don't like me? Oh, Billy, you never told me. I knew he wouldn't think I was good enough for you.'

'It doesn't matter, I tell you. One day—'

'One day. One day. You're always saying that. What am I to do?'

There was no answer to that question. 'Tell you what. I'll take you to a place I know down St Katherine's Docks way. We can eat and play skittles after.'

The Tower Bridge Hotel had been built a few years before the turn of the century, but there was already a well-worn look about it. Sitting proudly on a corner of Tower Bridge Road, it was built of red brick, rising three full floors, with an attic on top well supplied with dormer windows. Then, to show what an important building it was, there was a tower with a clock, and a cupola, which in turn supported a short spire and weather vane. The dining-room and the bar dispensed vast quantities of rum, gin and whisky, and unimaginable amounts of beer. Customers wined and dined with abandon, so much so that the hotel had to maintain a small team of enforcers to keep order.

A good meal could be had for as little as one shilling and sixpence. Even so, most inhabitants of this part of London could come no closer to the hot pies and palm trees of the Tower Bridge Hotel than the pavement outside, or the kitchen door, where an outstretched hand was invariably ignored.

As Billy and Molly arrived, a man in grey rags and a long beard began to stir from his position against the lamppost that would very soon illuminate the front door. The street was crowded and noisy with Friday night revellers, but Molly's attention was caught by a silent, barefooted flower girl of seven or eight.

Seeing her compassion, Billy swaggered over to the child and with a flourish bought her remaining sprigs of heliotrope for threepence. 'Oh, Billy,' said Molly when he presented them to her, 'you're ever so kind. Poor little thing. And, you know, no-one ain't never give me flowers before.'

The child was whiningly grateful, but Billy's whispered, 'Git out of 'ere' sent her on her way. He took firm hold of Molly's arm and pushed her indoors, before the dozens of other street folk could collect their wits and join in the bustle to claim his spare change.

The hotel catered for the working man and his woman, and was so busy on this night that Billy doubted if he could make himself heard to Molly across the table. Her eyes were everywhere at once, as a sweating waiter led them between tightly packed white cloth-covered tables and joyous diners. Her innocent happiness, the high-collared blouse that was chafing her neck and the rough gloveless hands affected him strongly. She deserved this night out. He would do her proud.

Molly drank several neat gins in short order, but didn't seem to lose her self-control. She had a healthy appetite, as well as an unending thirst, and finished her dinner with gusto.

'What do you suppose they have for pudding? Something grand, I'll bet. You are ever so kind to me, Billy.'

He squeezed her hand. 'Take it easy, old girl. The night is young. You don't want to race through the meal. There's plenty of time to play skittles after. Waiter! My lady friend and I wish to step out of doors for a minute or two to view Tower Bridge. Will you bring us two of your steamed puddings? And keep this table for us.'

The waiter was young, but up to every trick. 'I can't do that, sir. Not unless you pay your account first.'

Billy brought out his purse. 'Here's the bunce, me lad, and twopence for you. Now then, save this table, or I might be a little annoyed. Understand me?'

Billy helped Molly to rise from the table. She was a little unsteady, giving him the perfect excuse to put an arm around her waist. She looked up at him with adoring eyes and giggled a little.

Tower Bridge performed as if on cue, lifting its two halves so that a tall ship could pass. Molly cheered, but as soon as the bridge had returned to its normal position and traffic was once more flowing across it, she remembered her pudding and asked to return to the dining-room.

They had almost scraped their plates clean when she glanced up, then looked intently past his shoulder, as if seeing someone she knew. It made the hairs stand up on the back of his neck. Please God, let it not be his father approaching. He just had time to prepare himself for disaster when he received a hearty slap on the back.

'Billy, me dear fellow,' said Brock. 'Is this the lady love? Very pleased to meet you, ma'am. Name's Brock.'

Billy leapt to his feet. 'Arthur, this is Miss Molly O'Rourke what works for Charlotte. I'd a lief you didn't mention seeing us to Charlotte or me dad.'

'I understand perfectly, old boy,' said Brock with great good humour. He winked broadly at Molly, who looked stricken. 'As a matter of fact, I am here with a dear friend of my family. She is just attending to a few things and will be back directly. It's stuffy in here and far too noisy. Perhaps we four can have a stroll along the water. What say? I'll go and fetch Miss Fan and meet you at the door.'

'What about the skittles?' demanded Molly when Brock had left them.

'It can't be helped. We'll walk a short way with them, then cut off back to King Street. He's a tout. Racing. A friend of my dad's, or I wouldn't give him two minutes.'

'You promised me.'

'Another time.'

'He'll tell.'

'He won't. He's a good sort. But God alone knows what his lady friend is like.'

It was dark when they emerged from the hotel, and the gas lamps were hissing merrily. The moonless night blanketed the ugliness of St Katherine's Dock as reflections of gas light danced on the greasy water. From somewhere came an accordion's plaintive wheeze, while laughter and shouts issued from dark alleyways. Molly clung to Billy's arm as she sized up Miss Queenie Fan.

Queenie was a brassy woman of Brock's own age. Her hair was a trifle too yellow, her magenta gown too skimpy. Billy ran a professional eye over it, decided it wouldn't fetch more than half a crown in any pawnshop, and knew he had the measure of Arthur Brock's family friend.

Queenie turned out to be the sort of woman who took charge of any company in which she found herself. Apparently bored with Arthur Brock, she tugged Molly away from Billy's protective arm and announced that the women would walk ahead.

'Let the men talk business,' she said flatly. 'You and I can talk about interesting things. Where'd you get that outfit, lass? Did you buy it new?'

'Care for a Turkish cigarette, Billy?' said Arthur. 'Fine flavour. Six shillings the hundred from a man I know in the City.'

Billy accepted, noticing that Arthur's hand shook badly as he held out his cigarette case. 'How is the world treating you?'

'Rum, sir, rum. Times are hard and, as you see, I have this little charmer.'

'Beneath your touch, Arthur. Not your sort, surely.'

'Needs must when the devil drives. Your old man has not come through as promised.'

'He'll have you in Pentonville.'

'He won't,' said Arthur harshly. 'By God, he won't. But I ain't seen a penny yet. Got to nurse my resources, you know. Five hundred safely in the funds. Well, three hundred. I had a few purchases to make. Three hundred brings me in fifteen quid a year. Not enough. The country's going to the dogs and I can't earn a decent living at the track. And now Queenie. Shouldn't have got involved with her. I don't suppose you could put it to your old man that it's time he stumped up. We were promised. I'm a director of that damned company. Can't you do something?'

' 'Ere!' said Billy, a mild man who was occasionally driven to sudden rages. 'I can't so much as speak to my dad about that bloody company. You notice *I* didn't get invited in. Nobody asked *me* to be a director. If you're not happy with the way things are going, get the sainted Charlotte to speak for you. She's the director, not me.'

Brock took a drag of his cigarette. 'Queer that. Him making Charlotte a director and not you. Your old man hasn't got . . . designs on the girl, has he?'

'Certainly not. Look, Arthur. You take your lady friend wherever you two usually go. I want to get Molly home at a decent hour. Mind you don't tell anybody you seen us. I wouldn't take it well.'

Brock nodded wearily and quickened his pace in order to drag Queenie away from Molly.

Billy and Molly scarcely said a word on the way home, but when the lamp was lit in the rooms above the shop and Molly had put a few coals on the small fire, she tore the tam from her head and tossed it onto the table.

'She was a tart. A plain old tart. Fine people you introduce me to.'

'I'm sorry. Give me a kiss.'

'No,' she said, pouting. 'They spoiled the evening. It was so wonderful and they spoiled it.'

'I took you some place nice, didn't I? One kiss, Molly. Don't deny me that small reward.'

'Well,' she said, but got no further. A tender kiss on her lips settled the matter. He felt her stiffen, distancing herself from what he was doing. Gently, he forced her mouth open and thrust his tongue inside, while holding her so close that she couldn't push him away. After a second or two, she seemed to take the course of least resistance, not objecting, yet not encouraging. The fierceness of the embrace frightened her a little, but he held her tight. Suddenly, she gave in and kissed him back, clasping him around the neck with both arms, murmuring pleasurable sounds as he kissed her cheek, her throat.

'Let me,' he whispered. 'Let me do it. You know what I mean. Let me, darling. I'll move away before it's too late, I promise you.'

She laughed knowingly, a jarring sound. 'You can't be sure. That's how me little brother got born.'

He was reminded with a jolt that Molly's virginity had nothing to do with ignorance. Two adults and ten children living in close proximity had given her an education about which Billy had often speculated.

Eventually, she let him into her bed, whispering of her love, knowing the dangers and not caring. Much later, lying alone in his own comfortable bed, he remembered the staggering number of gins she had consumed and felt a little guilty. Nevertheless, he knew he would be with her on Saturday night, and whenever he could find the opportunity, taking chances, courting disaster and possibly a beating from her old man. He loved Molly – almost as much as he feared his father.

Charlotte had just come indoors after inspecting the orchids when the telephone rang. Before Rachel could come into the hall, she answered it herself.

'Is that you, Charlotte? What are you doing answering your own telephone? Why keep a dog and bark, too?'

'Hello, Vic,' said Charlotte wearily. 'How are you? How did you know I was here?'

'I've got spies. Listen, girl, we're coming out tomorrow. Popple and Florence and me. Arthur's going racing. We'll see you for dinner or supper, or whatever you choose to call it. Expect us some time after three o'clock. I've a few things to attend to tomorrow. All right?'

'Yes, all right.'

'Charlotte, have there been any letters for us?'

She was standing by the hall table and leaned across to pick up the pile of letters from the little tray. 'About twenty-five. I could bring them to you on Monday morning.'

'What's the matter? Don't want to see us? Florence talks of nothing else but coming back to Capel. She really loved her stay with you.'

'That's . . .' She couldn't think of anything to say and was too tired to make polite conversation with a man she knew so well. 'Look, Vic. I must go now, but I will be ready to meet you whenever you arrive. I must order some food. Goodbye.'

They arrived at half past three, cross because they had experienced some delay in finding a cab and had been forced to carry their own luggage a short distance. Charlotte knew that Vic was accustomed to carrying his own possessions at all times, so she failed to offer him the sympathy he seemed to think he deserved.

'You could have sent one of your layabouts to fetch us,' he said, slapping his hat onto the hall table. 'You could have done that. I think you're getting a little above yourself, old girl.'

'You didn't tell me exactly what time you planned to arrive, Vic.'

'I did so!' he exclaimed. 'I know I did. You don't listen to nothing I say any more.'

'Vic, old chap,' said Popple soothingly, 'it doesn't matter now. Are Florence and I to have the same rooms we had before?'

'I've got a headache,' said Florence in a whining voice. 'If you could possibly have one of those women carry up my bag, I would like to lie down.'

At that moment, Rachel appeared looking flustered. 'I'll take it, Miss. I'm ever so sorry, Miss Blair. There was a bit of a fire . . . that is, the meat juices caught in the oven. There's no harm—'

'My dinner, I suppose,' bellowed Vic, making the maid jump. 'Why can't you control your staff, Charlotte?'

Charlotte searched her mind for a cutting answer, but couldn't think of anything. Rachel managed to pick up all the bags at once and headed for the stairs.

Charlotte detained Vic by the sleeve as the others left the hall. 'Don't you ever speak to me like that again in front of my staff. Do you understand me? And,' she added, seeing that he was about to interrupt, 'don't tell me how grateful I should be to you, because I'm sick of hearing it. I don't mind what you say to me when we're alone, but keep a civil tongue in your head when others are around.'

Vic was never angry if she stood up to him. 'I don't get a chance to say anything to you when we're alone, you little harpy. I wish you wouldn't be so aggressive. It ain't ladylike.'

Charlotte was in the mood for a quarrel and would have welcomed the chance to vent her feelings, but Vic suddenly remembered that on his last visit Rachel had unpacked for him. For some reason, he was most anxious to prevent her from doing so again. He hurried away, calling over his shoulder that a strong gin would improve Charlotte's disposition no end.

She thought salvation lay in a little peace, but she headed for the kitchen to determine the extent of the damage that had been done to the evening meal. Mrs Duck had rolled up her sleeve and applied a little butter to a large burn on her arm.

'The mutton's all right, Miss Blair. I didn't burn it none. It's just this—'

'Sit down. Have a cup of tea. Where's the teapot?'

'Rachel laid it out on the trolley. They'll be wanting tea directly, I expect.'

'I've no idea.' Charlotte measured tea into a homely brown jug from the dresser, poured boiling water into it and set it down by the cook. 'I had better go upstairs and see how Miss Douse is feeling. I'll let you know if they want tea. I'll fetch the milk and sugar. Sit down and have a cup before you try to do anything else. In my experience, one accident leads to another. Do try to be careful.'

A few minutes later, she tapped gently on Florence's bedroom door and entered immediately, expecting to see her guest lying on the bed. Florence, fully dressed and looking perfectly fit, was standing at the window, gazing at the south lawn as Jacko guided the pony and mower.

'That horse has got boots on!' she said, having apparently forgotten that she was unwell. 'Do they make boots for horses?'

'They do, indeed. Otherwise, the pony would leave hoof prints all over the lawn. It's probably the first cut of the year and Jacko Boon will want to be very careful on the soft ground.'

'I expect this Jacko is a very good gardener.'

Charlotte laughed harshly. 'He can't grow orchids for toffee. I suppose he is fairly adept. He's sly. I never know what he gets up to.'

Florence turned. 'Oh, Charlotte, you are horridly critical. I've never known anyone who has such a low opinion of the rest of the world. I wonder, sometimes, how you can live with yourself. I pity anyone who has to work for you.'

Charlotte took a deep breath before speaking softly. 'The cook wants to know if you will all be having a cup of tea in the morning-room. I expected to find you on your bed, but you are obviously perfectly well.'

'I'll come down for some tea. I know Popple is gasping for a drink, and I expect Vic is, too.' She turned back to the window, then said in dismissal, 'Thank you, Charlotte. I will be down in a minute or two.'

Charlotte returned to the kitchen. 'Tea for three in the morning-room, Mrs Duck. I'm going for a walk to calm my nerves. Have you some madeira cake? Give them some of that. I will be back in time to change for dinner, but certainly not much before then, so they needn't expect me. We'll eat at six o'clock.'

'I'm sorry about the meat, ma'am. It's all right, really.'

'No matter.' Charlotte waved aside her apology and left the house by way of the back door. The lawn stretched out behind the house all the way to the grotto and the pond. Pines and rhododendrons shielded the western boundary (the house was built about thirty yards from the fence). Down the right side of the lawn lay a yew hedge in need of trimming, and behind this was an attractive garden with a winding path which Jacko Boon proposed to enliven with carpet bedding. Beyond this was a rose arbour where nearly a hundred bushes had been pruned hard and surrounded by rotting clumps of horse manure. Charlotte awaited the flowering of this part of the grounds with considerable interest. She thought it looked as promising as any public park she had ever visited.

On this day, however, she sought the wilder parts of the grounds, the rough earth and scrub where the gardeners had no interest. And she thought she might walk a bit farther and see for herself Temple Bar which had been one of the old gateways to the City of London. There would be no need to trespass onto the grounds of Theobalds, since she understood the stone structure was now the entrance to the estate and easily viewed from the road.

Matthew was very grateful for the kindness of the Admiral, whom he had met recently, because his rooms in Hanover Square were far from comfortable. He had engaged a valet, and there was barely room for the two of them to move about, now that Matthew had put his own possessions on display. Admiral Meux, upon discovering that he was the owner of Capel Manor and that it was rented out, immediately invited him to spend a couple of weeks at Theobalds Park.

The house was extremely pretty and very large. A set of rooms for himself in the north wing, and comfortable accommodation for Chalker, the valet, nearby, proved to be no problem at all for his host. The house had thirty-five bedrooms, and he was soon made to understand that he could stay as long as he liked and come and go as he pleased, provided that he made no advances to the five daughters of Lady Meux by her first marriage.

As Matthew hadn't enough money to keep himself or Capel Manor in style, he was not on the immediate lookout for a bride. They were a charming and lively family, but on this beautiful March day, he found the need to behave himself, mind his manners, make conversation with six women and show proper respect to an admiral who had a passion for racing, was more than he could bear.

Having nowhere in particular to go, he invented an intense need to sketch the countryside, and accordingly climbed the spiral staircase of the impressive water tower and let himself out onto the pitched lead flashing between the various slopes of the roof. Four floors up, and so precariously situated that he could not possibly be followed, he turned a page in his sketch book and took out a pencil from his breast pocket. The view was magnificent. He could see for miles, out over Waltham Cross and almost as far as the ancient town of Waltham Abbey in Essex. Assorted parapets and chimneys obstructed his view of Theobalds' extensive Italian garden. However, he had an excellent view of it from his bedroom window, so he didn't mind being cut off from it now. He had a clear view of Temple Bar, which was the principal entrance to the estate, and of the long drive bordered on both sides by rose bushes.

The late Valerie, Lady Meux, he had been told, had persuaded the City authorities to let her have Temple Bar. It weighed four hundred tons and had cost twelve thousand pounds to transport it to Theobalds, where it had been erected, together with a new gate-keeper's cottage.

Matthew was a connoisseur, a man who derived intense pleasure from all works of art, but especially porcelain. He had a small collection which he had expanded carefully during his years in the Far East. He was occasionally driven to attempt to create something that would give him the same buzz of pleasure that collecting did, and at these times he reached for his drawing pad. He was invariably disappointed by his efforts, but this never deterred him for very long. The perfection of this small architectural masterpiece seemed to cry out for a careful rendering, and the angle from which he was to draw it seemed an interesting challenge. The first two drawings were disappointments because of difficulties with the perspective. Picking up his binoculars, he focussed on Wren's work in the hope that he could make a better job of his next attempt. It was then that he saw Miss Charlotte Blair trying to pass through the gateway. The gate-keeper seemed to have other ideas.

Quickly abandoning all thoughts of trying to attract her attention from the roof, he scrambled back along the roof, climbed through a small window and ran down countless stairs and out of the front door, miraculously avoiding not only the family, but also every one of the twenty-five indoor servants.

By the time he had run along fifty or sixty yards of private drive, he was quite out of breath. However, he needn't have been afraid that Charlotte would leave in defeat.

'I only want to see the other side of Temple Bar,' she was saying to the gate-keeper. 'There was a time when this monument would have been available to all.'

'Not since 1880, ma'am. And I'm not rightly sure where it was before then.'

'I don't intend to steal so much as a dandelion, nor to visit the family.'

'I don't know you, miss,' the gate-keeper replied with a nice mixture of irritation and respect (in case she turned out to be someone important, after all).

Matthew waved, too puffed to speak at all, and Charlotte stared at him in surprise. 'Mr Warrender! What are you doing here?'

He took her by the arm, walked her past the solid gates that closed off the arch of Temple Bar each night, pointed to the dressed stone and gasped, 'Got a dining-room upstairs. See the window?'

'Upstairs?' she cried, fascinated. 'You mean a person can get inside it? There's a room? Could we—'

'Ahem!' said the gate-keeper.

'Not today, perhaps,' said Matthew, hastily. 'I will take you inside on another occasion. Shall we walk back towards Capel Manor?'

She was reluctant, but he whispered to her that on another occasion he would grease the gate-keeper's fist, after which it would probably be allowed. 'But I haven't twopence on me at the moment. I was sketching, up on the roof, and saw you from there. I ran all the way, afraid I would miss you, and I'm very out of breath.'

'Come on, then,' she said. 'Let's go where that horrid

man can't spy on us. I don't see that I did anything wrong by asking to see both sides of the thing. It shouldn't be here, anyway. It belongs to the City. Why ever did they allow it to come out here?'

'I haven't the faintest idea. Never mind that. It's good to see you.'

'And it is good to see you. You would always be welcome at Capel, you know. How is it that . . . What I mean is, are you staying at Theobalds Park?'

'Yes, I am.' He explained to her about how the previous Lady Meux had left the property to Admiral Lambton, provided he change his name to Meux, and how he had married Lady Chelsea, a widow with five daughters. 'So, you see, it is all a very interesting arrangement. The late Lady Meux was not received in the neighbourhood, but the Admiral and his wife are quite acceptable, so they entertain and—'

'Not received? Not invited to the homes of the gentry living around here? Why, that's just like me! What did she do wrong?'

'Nothing. Not like you. I mean, you have not done anything wrong, either, but—'

'But we're both not good enough. The difference is that I am not Lady anything and I don't own the grandest home for miles around. What was wrong with her?'

He had no desire to spend this fine afternoon discussing the background of the late Lady Meux. 'How is your business doing? There must be a great many parties and events of all sorts requiring your talents.'

She stopped to lean against a tree, dug her hands into her jacket pockets and smiled bitterly. 'There may be, but none have come my way. I can't regret having rented Capel, but . . . oh well, perhaps I do regret it. I can't afford it, at all events. And Vic . . .'

'Your friends are a sore trial, Miss Blair. I feel for you. I think they do you no credit. Perhaps you would do better to cut yourself off from them.'

'Not receive them, you mean? Because they aren't acceptable? Such a thing never occurred to me. Vic and Popple Douse are staying this weekend, and—'

'And that flirtatious daughter of Douse's? You must wish them in purgatory.'

She didn't answer immediately, but looked at him so sweetly that her whole face was transformed. 'Only occasionally. Everyone thinks I am very hard-hearted. Don't you? Are you not going to scold me for my critical nature?'

'No indeed. I think you are misunderstood and that all those around you are jealous of your beauty, success and willingness to work hard. They are a pack of vultures. Miss Douse is harmless enough, but I would warn you about Billy Tavern. He's very jealous, you know.'

'Vic treats him badly. I can't think why. Billy has been difficult in the past, but he has settled down recently. What must he think when his father gives me enough money to rent Capel Manor for eighteen months, but won't even allow Billy to drive his motor car whenever he wants to?'

'I can't imagine, but let's not talk about them. Tell me about Capel. Are the staff behaving themselves? How do the gardens look?'

'The staff are . . . the staff. The grounds look well, although from what I could see of Theobalds, the Admiral's gardeners are rather more experienced. I do believe, however, that Capel has the finest kitchen garden in the neighbourhood. The fruit and vegetables look prettier than some of the flower beds. The snowdrops are finished, and even some of the crocuses. Early tulips and daffodils come next. Something has happened to the grass on either side of the drive. I suspect Jacko. He was going to kill the weeds in the drive by putting down salt. Perhaps the salt was washed by the rains onto the lawn. In any case, it looks rather sad. But I don't want to think about that at the moment. May I ask you a question? There's some sort of canal on the property and—'

'The New River. It's not a river at all, of course, but a man-made canal, dug hundreds of years ago to bring fresh water to London. It begins in Amwell, I believe. In any case, Gussie Bowles's father was a director of the New River Company, before it was taken over by the water board.'

'It must be famous. I should have known about it.'

'Not at all. We all know our own particular subject, but may be mystified by something outside our experience. I lived with that canal, don't forget, and knew one of its directors. Now, I have a question for you. What is an auricula?'

'An auricula is a gold-laced polyanthus. They are very pretty. As many as fifteen flowers are carried in a bunch at the top of a short stem. Each flower has little petals around the edge, and these should be of a very dark colour, as near black as possible. They're small plants, you see, and poor people like my father could always find somewhere to grow them in pots. There has always been keen competition among the working class growers at shows. *Burnard's Formosa* was my father's favourite. He won several prizes with it. Mr Burnard of Formosa Cottage in Holloway bred the plant; just an ordinary man, you see, not some grand head gardener in some grand country garden. I daresay people whose hobby is growing auriculas would not be received in the neighbourhood, although I doubt if that was the reason Lady Meux wasn't received.'

'Aren't we all a strange lot? As if it mattered! You must point out to me an auricula one day. By the way, will you be having carpet bedding at Capel this year?'

'I most certainly will. Jacko Boon has been bringing on all the little foliage plants necessary. Carpet bedding takes great skill and thousands of plants, you know. It should make a marvellous display, and there's to be a bedding scheme of bright red geraniums, blue lobelias and white alyssum. You must visit us to see them.'

He decided not to tell her that Gussie Bowles's

worst fears were about to be realized. He could not see the dangers inherent in planting flowers of a bright hue in neat rows, although he was certain that the great Mr Bowles would be happy to explain.

'Are you really having difficulty finding clients?'

'Yes. I believe Lady Smythe has been abroad. She was my only contact among people who are received in their neighbourhood. Business has been slow, mainly funeral work. I say, why don't you come back to Capel for dinner? Everyone would be very happy to see you.'

'How kind, but I'm committed here, I'm afraid.'

'Tomorrow?' she asked, her cheeks going a little pink.

He touched her arm. 'Believe me, I would love to join you, but the family here has plans. I have a better idea. How about meeting in London? I imagine you will be returning on Sunday night, won't you?'

'Yes, I'll be in Town all of next week. I should like it very much.'

'Friday? Shall we have dinner at the Ritz? Where shall I call for you?'

Her smile disappeared. 'It won't be necessary to call for me. I'd much rather make my own way. I'll meet you there. Just tell me what time. Eight o'clock? Is that all right? It's fancy, isn't it, the Ritz. Shall I wear an evening gown? I have a nice one that won't embarrass you.'

'You always look charming.'

'It will be lovely. I expect the entire hotel is decked out in flowers. I'll bring my notebook to jot down a few ideas. Do you dine there often?'

'From time to time.'

She laughed, throwing back her head and looking infinitely more relaxed than when he had first met her at the gate. 'I do wish I could talk the way you do.'

'You speak very well—'

'No, no. It's the way you say "Indeed" when you wish to be sarcastic. And the way you said my Christmas decorations were "seasonal" when you didn't like them.'

'No, I assure you, I—'

'And just now when I asked if you often dine at the Ritz. "From time to time," you said. Whereas I would have said, "Oh, dozens of times! They know me well." What you say is so different from the sort of things Vic says.'

'I'm very pleased to hear it. There, I've just given you another phrase with which to taunt me.'

'I expect so,' she said, and laughed at a joke he couldn't see. 'That's another one. "I expect so." I only wish to tease you, Mr Warrender, but not cruelly, because you have cheered me up so much! Goodbye. I'll see you at the Ritz on Friday night.' She held out her hand to him, so full of joy that he couldn't be annoyed, even if she had made sport of him.

He clasped her hand, then impulsively raised it to his lips. Now it was her turn to be put out! 'Goodbye, Miss Blair. Until Friday night at eight o'clock.'

Chapter Nine

Popple Douse looked down at his brogues and frowned at the mud that had already encompassed the soles and was inching its way towards the laces with each step he took. It had been raining hard for an hour, and he would not have agreed to trudge through the holly walk that bordered the western boundary if he hadn't a few desperately important private things to say to Vic. Rightly assuming that umbrellas would be a useless encumbrance along the narrow path, the two town men had put on their macs and flat caps, and hurried to what they supposed would be the shelter of the trees. Unfortunately the holly trees offered very little shelter; galoshes would have been a help, but neither man possessed a pair.

'Nearly a thousand pounds in them envelopes, Popple,' said Vic, hunching his shoulders against the rain. 'How much does that make altogether?'

'Ten thousand, if you don't count the five thousand that we had to pay back because twenty investors smelled a rat.'

'You shouldn't have given it back.'

'Of course I should have! Those men would have begun to cut up rough, asking awkward questions. Our prospectus is a little dicey, you know. It could hardly be otherwise.'

'Arthur is the one asking awkward questions. Wants some ready cash. You'd better give him something on account.'

Vic pronounced Brock's name as 'Arfur', which irritated Popple. He frequently asked himself what he had been thinking of to go into business with a man who couldn't say Arthur. And Brock! A racing tout, a man who smelled of horses even though he had probably never ridden one. He wished he had not got involved with these two men who were far beneath him socially; but it was too late to draw back now. 'I have to tell you something, Vic, and I want you to damn well listen carefully.'

Glancing to his right, Popple chanced to see Florence walking down the lawn. The rain had stopped, but a strong breeze was tearing at her tam, causing her to put up one hand to hold it in place. She, too, was wearing a mac, a handsome beige one with a belt that skimmed her hips, and her feet were sensibly enclosed in overshoes. Her expression worried him, too solemn and strained for such a flighty youngster. He had told her that Matthew Warrender was staying at Theobalds Park, a piece of information that had come to him quite by chance.

Florence had made a face at the mention of the man's name, but she had been quite willing to visit Capel again when he suggested he might be able to arrange a meeting with Warrender. The girl was not in the habit of doing as her father wished without a great deal of persuading, so he had been naturally suspicious of such ready compliance. Now, here she was in the open air, dressed against the elements and quite alone, unusual circumstances to say the least. Florence abhorred the open air, preferring to spend her days indoors, or shopping, or going to the theatre. Her mackintosh looked expensive. Not for the first time he wondered how she managed to dress so well on the money he gave her.

And here came one of the gardeners, walking right up to her as if certain of a welcome! They began to walk side by side, in step, almost rubbing shoulders.

'Will you finish your bleeding sentence?' asked Vic. 'What's up with you? You look a bit queer.'

Popple ran a hand over his face as if trying to scrub away the worrying thoughts about Florence. 'There have been a few arrests for fraud, one or two convictions, that's all. I'm afraid we might be rumbled.'

'You've got no nerves, that's your trouble, Popple. Your blood's too thin. It's exciting, us pitting our wits against all them rich men. Are you sure you've got it right about unlimited liability if the law rumbles us?'

The gardener and Florence, deep in conversation, had walked off eastward. Within a minute or two they would be out of Popple's sight. He couldn't hear anything they said, but one image sent a shiver up his spine. Florence suddenly laughed loudly, turning her face towards the gardener and looking at him with . . . affection? He would send a message to Theobalds Park, just a casual note, saying he hoped to see Mr Warrender at Capel during the weekend. There was no time to lose in getting his girl settled in life.

'Was that your Florence walking off with a gardener? I expect she's a bit lonely for male company,' said Vic, peering through the trees. 'Likes the opposite sex, does your girl. Pity Billy ain't here to keep her company. She likes Billy.'

'Does she? She never mentions him, I assure you. Vic, I shall try to get our business on a safe footing, because it is perfectly true that we lose the protection of a limited company should we be convicted of fraud. I pay all bills promptly. I've bought almost all the shares we are required by law to own, and I've been careful not to oversell our chances of finding gold when I talk to prospective investors; but there is one more move I believe to be essential. We must declare a half-yearly dividend at the end of June. Eight per cent, I think. Of course, the dividend won't come from profits, since there are none. We'll use some of the money we've received from share purchases to pay out a dividend. No-one will question it.

They never get suspicious when they're making money.'

'Arthur will go spare. He's living beyond his income and needs whatever he can get from Goldseekers.'

'He will get his dividend, the same as everyone else. We'll do it that way. I'm not a clever man, Vic. I'm just a capable solicitor who got into a little trouble. I can only do what I think is wise and pray that everything will turn out for the best. Look, my dear fellow, I'm soaking wet and tired of walking under these trees. Let's cross the lawn.'

Vic laughed harshly. 'You won't catch Florence at anything naughty, if that's what's bothering you. The gardener wouldn't dare. Let her be. I want to go back to the house. I don't know why I decided to come out here for the weekend. This is the most boring place in the world.'

The men reached the entrance hall at the very moment when Charlotte was coming in through the front. Popple was able to see her glowing cheeks and to marvel at the carefree smile, such a transformation from the grim young business woman who had left the house an hour earlier.

'I got caught in the rain!' she laughed, shaking out her thin coat. 'I think my hat is ruined.'

'You've had a long walk. Was there nowhere to shelter?'

Charlotte tugged the bell pull in the hall and headed for the morning-room. 'I decided to see what Temple Bar looked like, and you'll never guess who I met.'

'Matthew Warrender,' said Popple. 'I heard that he was visiting the Admiral and Lady Meux.'

'Why yes! I invited him for dinner tonight or to come over tomorrow, but he said he couldn't manage it. The Meuxs have other plans for him.'

'They have five daughters. I expect he figures in the future of one of them,' said Popple maliciously. From long experience of fatherhood, he knew all the telltale signs of feminine joy. Warrender had been flirting with

Charlotte. Damn the man! And Florence was nowhere about. The weekend was wasted. He could have said all he needed to say to Vic, opened the letters and taken them away, within hours. They were expected to stay until Monday morning, but he would speak to Florence about inventing an excuse to leave on Sunday morning. He was almost certain she, too, would be bored by then.

The maid entered the room and Charlotte ordered a sherry, asking the men if they would care for a drink. She was pleased with herself! What had the man said to her that could possibly be a cause for celebration? Vic preferred gin to sherry, and Popple, his mind on other things, said he would have the same, although he liked neither gin nor sherry.

'Vic,' said Charlotte pleasantly, 'I received the thousand pounds worth of shares in my name. It was very generous of you, but I think I would prefer to have the cash. Will you arrange to sell my shares to someone else? I'm not cut out to be a company director. I don't know anything about it. You'll do that, won't you? And change the company address. You can't continue to use Capel Manor, you know. I shan't be living here for ever.'

Vic's reaction startled everyone. 'Greedy bitch! I didn't give you a thousand pounds. I bought some shares in your name because I had to. *I'll* decide what I'm going to do and how I'm going to do it.' He had been seated in one of the deep armchairs, but he bounded to his feet and stood over Charlotte menacingly. 'Ungrateful little trollop. How dare you treat me like this?'

'Vic!' cried Popple, standing up as quickly as he could. He was afraid that his unpredictable fellow director would strike the girl before he was able to protect her.

Charlotte, he noticed with surprise, was angry but not at all afraid. 'Don't ever speak to me like that again. I'm tired of your bullying. If you don't mind your tongue, I'll not let you set foot in Capel. What if the servants heard you?'

Now Vic was speechless. He sputtered something about 'cheek' and 'ingratitude' and 'whose house was it, anyway', but he was defeated by her cool composure.

'I think she is quite right, Vic,' said Popple coldly. 'You must not speak so. It's improper. Especially as we should have no difficulty in convincing Charlotte that she cannot get out of her commitments so easily. You are a part of our business, my dear girl, and you had better behave yourself. If not, you could find your hopes of running a successful business ruined and all chance of becoming a great floral decorator dashed for ever. You wouldn't like that, would you?'

It pleased him to see that Charlotte was as frightened by his words as she had been indifferent to Vic's. Florence never gave Popple the satisfaction of being cowed so effectively. But then, there was nothing with which Popple could threaten Florence. Charlotte was an ambitious woman, determined to be a success. She had much to lose.

Florence came into the room as the maid entered with the drinks tray, ordered a sherry for herself, then draped her elegant form on the arm of her father's chair. They all finished their drinks with great speed and no cheer whatsoever, and agreed to part in order to dress for dinner. Popple allowed his daughter to mount the stairs alone, then tiptoed to her room and knocked softly.

Ten minutes later, Florence knocked just as softly on Charlotte's door and entered when invited to do so. She hoped Charlotte wouldn't notice that she had been crying. Popple had been in a vicious mood. She had never known him to be so cruel, and knew she must follow his instructions exactly on this occasion. He suspected her of warm feelings for a gardener and had accused her of loose behaviour. There would be no further occasion to speak to Jacko Boon during the weekend.

'I just came in for a chat. I've been for a tour of your gardens this afternoon. That nice gardener, Mr Boon, showed me round. Fancy me in a greenhouse and admiring rhododendrons! I'm afraid country life doesn't appeal to me. As my father is feeling a little unwell, I hope you don't mind if we go home tomorrow morning. Popple tells me you saw Matthew Warrender this afternoon. My father is such a fuddy duddy. Can you imagine it? He wants me to set my cap, as he calls it, for Mr Warrender. No hope, I'm afraid. That man just looks right through me. And I don't fancy him, either. He has a stern look, and he's old. I could tell right away that he liked you, though. His eyes light up when he looks at you. Will you be seeing him again?'

Charlotte, wearing a corset cover and French drawers, black stockings and dainty black satin shoes, was applying a dusting of powder to her small, straight nose. She had a good figure, Florence silently acknowledged. Florence wore a bosom amplifier, a delicious, lacy concoction of tightly spaced rows of ruffles, but Charlotte had no need of such a garment. Florence hadn't noticed it in the morning-room, but Popple was right; Charlotte wore the flush of love.

'I'm sorry you aren't having a good time, Florence. I'm afraid I can't offer you any entertainment, as I don't know anybody in the neighbourhood. Of course I don't mind if you and your father go home tomorrow morning. I have a feeling Vic won't stay, either.' Charlotte turned from the cheval mirror to put the powder puff on the dressing table. 'As a matter of fact, Mr Warrender has invited me to dinner at the Ritz on Friday!'

Florence tried to hide her surprise. 'Have you anything suitable to wear?'

'Not a thing. I suppose I could go into Town tomorrow, if Vic goes away, but, really, I should work with Molly on Monday. I'll have to find the time to alter something.'

'You'll make a mess of it. You're just not sufficiently interested in clothes to do the best by yourself. Why must you persist in buying old theatre costumes? Who will ever forget that theatrical concoction you wore at Christmas?'

Charlotte laughed. 'Not you, apparently! I like old costumes and stage jewellery.'

'You could borrow one of my gowns, the one that you thought was a couture gown. I paid five guineas for it. You won't want to spend that much money. And, believe me, if he invites you out often, you will be hard pushed to come up with a different elegant gown for every occasion. Borrow my green gown. I know he saw me in it, but I'm sure he won't remember.'

'Thank you for the kind offer, I'd like to wear the gown. I'm sure he won't remember that you wore it all those weeks ago. You know what men are like.'

'Yes, I do. You are the one who doesn't know what men are like.' Florence sat down on the bed and fingered the ruby crushed-velvet gown that Charlotte had laid out. It was not new, but it could be greatly improved with a few ostrich feathers around the neckline. 'I realize that you are a few years older than I am, but I'm going to give you some advice anyway. He won't marry you. If he had fancied me, he might have considered marriage. I'm closer to his own class, you see. But he won't even consider the daughter of a Covent Garden porter. Now, if you had stayed in the theatre, that might have been different. Gentlemen find themselves able to marry actresses, for some reason or other. But not flower girls. So have your fun and don't let him break your heart. I'll send round the dress by a carrier to your shop on King Street.' She scanned Charlotte's face for signs that she had struck a blow to the heart. She didn't want Mr Warrender for herself, but she hated to think that Charlotte might make such a catch. 'I hope you will remember this favour, because I have one to ask in return. Popple is determined that Mr Warrender should fall in love with me. I would appreciate it if you didn't tell my father that you're going out with him. It would make my life more peaceful, I can tell you. I do so envy you your independence.'

'I've no intention of discussing Mr Warrender, or anything else, with Mr Douse. He's like a bear with a sore head at the moment. So there you are, a favour for a favour.'

Florence slid off the bed and gave Charlotte a fleeting peck on the cheek. 'Enjoy yourself, and don't do anything I wouldn't do.'

'That should give me a fair degree of freedom,' said Charlotte drily, and Florence forced herself to laugh as she closed the door.

He knew the type as soon as they walked into the shop. Bad men. Burglars. Eyes darting suspiciously everywhere. The two of them, wearing ragged collarless shirts with grimy white silk scarves knotted around their throats and caps pulled low over their eyes, slunk up to the counter and fixed Billy with a hard stare. He stared back. They could trust him – to a point – and he could trust them about as far. The younger one had an eye that wandered independently of its partner, and a stupid look about him. His friend had slit nostrils and assorted livid scars about the face, the result of fights he had lost, no doubt. There was a desperate look about him.

'This better be good,' Billy murmured. Then to his father's clerk, Robinson, who was hovering uncertainly, 'Tidy up round the back. I'll handle this.'

'Well . . . yes, sir,' said Robinson. Billy was thankful that Vic wasn't on the premises because, if he had been, Robinson would surely have called him to the front.

'Have you got something to show me or not? Hurry up about it. The rozzers come round here all the time.'

Wall–eye reached into a bulging pocket and pulled out a red patterned handkerchief. Untying the loose knot, he revealed a sparkling tiara. 'Worth five thousand,' he bragged. 'Neatest little job you ever seen. The old girl what owned it won't miss it for another month.'

The spring sun filtered through the front window and bounced off the diamonds. Billy, his heart pounding, swiftly covered the tiara, while one of the men told him it could be detached from its frame to make a necklace.

'I'll have to have a look at it in the back room,' he said, and scooped up the handkerchief before the men could object.

Robinson was leaning against the desk, sucking on a toothpick. He was twice Billy's age and had worked for Vic for twenty years. A quiet man with good handwriting and a head for figures, he had married rather late in life and produced five children within seven years, which made him excessively anxious not to lose his job.

'What do you think?' whispered Billy.

'Very pretty. Very dangerous. Don't touch it, Mr Billy. Your old man wouldn't touch it, I'm sure.'

'I ain't my old man. Where's that catalogue from the Association of Diamond Merchants? Ah, here. Look, a tiara very like this one. Five thousand quid.'

'Not as fancy. Nowhere near as many stones. Your dad wouldn't pay more than two hundred, if that. And probably he wouldn't touch it.'

Billy reached into a drawer of the desk, released the secret catch and pulled it out far enough to get his hands on three hundred pounds in big, white five-pound notes.

Returning to the front of the shop, he soon discovered that the men wanted four hundred pounds, but Billy, with the determination borne of his having only three hundred pounds to spend, beat them down.

'This ain't got nothing to do with me,' said Robinson, when Billy returned to the back room with his prize. 'For God's sake, get it out of the shop as soon as you can!'

'I'm going to the fence right now. Old Grimsdyke. He'll take it. I'll have the money back in my dad's drawer before he ever comes in to work.'

'What I'm wondering, sir, is why they didn't go to old Grimsdyke. They must know who he is. Was they hoping to get a better price from you?'

Billy could feel the sweat forming on the back of

his neck. He pulled off his sleeve protectors as fast as he could, reached for his jacket and attempted to stuff the tiara into an inside pocket. It wouldn't fit, of course, so he was delayed in looking for a suitable carrier. All the way to Grimsdyke's, which was only a short distance away on Henrietta Street, he was terrified that the two villains would waylay him and steal back the jewellery. He had heard of this happening many times.

Grimsdyke, who could have been any age from fifty to eighty, operated from the cover of his son-in-law's grocer shop, shoe-horning himself into a little cupboard of a room that barely had space for his high work table, a strong light and a jeweller's eyepiece. Muffled against the mild spring air, he wheezed a greeting, clutched at the tiara with one hand and his eyepiece with the other. It didn't take the old man long to pronounce on the tiara.

'A fake,' he rasped. 'Can't you see the silver foil under the stones? You been done, old son. Done proper. This is paste. I'll give you three quid for it, but you'll maybe get more selling it in the auction rooms. There's lots of fancy ladies what needs jewels like these. Mind, this ain't even a good fake. What's old Vic thinking of allowing hisself to be taken in?'

'He doesn't know, Mr Grimsdyke.'

Grimsdyke whistled, rested his bloodshot eyes on Billy and wheezed out an unsympathetic laugh. 'Where'd you get the lolly? By the way, how much did you pay? Not over a hundred, I hope. Even if it was genuine, it wouldn't have been worth more than five hundred to me.'

'I'd appreciate it if you wouldn't mention it to my old man.'

'What, Vic?' laughed Grimsdyke. 'I ain't seen the old bastard for donkey's years. Used to send me stuff regular, but he lost his nerve. I won't squeal on you. You're going to be in enough bother without me adding to it.'

Geographically, she had not travelled far, a few miles only, but the distance from Charlotte's florist shop to the Ritz hotel was socially immense. The cabbie thanked her politely for his fare and tip, and left her standing on Piccadilly amid the noise and lights, the elegant women and drawling men. It took her a moment to get up her courage to enter the grand hotel, to walk up the broad steps to the winter garden where a small orchestra was playing and a gilded female statue reclined, naked as God made her, in a spectacular niche on the wall ahead of her. So busy was Charlotte in looking at this statue while pretending not to, that she didn't see Mr Warrender approaching.

'How good to see you! Let me take your cloak.' He lifted the cape from her shoulders and a porter appeared as if by magic to relieve him of it. She smiled, gave her feathered turban a hitch in the right direction and took the arm extended to her. She was sure she would not be able to think of a thing to say all evening, but Matthew didn't give her the opportunity to be shy.

'A beautiful hotel, don't you think? It's only six years old, but done entirely in the style of Louis the Sixteenth. The painted ceiling in the dining-room is particularly fine.'

Charlotte nearly tripped over her own feet as she admired the gilded metal flower swags and the richly painted ceiling of the dining-room, but Matthew Warrender's hand on her elbow steadied her.

They were shown to their table in a corner of the great room. She wished they had been shown to the centre of the room, because her escort looked so handsome in his evening wear, finer than any man present. He smiled warmly whenever their eyes met, and casually offered to order for her. Having glimpsed the menu and seen that it was written in French, she gratefully agreed.

Mr Warrender dealt with the business of choosing the dinner, pronouncing all the difficult French words as if he could do it in his sleep. 'And now,' he said, 'for the wines. Sherry with the onion soup, I think. Claret with the main course and Sauternes to end with.'

'It sounds delicious,' she said shyly. 'I'm sure your choice is perfect. I wouldn't have known what to choose.'

'You know, you are looking much happier than when I last saw you. Perhaps your house guests were a trifle burdensome. Vic Tavern has a rough tongue.'

She looked at him sharply. Had he heard tales of the rows at Capel? 'Vic is a . . . a rough diamond, you might say. However, as I've known him all my life, he doesn't have the power to bully me. Everyone went home on Sunday morning, leaving me free for the day. I was able to gather quite a lot of material from the grounds and the houses. I must confess, I find Mr Douse more intimidating than Vic.'

'Douse? Has he been unpleasant to you?'

She was about to say that he had. It would have been wonderful to unburden herself, to tell him about Goldseekers Limited and ask his advice, to complain about the gardening staff and their failure with the orchids, but years spent listening to her mother's suspicious maxims caused her to forego the pleasure. Maud Blair trusted no man, woman or beast, but above all she believed that telling your troubles to anyone furnished them with a weapon. How could it be otherwise, she used to say, since the enemy would then know precisely where you were vulnerable?

Besides, Charlotte was afraid of boring Matthew. At this moment, boring her dinner companion was the greatest sin she could imagine. He must be entertained, made to laugh, encouraged to feel that the money he was about to spend at the Ritz was worth every penny. She denied, therefore, that there were any problems in her life and changed the subject, urging him to tell her about his early years.

'My early years? Very lonely, I assure you. My father was an adventurer and traveller of some renown. He and my mother went everywhere in the world together. I was sent away to school at six and saw very little of them. They died at sea, sailing to Greece. I was sixteen at the time, and it took me many years to forgive them for abandoning me.'

'Poor you,' she said with feeling. 'My father died when I was eight, but my mother was always nearby. She passed away over two years ago and I still miss her dreadfully. She was my companion and my adviser. I'm sure I've done any number of very foolish things since she left me on my own. And Hong Kong? Was it exotic and exciting?'

'Exotic, yes. Not very exciting for cadets like myself. I believe I met rather more Chinese than most of my compatriots did, but I can't say I ever got to know them. They are a mysterious people. Nor did I get to know my fellow Britons well. I feel as if I spent eleven years abroad with my nose pressed permanently against the window-pane of superior households. There was always a party indoors, or so it seemed, but I was forever outside looking in.'

'But how could that be? You're a gentleman!'

'A gentleman adrift. I envy your sense of purpose, your talent and the pleasure it gives you. I don't know what to do with my life.'

Charlotte blinked in surprise. Several people, it seemed, envied her, but all for different reasons. Billy wished for the affection that Vic showed to her. Florence envied her independence. And now Mr Warrender envied her business interests.

'My business has picked up since I last saw you. I've been waiting for three days to tell you about it. Lady Smythe telephoned me at eight o'clock on Monday morning. You know, Vic has always insisted that a telephone is a great waste of money, but what would have happened if I hadn't one? She might have telephoned some other floral decorator. She was planning to have a few friends in to dinner on Wednesday night and had forgotten to order any flowers. I rushed around to see her and we quickly decided what would be most appropriate for a dinner table in the spring. I used yellow silk as a runner down the centre of the table, waves of it, frothing and folding every which way, yellow tulips and orange ones, green smilax and . . . but you won't want to hear all of this. The important thing is, there was a certain Lady Briggs at the dinner party.

'After supper, I returned for my silk and the smilax, which can be used again if you submerge it in water overnight. Lady Smythe sent for me, and I was introduced to her guest.' Charlotte's eyes sparkled with excitement. 'I am to decorate her entire home on the night of April the sixteenth for a private ball. She lives in Wimpole Street.'

Warrender didn't seem at all surprised by her good fortune, although he was obviously pleased. 'I have met Lady Briggs. She is a formidable lady. Her son is a cadet in Hong Kong. I suspect she is a stern taskmaster, so I advise you to handle her with great care. How will you manage to do so much work single-handed?'

'I have engaged an entire gang of willing workers: Molly, my girl, of course, but also Vic and Billy and Mr Green and Jacko Boon, and even Florence Douse, who is dying to try her hand at flower arranging. Oh yes, and Arthur Brock. He has a new motorcycle and sidecar. He took me and my flowers to Lady Smythe's and returned with me to fetch my things. Little do they all know that they will have to work like navvies! Oh, you may be sure the lady won't regret having hired me. I have spoken to her by telephone. I really must tell Vic how useful the instrument has been.'

'Wretchedly expensive to install, I believe. I don't have one in my rooms in Hanover Square.'

'Oh, I had forgotten you live in Hanover Square!'

'Yes, I do,' he replied, surprised to see a rather demonic gleam in her eye.

'Then will you spy on Felton's, and Wills and Segar

for me? Make a note of what you see in their shops and any arrangements you see about to be delivered. I am very curious to know what sort of competition I have.'

'A spy!' he laughed. 'I can hardly wait to begin my duties. I'll make sketches, shall I? Now then. Here is the lamb.'

Charlotte scarcely recognized the lamb as being from the same animal that provided her familiar roasts. The chef had done curious things with the vegetables, as well. She pronounced the food delicious and drank an entire glass of claret rather quickly to drown the taste of the rich meat sauce.

'Will you . . . that is, do you think you might possibly return to Theobalds Park occasionally?' she asked as the waiter refilled the glass.

'Most probably. I have been given a set of rooms there for myself and my man. I am to come and go as I please. Most generous of the Admiral.'

'I believe you said Lady Meux has five daughters by a previous marriage.'

He laughed. 'Yes, she does and it has been made plain to me that I have no hopes in that direction. They will all make brilliant marriages, I'm sure.'

'I can't see what they have against you, but then the upper classes often surprise me. Did you ever meet the other Lady Meux? Valerie, the one no-one received.'

He admitted that he had, and made her laugh by telling her about his experience in Lady Meux's swimming pool.

'And was she really so wicked that no decent woman would want to know her?'

'Possibly. Recently, when Admiral Meux was having the principal bedroom refurbished for his new bride, the floorboards were lifted for some reason and several hundredweights of sea shells were found packed between the joists.'

'Why ever were they put there?'

'Apparently, sea shells between the joists are a means of deadening sound, and the late Lady Meux was a . . . noisy sleeper.'

Charlotte blinked, then burst out laughing when she realized the true purpose of the shells.

'I beg your pardon,' he said stiffly. 'That was too near the knuckle. I should not have mentioned it. Very indelicate of me.'

Charlotte put her napkin to her mouth; people were looking at her with disapproval. 'I should not have laughed. I'm sorry. I should have pretended not to understand you. I simply must learn to behave like a lady. That is, I must learn to imitate the manners of a lady, although I don't think I wish to imitate the behaviour of some of them. What sort of man was Lady Valerie's husband?'

'Sir Henry drank himself to death at an early age.'

She took another sip of the claret, decided that she hated it, and now had to eat the lamb to disguise the taste of the red wine. 'I suspect she was a rather fast woman and that is why she was not received. I am not received, either, but at least I'm respectable. My fault lies with being working-class.'

'Oh, not working-class!' he said earnestly. 'I would not describe you as working-class. Artisan; a craftswoman. Yes, that is what you might say. Artisan. And entrepreneurial.'

'What is that?'

'Many a person from humble beginnings has risen by talent and effort to a position of importance in a business way. And I suspect your mother was—'

'My mother's father was a railway clerk.'

'There you are!' he cried, clearly relieved. 'She was middle-class. Well, lower middle-class. They are the salt of the earth, people who set us all a good example by their hard work and temperate ways.'

'Does it matter what my grandfather was?'

'No, of course not. Forgive me for rattling on.'

She allowed the subject to drop, because it was impossible to think of disagreeing with him on any subject on this wonderful night. However, she did remember Florence's warning. And Florence knew all about men. Charlotte most definitely didn't want to be snubbed by Matthew Warrender or anyone she might meet while in his company. Her mother, wise in the ways of a wicked world, would certainly advise caution.

After dinner, they left the Ritz and visited a very grand dance hall where Matthew Warrender good-humouredly taught Charlotte the bouncy dance so appropriate for 'Alexander's Ragtime Band'. She had intended to ask him to summon a cab for her, and to travel to King Street on her own. In the end, she didn't care if he saw her home, at least from the outside. Never would she allow him to see her domestic arrangements in King Street. They sat close together in the cab, now calling each other Charlotte and Matthew, and laughing inanely about nothing in particular.

'So this is your shop! So much activity from such a small place,' he said when they had alighted.

'It's all the room that's necessary, but I wish I had a better address. I tell customers my address is Capel Manor in Enfield these days. I say that my business phone is in Covent Garden so that I can be close to all the latest flower imports.'

'And when does the market open? Within the next hour?'

'No, it's only one o'clock. The market opens at three. I shall have two hours' sleep before I must get up to make my purchases: just one or two small orders to be delivered tomorrow. I shall stay in town over the weekend.'

'One of these days, I shall surprise you and arrive on your doorstep at the stroke of three to help you shop for bargains in the market. It must be very exciting.'

'Why don't you come next Thursday morning? I

shall be buying flowers for a wedding which is to take place at St Paul's across the road on Saturday morning. Just a small wedding, really. The wedding breakfast is in a hotel, so I won't get any further business. The hotel makes its own arrangements.'

He held both her hands and looked into her eyes by the light of the gas lamp. 'I think it would be the greatest fun. Will you have all your labourers with you?'

'Oh, no! Just you.'

He raised her hands and kissed each one in turn. 'Good night, dear Charlotte. I will see you on this spot at three o'clock on Thursday morning.'

'Thank you for taking me out.' She withdrew her hands from his grasp, afraid that she had, by some sign known only to the gentry, indicated that he might take liberties. His smile seemed genuine. She thought he liked her. For him the evening had been a relaxing interlude, while for her the few hours spent in the company of a gentleman had been exhausting. There was nothing so tiring as wondering if one was making a fool of oneself!

Chapter Ten

Arthur Brock, dressed in his underwear, socks and slippers, wrapped a kimono around his slender form and shuffled into the dining-room of his flat off Russell Square, catching a gratifying glimpse of himself in the hall looking-glass. The kimono was silk damask in blue, green and purple, embroidered with a design of birds and clouds. It had cost him thirty-five shillings at Liberty's. Few men could claim to possess so handsome a garment. Brock thought it was vital for a man in his position.

An inheritance of five hundred pounds had been severely dented by the renting of his present establishment and the furnishing of it. His drawing-room was in the Saracen style, the walls covered in Moorish designs, with matching bench seating built into either side of the fireplace. The fire, when lit, threw out about as much heat as when the grate was empty, but the hanging lamps set above the banquette seats, the many pots and heavily carved occasional tables added greatly to the atmosphere he was attempting to create, as did the seven richly patterned oriental rugs. Brock even had a Turkish hookah pipe into which he blew bubbles of an evening.

His manservant, about to serve breakfast, showed little signs of being stirred by such a splendid garment. Brock had hopes of entertaining a few notable guests in the near future, which might well impress Perkins favourably. All that was required was that he should happen to meet a few people worthy of the invitation.

He met any number of great gentlemen at the track,

men who owned strings of race horses, had town as well as country homes, and spoke to him with the easy camaraderie of the sport of kings that stopped just short of actual friendship. It was the frustration that this distancing caused him that led Brock to accept Charlotte Blair's request for help in her work.

How eagerly did he fetch his motorcycle and sidecar, how dangerously did he make his way to Covent Garden, with what hopes of success had he entered the kitchen of Lady Smythe! From then on, the morning had spiralled down into farce. The first humiliation was being required to remove his shoes before he was allowed to enter the Smythe dining-room. Charlotte, dressed for work in one of her less flattering skirts and blouses, had brought with her a pair of ancient slippers. He tiptoed in his stocking feet. She spoke to the housekeeper in deferential tones, kept her head lowered and hurried him and their paraphernalia into the dining-room, where the table cloth was already in place.

Charlotte worked quickly and neatly, throwing out yards of diaphanous yellow silk, arranging it artfully down the centre of the table, placing low vases of yellow and orange tulips, with a tall arrangement at either end. That green stuff with the murderous thorns – smilax – was removed from tissue paper and laid along either side of the silk, then trailed to the edge of the table between each cover. The occasional tulip was laid, bare, on the silk, the cut end of its stem hidden in the folds.

The mantelpiece had all its ornaments removed, except for two shaded electric lights, then trays of moss were placed end to end. With great speed, Charlotte inserted tulips in the chosen colours. Still working like a demon, she extracted bundles of ivy – yards of it – and with these she draped every painting hanging from the picture rail and the huge mirror that dominated the fire-place.

The butler came into the room and paid her a few grudging compliments. Charlotte nodded shyly and set about transferring all of her scraps and tools into a large piece of sheeting which she then handed to Brock to carry out. They had been in Lady Smythe's home for exactly half an hour, and he had not caught so much as a glimpse of the lady herself.

The butler was just about to close the door behind them – this at half past two in the afternoon – when a remarkably uncultured female voice instructed them to stay right where they were. Brock turned, and had his first sighting of Lady Smythe, a handsome, plump woman of about forty-five.

Charlotte said how pleased she was to have the opportunity of a word with Lady Smythe. Would the lady care to inspect the dining-room?

The lady most decidedly would! How dared Charlotte creep away before making sure that her client was satisfied?

So they all returned to the dining-room: Lady Smythe, the butler, Charlotte and himself. Fortunately, Lady Smythe was almost thunderstruck with pleasure. The decorations were admitted to being a success.

'My lady,' said Brock, snatching his opportunity as Charlotte seemed too relieved to speak, 'you see before you the finest floral decorator in the whole of London. I say nothing of the others – mere men. Miss Blair is exceptional.'

Lady Smythe looked Arthur over from head to toe very deliberately. The inspection seemed to take minutes rather than seconds, but he stuck it out, smiling at her in a familiar way, trying with all his being to impress her favourably.

'And you are Miss Blair's assistant?'

'By no means, your ladyship. I have known the young lady since she was a nipper. My card.' He whipped from his pocket a calling card with his address on it. 'I plan to use her services very soon for a little soirée of my own. I find her work impeccable. Why, if she were not so clever, would she now be living at Capel Manor, my lady?'

Lady Smythe now directed her attention to Charlotte. 'You live at Capel Manor, Miss Blair? The Capel Manor owned by Mr and Mrs Gryce, to which I directed you some months ago?'

'Mr and Mrs Gryce have die . . . passed away,' said Charlotte quietly. 'I have rented the estate from Mr Warrender.'

Lady Smythe's eyebrows rose. She looked from Charlotte to Brock. He smiled again, his face aching with the effort to be charming and attractive.

'You will return to clean away this evening, won't you? You may wait in the servants' parlour until all the guests have left.'

'I always clear up immediately after a party, unless requested not to come back,' Charlotte assured Lady Smythe.

'And you, Mr Brock? Will you be . . . helping?'

'I am always pleased to assist my protégée, if your ladyship pleases.'

Charlotte had not been too pleased by his last words, as she told him most forcefully on the way home. He insisted that his comments could do Charlotte no harm and might help him to achieve his ambition. He was then obliged to explain his ambition in detail, how he hoped to snare a bride exactly like Lady Smythe. She must be a rich widow but not high-born, in short, someone who had married money. Charlotte must admit that Lady Smythe was not top drawer, yet she must be wealthy and she must be on the lookout for a younger man to enliven her declining years. Mercifully, Charlotte had not laughed, nor had she poured scorn on his ambitions. She had simply warned him that Lady Smythe was a demanding woman with few graces.

When they returned to the house at eleven o'clock that evening, she was led away immediately to meet some lady who might or might not want a few flowers arranged, while Brock was left in the kitchen to cool his heels.

The very next Saturday, he met Lady Smythe quite by chance at Cheltenham races, dressed to the nines and talking to four or five wealthy men. There followed a heady afternoon. At first, she hadn't recognized him. He was quick to remind her where they had met, to take credit for setting Charlotte up in business and to tell her that he was a director of Goldseekers Limited. For his part, he learned that she had been on the stage, that the late Sir Rupert Smythe had been thirty years her senior and stone deaf. During the course of the day's racing, he won twenty pounds, actually came out on top, which was an increasingly rare occurrence for him.

One of the gentlemen to whom Lady Smythe introduced him was Tristram Fotherby, a young man whose name was known to him. Younger son of somebody or other. They travelled back to London together and Brock (having sent a telegram to his manservant) invited Fotherby to supper. They drank quite a few jars together and seemed to be getting along famously, but when it came time to leave, the wretched young sprig succeeded in borrowing the twenty pounds from him!

Brock was no fool. Desperate for money he might be, but the upper classes were as voracious at hottentots, and about as comprehensible. They were not for him, and that included the actress who had married a fortune. At first blush, she had seemed like the perfect bride for him, but she was inclined to order him about. He found himself running all over the grounds to place her bets, fetch her refreshment and offer advice. Arthur Brock had not taken orders from a woman since he was in short coats and would not be under any actress's thumb! He would pin his hopes on Goldseekers and pray that the money started coming in before he had to relinquish his new-found way of life.

However, just as he had made a firm resolve to rub shoulders only with his own class, up popped Charlotte with a plea for help as she'd got this absolutely spiffing commission to provide decoration for a private ball at the home of Lady Briggs. Should he make one more attempt at wealthy wedded bliss? He had flipped a coin, heads he'd go, tails he wouldn't. Heads it was. He informed Charlotte. Two days later, he discovered that Lady Briggs was sixty, married and had a beard on her that wouldn't shame a purveyor of cough drops. It was enough to drive a chap to drink.

He had doted on them during the winter, giving them a sip of water from time to time, removing any dead leaves, as anxious about disease as any parent with a sickly child. In February, he had delicately scraped away the spent soil around each one before repotting it in a fresh mixture of his own concoction. March had brought the excitement of taking cuttings, hundreds of them, from the thirty varieties he grew. Fuchsias for basket work, fuchsias for standards and half standards. *Triphilla* fuchsias like 'Andenken an Heinrich Henkel', with long carmine flowers born in clusters, and 'Coralle', having dark green foliage and coral tubular blooms.

Of course he loved the other fuchsias, the ones that made people gasp when they saw them in public parks. John was particularly fond of the German varieties. People could say what they liked, the Germans certainly could breed wonderful fuchsias, like 'Alice Hoffmann' and 'Schneewittchen', so good for bedding out. Then again, you couldn't beat good old 'Amy Lye', raised by the greatest of British growers.

In April, he was continuing to pinch the tips to make the plants bushier, to increase the number of blooms. Now was the time to plant up the baskets, which would be brought out of doors in the summer and placed where their arching stems and profuse flowers would tremble in the breeze.

He reached for a wire basket with his left hand, for a bundle of moss with his right, then shook his head. He couldn't work, couldn't give his babies the love they deserved.

It wasn't just that he had come to hate the sound of Mabel's whining voice or the sight of her puffy, tear-stained eyelids. It wasn't that he thought he might one day do some serious damage to Mrs Wheems if she didn't stop making mischief between him and Mabel. It was worse than that. He had been found out. He had stolen money from Miss Blair, and in a weak moment he had told Mabel all about it. There had followed one of the worst battles he and Mabel had ever fought. Her first reaction had been to demand the extra money.

'If you got paid extra by Miss Blair, I should get it. You cheated me.'

'Cheated *you*?' he said. 'What about Miss Blair? I robbed her. I don't know why she keeps me on. She could sack me. We could end up on the street. I could go to prison!'

'Why ever did you do it? It was for beer money, wasn't it? Mum says you're a drunken wastrel. Wait till I tell her what you done. Then you'll get what for.' That stung him. She told her mother everything, probably everything they said in bed and all. 'If you do go to jail,' she continued, 'I'll not wait for you. I'll go home, that's what I'll do. I'm not having a jail bird.'

They were standing in the kitchen, yelling at each other like screech owls, and both of them had no trouble envisaging John tried, convicted and imprisoned. 'I couldn't go to prison. Wouldn't live through it, shut away in some dark cell without my fuchsias. They would die without me and I would die without them.'

'You love them stupid flowers more than you do me.'

'I've got a cousin in America,' he mused. 'I could emigrate. If they come for me, I'll go to America and find my cousin.' Actually, he had no idea where his cousin was, hadn't heard from the man in ten years. However, the threat was sufficient to send Mabel into loud cries of distress. He left the house, satisfied that he had frightened her good and proper.

The next day, Mrs Wheems, having heard about

179

John's disgrace, taunted him with the knowledge. 'Run away to America, would you? You useless idle swine. I never heard of any cousin in America, and I've known your family for thirty years. I'll bet you made him up. Not that I'd put it past you to desert Mabel.'

There was more of the same for half an hour, and the more she talked the more he thought about how he really would like to emigrate. What bliss! Everybody was rich on the other side of the Atlantic. The sun always shone, and no-one would call him a fool.

For several days he entertained the dream, happy just to think about it. This morning he had arisen filled with the conviction that he would go abroad. Mabel and her mother would be sorry they had ever raised their voices to him.

They grew fuchsias in the United States, he knew they did. What was more, he was quite sure no-one across the Atlantic could grow them as well as he could. He would get work and start a new life. There were a few obstacles to his dream, like where he was going to find the money. And, did you have to have a passport or other document? He liked to think he was a caring man. He would want to be sure that Mabel didn't suffer on his account. He knew, of course, that she would suffer. She would be losing a husband, after all. He just didn't want her to be held responsible for his crimes. Her parents would have her back to live with them. She might marry again with him abroad. He ground his teeth. She'd have to learn to cook and clean and smile, before she would find another man to take her on. As for himself, he was finished with women. They were too much trouble.

Jacko came through the open door of the greenhouse and had almost reached his side before John realized he was there.

'Are you all right, Mr Green?'

'Yes, of course, I am! What's the matter with you?' John could scarcely bear to look at Jacko since the day when Miss Blair had told him off for paying Mabel more than she had earned. Jacko had also helped himself to some of the woman's money, but Jacko didn't seem troubled at all.

'I came to talk to you about this business of helping Miss Blair do up Lady Briggs's place. I've bought four of them Hamilton self-acting table fountains, and three dozen fairy lights. I never heard of this business of having a colour theme for the decorations, have you?'

'No,' said John. He began assembling a basket, lining the wire cage with moss.

'Even some of the food is going to be green. Asparagus soup, sort of thing. Ferns! Palms! I've been to Rochford's this morning, arranging to hire four dozen palms and tree ferns. I hear Miss Blair sent that young lady, Miss Douse, to Liberty's to buy some sort of fancy vases. Florian Ware, it's called. Two dozen – you may think I'm exaggerating, but I'm not – two dozen twelve-inch vases, sixteen shillings each. There's some money being laid out on this affair. Fifty maidenhair ferns in pots, and a lot more cut stems. Lily of the valley and the other white flowers will have to be bought in the market. I'm told Lady Briggs fully expects to pay more for the flowers than for the food and drink.'

John had not been listening carefully. He wasn't at all certain that he would still be in England, come April the sixteenth. However, Jacko's words penetrated his gloom and he blinked in surprise.

'How do you know Miss Douse has been out buying vases from Liberty's? Who told you? You ain't by any chance been seeing that young woman, have you?'

Jacko licked his lips, giving a little embarrassed laugh. 'That wedding the other Saturday, remember? I went up to Covent Garden to move the potted palms into St Paul's Church. Miss Douse was there. We exchanged a few words, sort of thing. The church looked a treat. Miss Blair had made the wedding bouquet. Fifty white roses and asparagus fern. It was what the bride wanted, but she could scarcely lift it. Mr Warrender was there, too. Seems he had come up to the market on the Thursday before to look around, sort of thing. I believe he enjoyed himself. I don't want to worry you, Mr Green, but I wouldn't be surprised if them two didn't get theirselves hitched. We could be having her as the lady of the house permanent like.'

Charlotte was so tired she could scarcely keep awake. On the other hand, she was so nervous and anxious about the ball at Lady Briggs that she found it impossible to sleep at night. Molly had been making boxwood swags for the past week. The poor girl was nursing bleeding fingers and looked very tired. Billy had surprised everyone by volunteering to help make the swags – they needed fifty yards – and Molly had begged her to accept Billy's offer.

Charlotte had taken measurements of the rooms she was to decorate, had drawn out the decorations on squared paper and counted every flower, leaf and plant she would need. Allowing for accidents, last-minute changes, flowers being unavailable and substitutes being more expensive, she had invested a hundred and fifty pounds in supplies. Green plush for the table runner and the short, individual pieces that would go under each plate and hang down the length of the cloth, the green ribbon for tying each individual posy of lily of the valley and fern, plus the twenty-four green and cream vases, had all added up to a sum that terrified her. She would have to make a rental charge for the non-floral material, and thought ten per cent sounded reasonable. She knew all about the rich and how they managed to stay that way. Although she had been forced to pay cash for all her supplies, Lady Briggs would not pay her until the end of the second quarter: July.

The doorbell clanged. Charlotte heard Florence being directed to the small back room by Molly. 'I'm in here, Florence, just working on my figures.'

'You look dreadful,' said Florence. 'You're working too hard, Charlotte.'

'I don't see that I have a choice!' She then patted Florence's arm to indicate that she had not meant to be so sharp. 'I have so much money invested in this ball. And so much of my future, as well. Lady Briggs has actually recommended me to a few of her friends. I have valuable work right up until the beginning of June. The trouble is, my capital is dangerously low, and I can't expect to be paid immediately. The vases have arrived from Liberty's, by the way. Thank you very much for buying them for me. Rochford's will deliver the palms to Wimpole Street at half past nine tomorrow morning. Jacko Boon and Mr Green will bring up other necessary things from Capel Manor in the fly. They will reach Wimpole Street at about the same time. Lady Briggs doesn't want us to start work before then. We'll be in the way, she says. You will come, won't you, Florence?'

'Of course. I wouldn't miss it, although I'm not usually abroad so early in the morning. Will Arthur Brock collect you?'

'Yes, I shall be taking the green ribbon and the green plush table centre and individual place runners, but Molly will ride in Vic's car with Billy and Vic and the fifty yards of box swag and the vases. It's going to be beautiful. Three shades of green glasses on the table, green and cream dishes, menus in bronze green printed in copper. This is my greatest chance. I just wish it was all over.'

Florence left the shop soon after. Charlotte made a cup of tea for herself, Billy and Molly, then began making up the bunches of lily of the valley and fern that were to be placed at each cover. Thirty guests would sit down to dinner. One hundred and fifty were expected for dancing in the ballroom. Two bands had been engaged. A caterer was dealing with the food. And every person who set foot in Lady Briggs's home on the following day could well bring more business to Charlotte. Her stomach churned every time she thought about it.

At nine o'clock that night, Molly closed the shop and went off to eat with Billy. The street was exceptionally noisy for a Monday night. Molly and Billy had been full of some news, but Charlotte had told them firmly that she wasn't interested in anyone's troubles but her own. She was going to fry herself an egg and then go to bed. She had to be up at three o'clock in the morning.

'Wretched,' said Arthur Brock when he came to fetch her the next morning. 'Terrible thing to happen.'

Charlotte climbed into the sidecar, holding the cardboard box of cloth and flowers in her lap. 'I'm not interested in anything but my work. Terrible things go on in this world, but I must concentrate. No-one wanted to discuss my order this morning. All they wanted to do was gossip. Now let us get as quickly as possible to Wimpole Street.'

Arthur gave her a puzzled look, then shrugged his shoulders and concentrated on getting his machine going. It took him a minute or two to accomplish it, and Charlotte bit her lip and dug her fingernails into her palms to keep from screaming at him. Just when she thought she would have to get out and hail a cab, the motor turned over and they were away. Even so, they were almost the last to arrive.

Rochford's wagon was drawn up to the curb, Billy was behind the wheel of his father's car. Vic was pacing the pavement in front of the handsome house. Arthur pulled up and called a muted greeting to Vic just as Mr Green and Jacko Boon arrived in the fly. As everyone was accounted for except Florence, it remained only for the butler to unlock the gate at pavement level that led downstairs to the servants' quarters so that everyone could begin to unload.

Wearing his morning uniform, a footman opened the wrought iron gate. Rochford's men, who were anxious to unload and get away, were first down the narrow, steep stairs – three men carrying huge potted palms and tree ferns. Billy, Vic and Molly negotiated the stairs with the yards of swag, before the butler managed to fight his way up the concrete steps to summon Charlotte.

'Lady Briggs must see you urgently, Miss Blair.'

Charlotte followed the butler to the morning-room where Lady Briggs was seated, wearing a maroon dressing gown and old slippers. She was crying, a startling figure with a single plait of white hair hanging down her back almost to her waist, watery blue eyes brimming with tears and tufts of sparse white hairs quivering on her jowls.

'I presume you have heard the news,' she said hoarsely.

'About the *Titantic* sinking? Yes, ma'am. It's terrible. So many people dead.'

'I've lost two cousins and any number of friends. It will be days before we know who died and who was saved. Over a thousand people! I can't believe it.'

A prickle of fear slithered down Charlotte's back. It was terrible, but she had been so wrapped up in her own affairs that she had not paused to consider the horror of the tragedy. Lady Briggs cancelled the party. Charlotte, her mind refusing to envision drowning men, women and children, focused on fifty yards of boxwood swag and the possibility of keeping it in decent shape for a week or more.

'You must get your things out of my house immediately.'

There was no point in arguing. Charlotte summoned up her courage to speak. 'Will you . . . will you be giving this party at a later date?'

Lady Briggs stood up. 'How can you ask such a question at this time? No, I will not be giving this party at a later date, but don't you dare to use the green theme for any other party. That idea was for *me*. You promised it to me.'

'I've had a great deal of expense, Lady Briggs. I've paid out a considerable amount of money. I would expect—'

'I've had nothing, do you understand? Nothing. What you have spent can be used elsewhere, in other ways. I am amazed at your insensitivity. Please leave my house as quietly as possible. I want no mess left behind.'

In the street, Charlotte met the caterer, Mr Fouchard, and told him that his services would not be required. He, too, was dismayed, and she was certain he would sustain a considerable loss, but he managed to sound more sympathetic than she had done. Rochford's men were told to remove the palms and tree ferns they had already delivered.

'I am cancelling the order,' she said firmly, hoping that would be the end of the matter.

'I'm sure there will be some sort of charge, ma'am,' said the foreman. 'The firm lost a thousand pounds worth of palm trees on the *Titanic*. That's a terrible loss, you know, even for a company like Rochford's. I'm sure there will be a charge, but the bill will be sent to your business.'

Vic, Molly and Billy awkwardly replaced the swag in the motor and drove off. Arthur whispered that they would have to go back to the dining-room, because he had already delivered the lily of the valley and the green plush. At that moment, Mr Green and Jacko mounted the stairs to the pavement. Florence, whom Charlotte had not seen arrive, was helping them to carry the vases which she said would be taken back to Capel Manor.

'Well, let's get on with it,' Charlotte said, and turned her head away so that no one could see the tears in her eyes.

The day dragged on. There was much to do. Everything had to be stored somewhere, and by the time the shop closed on Tuesday evening, the cellar and her small flat were full. She had scarcely spoken all day, and was very relieved to say good night to Molly. Having no appetite, she ate a piece of bread and butter and sat down in the chair with shiny wooden arms that had been her mother's favourite resting place. She was ruined. The debts had been mounting as she purchased supplies, but this cancellation was a blow from which she could not hope to recover.

Closing her eyes, she fell into an exhausted sleep, but instead of dreaming of the ball that never was, she found herself at sea, drowning, crying for help, witnessing a gigantic ocean-going liner sinking to the bottom of the ocean on its maiden voyage.

Chapter Eleven

Billy was behind the wheel, as usual, when he, Vic and Molly pulled away from the kerb in Wimpole Street. 'We'll go straight to Charlotte's shop and return this damned swag,' said Vic. 'I've got work to do.'

Molly had put on her only decent skirt, made of blue serge with several large buttons on the side. Her shoes had been polished until they glowed, and her white blouse had been starched so stiffly, Billy was amazed that she could move her head at all. She didn't normally dress this way for work, but wanted to look her very best when visiting the home of Lady Briggs. It was to have been a wonderful occasion, something to dream about for ever. For several minutes after she heard that the party had been cancelled, she had made a monumental effort to keep her composure; now she sat crying quietly in the back seat. The swag lay heaped every which way over the seat beside her and on the floor.

'Isn't it awful? I don't know what Miss Blair is going to do. She won't be able to find a use for all this greenery before it dries to a crisp. Nor the vases. Oh, Billy . . . *Mr* Billy, we forgot the vases!'

Billy braked, but Vic ordered him to drive on. 'Someone will take them. Maybe them gardeners from Capel. They got to be good for something, them two. I want to get back to my shop, dammit. Watch out for that tram, Billy! Ain't you got no sense?'

Traffic was heavy, but it took them only about twenty

minutes to reach King Street. Despite his father's complaints, Billy got out of the motor and helped Molly to unload the car. Charlotte had not yet arrived, so Molly had to use her key to get in. With his father seated a few yards away, Billy didn't dare say more to Molly than, 'I'll speak to you soon.'

'Leave the motor parked here,' said Vic. 'We can get Robinson to drive it to our house. I've got business.'

He stormed into the shop and walked straight to the back room. Billy followed after telling Robinson to drive the motor car to the Tavern house.

'Close that door behind you,' said Vic. 'Charlotte's going to need a little money to tide her over. This will be a mortal blow to her.' Billy's stomach lurched as his father approached the rolltop desk. 'Fancy that Lady Briggs not paying her anything on account. The girl should have left it to me. I'd 'ave made sure the old harpy coughed up.'

Vic pulled the drawer out six inches, reached for the secret catch and opened it up its full length. The place where the three hundred pounds should have been was empty; in its stead was the paste tiara. Vic turned slowly to face Billy. Only the two of them knew how to activate the hidden catch, or so Vic thought. He never doubted that Billy had taken the money.

'I can explain, Dad.'

'I don't doubt it. What have you done with my money? And what's this?' He picked up the tiara gingerly between thumb and forefinger, looked at it closely and tossed it on the desk. 'What's this piece of trash? You're not going to tell me you bought it for three hundred quid!'

'I was a fool. You see—'

'I see, all right. Bloody fool, that's what you are. And I suppose the police have been round asking about it.'

'No!'

'No, of course not. Who would report the theft of a paste tiara?' Vic rubbed his chin and paced the floor.

'Still and all, they might. Somebody, perhaps the wife, will have sold the real tiara without telling the insurance company. Happens all the time. The owners will have to make a claim, and the police will turn up on our doorstep sooner or later. Later rather than sooner, I'm thinking, because they know I can tell diamonds from glass. They'll never guess I'd be so stupid.'

'I'm sorry, Dad.'

'Not as sorry as you're going to be. You've had it now, my lad. Always whining about how I put myself out for Charlotte and won't do nothing for you. Damned right, I won't. She's smart, hard working. That young woman has got a head on her shoulders. As for you, anything I might have considered giving you has been spent. Got that? Spent! You won't get a penny piece from me now or any other time. Your inheritance went into the pockets of a thief.'

'That's not fair. I'm entitled to something.'

Vic turned to look at his son, coming up so close that their noses almost touched. 'Over my dead body. When I'm dead and gone, you'll get what's left. But I warn you, I'm tired of spending my days in this stinking hole. I want out. I'm going to be respectable. A company director, a gentleman, see? As soon as this Goldseekers thing comes off, I'm closing the place down. Well, selling it. But not to you, because you ain't got two ha'pence to rub together, have you? You couldn't buy it. I reckon I could get near enough four thousand for it. That and my income from Goldseekers will take care of my old age. I'm tired of living off the poor, watching pinch-faced women coming in here week after week, popping their laundry, the old man's overcoat, the kid's shoes.'

'You always said a pawnshop was necessary for the poor. You always said you was like a bank to them.'

'So it is and so I did. But I'm tired of it, don't you understand simple English? I done all right off these poor people. Now I want to take a little from

190

the rich. They deserve to have their pockets picked. They're greedy and stupid and they don't think. Serve them right.' Vic hitched one hip up on the desk, folded his arms and looked at his son. 'Just tell me one thing. What got into you? We never take chances here. If I know the tea leaf, I might do him a favour. But a couple of chancers come in here with a tiara of all things, I'd give 'em a flea in their ear. Why did you do it?'

'I thought if I could buy it for three hundred and sell it for much more, I'd have my stake for the future. You won't do anything for me. It's Charlotte this and Charlotte that. I'm your son!'

'Yes, and I wish you wasn't. Must take after your mother, wherever she is. Get out of my sight. I don't want you sleeping at home tonight. You can come home tomorrow night.'

Billy, red in the face, turned to go.

'Poor Charlotte,' moaned Vic. 'I've a good mind to tell her I can't help her over her present difficulty, because my bleeding son spent all my money.'

'Mr Green,' said Florence softly, as the footman locked the gate to Lady Briggs's kitchen. 'This has been very upsetting. I can't imagine what my poor dear friend, Miss Blair, is going to do now. She's left without her vases. Two dozen of them. I think they should be taken to Capel Manor, don't you? Her shop is ever so crowded. I think you should take them home with you.'

'Yes, I reckon,' said John Green, sounding not at all certain.

'And I am going to ask a favour of you. Could Mr Boon see me home in a cab? Oh, I'll pay the fare, don't worry about that, but you see, I'm feeling rather queer. I could walk up the street and hail a cab, but, you know, I'm so faint, I might not manage to get home safely.'

'Well—' began Green, but Jacko interrupted.

'I'll see Miss Douse to her home, Mr Green. Then

I'll take the train to Enfield. I won't be long. Probably get back to Capel before you do, sir.'

John Green looked from one to the other of them very suspiciously, but Florence had adopted her haughtiest expression. The head gardener didn't dare to refuse her. She leaned against a nearby lamppost with a tiny white scrap of lace handkerchief to her nose until the Capel Manor two-wheeler had travelled down Wimpole Street and turned the corner out of sight. Then she looked at her companion and smiled broadly.

'That was well done, if I say so myself. You're very quick-witted Jacko. I like that in a man.'

'Miss Douse, I'm a fool. I shouldn't have done it, except I didn't know what you'd get up to if I failed to speak up. You're naughty, you know that.'

She hung her head, looking up at him coquettishly. 'Yes, I'm a naughty girl, and I need a big strong man to keep me out of trouble. Anyway,' a sudden change of mood and tone, 'that terrible accident to the *Titanic* is so horrible, every time I close my eyes, I see just how it must have been. I need a cup of tea. And a cake. Perhaps two cakes.'

'I can't go anywhere decent in my work clothes, ma'am.'

'I think you look splendid. Very manly. We'll find somewhere. Take me to a café where the working class eat. I shall enjoy it. I'm not snobbish, you know.'

'Not much, you ain't. How does your father deal with you? I don't know my way round the West End at all, but we'll manage. I ain't got much time and I want to make the most of it. I want to watch your beautiful face, hear your sweet voice. It's got a song in it, sort of thing.'

She laughed and gave him a teasing look, enjoying the effect she was having on him. It was a glorious spring day, the sky hadn't a cloud in it. People were beginning to come out of their houses, to promenade in their elegant walking costumes or to step into their carriages or motor cars. How sad about the *Titanic*. How sad about Charlotte. Never mind, Florence would have her hour with Jacko. That was all that mattered: their happiness, Jacko's and hers.

Florence walked him briskly to Lyon's Corner House in Coventry Street, Haymarket, which seemed to fill all requirements, as no-one paid any attention to them. The tea and cakes were expensive, but Florence had already slipped a pound note into Jacko's hand. He said he hated to take it and wished he could afford to pay for her, but he hadn't brought but half a crown with him, never thinking that he might need money. Never thinking that he might have to travel home by train or tram, either.

'Don't you worry about that,' she said gaily. 'I shall take you to Liverpool Street station in a cab and . . . and kiss you goodbye.'

He blushed. She giggled at his embarrassment and laid a hand on his arm. He closed his eyes, as if to savour the pain her touch caused him. *I love him*, thought Florence. *I really do love him. This is the man I'm going to marry. And I won't ever look at another man again. He'll be good to me and keep me from getting into trouble. And it will all be wonderful.*

'Jacko,' she said quietly. 'Tell me about yourself. You don't want to be a gardener at Capel Manor for the rest of your life, do you?'

'No, ma'am, I surely don't. I want to have my own nursery. Growing roses, I think. That would be just the ticket. I could do it. I'd be as big a success as Rochford's or Stuart Low, if I had the money to buy the nursery, of course. But I'm saving up. I've got ten pounds in the bank already. I'm an ambitious man and I know my business.' As he spoke, he seemed to grow in stature. His face glowed with confidence, making him more attractive than ever. 'You must come out to Capel beginning of June, sort of thing. By that time, I'll have planted a couple of thousand plants. Carpet bedding. I believe it was invented by the head gardener at Cliveden. Some head gardeners are real clever. Not Mr Green, though. He don't care for nothing but fuchsias.'

'And what do you do in the garden at Capel Manor?'

'I'm doing a real nice design on a great bed twenty feet across, comes up in the middle like a hill. It's marked out like the petals on a flower with six triangles in between. *Herniaria glabra* for edging. The groundwork's to be *Sedum glaucum*, with *Alternanthera, Mesembryanthemum* and a central plant of *Echeveria metallica*. Then there's . . .'

Florence let her mind wander, as his words were not important. What mattered was that he was being given the opportunity to show off his knowledge of Latin names and to impress her with his skill as a gardener. She didn't tell him that she had seen a great deal of very fine carpet bedding in the public parks the previous year, during the celebrations for the coronation of George V. Florence knew about men. You let them boast as much as they wished. The more they boasted to you, the better they liked you.

'It's a devil of a lot of work,' he was saying, 'and you have to plan out the whole thing very carefully. Then keeping it in order, that's delicate work. None of the plants is allowed to bloom, you see. Pinching, replacing dead plants, keeping the lines neat, getting down to the plants without damaging any and clipping them close. The effect is created with different colours and shades of foliage, you know.'

'I think you're very clever. I saw that straight away, the first time I met you. But I don't know anything about you. What sort of home did you come from? What sort of little boy were you?'

Like every man she had ever met, he loved to talk about himself, but she was unprepared for the story of this man's life, for the tale of hardship and neglect and lack of any sort of parental love. When he had finished, fifteen minutes later, the tears were standing in her eyes.

'Oh, Jacko, you need someone to love you and cuddle you and make up to you for all that you missed out on when you were a boy. I daresay you didn't even have a hobby horse or a hoop when you were little. And I need someone to look after me and make me behave. I think we were meant for each other.'

'Don't talk that way!' he growled, suddenly not only embarrassed but frightened. 'Come on, we better get out of here. I must go back to Capel. What have I been dreaming of?'

As good as her word, she rode in a cab with him to Liverpool Street station, pressing the money on him to pay for it, and more to buy his ticket to Enfield. 'Over here,' she whispered, dragging him by the arm to a dark recess. She manoeuvred him into the corner with his back to the wall, then kissed him on the lips.

He pushed her away roughly. He was breathing hard, but then, so was she. 'Jacko, don't be angry.'

'Don't you never kiss a man like that again!'

'I won't! Oh, I promise you I won't. Only you.'

He made a noise in his throat, something between a snort and a groan. Their eyes met and held. Suddenly, he reached for her and laid his lips against hers, not in a snatched kiss, but long and thrillingly gentle, the kiss of a man in love. Florence leant against him, let him take her weight as she put her arms around his neck. They parted only when neither could survive without taking a breath.

'You're a vixen,' he said, and she smiled, because he had said it lovingly.

'Yes, my darling, a vixen. But all for you, because I love you. That's your train being called. Dream of me tonight. And on Sunday night you come to town. You meet me at the Lyons Corner House in the Strand at five o'clock.'

'Your old man won't let you out. What could you possibly tell him?'

'He'll let me out. He can't hold me. And what I'll

tell him will be my business. Goodbye, Jacko. Hurry! You'll miss the train!'

Matthew removed his goggles, flat hat and dust coat, before handing the butler his card. He was called up to Lady Briggs's drawing-room almost immediately. Like the other guests, he had received a telegram on the morning of the sixteenth telling him that the ball had been cancelled. Rumour had it that Lady Briggs lost two cousins on the ship, so he had waited three days before calling upon her.

'Matthew!' she cried, as he entered her drawing-room. 'I'm so glad you arrived before the others. Did you drive yourself in that motor of yours? Sit down and tell me how you are.'

He was pleased to see that her old spirit had returned. She was a formidable woman, with the largest bosom he had ever seen. As a boy, he had been rather frightened of her when visiting his friend, Pelham. Sir Grover Briggs was a surgeon who operated almost exclusively on wealthy members of the upper classes, and had developed a professional manner that owed more to sycophancy than medical concern. Although Matthew used to imagine the round-shouldered little man wielding knives and saws and drills, he was never so nervous of the quiet Sir Grover as of his booming wife.

'I did come in a motor, as a matter of fact. I inherited it from my grandfather. It's parked directly in front of the house, and I'm very well, Lady Briggs. But what news have you?'

'Safe,' she smiled. 'My cousins, Lucinda and Isobel Fewkes-Dawn, were in the very first lifeboat. There weren't enough lifeboats, you know. Fifteen hundred people drowned because there weren't enough lifeboats. Mind you, some extremely rich gentlemen survived, while others went down. They say the band played as the ship sank. I received a cable from Nova Scotia telling me the good news. It has been a dreadful time,

Matthew. I wish Pelham was here. I do miss him so. Is he happy in Hong Kong? He never writes to me.'

'That is too bad of him.' Matthew knew for certain that Pelham resided on the far side of the world in order to escape his mother's intrusive love.

She poured him a cup of tea; in the distance they heard the front door bell ring. 'Tell me quickly. Does he have a mistress?'

'Lady Briggs!'

'He's thirty-five, Matthew. Older than you, and unmarried. I have never known him to show an interest in any girl and would be relieved to know that he has a mistress.'

'A very beautiful young Chinese. You may rest easy, although I shan't, if Pelham ever discovers that I have told you about her.'

Two women in very large hats were shown into the room. He was introduced to Mrs John Wingate, whose husband was a physician, and to Mrs Horace Templeton, whose husband specialized in infectious diseases. The three women intrigued him. Not only were they much the same age, with husbands in similar work, but they were all exceptionally ugly. His hostess reminded him of nothing so much as an old walrus, while Mrs Wingate, with her long thick neck and very mobile lips was a camel, and Mrs Templeton brought to mind an ageing stork, all long neck, skinny arms and feathers lying every which way. Perhaps they were friends because they felt secure in each other's company.

Lady Briggs poured, while Matthew busied himself handing out the tea, milk, sugar, sandwiches and cakes. When he at last sat down to drink his own, now cold, tea, Lady Briggs gave him an approving smile.

'That young woman you recommended to provide the floral decorations for my ball was a bit of a disappointment, Matthew,' she said.

'I can't believe—'

'Oh, not her designs. Not her ideas. Very clever

indeed. But when she arrived in the morning and I was forced to tell her the ball was cancelled, she was extremely put out. She didn't seem to have any regard for my feelings at all. I told her I had lost two cousins, as I then thought. All she could speak of was how much money she had spent on flowers and materials. Really, Matthew, if you ever see her again, you must warn her that such a mercenary approach is most unbecoming.'

Matthew struggled for an acceptable explanation. 'She is dedicated to her work. I'm sure she's neither callous nor mercenary. However, she does run a business. She will have had considerable expense—'

'How do you know her?' enquired Mrs Templeton. 'You seem to enter so wholly into her feelings. Is she from a good family?'

'No, that is, I have no idea. She has rented Capel Manor from me.'

'I beg your pardon?' said Lady Briggs in a bellow that was only this side of vulgar. 'I don't like this, Matthew. You haven't—'

'You misunderstand! My agent rented the estate to her at a time when I thought I would remain in Hong Kong. I changed my mind and came home, only to find that someone else had possession of Capel Manor. She offered to move out, but I thought it would be dishonourable to expect her to do so. That is how I know her, how I have come to admire her work, how I presumed to recommend her work to you.'

Lady Briggs held out her hand for his cup, which he mutely gave up. She emptied the cold dregs into a bowl, while her two lady guests watched her eagerly, waiting for her judgement. 'She is very pretty. Thick, blond hair,' she explained to her friends. 'But too solemn, almost sour.'

'Shyness,' ventured Matthew. 'A dedication to her work.'

'Dresses like a fishwife.'

'Oh, surely not—'

'Or an artist.'

He could think of nothing to say, had exhausted his fund of excuses and really wondered if he was doing Charlotte any good by such a vigorous defence.

'Talented women, artistic women, quite often have no taste in personal adornment,' said Mrs Wingate. 'I've observed it many times.'

Eventually the subject changed from Charlotte's shortcomings to the International Flower Exhibition, which was to be held the following month in the grounds of the Chelsea Hospital. All three ladies had every intention of being there on the first day. Neither rain nor hail nor dark of night would keep them away.

Matthew put two cubes of sugar into his fresh cup of tea and remained silent. A few weeks ago he had been roused from his bed at two o'clock so that he could join Charlotte at Covent Garden market. The idea was not so amusing at that hour as it had been when he first suggested it. Cranking up his grandfather's small motor car in the chilly dark morning, it struck him that the air was quite different when one was coming *home* at half past two in the morning from what it was when one was going *out* at half past two.

He rumbled through empty streets without a hitch, until he reached the vicinity of the market. Here, he found every road blocked. There was no possibility of driving down King Street. He moved away from the market area, parked his motor and joined the throng on foot. Many of those claiming the roadway and pavements had clearly walked great distances, some carrying tall woven baskets of produce on their heads. Carts rumbled over cobbles, horses snorted as if in response to the curses of their drivers, and the closer he came to the market, the more intense was the smell of rotting vegetation.

He was ten minutes late. A minute or two before he was able to fight his way to her side, he could see her standing on the pavement looking around her. The bright yellow hair was worn in a long plait, rather than her usual splendid pompadour. Her shoes were sturdy, her skirt a slightly flared brown material, hemmed well above the ground, except where the stitching had come undone. For some reason, she had chosen to wear a bright green satin overblouse of the sort said to be favoured by Russian Cossacks. It must have been part of a theatrical costume. She had belted it with a long scarf, which on closer inspection he saw to be a rather fine Liberty print. A knitted woollen hat pulled over her ears completed what could only be described as a highly individual style of dress.

But then, as he studied other people in the market, he realized that he was the odd man out, the person who had not donned the first garment that came to hand. He had dressed with care in a tweed suit.

'There you are!' she cried, pushing aside a barefooted woman with a pipe in her mouth and a basket of greens on her head. The woman cursed at her in an Irish accent, but Charlotte appeared not to notice. 'Hurry, all the best flowers will be sold.'

Without further conversation, she took his arm and led him through the press, giving him an opportunity to smell the people as well as the cabbages. A group of boys were washing by the pump, splashing icy water at each other and yelling dares. The general level of noise rose steadily until, by the time they reached the flower markets, his ears were ringing with the din.

Charlotte was greeted warmly everywhere they went. She spoke to everyone with a distracted air, touching a flower here, turning up her nose at a plant there, ignoring the salesmen's urging, laughing at their loudly expressed disappointment when she refused to buy. No-one actually took offence at the failure to make a sale, since whatever Charlotte refused to buy was snatched up by the customers behind her. Money changed hands with great speed. Bemused as he was by the unfamiliarity of the floral hall, the speed of Charlotte's decisions and the noisy crowds, he noticed that Charlotte was among the few customers who paid cash, whereas almost all the men who placed orders seemed to have accounts.

She handed Matthew her purchases and pressed on, determined to get the finest white roses for the keenest prices. Five dozen white roses, all in bud, none with so much as a single blemish, cost her two pounds. A dozen tuberoses, two shillings, a dozen bunches of maidenhair fern at eight shillings and, finally, a dozen bunches of French myrtle. All these purchases were, she said, for the bridal bouquet, because the bride *would* have a bouquet as large as those carried by debutantes at their presentations. 'And a circlet for her veil,' added Charlotte. 'My materials for the bride have cost me two pounds twelve shillings. I shall charge eight guineas. The three bridesmaids must make do with smaller bouquets of white carnations, lily of the valley, myrtle and fern. I daren't charge more than two guineas for them. Now, I must hire two dozen large palms and tree ferns for the church. A simple wedding, really. No flowers in the church. Just the greenery, making a total of seventeen pounds, seventeen shillings. Perhaps I might dare to round the figure up to eighteen pounds.'

'Do foolish women actually spend so much?' he had asked, slipping on a cabbage leaf and nearly falling down.

'It's not foolish at all. Flowers scent the air and turn an ordinary occasion into an exceptional one. I shall make something spectacular for Lady Briggs. I wish you could see it.'

He lacked the nerve to tell her that he had been invited to the ball, because then she would know that the commission was his doing. Matthew was extremely fond of Charlotte and liked and admired her more each time he met her, but her reactions were unpredictable.

As he sat drinking tea in Wimpole Street, he began to wonder if he had actually done Charlotte a favour by recommending her to Lady Briggs. 'Lady Briggs,' he said, when there was a break in the conversation, 'please forgive me. I have overstayed my welcome.'

'Nonsense. Sit down. Mrs Wingate and Mrs Templeton are leaving. I want a word with you in private.'

He guessed that he was due for a lecture on some subject or other, and waited impatiently while she saw off her other guests. How wise of Pelham to have moved so far away!

'You're a strange boy,' she began.

'Hardly a boy. I'm nearly thirty-three years old.'

'I repeat: a strange boy. No, perhaps confused would be a better word. But it's not to be wondered at. Your mother had the odd idea that she ought to raise you herself. Then your father (I never could understand him) decided that he wanted his son to be a chum! Then they would take it into their heads to travel to foreign parts, leaving you in the charge of some unimaginative nanny. Your mother had no sense when it came to employing staff, and I told her so many times. No wonder you have found yourself on the fringes of society. Strange. Quite presentable, but not sufficiently willing to put yourself out to be charming. And you have not been assiduous in breaking into the right circles. Inferior birth need not be an obstacle, you know. I, myself, am humbly born,' she said with all the complacency of a woman born to a farmer with a thousand prime acres. 'Briggs has concentrated on choosing his patients with care and—'

'Not the other way around?'

'I sincerely hope not! Although I occasionally have cause to mistrust my husband's judgement. He does more charitable work than he dares to tell me of. However, we are talking of you. What are you going to do with the rest of your life? You have your little estate, and I presume there is a home farm.'

'And a beer house called the Spotted Cow,' he could not resist telling her.

'Well, that lot won't keep you in stiff collars! You must marry money. I have to say very few of our most suitable girls are quite so noticeably pretty as the floral decorator.

If you allow yourself to be seen with her – oh, yes, I've heard rumours. The Ritz hotel, no less, and fashionably dressed, I'm told.' Matthew had recognized Charlotte's gown as belonging to Florence, and had been greatly relieved to see her so conventionally turned out. 'If you allow yourself to be seen with her, you cannot expect a suitable girl to be willing to stand the comparison. Have some sense, Matthew. I have a fair idea of what sort of income you are existing on. Show that you are a worthy successor to your maternal grandfather and think of your future.'

Matthew's collar had become uncomfortably tight, and he was sure his colour had risen, but he managed to smile and to keep his voice level. 'I'm far from wealthy, Lady Briggs. Fortunately, my grandfather left me no less than three splendid automobiles. I am considering going into business. Opening an agency and selling motors, you know.'

'Don't be a fool!'

'There should be money in it.'

'But not a wife. Consider banking. You speak Chinese. But no, there is no value in that. I daresay they can't read or write, much less do business.'

Matthew drew in his breath and held it, calculating the distance to the door and how soon he could exit through it. 'I speak French, German, Cantonese, Mandarin and Japanese.'

'Not stock jobbing,' she said, ignoring him. 'That is definitely not good enough. Try to get yourself appointed as a director on a few boards. That would be nice. I'm sure you know nothing about the management of land, so you mustn't consider it. But a company director of say, Lever Brothers, or, better still . . .' she smiled excitedly; he wondered what hideous fate she had in mind for him, 'an American company. You have visited the United States, haven't you? An American company it shall be.'

'How on earth,' his temper was slipping out of

control, 'how on earth am I to get myself appointed to an American company, when I don't know a single American? I have no skills that would be of value to any company, much less an American one, and there is no reason why anyone should choose to employ me for any reason, except possibly the Civil Service. And I will tell you now, I never want to be a part of any government of any sort in any capacity.'

She clapped her hands together with delight, having heard not one word of his outburst. 'I have it! You shall stand for Parliament. I suppose it would have to be as a Liberal, but never mind!' She beamed at him, as he sat silent, defeated at last. 'And to set you on your way, I shall give my ball. Possibly on the night – no, two nights – before the International Flower Show. I would hold it the night before – so prestigious – but I'm too late. I, myself, am engaged for an event that evening. Now you may go, Matthew. I'm pleased that you understand what I have been telling you.'

Outside, traffic passed up and down Wimpole Street while Matthew sat in his motor, trying to recover his composure enough to drive off. He was parked for almost ten minutes.

His grandfather had left him three motor cars, all handsome vehicles. Reasoning that he could not drive more than one, he chose the least ostentatious of them and sold the other two for two hundred and fifty pounds. He was well aware that the majority of men in England would have been content to have so much money in the bank, but he also knew that the owner of Capel Manor could not possibly maintain his position for more than a few months on such a sum. Lady Briggs had, therefore, touched a raw nerve. Something must be done.

As so often in the past, Matthew had a stroke of luck just when he was beginning to worry about the future. The day after his visit to Lady Briggs, an old friend, Buffy Morrison, came to call. They had been friendly acquaintances in school, and Buffy had once travelled to Hong Kong, where they spent a fairly riotous two weeks together, during which they became close friends. That had been five years earlier; Matthew had not written to Buffy, so he was surprised that his old drinking companion knew of his return to London.

'Tracked you down, old boy. Got word you were in town. My mother knows the Bowleses of Forty Hall. Word travels fast, you know.'

Buffy was a pudgy man whose small round nose was not enhanced by the wire-framed spectacles he constantly pushed against the bridge. Thinning, mousy hair was moulded to his skull, giving him the appearance, Matthew always thought, of a near-sighted, blinking mole. The man had an excellent sense of humour, an eye for the main chance and a fund of money-making schemes. He had one on this day.

'I say, Warrender, this is a cosy little establishment. It can't be above half the size of your little place in Hong Kong. Rotten luck, coming home to find Capel Manor had been let out to a flower seller. I hear she's a peach. Oh, I say, what's this?'

'A teapot, you idiot.'

Buffy laughed. 'I know that, but it's a trifle strange, wouldn't you say?'

Matthew gently took the pot from Buffy's hands and caressed it lovingly. 'Black stoneware. Chinese. It looks like an official seal wrapped in cloth. Very clever and probably sixteenth century.'

'And this one?' asked Buffy. 'This silver one must be worth a small fortune.'

'Hardly. It's less than five inches tall. Forty years old. Woshing, Shanghai. Notice how there are panels in the silver that look like bark. The alternating panels show tea plant blossom. Here is a favourite of mine. Boy with Outstretched Hand. Chinese, but not at all valuable. Why are you quizzing me on my oriental collection? You're up to something.'

205

Buffy sprawled in an arm chair. 'Going into the house-building business. Going to make a fortune this time and no mistake. It's time I settled down and stopped chasing hares. This project is sound as a dollar. I've got Voysey and Lutyens interested, I can tell you in confidence. Houses for the masses, Warrender. I'm buying up land in the suburbs and I'm going to build houses by the dozen.'

'The masses can't afford houses designed by Voysey and Lutyens.'

'Well, perhaps not,' laughed Buffy, resting his head on the chair back and closing his eyes. 'But they were interested when I mentioned my scheme to them. How about coming into the project with me?'

'Invest, you mean?' asked Matthew. 'I haven't a sou.'

Buffy opened his eyes and smiled slyly. 'Sell some of your treasures. We'll make so much money, you can return to Hong Kong as a tycoon and buy up every blooming teapot on the islands. I must raise twenty thousand, but you can buy in for a thousand pounds or two.'

Matthew looked around the cramped sitting-room, his eyes resting on the Imari, Satsuma and Yixing ware. Collecting Chinese and Japanese objects was a passion. He knew what he liked. He knew when he was holding an object of value and when he was being offered a bargain. However, his oriental treasures would not fetch very much, as they were not old enough to be very valuable. On the other hand, he had crates of porcelain in storage, his inheritance from his mother. He could perhaps sell some of it to raise capital which he could invest in Buffy's scheme. To make enough money to return to Hong Kong as a wealthy gentleman in search of *objets d'art* would be a suitable revenge for years spent half way up the hill to Victoria Park. Developing property was an acceptable occupation for a gentleman lately retired from the foreign service. Why not?

'Give me some time to think about it, will you? I must consider my future.'

Buffy wriggled deeper into the overstuffed chair and sighed with satisfaction. 'Jolly good. Now, let's forget all about business. What about that dasher you had in Hong Kong? Whatever happened to her?'

Chapter Twelve

Jacko had withdrawn five pounds from the bank, and it was now folded into his pocket book, tucked into an inside jacket pocket next to his heart. He dreaded the possibility of its being stolen, in fact, he dreaded the possibility of having to spend it. Yet he was afraid that this Sunday rendezvous with Miss Douse was going to cost him dearly.

Since their last meeting, he had found it very difficult to concentrate on his work. She was the most beautiful woman he had ever seen, a woman whose remembered kiss haunted his dreams, but he wished profoundly that he had never met her. The story of their meeting and possible future played in his mind continually, with wildly differing endings. Perhaps he would find the strength to break off with her this evening.

I'm sorry, Miss Douse. We come from different worlds. I am but a humble gardener. You are the daughter of a solicitor, far above me. Farewell . . . He couldn't do it. The thought of never seeing her again was too much to bear.

No, Jacko, I won't let you go. I will live with you in two rooms, if necessary. I will cook and clean and bear your children. Never will I utter one word of complaint if you will but love me all our lives together. This was such an absurd thought that he had to smile to himself.

Then there was his favourite day-dream. *Well, Boon, since you and my daughter insist on marrying, I will just have to buy you a rose nursery. Would five acres under glass and a six-bedroom home be enough to make the two of you happy?*

This dream sustained him for many an hour behind the pony as he cut the lawn, or in the houses as he watered the plants. Surely her father was a rich man. Surely he would buy a nursery for the man Miss Douse loved. Surely he wouldn't reach for a horsewhip instead!

On days when it rained, when he woke to leaden skies and rolled off his thin, lumpy mattress to wash in cold water, put on sweaty clothes that he had worn all week and eat what was put before him by Mrs Horn, on those days it was another story. In this version of his future, Jacko was tied for ever to a beautiful wife who would not, could not cook, who had no strength for the chores that made a man's life comfortable. And her father, whose face glimpsed from afar seemed so cruel, would make demands on Jacko that he couldn't meet. He would be exchanging one mistress – Miss Blair – for another, only this time he wouldn't be able to hand in his notice and travel to a new place and start anew. This version made him sweat, and it was the one uppermost in his mind as he left the train and headed for the tube station.

The Strand Corner House was in a big stone building with a bewildering variety of windows. The large plate glass ones at pavement level displayed ornate cakes on stands of different heights, the cakes tilted dangerously forward, the better to entice customers.

Miss Douse was pacing up and down, looking elegant and unobtainable in a straw boater and a white linen costume. He was tempted to cut and run, but she turned, saw him, and her face lit up with pleasure. He wished he had spent more time cleaning up his finger nails, but was relieved that he had taken the trouble to put on a fresh collar.

In such a public situation, they could do nothing more than shake hands, but he held on to hers for several seconds. 'So you did get away from your father.'

'Of course. When I say that I am to visit my friend, Katherine Nevis, just off the Strand, Popple doesn't object. I think he is relieved, because then he can do whatever it is that widowers do. I've packed a few things into a bag and will take a cab to her home later. I won't stay out all night,' she said, teasing him, 'because you wouldn't ask it of me, would you?'

'Of course not! How can you say such things?' He was determined to tell her that they must never meet again. He would stress the difference in their stations, the life she was accustomed to, the very different life he had to endure. He wondered when and where he should do this. Not in the middle of the Strand, that was certain.

'Shall we go in?' she asked.

'Is it open? It's Sunday and five o'clock.'

'Silly man. This branch stays open all night.'

He was intrigued. 'I say, how do you know that?'

'The sign says so.' She laughed at his confusion and headed for the door, waiting for him to open it. The restaurant was crowded, the customers all appearing to be wealthy and fashionably dressed. He held his bowler hat in both hands and managed to ask for a table for two. The menu was brief; it didn't take him long to locate the cheapest dish.

'I'll have tomato soup, meat pie and vegetables, please,' Florence told the nippy. 'I don't know what I want for dessert. And a pot of tea, of course.'

Mrs Horn had prepared a roast dinner at Capel Manor bothy, as she did every Sunday. They had sat down to it promptly at one o'clock. Jacko wasn't hungry so soon after a large meal. However, he mumbled that he would have the same and began to calculate the cost.

'Miss Douse—'

'Yes?' She put her elbows on the table, folded her hands and rested her chin on them. 'What is it, darling Jacko?'

'This is all wrong. I mustn't do this again. You and me, we—'

'Do you love me?'

A voice that he could barely recognize as his own whispered, 'Yes, I think I do, but—'

'When are you going to understand that I need you and love you, Jacko? I am well aware of the differences in our background and I don't care. I've made up my mind, you see. You must save me from myself. I'm a naughty girl and one day I shall get into terrible trouble. Charlotte has told me so. You see, my mother died and I haven't been able to think straight ever since. I was fourteen, a terrible age to lose one's mother. There was no-one to teach me how to go on. I want to be loved, Jacko. I want a home of my own and someone who will take care of me. I'm very foolish.'

He couldn't meet her eyes, knew that he would be lost if he did. 'I refuse to believe that you have been really naughty. I refuse to believe it.'

'I meet strange men in hotels,' she whispered.

'You haven't . . . you haven't . . .'

'Misbehaved with them? No, not yet. But you see how out of control I am. You could stop me from doing such things. It's only loneliness that causes me to do it, and I haven't done it at all since I met you.'

'Dear God,' he said, feeling the sweat on his forehead. He had forgotten to bring a handkerchief and wiped it away with his hand. 'But you don't understand. I have a bed in a bare room, fortunate not to have to share with two other gardeners. Mrs Horn cooks my meals. I'm up at half past five and working by six. I finish working at six o'clock in the evening and by that time I'm often too tired to do anything but go down to the Spotted Cow, have a jar and go to bed. I make a quid a week. *I* could live on that with a wife, but *you* couldn't. You ain't used to it. The hard work would kill you, even supposing you was willing to do it. And gardening is all I know. I ain't had no schooling. You must be mad.'

'Of course we couldn't live on a pound a week. What a thing to say! Popple will buy you a nursery. I suppose they would be cheaper out near Capel Manor. I believe the area is full of nurseries. The Lea Valley. That's true, isn't it? What sort of nursery? Oh, yes, roses. How

211

lovely. So you see everything is settled. I'm to have my strong man.'

The soup arrived. Jacko discovered that he was hungry, after all. Florence chatted on about a play she had seen, a gown she wished to buy, a ragtime band she had heard. Jacko finished the soup, tilting the plate to get the last drop, accepted a second roll when it was offered, yet wondered how he could eat at all, considering his worries. Mr Douse would never agree. And yet . . . and yet.

Florence looked up, her voice trailing away in midsentence. Jacko turned to see what had attracted her attention, and met the cold eyes of Mr Billy Tavern as he strode between the tables in their direction.

Mr Tavern reached the table within a second or two, too quickly for Jacko to jump up and leave. 'Well, Florence, my dear. You are a first class fool,' said the young man, his voice quiet but full of menace. 'If you must meet Charlotte's gardener on the sly, why come to this neighbourhood? Don't you know Dad and me live two minutes away? You have only to step out of this place and you could come face to face with him. I saw you two through the window.'

'I didn't know you lived around here, Billy,' said Florence, unconcerned. 'I don't suppose I gave it a thought. But you see, Jacko doesn't know London terribly well and—'

'I do so! I was born here, well, not too far from here. We could've—'

'If my dad finds out, he'll tell Mr Douse and then you'll be in the soup,' said Billy, ignoring Jacko.

Florence reached out and touched Jacko on the arm, a reassuring gesture. She may have realized that he wanted to run away. 'It's all right. He'll have to know some time. Jacko and I are going to be married.'

Tavern's eyebrows rose. He smiled sardonically as he slapped Jacko on the back. 'You poor beggar,' he said, cheerfully. 'I don't envy you one bit, but I have to tell you I'm very happy about the whole business. My dad fancied Florence as a daughter-in-law, but Florence and me understand each other too well. She needs a strong hand. I suggest you beat her every Saturday night.'

'I intend to—' began Jacko, but his voice died away as Florence and Tavern laughed. Billy Tavern and Florence Douse *were* perfectly suited. Their quick wit and easy camaraderie left him isolated. He almost said as much, but watching them as they joked and laughed, he suddenly felt a gut-wrenching jealousy and knew that he must have her, come what may. 'I'd be obliged if you wouldn't mention—' he began.

'He won't,' said Florence. 'I've seen how he looks at Charlotte Blair's assistant. We can keep each other's secrets, can't we, Billy?'

Billy Tavern pulled out a chair, without a by-your-leave, and grinned at Jacko. 'Think I'll join you. What are you having? Pie? Good idea.' Jacko put a hand to his heart, feeling his pocket book. 'This is my treat,' continued Tavern. 'A celebration. I'll tell you what. After we leave here, we can go to a little place I know. They've a good band. We'll go over to King Street and knock for Molly. She's staying there this weekend, because Charlotte is in the country.'

The evening passed with bewildering speed, a golden time that Jacko would think about for weeks to come. Miss Molly O'Rourke was a sweet child who clearly adored Billy Tavern. Florence talked down to her, but the girl didn't seem to notice. Billy Tavern had money to burn and refused to let Jacko pay for anything. He was being kind without allowing the gardener to feel indebted. The ragtime band – three banjos, a piano and a violin – was the finest thing Jacko had ever heard. They all drank a great deal and laughed a lot. In no time at all, they were on first-name terms. He had never enjoyed himself so much, had never known that people, ordinary people, could have such fun. But it was too expensive for him.

Was this what Florence was accustomed to? How could

he possibly give her such a life? Now and then, when everyone was talking at once, Jacko reflected on what had happened to him. Florence wanted a strong man, but Jacko had not been strong since Florence decided she loved him. He had been willing to follow where she led. Whenever he thought about her and her strong will, he had to admit that he was a trifle frightened of her.

He shook his head, taking himself to task for harbouring weak thoughts. He was a strong man, in the sense that Florence meant it. He would work for her and make his nursery a success. He would earn enough money to give her a comfortable life. Her father would be impressed. Jacko made up his mind he would marry the girl, but only if her old man bought him a nursery. How else was he to fulfil his dream?

Charlotte had very little time to mourn the loss of the Briggs commission. She must do something quickly, or see her business fail. Since one of her mother's favourite maxims had been that you had to spend money to make money, she lashed out on a prominent advertisement in *The Lady* magazine and another in *The Illustrated London News*, which was very expensive.

In the meantime, while the fifty yards of swag was immersed in water in the cellar, she managed to sell off the flowers she had bought for Lady Briggs's home. Funeral work paid the day-to-day expenses, and as the weather got warmer she depended more and more on whatever she could bring back with her from her regular visits to Capel Manor. Occasionally, she thought of her early dreams about making friends among the wealthy people who lived near Capel, of being invited to their homes and obtaining work from them. How naïve she had been! She had been incredibly foolish, but at least she had not spoken of her daydreams to anyone but Vic. And, as she well knew, Vic listened to her with half an ear. There was no time for tears of regret. She had to continue struggling for business.

The very day that her advertisement appeared in *The Lady*, she received a telephone call from the housekeeper of Mrs de Freyne in Hans Crescent, asking her to call. The next day there were two more commissions, and the following day yet another one. She was obliged to tell Molly that there was a job waiting for her next younger sister, Ruth, if the girl should wish. Molly was reluctant to involve her sister, seemingly unwilling to share her own good fortune. In the end, Ruth appeared, a pretty little girl of fourteen who proved that she knew how to work hard. Naturally, she lacked Molly's skill and experience, so Charlotte put her to work carrying flower vases from cellar to shop and back down again, and to sweeping up.

The de Freyne commission was a large one, and Charlotte had just four days to prepare it. Madam wanted flowers in every guest room, the curving staircase decorated, the dining-room dressed for an evening reception for a sister of Mrs de Freyne who had married for the second time, a few days earlier.

The monstrous garland, so carefully prepared for Lady Briggs, was removed from its wet bed and had its rotting bits snipped away. Part of it was draped in great loops down the staircase, more was pinned on the wall behind the dining chairs where the bridal couple would be sitting, and the remainder decorated the pictures in the lobby. Yellow and white flowers filled the dining table and tumbled down the three tiers of the cake.

With touching friendship, everyone agreed to help – Florence and Billy, Molly and Ruth, Arthur Brock and the two gardeners from Capel Manor. Mrs de Freyne was deeply impressed by Charlotte's ability to mount so magnificent a display in four days.

That evening, when Brock took her on his motor-bike to recover her possessions and clear away, they met Matthew Warrender leaving the house with the last of the guests.

'Miss Blair!' he called, leaving his companions to go

their own way. 'Were those magnificent flowers yours? Everyone was talking about them.'

'They were, and I have half a dozen more commissions during May. This morning I received a telephone call from Lady Briggs's social secretary. I had been about to arrange a wonderful display there, but it was cancelled at the last minute, because of the sinking of the *Titanic*. However, the ball is to go ahead on the twentieth of May. Isn't that wonderful?'

'It certainly is. Will you be helping out, Brock? That's a splendid motorbike you have there.'

'I wouldn't let my old friend down,' said Brock, shaking hands with Matthew. 'I don't mind helping Charlotte. Man of leisure, you know. May as well be occupied. We all do our bit, even Billy Tavern, whom I had not thought would be prepared to put himself out. I believe he has had a bit of a tiff with his father and is staying out of the way for a few days, until Vic forgets whatever it was that made him angry. That's wise of him, I think. And Miss Douse is helping! She is not only very decorative, but has proved she has quite nimble fingers.'

'I am amazed,' laughed Matthew. 'But surely you will have time to return to Capel in order to visit Mr Bowles's tulip tea, Charlotte, I mean Miss Blair.'

'I haven't been invited,' she said briskly. 'There's too much stuff here, Arthur, and no room for me. You go ahead. I shall take a cab.'

Brock looked from one to the other of them, gave a little salute and gunned his machine into life.

'You shall drive home with me,' said Matthew. 'My motor is right here.'

'You're a very good driver,' she said a few minutes later. 'I don't feel at all afraid, as I do when I'm riding with Arthur or Billy. I hope you have a pleasant time at the tulip tea or whatever it's called.'

'Charlotte, do come with me. John Green, as Capel's head gardener, is sure to have been invited. This is not a grand occasion for Mr Bowles's dearest friends. It's more of an open house. The grounds are filled with all sorts of people, and there is tea for everyone. It will give you an opportunity to see his grounds. Head gardeners are always welcome at these events, because Bowles is one of the greatest authorities in the country, and his head gardener was trained at Kew Gardens. He wishes only to share his knowledge with others. You know, he often has small flower shows for children, to encourage them to have an interest in plants. They turn up with their jam jars of flowers and he solemnly judges them. It's to be on the eighteenth of May. Do say you will come.'

'I'll come with you. That way he's unlikely to turn me away, but I shall have to return to London that evening. I am extremely busy, I'm happy to say.'

'Have dinner with me tomorrow night,' he begged. 'You work too hard. I'll take you to the Café Royal. It's very pretty, and you will be able to study the flowers.'

Of course she accepted, and since he now knew where she lived, allowed him to call for her at eight o'clock.

She was waiting for him on the pavement, wearing a narrow gown of rose pink crêpe, with a tiered skirt and a wrap-over bodice, and for once added only six strands of her collection of glass bead necklaces.

He drove up in style, parked the car with a flourish and leapt out to greet her. 'You look magnificent.' She held out her arms and turned round once for his benefit. 'Florence?' he asked.

She laughed. 'Of course! I don't possess such a lovely gown, and I haven't the time or the money to buy one. You should have pretended not to notice.'

'No, I think I know you well enough to be honest with you.' He took her hand and squeezed it as he led her to the motor.

The joke about her borrowed gown set the tone for the evening. They laughed and danced and laughed some more. As they drew up at her door, the bells of St Paul's chimed just once.

'I've kept you out too late!' he exclaimed. 'You'll get just two hours' sleep.'

'Much more. I have no need to visit the market tomorrow morning, and believe me, I can sleep through the noise when I'm really tired. Thank you for a lovely evening, Matthew. It was heavenly.'

He put his arm around her and kissed her, not caring that anyone who happened to be about at one o'clock in the morning could see them plainly. Charlotte responded with diffidence, afraid of seeming too forward or too eager, unsure of how to behave in such a novel situation. In an effort to deal satisfactorily with her wealthy clients, she had lately been reading every book and magazine article she could find on good manners, but there was no guidance on the subject of first kisses.

'I must go.'

'Charlotte.'

'Good night, Matthew. I won't see you again until the eighteenth. You will call for me at Capel Manor, won't you?'

She was intent on getting the door open, but he gripped her wrist. 'Don't run away. I shan't devour you, much as I would like to.'

She laughed a little, but pulled away. 'Good night.' Her key was in her hand. She heard him drive away as she closed her door behind her.

May the eighteenth was extremely hot. A week earlier the temperature had reached eighty degrees. Matthew had put on a pair of light trousers and his linen jacket, and looked forward with some amusement to discovering what Charlotte was wearing.

Not even his wildest imaginings came up to reality. Her narrow gown was made up of bright, solid pink bands of silk alternating with bands of a glaring pink print on a white ground. There were huge tassels on a shoulder drape and down the right side. The material was caught with machine-cut steel buttons down the top of each sleeve, thus revealing the flesh of her arm every few inches. A Liberty print scarf was wrapped twice round her body just below the bust, while a straw hat, fully two feet across, was decorated with a wide black bow and streamers that she had not bothered to tie beneath her chin.

'You don't like it,' she said, studying his surprised expression. 'I could change.'

'You look lovely.'

'Do you think so?' she cried happily. (She believed him! He had not realized what an accomplished liar he could be.) 'It's the boldness of the design that fascinates me,' she was saying, 'the asymmetrical lines. Women so often look like trussed dolls, don't you agree? Oh, this dress makes me feel free! I'm so glad you approve.'

'Perhaps,' he ventured, 'you might remove six or seven of your necklaces to allow the gown to be seen properly.'

She was doubtful. 'Do you think so? Don't you like the effect? Excess, abundance, like a garden that is overwhelmed with flowers. However . . .' She took off the necklaces and laid them in a heap on the hall table, looking so adorable, so vulnerable, that he couldn't resist leaning forward to steal a kiss. Unfortunately, Rachel, the parlour maid, entered the hall at that moment forcing Matthew to stifle the impulse to express his love.

For it was love that he felt. He had known he loved Charlotte the instant Lady Briggs began to lecture him about her. Matthew did not like to have his behaviour criticized. Even as a young boy, a firm negative invariably set him on the forbidden course. Lady Briggs thought he should distance himself from Charlotte? Very well, he would marry her. Thank God, he could soon afford to do so if he chose.

Buffy's suggestion that he sell some of his oriental

collection had shown him how to establish himself creditably. Not by selling his beloved oriental china, of course, but by taking his inheritance round to Christie's.

To his surprise and delight, four Bristol china children representing the seasons had fetched six hundred guineas. He had always hated them. A single Limoges enamel candlestick was bought by some uncomprehending fool for four thousand, one hundred guineas, simply because the maker was Jean Courtois. Finally, a majolica dish that the family had always regarded as hideous brought him two thousand, seven hundred guineas.

At first, he had felt like Lord Rothschild, but a few quick calculations led him to understand that a little under eight thousand pounds would bring him in an income of less than four hundred a year. As such a sum was not sufficient to maintain himself and Capel, he knew that he must invest in Buffy's scheme, which was sure to make him extremely comfortable within a year or two. How grateful Charlotte would be when he proposed to her and assured her that she need not continue to struggle to run a business.

They walked to Myddleton House at a leisurely pace and largely in silence, each taken up with thoughts of money-making, joining other guests only as they trudged up the curving drive to the handsome yellow brick house.

Mr Bowles greeted them with considerable warmth and Charlotte, assured at last that she was welcome, relaxed in the great man's presence. They strolled among the guests and paused to admire the large pond which had been specially dug by Bowles's men. Then, on a sudden impulse, Bowles offered to abandon his other guests in order to take them on a walk through his 'few acres'.

Although the Myddleton House grounds were considerably smaller than those at Capel, the land had been put to excellent use. Flower beds abounded, filled with rarities which had been collected by Mr Bowles himself, and by other energetic plant hunters. There was probably a quarter of a mile of walkway in the vast rockery, which was his great pride, and all the while they walked, he explained. Mr Bowles, a very great plantsman whose knowledge was encyclopedic, assumed that everyone dealt in Latin tags as readily as he did. He also had a witty, florid style of speaking that at once amused and irritated his listeners.

'My *Wisteria multijuga* is one of my prides,' he said, indicating a wisteria that had been trained as a tree. '*Multijuga* is supposed to be a shy flowerer, but this standard has flowered magnificently in the past, and I hope it will continue to appear at Queen Summer's State Ball. The poor plant is often thirsty about flowering time, and flings the buds off the central rachis as crabs are said to do with their legs and claws, unless packed too closely for kicking in the boiling pot.'

'What a bewildering selection of plants!' exclaimed Matthew. 'Which ones are your favourites?'

Bowles thought for a moment. 'I can admire and enjoy most flowers, but just a few I positively dislike. Collerette dahlias and those superlatively double African marigolds that look like India-rubber bath sponges offend me most.'

'But—' began Charlotte, ready to argue.

'I dislike the cheap thin texture of godetias almost as much as I do the sinful magenta streaks and splotches that run in the blood of that family. I loathe celosias equally with dyed pampas grass; and coxcombs, and spotty, marbled, double balsams I should like to smash up with a coal-hammer; and certain great flaunting mauve and purple *Cattleya* orchids cloy my nose and annoy my eye. There! I feel ever so much better for that denunciation,' said Bowles. Then on seeing Charlotte's expression, 'But I gather you disagree. Ah, I was forgetting. You are a floral decorator. I imagine your customers demand such excesses.'

'All flowers can be loved, don't you think?'

'Yes, of course. I simply wish that the plants I've just spoken of could all turn white with fear of the public exhibition of their decapitated heads, for I can love an albino *cattleya*.'

'You have a special interest in weird specimens, don't you?' said Matthew, hoping to prevent an unseemly row.

'My "lunatic asylum", I call it. I will take you there.' Bowles turned to Charlotte. 'I sometimes feel that cutting flowers to decorate one's rooms is a practice unworthy of the true lover of a garden, for I am convinced that most flowers look best when growing on the plant.' He gave her a challenging look. 'Yet I could not be happy for long without cut flowers in the house, for there are so many dark hours and cold days when one can best enjoy their beauty indoors. It gives me such pleasure to group and arrange them in vases for effects that are never produced in the plants themselves.'

'I have made a career of that, Mr Bowles.'

'Ah, yes indeed. Artificial light brings out fresh and unsuspected charms in some flowers, even converting ferocious militant magentas into a saintly beneficent rose colour at times.'

'The use of blue after dark is—'

'The scent of fresh flowers in rooms is one of the joys of life, if sufficiently understood and controlled. I have been poisoned olfactorily, which means headache and a fearful longing for a whiff of the clean outdoor smell of greenery, by rooms with too many *Lilium auratum* or *Azalea mollis* in them. And I do not think I could be polite and good-tempered for long in a room with many bunches of phloxes in it. A dinner table decorated heavily with sweet peas spoils my dinner, as I taste sweet peas with every course, and they are horrible as a sauce for fish, whilst they ruin the bouquet of good wine.'

'All scented flowers must be treated with care,' said Charlotte through gritted teeth.

'But I believe there is a wider evil lurking in the apparently harmless practice of growing flowers chiefly for cutting. I mean that it tends towards regarding flowers merely as decorations, and plants are chosen because they will produce so many masses of colour of some particular shade, much as one would buy silks by the yard. It seems to me a waste of energy and intellectual powers to grow plants merely to fill a dozen large bowls with soft mauve or pale pink to place in the drawing-room because they go well with the curtains or wallpaper.'

'Many people would disagree with you, Mr Bowles,' said Matthew.

'I know, but I have my own opinion on the subject. I have ceased to care for forced lily of the valley now that, thanks to cold storage, it is so much like the poor, in being wan and pale and ever with us. Indeed, I feel disposed to found a Society for the Prevention of Cruelty to Plants. Even the winter-flowering carnations that the last few years have brought to perfection leave me as cold and indifferent as do the silk and velvet counterfeit blossoms for wearing in hats, that I see in shop windows. I do not want carnations all the year round, nor do I admire half a yard of stem with scars at intervals where buds have been picked off in the fair promise of their youth, so that the one terminal flower may be as round and fringy and perfect as if it were made of pinked-out paper, like a ham frill.'

Charlotte twirled the handle of her parasol, transferring her irritation to an inanimate object. 'I would be out of business if it weren't for carnations, and my customers demand flowers on long stems, Mr Bowles.'

He smiled warmly at her, well aware that he had teased her beyond what was acceptable in a well-mannered host. 'But perhaps you could educate your customers to a finer feeling.'

'Not if I must starve in the process,' she said fiercely. Bowles, his lecture over, laughed heartily as he urged her along to see his freaks.

Chapter Thirteen

Matthew had planned the day very carefully. Once they were safely free of Mr Bowles's provocative presence, he introduced Charlotte to Admiral Sir Hedworth and Lady Meux, who graciously invited her to call on them on the last Friday in the month, Friday being Lady Meux's day for receiving callers.

The brother of E. A. Bowles, Colonel Bowles of Forty Hall, was also introduced to her, but no invitation to tea was forthcoming. She already knew the vicar of Forty Hill church, and then greeted John Green the gardener with such relief and warmth that Matthew suddenly realized what a desperate strain Charlotte was under on this informal occasion.

As early as was permissible, he removed her from the gardens of Myddleton House and helped her into his motor. They were to take a short mystery tour, he told her, and drove directly to Temple Bar at the entrance to Theobalds Park.

With uncharacteristic forward planning, Matthew had arranged for the gatekeeper to unlock the door to the staircase that led to the room above, after which the old man would quickly walk up the long drive to the vast kitchens of Theobalds for a cup of tea, leaving Matthew and Charlotte alone.

Everything had been done to provide them with a romantic setting and complete privacy so that he might take his time in proposing marriage. For days he had savoured the moment when he would say, 'Will you be my wife?' Over and over, he imagined Charlotte's surprise and delight, her tenderness and gratitude for the offer of respectability and a safe haven. No longer would she have to rise at two in the morning merely to purchase flowers for the tables of others. She could lie in bed and have her breakfast brought to her. He would guide her towards a less sensational mode of dress, select a reading list for her education and train her in all the little ways of Society without which she would never be accepted.

He parked the motor by the old gate, and they stood outside to gaze at its three arches, narrow ones for pedestrians either side of the wide main gate. Deeply carved stonework rose above the central arch. There were two statues in niches and a barrel roof topping all. From the front, it hardly seemed possible that a small room could exist above the main gateway, yet two long, leaded windows could be plainly seen on the front and back. Passing through the foot gate on the left, they met the gate-keeper, who soon had the small door to the staircase unlocked.

'Oh, isn't it delightful! It reminds me of the Old Bailey,' she exclaimed as she lifted her skirt to dash up the stone steps. 'And pink walls! How wonderfully absurd to furnish the room above this great old City gate and paint the walls pink. Pink is a favourite colour of mine. You know, one could be very comfortable here, there are such magnificent views.'

'I believe Valerie, Lady Meux used to entertain here many years ago.'

Charlotte frowned. 'And the poor servants had to take the food all the way down that long drive from the kitchens? I don't suppose grand ladies ever think about what troubles they cause their staff. I've seen some amazing sights in good homes, I can tell you.'

He smiled at her indulgently and suggested that she sit down on the settee. She almost did so, but decided that it smelled musty and that she would rather look out of the windows on either side of the room.

Impulsively, she turned to him. 'I don't suppose you

will be attending the International Flower Exhibition at Chelsea?'

'Of course I will. Everyone will be there. I am a member of the Royal Horticultural Society.'

'But you aren't interested in gardens or flowers.'

'No,' he said, 'but I am very interested in being a member of the RHS. Will you attend as my guest?'

'I will be delighted to, but you must excuse me if I yawn a great deal. I am to be there as one of the helpers of an exhibitor, and we may not have everything in place until five o'clock in the morning. I shall try to snatch a few hours sleep. If we are to see all the dignitaries arrive, we must be in the grounds shortly after eleven o'clock, so I will meet you at the main entrance on the Chelsea Embankment at half past ten.'

'What can a flower arranger do for an exhibitor?'

'Mr Kitson is a topiarist in Broxbourne, and he has asked me to help arrange his plants at the show. He clips box plants into many different shapes, you see, balls, pyramids, peacocks, corkscrews. He has been allocated a space, but doesn't know exactly how to arrange his display to get attention. He will have formidable competition. There is a very big grower whose name springs to mind: Mr Cutbush, who sells cut bushes, among other things. I've arranged for Mr Kitson to bring some plant stands of different heights, and I have bought an old piece of stage scenery which depicts the door of a house, and has windows painted on it. The door actually opens, so we will have it ajar and try to give the impression that Mr Kitson's display is the front garden of a fine town house. It could be very effective.'

'But how witty! Will other people be up to such clever wheezes?'

'I sincerely hope not. A grand rock garden, covering a very large area, is to be built, and there is to be an entire section given over to Japanese gardening.'

'Arranging this exhibition will be heavy work, Charlotte, and I believe you labour too long as it is.'

'No! Do you? I believe I am quite idle. You must know that women need to work harder than men if they are to succeed. No-one will extend me credit, you know, although I have been in business for over eighteen months. A man would have been given credit straight away. My sex is unfairly treated.'

'I agree,' he said heartily. 'Women should be given the vote.'

'I don't see that it matters. Women should be able to divorce useless husbands and retain custody of their children. Women should be paid as much as men when they do the same work. Those things are important, but what difference would the vote make? You don't suppose a woman would ever be allowed to help make our laws, do you?'

'But you must support the cause of suffragism, Charlotte. I shouldn't have to lecture you on the subject.'

She frowned. 'You shouldn't have to lecture me at all.'

'No, of course not. All I meant was—'

'I have to support myself. That is the only must. I care about nothing else. I will be as famous a floral decorator and as rich as Mr Felton one of these days. You can be sure he has no such foolish ideas about cut flowers as Mr Bowles does.'

Matthew, torn between the desire to defend the reputation of a local celebrity and the greater desire to propose to the woman he loved, was ready to drop the subject for the sake of harmony.

She, too, was eager to talk of other things. 'How was it that you went to Hong Kong, of all places?'

Resigning himself to the fact that the moment had not arrived for a declaration of love, he said, 'It was my grandfather's idea. In Hong Kong I was taught Cantonese and Mandarin, after which I acted as an interpreter. I thought Japanese might be useful, so I studied that as well.'

'And what did you do? Was it exciting?'

'I did as little as possible, working mostly in the post

office, which was deadly dull. Society is very rigid there, more so than here. I was not top drawer; many people had known me in England, knew my background. Pelham Briggs, for one. He soon told anyone who would listen that my father had been a dashing adventurer. People were intrigued, but I was marked out as being different, perhaps untrustworthy. I cannot say that I was totally happy in Hong Kong, except that no great effort was required of me. Languages come easily, you see.'

'You must be very clever,' she said. He shrugged, on the point of denying it, when she added, 'It's a pity you are so idle now.'

'Thank you. I am a gentleman and don't require an occupation.'

She smiled warmly, teasing him. 'You had a glorious opportunity to write a book about your adventures in the Far East, or – I seem to remember that you have some talent as an artist – you could have filled a hundred sketch books. The plants in Hong Kong must be truly wonderful.'

'Not particularly, so far as I know. The botanical department embarked on a great scheme to beautify the protectorate by planting conifers on the hills. I regret that you think I am idle. Needless to say, I have never regarded myself in that light.'

'I know, but something must fill your days. What will you do now that you have returned to England?'

He was spared the necessity to answer by the sound of a horse and carriage approaching. Charlotte peeped through the leaded window and whispered that she could see the Admiral and his wife returning.

'As soon as they have passed through the gate and reached their own front door, we must hurry away, Matthew. I couldn't bear for them to think I have looked over part of their property without their permission.'

Matthew smiled wryly. So much for the best laid plans! The moment was not propitious, after all. He had a better idea. Since he was to attend the opening day ceremony at the Flower Show, and Charlotte would be with him, he would propose in a floral bower. After a stroll around the grounds, he would take her to luncheon and ask her to marry him. For ever after, they would remember the day of their betrothal as the opening of the greatest flower show the country had ever known.

The work which came to Charlotte in the next few days kept her standing by the telephone for hours at a time. The social secretaries of Lady This and Mrs That made the wires sing with requests for her presence at various London addresses, to calculate possibilities and offer suggestions. Although she had some response from her advertisements, she was in no doubt that most of her business sprang from two sources: Lady Smythe and Lady Briggs, who had certainly come to her by way of her son's friend, Matthew. These two women were her entrée to London society, her guarantee for the future.

Molly was looking extremely pale these days; Charlotte knew she ought not to ask so much of the child, but tried to make up for the long hours by raising the girl's wages to a guinea a week. She also paid Billy five shillings a week for his occasional help. He seemed very grateful for the money, and for the trust she placed in him. As for Arthur Brock and his motorcycle, she could not have done without him. Even Florence gave generously of her time, occasionally arriving with Mr Green and Jacko Boon.

She made almost daily visits to Capel Manor, and with a pruning knife in one hand and a garden trug in the other, slashed at ivy trails, laburnum bushes and any conifer whose branches were within reach. The houses were denuded of ferns and smilax, carnations, camellias and forced lilac (although forcing lilac ruined the plant for several years to come). On some occasions, she took so much away that Arthur was obliged to meet her at the Liverpool Street station to fetch the tightly packed boxes from the goods wagon and cart them to King Street in his machine, while Charlotte walked.

The ball at Lady Briggs's home on May the twentieth tired them all: there was so much to be arranged and erected, and so much to be dismantled and carried back to the shop. Lady Briggs, tired and somewhat dishevelled, returned to the ballroom at four o'clock in the morning to watch them gathering the fading flowers. Sinking unceremoniously onto a small gold chair, she attempted unsuccessfully to smooth the wrinkles from her bronze satin gown, and to tuck in the numerous strands of hair that had come loose from their pinnings.

'A splendid affair, my dear. I'm afraid some of your vases were accidentally broken. Such a laugh! Some of our younger guests were a trifle high-spirited. Just tore the garland right off the dining-room wall! Just tore it off! Right off! "You naughty boys!" I said. "Shouldn't tear off the garland." '

Charlotte realized, with some amusement, that the dignified Lady Briggs had drunk too much champagne. Billy turned his back, grinning broadly and winking at Molly.

'Gave the party for a very good reason, you know, my dear,' continued the lady. 'Wanted to introduce my son's dearest friend to some suitable young women.' Charlotte, busy packing arrangements into cardboard boxes, lifted her head and stiffened, as if bracing herself for a painful blow. 'Mr Matthew Warrender,' confided Lady Briggs. 'Old friend of the family. Just back from Hong Kong. Friend of my son, Pelham. Mr Warrender is an intelligent young man, somewhat too easy in his manners, hates to offend. It is necessary to find him a suitable bride from his own class. You've met him, of course. He has been instrumental in finding work for you, my dear. But that's all it is, you know. Nothing more.'

Charlotte's helpers paused in their work, relishing the dramatic moment, while making every effort to appear uninvolved. Charlotte's face was hot and very probably a tell-tale red.

'Of course, Lady Briggs. And that reminds me. I have had some new calling cards printed. May I give you several? Just in case one of your friends should be in need of my services.'

Mrs Humphry's book, *Manners for Women*, had been her guide. Charlotte had made a study of the small volume, determined not to fail in the minor social niceties now that she was doing business with women of quality. Her new cards were exactly three and a half by two and a half inches, with her name in the centre in copperplate italic. Her address, in smaller type, was neatly printed in the lower left hand corner, the telephone number in the lower right. Whereas a lady might have printed the words 'At Home', Charlotte had 'Floral Decorator' in extremely small type directly beneath her name. Neat, correct, understated, and as good as any great lady's calling card.

Lady Briggs took the cards and read one with interest. 'Oh, my dear! Either a business card *or* a personal calling card, but not surely a combination of the two and . . .' She began to laugh. '*Convent* Garden? With two "n's"? How droll! I believe it was once a convent garden, but no longer.'

'Printing error,' murmured Charlotte, retrieving the cards. 'The printer will hear from me.'

On the pavement outside Lady Briggs's home, her friends gathered round to express their sympathy. 'Silly old cow,' said Florence. 'What does she know about Mr Warrender's intentions? And six vases broken! What sort of people does she entertain?'

'Drunken oafs, if you ask me,' added Billy.

Arthur Brock shook his head. 'No, my dear chap, you don't understand the upper classes. They don't have the same code of behaviour as your lesser orders. Can't be judged.'

'I don't care what she says or how many vases she

231

breaks.' Charlotte pushed past Arthur to place the remaining vases in the motorcycle's side car. 'I shall charge her for them. Thanks to her and Lady Smythe, I have commissions stretching all the way to Christmas. I'll willingly tug my forelock and curtsey to the likes of Lady Briggs, if only she will recommend me to her friends. Now, let's be off. I'm afraid you will arrive home very late tonight, Mr Green, or I should say very early in the morning. I do hope your wife will understand.'

John Green hung his head, a gesture that never failed to annoy Charlotte. 'I don't know whether she understands or not, but her old lady, that is her mother, is spending the night. Mabel don't like being on her own. I told them I had to come, because this ball was important. I think it went well, Miss Blair. The ballroom and the dining-room looked a treat.'

'Several of the palms have candle wax on them,' said Jacko Boon. 'And I was told people was taking the decorations apart and throwing the flowers at each other. *And* there's a couple of scorch marks in the long green table runner, and four of the individual ones is missing altogether. The butler thinks some of the guests took them home, sort of thing.'

'All to be billed. I shan't worry about it. It remains only for me to thank all of you for your help. I do appreciate it. Billy, can you drive Molly and me back to King Street? Arthur can follow. There's no room for me in the side car.'

Florence impulsively moved forward and kissed Charlotte on the cheek. 'I've enjoyed it,' she said simply. 'I look forward to helping you often.'

On the night before the grand opening of the horticultural show, Charlotte had to hire a carter, an old acquaintance of her mother who specialized in transporting theatrical material around the country, to take her newly-purchased backdrop to the grounds of the Chelsea Hospital. Since the position allotted to Mr Kitson was close to one of the bandstands, she and the carter entered the grounds from Chelsea Bridge Road. Flares and pressure lamps lit the way; there were people and vans everywhere, a buzz of voices, some with a hint of panic in them, and a sense of total confusion in the darkness.

The rock garden rose high into the air to her left, an eerie sight since men were busily planting between the stones by the light of flares. Her progress was slow, but by asking the way of every man who passed by, she eventually found Mr Kitson's allotted space, which turned out to be close to a tea pavilion, the Japanese and Canadian sections, and the tent which was to hold the science and education exhibition. Behind these was the long sundries tent and the ladies' cloakroom.

With the help of several pairs of willing hands, the carter unloaded the canvas, a hard-to-control wooden frame, twelve feet wide by fifteen feet high, held more or less rigid by tightly stretched painted canvas. Mr Kitson's helpers held it upright so that it could be studied by Mr Kitson and Charlotte.

'Doesn't look right, somehow, Miss Blair,' said Kitson. 'I mean to say, you'll have to have two by fours bracing it at the back, and people will be walking behind the scenery. What if someone trips over the bracing? Anyway, it doesn't look right.'

Charlotte took a deep breath, well aware that her client was speaking the truth. It had been extremely foolish of her to imagine that she could design a setting for the topiary when she had no idea what sort of site had been awarded to Mr Kitson.

'We'll have to hide it, by putting another piece of scenery behind it. The second piece can be braced the other way, all neat and tidy. Where's the carter? I believe there's another canvas flat inside.' There was, a narrow piece, even more awkward to handle since it was but five feet wide by fifteen feet high. It was in a sorry state, a flaking and highly inaccurate rendition of Swiss mountains.

'We can't have what's supposed to be the front door of a house opening onto a mountain,' said Mr Kitson. He had been on site for many hours, unloading dozens of plants, and he was extremely tired and short-tempered. Charlotte picked her way around the plants, trying desperately to think of a solution. Standing in no particular order were privet, box and yew topiary sundials, layered trees ten feet tall (which Mr Kitson described as cake stands) peacocks, dogs, spires and corkscrews and dozens of clipped balls in wicker baskets. In the darkness, Charlotte at first failed to see the quite remarkable box 'stone' topiary pillars linked by green 'picket' fencing.

'The topiary fence must go next to the public path, Mr Kitson,' she said excitedly. 'Then what should be the garden will be filled with all manner of bushes. The front of the house should stand about thirty feet back from the pathway with one of those six foot box spirals on either side of the open door. I hope you have some gravel to lay a path from the gateway to the door. Five feet back from the door will be the second flat. Yes, yes, I know it shows mountains, but I shall repaint it tonight. I see some white trellis work lying on the ground. Does that belong to you or some other exhibitor?'

'To me,' said Kitson. 'I don't see how you can paint that scenery by the light of a few lamps. And where's the paint to come from at this hour? It's ten o'clock and we've to be off the site by five in the morning.'

'Erect the trellis on either side of the "house". I will go and fetch some paint. Or no. I think I know someone who can paper it with proper wallpaper. I'll hang a mirror, put an occasional table before it and have one of my big floral designs in a brass bowl sitting on the table. The flower market opens at two. We'll make it. I must leave now to get my paper hanger.'

Mr Kitson was not convinced. 'And where will you find wallpaper at this hour?'

'Trust me,' she said and ran towards the entrance on

Chelsea Bridge Road, before he could raise any more objections.

As luck would have it, both Billy and Vic were at home. Vic scolded her for having failed to plan adequately for this important display, but went up to the attic to find two rolls of wallpaper from six years earlier when he and Billy had papered the dining-room. The pattern was yellow with small red flowers on it.

Billy fetched his paper-hanging equipment and a five pound bag of flour, having been assured by Charlotte that water could be had on site.

'I'll load up the motor,' he said as his father came downstairs from the attic.

Charlotte put a hand on Vic's shoulder to detain him. 'I'll need a hall table. Do you mind?'

'That table?' asked Vic, amazed. 'To let it sit out in the open for eight bloody days and nights, rain or shine, wind and frost? Not my good oak one, you ain't having.'

'Please, Vic. I'll buy you a new one if this one is ruined. Go on, put it in, Billy. I'm tired and I can't waste time arguing.'

'You're trying to kill yourself,' said Vic, 'working too hard.' He picked up the table, nearly dropping it when he saw her remove the round, oak-framed mirror that normally hung above the table.

She gave them her exhibitor's pass without which they would not be able to enter the grounds, and walked home to King Street.

Molly was sleeping at her own home on this night. Charlotte fetched a large brass bowl from the shop and carried it upstairs to polish. When she finished, it was half past eleven. She set the alarm clock for three, sat down in the chair and fell asleep. It seemed like no more than three seconds later that the bell clanged, warning her it was time to get up. She struggled out of the chair, splashed cold water on her face and headed for the market, which was in full swing. Three dozen red roses were needed to fill the brass vase. She pocketed her pruning knife, slung a large bag of moss over her shoulder, then had a long run to the Strand where she was fortunate to be able to hail a passing cab. At the Chelsea Bridge Road gate, she needed all her persuasive skills to gain entrance without a pass, but fortunately the guard was tired. He waved her inside and sat down again on his camp stool.

Vic and Billy had done an excellent job of papering the scenery. All was in place and Mr Kitson, now so tired he could scarcely put one foot before the other, found the energy to tell her the display looked brilliant, at least he assumed it would in daylight. Six hundred pounds had been spent on installing electric light on the twenty-eight acre site, he told her, but the bulbs were never where you wanted them.

Someone brought a tray with cups of tea and hot buns. There was an air of suppressed excitement in the grounds, a sense of friendly rivalry and a general weariness. It was nearly five o'clock; the sky was brightening; everybody was heading for home, the exhibitors filled with last-minute doubts, secret dreams of medals and a determination to dress up for the arrival of Queen Mary and King George. The weather, they said, was going to be glorious: a reliably hot, sunny day in May for a change.

Matthew arrived at the Chelsea Embankment entrance to the show at a quarter past ten, to be sure of meeting Charlotte. He found that he was not the only person to believe in arriving early. The pavement was crowded, and the Piggott Brothers' entrance marquee, with its small gateways, looked inadequate for the throng that would soon be passing through. Although the flower show had not been organized by the Royal Horticultural Society, they had supplied many members for the committees, and had backed the eight day show against loss. Members of the RHS were able, therefore, to purchase tickets for the first day for two guineas apiece. Matthew soon had his, ready to shepherd Charlotte inside the moment she arrived.

There was to be an invasion of dignitaries on this beautiful morning. Not only Queen Mary and King George, but also Princess Mary, Princess Victoria and Princess Henry. Due to recent deaths in the Royal family, there was to be no formal opening, but the Duke of Portland would be on hand to greet British royalty, as well as their Royal Highnesses the Archduke and Archduchess Franz Ferdinand of Austria.

It was with some disappointment that Matthew saw Charlotte from a distance, walking briskly in her lurid pink gown and huge black-ribboned straw bonnet. He had intended to present her to as many distinguished people as possible, but was rapidly readjusting their schedule.

'My dear, are you all right?' he asked as soon as she held out her hand to him. 'You do look rather tired and flustered.'

She smiled. 'It has been a long night, but I'm very excited. You look handsome in your top hat and frock coat. Am I sufficiently dressed up? Will I do?'

'Of course. Let us go in before they start clearing the way for the special visitors.'

The many guests arrived at half past eleven in their carriages, and there was a certain amount of good-natured jostling among those who had two-guinea tickets and a determination to see royalty. Charlotte clung to Matthew's arm, murmuring 'I'm wrongly dressed' over and over again, to which he made no reply.

When the excitement was over, they turned to their left, having seen from the catalogue that the French, Dutch and Belgian sections were nearby. A tent containing cut flowers was directly behind these foreign displays, and next door was a tea tent. Charlotte confessed that she had forgotten to eat breakfast, so they went inside for a cup of tea and a bun, before touring the remainder of the show.

'Mr Warrender!' cried a young lady in a smart crêpe, pearl-grey two-piece with a fur collar. 'Isn't it marvellous?' She was fair and had a long face with a very short upper lip, giving her an unfortunate permanent sneer. She looked at Charlotte curiously, awaiting an introduction.

Matthew stood up. 'Miss Windscome, Miss Blair. Miss Windscome's brother and I were at school together. Did you see the crowned heads?'

'Yes, and Buffy Morrison and Lady Briggs and Charles Fanshaw. Oh, it's glorious! Just like a point-to-point. I must be going. I think I see . . .' and she was off, waving to someone outside the tea tent, although too well bred to call to him.

'I must see the orchids. I understand they are wonderful,' said Charlotte. 'And of course, I must introduce you to Mr Kitson and show off my display.'

On their way to the orchids, they passed a tent marked 'First Class Refreshments'. Matthew made a note of its position so that they could return at one o'clock.

The orchids were beautiful, but Charlotte was clearly too tired to enjoy them. Revising his plans yet again, Matthew decided to take her to luncheon at half past twelve, ask her to marry him and then take her home to rest. She was a small-boned woman; he couldn't imagine how she managed to work so hard. She might consider him lazy; he thought she was mad to rush about all day and half the night.

Mr Kitson's topiary display was attracting such an enormous amount of attention that they had trouble getting close enough to see it properly. The topiarist got up from his folding chair to shake her by the hand and to greet Matthew warmly.

'There's any number of people wanting to meet you, Miss Blair. Near neighbours, you might say. Mr Perry of Perry's Hardy Plant Farm in Enfield, showing ferns, I believe. Then there's Stuart Low with his orchids, not too far from Capel Manor, are they? Mr Paul of Waltham Cross. Do you buy his roses? Then there's Mr Harkness from Hitchin. He asked me who had done my business.

238

I told him, Miss Blair of Capel Manor. Just to be polite, I said those are Harkness roses in the bowl, but he shook his head. Knows every one of his varieties. Wouldn't let me pull the wool over his eyes. Mr Felton's exhibiting. Did you know?'

'No!' exclaimed Charlotte. 'Oh, Matthew, I must see his display. There is so much to learn.'

'But I want to introduce you to a few people,' said Mr Kitson. He looked at Matthew. 'Could you spare this fair lady for half an hour?'

In response to Charlotte's pleading gaze, Matthew withdrew gracefully, and was quickly caught up in a throng of old acquaintances. It was, indeed, like a point-to-point. Half an hour later, he collected Charlotte from Mr Kitson's stand and she was in a very different mood from the tired condition in which he had left her, being buoyed up by the compliments she had received from members of the horticultural trade.

Matthew was also in a different mood. Tucking her hand in the crook of his arm so that she could not move even a few inches away from him, he guided her towards the rock garden which covered several acres. 'I have been speaking to Lady Briggs.'

She cocked her head to one side and looked at him solemnly. 'What is it? What's wrong? She was very pleased with my work. She told me so.'

'She has had a burglary.'

'Oh, I'm very sorry to hear it. Did they steal much?'

'Jewellery, a Ming vase, a painting or two.'

'I hope she is insured.'

'I hope *you* are,' he said grimly. 'Lady Briggs is not the only person to have sustained a burglary in the past ten days. Every one of your recent customers has been burgled within two days of your decorating their homes. Your customers have been putting two and two together and getting four.'

All the time he spoke, he guided her higher and higher among the rocks, following narrow paths, brushing against rhododendrons and tulips, miniature pines, aubretias and daffodils, which all looked as if they had been growing on the site for years.

'I have not stolen anything,' Charlotte said after she had recovered her breath. 'It is my ambition to be a famous floral decorator. Why should I risk everything by stealing from my customers?'

'I don't for one moment suspect you of stealing, you little idiot! It is your so-called friends who have let you down. A more likely gang of thieves I have never seen assembled in one place. I've told you before, they do you no credit. Cut off your links with them. I think I have managed to convince Lady Briggs that you are not in any way, knowingly or unknowingly, involved in the thefts. However, if your friends continue to take advantage of you, I cannot guarantee to save your good name.'

With some difficulty, she prised her arm free from his, mounted two steps and, turning, blocked his way forward. 'Without that gang of thieves, as you choose to call them, I would not be able to carry on my business at all. Even Florence, who I always thought was a lazy fool, has worked tirelessly on my behalf. It's a pity you are not so energetic.'

'Ha!' he said, not caring who might be listening. 'You are so self-absorbed, you can't see what is before your eyes. No wife of mine is going to—'

'*No wife of yours?*'

'Well, I had not intended to mention it in this way, but I meant to ask you to—'

'Don't go on. I do not wish to hear anything you may have meant to say. You are high-handed, snobbish, arrogant, lazy and . . . and, I can't think of anything more. You have no friends to equal mine. How foolish I was to imagine myself superior to them. Serves me right. I'll not make that mistake again. What they do for me, they do out of friendship and concern for my future. What a pity you can't claim friends of a similar calibre.'

'Open your eyes, Charlotte. They are all making use of you and your business for their own purposes. Unless I am very much mistaken, Miss Molly O'Rourke is expecting a child and Billy Tavern is the father. You provide them with an excuse to be together. Arthur Brock is using you to insinuate himself among a better class of person. Florence Douse has run mad and fancies your gardener, Jacko Boon, who doubtless intends to hold her father to ransom. As for Vic Tavern, I strongly suspect he has designs on you.'

'You can't know these things. You are merely guessing.'

'No,' he said with a sad smile. 'But my guesses are based on observation. Molly has the look of a woman in the early stages of pregnancy. Haven't you ever noticed it? The faint shadowing around the eyes? The grimace at the sight of food? And have you not heard the way Miss Douse speaks to Boon? There is an intimacy, unmistakable if one is listening out for it. He approaches her casually, touches her arm in passing. Strangers, people who have no special interest in one another, do not exchange glances so frequently. As for Mr Brock—'

'And you have so much time on your hands that you can spend hours gazing at others while they work, concocting stories about them, making up mean motives for their every word and gesture. I'm sorry to say you are a worthless but perfectly healthy man who despises honest endeavour.'

'And I am sorry to say you have no heart. You think of no-one but yourself, and make the mistake of thinking that others are equally enthralled by you. But they have their own lives, their own ambitions. I tell you they are using you to further their dreams. And one or more of them is informing burglars where to look.'

Standing two steps above him, she closed her eyes and swayed slightly. He could easily reach out to her, apologize for his brutal honesty and offer to help her to recover from this blow. She needn't have a business at all. They could live as a lady and gentleman should, except that . . .

'You don't understand,' she said, and her voice was quiet now, reasonable. 'I must never be poor again. *I want to be rich!*'

'There's no reason why you should starve. Good heavens, I'm sure even Vic would—'

'And what if he dies? He's not all that young, you know. People die and leave you alone. Men forget their responsibilities or choose someone else on whom to lavish their attention. Vic could lose all his money, or decide to give it to Billy.'

'Charlotte, this is madness. Could you not depend on Billy? Or Mr Douse? Or me?'

'No. None of you knows how to make money. You only know how to spend it. You are parasites, all of you. Now that my mother is dead, there is no-one. I must carry on. I must work. And if I have to start again to build my reputation, I will do so.'

Matthew did not care to be called a parasite, nor did he like being compared to Billy Tavern and Popple Douse. Had she kept control of her tongue, he might have been sympathetic towards someone whose insecurity was intense to the point of madness. Yes, that was it! She was mad to be so obsessed with money. Thank heaven he had discovered it in time! How grateful he was that he hadn't sprung from a class that was obsessed with money. Vulgar, that's what she was. Well, she had her chance. He could have given her a decent life. Now his offer, never made, was withdrawn. Parasite? Idle? No man or woman had ever damaged his self-esteem so seriously in all his thirty-three years. Damn the woman.

Charlotte had run off, stepping blindly over nameless rarities, leaping the narrow stream as she negotiated the hazardous rockery like a mountain goat. From this height, he had a good view of her running along the paths to the Chelsea Bridge Road exit.

Matthew made a more dignified descent, suave and unconcerned, greeting friends casually. 'Luncheon tomorrow at Whites? Of course, old chap, be delighted. Excuse me, must see a few people.' No outward sign of his seething emotions marred his handsome face, but when he happened to pass the Japanese exhibition of the Tokyo Nursery Company, he paused briefly to take several deep breaths, standing before the maples and bamboos, the bronze and stone garden ornaments. Tokyo Nursery Company announced that it had branches in Tokyo, New York and Kingsway, London. However, at that moment there were four Japanese gentlemen enquiring about something, and three frustrated and embarrassed English employees attempting to understand.

Damned fools! Matthew was continually amazed by the mental laziness of his fellow countrymen. Their refusal or inability to learn the languages of the world frequently shocked him. 'May I help? Do none of you men speak Japanese?'

'We deal with English customers,' said the shamefaced individual who claimed to be the manager. 'We don't generally need to speak to oriental gentlemen. And I don't even know if these gentlemen are Chinese or Japanese.'

Matthew approached the visitors and attempted a little Japanese. '*Ohayo gozaimasu.*'

His accent was good, and 'good morning' was a common expression. The Japanese, mistaking his fluency in this simple phrase for a thorough knowledge of their language, launched into a flood of questions and comments. It was a minute or two before he began to 'hear' the language again and was able to begin the long and difficult process of translating for the Japanese to the British and back again. Tokyo Nursery Company made no sale, since the Japanese were merely intrigued to see a branch of this firm in London. However, the visitors seemed extremely pleased by the encounter and made

243

haste to present their calling cards to Matthew, who presented his to them, while the three bemused Englishmen looked on. Matthew refrained from asking the Japanese if the British growers had achieved an authentic flavour to their 'Japanese' garden. He reckoned he knew the answer.

'I should think,' said Matthew when the Japanese had moved away, 'that a company which has offices in Japan should employ someone capable of dealing with the Japanese in their own language. Apart from this being simple courtesy, how do you know, when making your purchases, that you aren't being cheated?'

'I am Mr Belper, the British manager, sir, and no-one has ever asked me that question before. However, perhaps I could call on your services if the necessity should arise.'

So Matthew exchanged cards with Mr Belper with considerably less ceremony than had accompanied the handing over of his card to the Japanese. The brief encounter, and Mr Belper's evident need of his talent, served to soothe his ruffled temper, but only until he rounded the corner to the next exhibit where he saw Lady Briggs, surrounded by friends, talking with great animation in a loud voice.

Chapter Fourteen

Charlotte hailed a hackney cab on the Embankment and rode to Covent Garden in a daze. The shop door was open; she could see Molly inside serving a customer, while her sister was moving water cans of bright flowers. Neither girl saw her, so she let herself into her flat, flinging off her hat and gloves as she mounted the stairs. By the time she reached her bedroom, she was wearing only her corset, drawers and shift. The corset had to be removed; she was suffocating, gasping for breath. Slipping between the sheets, she was asleep in seconds.

Nine hours later, she opened her eyes to darkness, and stumbled into the sitting-room in search of a candle and a box of matches. Someone had picked up her pink gown and laid it neatly on the chair. The grate was clean, the dishes, left unwashed for a day or more, had been scrubbed clean and replaced on the shelf. Molly? No, she remembered now. Else, who came in for half an hour once a week, must have borrowed Molly's key. The room smelled comfortingly of lavender polish. Two large potatoes had been peeled and put into a pan of water which was sitting on the small gas cooker. A fresh loaf lay on the table, loosely wrapped in the baker's white paper. She was ravenous, couldn't remember when she had last eaten a proper meal.

How kind they all were! Her friends. Matthew didn't have friends as kind and supportive as hers. How dare he call them a gang of thieves? He could not know that Molly was pregnant. And if she were, he could not possibly guess that Billy was the father. Either he had been eavesdropping on a private conversation, or he was making wild assumptions, as with the charge that one or more of her friends was a thief.

The day's takings lay on the oilcloth; five pounds ten shillings, which was quite satisfactory for a Monday. In her neat print, Molly had itemized each sale, a dozen sixpenny bunches of flowers, a two-guinea funeral spray, the rest five-and-sixpenny wreaths.

Next to the money the girl had neatly stacked Charlotte's letters. She began to open them, tearing at the envelopes with her fingernails. The first four were bills. She set them aside. The next letter was from Mrs John Wingate who would not be requiring Charlotte's services on August the fourth at her Surrey home. There followed three more letters from customers who had booked other occasions, and all of them were cancellations.

Bitterly, Charlotte noted that they had used the telephone when they wanted to employ her. It was 'I want this' and 'I think that' and 'What do you advise me to do?' Their cancellations, however, came by post on thick notepaper couched in a distant form: 'Mrs de Freyne wishes to inform Miss Blair that she will not be requiring . . . 'Mrs Horace Templeton is cancelling her . . .' The telephone was an instrument for doing business, whereas there was nothing so suitable as thick notepaper for delivering a snub.

Only Lady Smythe's letter was forthright. Charlotte could almost hear her speaking as she read the cancellation. 'Since I believe you have been at least partly responsible for the loss of some of my most treasured possessions, I don't want you to decorate my home in July. You ought to be ashamed of yourself. Yours in disappointment.'

It was probably hunger that made her feel faint. She sat down, put her face in her hands and released the tears that had been waiting to be shed. Matthew! How could she have guessed that he would want to marry her? Had she been too self-absorbed to notice his love for her? She thought not. No woman, not even one who was driven by a need to succeed, could fail to notice when she was loved. Therefore, he hadn't loved her. It followed that there must be some other reason for his intended proposal. Genuine emotion would have prevented him from so readily criticizing her. The only reason that came to mind for his surprising revelation was that he pitied her, and she couldn't marry him for that reason.

Yet, his company had been sweet. Now that she was quietly thinking about him and his charm, his handsome face and delightful sense of humour that could lift her mood in a flash, she realized the enormity of what she had denied herself in a few seconds of angry, exhausted vilification.

She stood up from the table, fetched the bread knife and hacked off a thick slice of soft, new bread. On the other hand, how could she marry a man who was incapable of understanding her? She had to make money; there could never be enough. And, now that she thought of it, how could she ever respect a man who did no work? Had she not seen enough of such men?

Her father had died in the same small bed from which Charlotte had just risen. He had gone to bed at eleven o'clock one morning after a gruelling shift portering in the market, had taken off his boots slowly, complaining of a pain in his chest. Maud Blair had brought him a cup of tea and helped him to undress, had tucked him under the covers and was about to hand him the hot drink when he cried out in agony, then fell back upon the pillow.

Little Charlotte, eight years old, had seen him die, had heard her mother wail with grief. The memory of that grim moment was strong. Several hours later, after his body had been removed, Maud Blair unburdened herself to her child, and her words had seared a place in Charlotte's memory, never to be expunged.

'What will we do now, baby? How will we manage?

I haven't had work for six weeks. What will we live on? How will we eat? There's no money, love, no money!'

Little Charlotte had experienced a sense of panic that held her speechless. They would starve! The child was enveloped in fear, although she couldn't fully understand why her mother felt so desperate. When she could find her voice, she whispered, 'Uncle Vic will help us, won't he?'

'Vic?' said her mother, her voice filled with scorn. 'Why should he help us? He's been living with that yellow-haired trollop for the past six weeks. Do you think Vic will give us a farthing while that trollop's in his house? He's got to feed her, hasn't he? And little Billy. They come first with Vic now. No point in looking in that direction. I'll probably have to go on the streets.'

Young Charlotte didn't know what a trollop was, nor what her mother meant by going on the streets. She did, however, recognize the despair and bitterness in the words and their underlying message. A woman couldn't trust anyone to help her in times of dire need. A woman had to rely upon herself. Catastrophe was always just around the corner, must be expected, must be provided for. Since that day, Charlotte had felt intensely insecure, afraid of extreme poverty, afraid of starving amidst the plenty of the vegetable market, the acres of cabbages and carrots, the punnets of strawberries and imported oranges.

Ironically, within a week 'that trollop' had left Vic's home and protection for ever, leaving Vic to bring up his five-year-old son by the black-haired beauty who had long since departed. Taking pity on the grieving widow, he had been as generous as his circumstances at that time allowed. Maud found work in the theatre within the month. The Blairs, mother and daughter, never went without a meal, although occasionally they were reduced to the most meagre of menus. Nevertheless, the fear would not subside, and to this day occasionally troubled Charlotte's dreams.

'As long as there's the two of us,' Maud Blair would say, 'as long as we're both bringing in a bit of money we'll be all right. But you can never depend on a man. Remember that, my girl, they're fickle and lazy. They drink and they gamble, and if they don't do such things, they chase women. You can't depend on anything but your own strong back.'

Mechanically, Charlotte finished eating the bread, put the potatoes on to boil and set about preparing some bacon and eggs. Anticipating her increased work load, she had made a number of purchases during the past few weeks. The King Street cellar was crammed to capacity with vases, wrought-iron pew-end stands, Ellen Terry stands and several dozen silk table runners in glorious colours and metallic threads, all carefully wrapped in tissue paper and neatly labelled. Charlotte had no intention of selling off these supplies. She couldn't expect a good price for them, and she would be drastically reducing her capacity to fill a grand order, should she have the opportunity. No plan of action occurred to her. She ate her supper while searching through her account book, hoping for inspiration.

Despair either destroys sleep or increases the need for it. Charlotte, having so recently slept for nine hours, went to bed early and slept for another seven. Consequently, she was late arriving in the shop and found Billy leaning against the counter with his arms folded, watching Molly pin laurel leaves onto a moss wreath.

'I happened to be passing,' was his opening remark.

Molly greeted her more conventionally, but her eyes were full of torment. Why had Charlotte not noticed this before, nor seen the way Billy's eyes lingered on Molly's young face as she spoke? Just as Charlotte couldn't stop herself from calculating how many leaves and in what way Molly was constructing a wreath, so Matthew couldn't stop himself from noticing all the little ways people had of revealing their innermost thoughts and feelings. While Charlotte's calculations were entirely

249

artistic and financial, his could be categorized as minding other people's business. She almost wished she wasn't aware of Billy's attitude to Molly. The knowledge was about to complicate her life.

'Where's your sister?'

'My mum's not well. She's stayed home to look after the little ones.'

Charlotte cleared her throat and asked the question to which she didn't really want an answer. 'Are you two expecting a baby?'

The effect of her blunt question was quite startling. Molly burst into tears. Billy was furious. 'You don't mince words, do you?'

'I don't have babies by men I'm not married to,' said Charlotte. 'How could you, Billy? You took advantage of this girl. You've ruined her life.'

Billy left Molly's side to confront Charlotte from several inches away. 'I beg your pardon.'

'She has talent. She could make money, be someone important. I suppose you were the man who knocked me down that night on my own stairs. Haven't you been busy? You've ruined everything for her and, incidentally, for me. How can she work here and look after her baby?'

'I don't want to be someone important,' said Molly. 'I love doing the flowers and all that, but work isn't everything, Miss Blair. Well, I know it is for you, but not for most people. I love Billy and we want to get married.'

'And don't ask us why we haven't already,' added Billy. 'You must know my dad will raise merry hell. And Molly's family are Catholic; they won't want me as a husband for their girl.'

Charlotte snorted, dismissing all excuses. 'They will prefer you to no husband at all. As for Vic, you're just afraid to confront him.'

'What are we going to live on?'

'The sweat of your brow, Billy. But don't look so stricken. I'll go down to the shop and tell your father what's happened. Between the pair of you, you would wait until the child was in short coats before finding the courage to speak up.'

'I have the right to something from my old man. He does enough for you.'

'And I'm sure he will set you up in business or make you a partner in his, now that you are going to be a married man and a father.'

Billy shook his head. 'I bought this tiara, see. I thought I'd sell it to a fence and then Molly and me could set ourselves up on the profits. Took three hundred of Dad's money to buy it. Well, how was I to know it was paste?'

'So Vic isn't on the friendliest of terms, is that it?' Charlotte thought of the accusations levelled against her friends by Matthew. How fortunate that he could not hear this tale! 'I'll see what I can do to put things right. Meanwhile, you must both tell your family, Molly. You aren't old enough to get married without your parents' permission. And you will need somewhere to live. You may have the rooms upstairs.'

'Are you going to move to Capel Manor?' asked Billy. 'Quite the fancy lady, aren't you? I'm betting you will be getting married, yourself, one day soon.'

She shook her head, briskly disabusing him of that happy thought. 'I have no intention of marrying Matthew Warrender. However, I have decided to spend more time at Capel Manor, at least until my lease runs out. By that time, I imagine you two will have found a house to rent. By the way, how does Matthew know that Molly is expecting?'

'I believe he overheard us when we were talking. I stopped as soon as I knew he was near, but I suppose he put two and two together,' said Molly.

'He's a sharp man, is Mr Warrender. Doesn't miss a thing.'

'Not a thing,' agreed Charlotte and left the shop to visit Vic.

On the way, she practised a number of subtle opening lines, for Vic had to be approached with care. He was a man with an explosive temper. Over the years, she had made something of a study of the best form of attack to get what she wanted from him. Never once had she succeeded in getting her way without a row, nor did she do so on this day.

'Vic, I want a word with you.'

'Well? Come into the back room. The shop's a bleeding madhouse today. Everybody's short of money, for some reason.'

He led her to a chair, went in search of a cigarette and a match, which he lit with a flick of his thumbnail. 'Out with it. What's the trouble?'

'Molly is pregnant. Billy's the father and you've got to do something to help them out.'

She waited calmly through the expected outburst. 'The boy's a bloody coward. Why did he send you with the bad news? I'll buy her off for a few quid. He don't want to saddle himself with someone like Molly.'

'If he is a coward, it's because you made him one. You've always treated him badly. I don't care if he is the spitting image of a woman you have come to hate. He deserves your love. He's your son. You've got to help him out. You should make him a partner now.'

'He ain't got no brains. If I was to tell you what he did the other day—'

'About the tiara? He's already told me. Do *you* accept stolen goods, Vic?'

'Not when it's obvious . . . that is, no, I don't. How can you ask such a question?'

She heard him out as he remembered every occasion in Billy's life when the boy had failed to live up to his father's expectations, taken the easy route, avoided responsibility, cheated, lied, hidden from expected punishment.

'He's accepting his responsibilities this time. He loves Molly and wants to marry her. Things will be hard for them. I have told them they can live in my rooms above the shop. I'm planning to—'

'Live at Capel Manor?' asked Vic sharply. 'Well, you needn't bother your head about all them letters arriving. I'll come out regular to collect them.'

Charlotte drew in her breath. Matthew had not guessed correctly about this friend. The thought of Vic's having designs on a woman he'd known since birth was ludicrous, and Charlotte had not given it a second thought. But Goldseekers was a venture of which Matthew was in complete ignorance. Goldseekers Limited was the reason for Vic's kind attentions and extraordinary generosity to Charlotte. Remembering Matthew's heated remark about her friends being a gang of thieves, Charlotte shivered. What other shocks were in store for her?

Over the next few days, she received several more cancellations of orders, some of which were for several months in advance. It wasn't fair, and she was beginning to get annoyed. Why should they all assume that she was in league with housebreakers? There was very little proof for these rich women to go on. Briefly, she considered consulting Popple Douse, but soon changed her mind. He, alone, could not have been involved in passing on information. On the other hand, she knew that he had ceased to practise as a solicitor due to some disgrace. His sympathies were likely to be with any miscreant.

May the twenty-seventh was a Bank Holiday. Charlotte visited Vic's house at half past seven in the morning, joining them for breakfast without an invitation.

'Several of my customers have been robbed immediately after having me to do their flowers, Vic. Do you understand? People are saying somebody who works for me is breaking into their homes, or else giving information to burglars. I'm asking you straight out. Have you or Billy been doing that?'

Vic set his coffee cup down in its saucer so fiercely that the saucer broke and coffee splashed over the white cloth in a rapidly widening brown stain. 'How dare you speak to me like that?' he bellowed. 'Mrs Clapper! Come in here and clean up this mess!'

The housekeeper, an ancient woman with a bent back, trotted in with a cloth and shooed them all to the far end of the table so that she could throw back the wet damask.

'You haven't answered my question,' persisted Charlotte. 'I was angry when I heard the accusations, too, but anger butters no parsnips. I must know if you have done such a thing. Tell me no and look me in the eye when you do it.'

'No, I haven't, damn it! You know your trouble, my girl. You must consort with them upper crust types what would steal the pennies off a dead man's eyes, while at the same time criticizing him for having died in brown boots.'

Charlotte was forced to smile, but she turned to Billy. 'And you? Do you swear you've never given information to anyone?'

'I may have talked about what I've seen and heard to Molly, but not to anyone else. What sort of man do you think I am, Charlotte?'

'Will you get out of here, woman?' said Vic to Mrs Clapper. 'How long does it take to clear up a little coffee?'

'Longer than it takes to spill it,' said the old woman with spirit. 'And broke a nice saucer, too. Now we've got three extra cups. I wish you'd stop slapping your cup down.'

Vic waved her away, not in the least offended by her familiar retort. They had known each other for twenty years, and he would not have been comfortable with a more respectful servant. 'And you can get Florence Douse and Brock out of your mind, too. They aren't thieves, nor they don't consort with thieves. I'm ashamed of you. You're looking for a thief? Try that head gardener of yours. He's got a shifty way with him. Never looks me in the eye. And then there's Jacko Boon.'

'Naw,' said Billy contemptuously. 'They've neither of them got the belly for that type of work.'

Charlotte knew that both John Green and Jacko were petty thieves, taking a shilling or two when the opportunity arose. However, like Billy, she couldn't believe either one was sufficiently organized to take part in major crimes.

'And another thing,' Vic said, bringing her up with a start. 'Billy's going to talk to Molly's folks today. I think they should be married at a register office and sort everything out with the priest later. They'll be living with me, so you can keep your rooms above the shop.'

Charlotte looked over at Billy, but he refused to meet her eyes. 'You're taking the girl away from me, aren't you, Vic? You're going to turn her into a housekeeper for you.'

'I've got a housekeeper. You don't think I'd get rid of Mrs Clapper at her time of life, do you? Molly will live better than she's ever done before. I've got a couple what lives in. The girl will be in clover and my grandson will be born with a bleeding silver spoon in his mouth. Why don't you train up her sister? I daresay one O'Rourke is as good as another.'

Billy's visit to Molly's family home tested his love for her quite severely. His first impression was of disgusting squalor. The family lived in two rooms, scarcely more spacious than Charlotte had to herself in King Street. There were no beds, just pallets on the floor. He could see no sign of running water or a means of cooking. He presumed the family existed on food bought from stall holders. The twins, Rory and Liam, were present, as were the three youngest – a boy of four who was naked below the waist, a girl of two in a dirty shift and a baby of unknown sex who sat on the floor bawling.

Mrs O'Rourke was thirty-five years old and looked ten or fifteen years older. Shapeless in her rags, she looked at him with loathing. Mr O'Rourke, despite his poverty and the grime on his face and hands, was a handsome man with broad shoulders and a narrow waist. He had small, deep-set eyes and a square chin, and a habit of staring at Billy as if he might at any moment leap forward and stick a knife into his future son-in-law. Naturally enough, he was not pleased to hear that Molly was expecting a baby, but he seemed to realize that she was marrying a man of substance, which helped him to keep his temper in check.

Mrs O'Rourke lacked her husband's calculating nature, and in any case saw the situation from a totally different point of view. 'You're a fool, Molly. Years of bringing babies into the world. You'll be worn out before you're twenty. What could you have been thinking of? Can't you see what it's done to me?' The baby scooted on its bottom towards its mother, reaching out to tug at her skirt. Mrs O'Rourke picked it up, felt its wet bottom and untied the stained rag that served as a nappy. The rag was dropped on the floor, the wet-bottomed child cuddled automatically on its mother's lap. 'I'd 'ave thought you would have had more sense, Molly,' went on her mother. 'That was a good job you had. You could've been independent.'

'What does a woman want to be independent for?' asked Mr O'Rourke. 'She could have worked till she dropped and not made the sort of money she's marrying into. Mind,' he said to Billy, wagging a finger, and looking menacing, 'I'll expect you to do something for my boys, here. Something for the twins. We'll all be one big family soon. We're having a hard time here. Jobs is hard to come by. We'll be losing what Molly brung home. You do your duty by your wife's family and you won't get no trouble from me. In fact, you could take me out for a pint right now and get to know your father-in-law.'

Billy, who was holding Molly's hand, felt its convulsive squeeze. 'Oh, I'm really sorry, Mr O'Rourke. Molly and me's going to Southend today. But here,' he withdrew a pound note. 'Why don't you take this and the whole family can celebrate our betrothal.'

Mrs O'Rourke was quicker off the mark than her husband, despite the hindrance of her child. She took possession of the money saying, 'Yes, I'll get some food in. We'll all celebrate today.'

During the entire visit, which had lasted no more than fifteen minutes, Molly had not spoken a word. When they left the building, which housed a dozen families like hers, Billy took a deep breath to clear his lungs of the smell of stale urine and boiled cabbage, then walked his fiancée towards the Strand as fast as her tired body would manage. Do something for the O'Rourkes? Given half a chance, he'd pay their way to Australia!

John and his Mabel were on their way this Bank Holiday Monday to visit the great exhibition at Chelsea. John should have been taken to Chelsea on the first day by either Miss Blair or Mr Warrender. However, neither of them seemed to know the proper way to treat a head gardener, so he was happy enough to take his wife on this last day. The entrance fee on the last two days was a shilling, an affordable price. Mabel sat in the train with the hard brim of her straw boater bumping against the glass as she watched the houses flash by. She was excited by the outing, grateful to be taken to town. There were no tears today. Mrs Wheems had decided to spend some time in her own home, for a change, leaving John to contemplate his wife's plain face, and to feel guilty about his plans to desert her. But mostly he thought about his fuchsias.

It was a peculiarity of the plant that you could calculate how many blooms you would get on a particular one and almost exactly when those blooms would appear. With a clever pinching of thumb and forefinger, you could 'stop' a plant, so that by careful training you could make a pot carry that many flowers it was a wonder the branches would hold them.

He was sure he had a winner, but he had to wait. When his young plants, nurtured back to life after their long winter rest, had produced stems with three pairs of leaves, he had pinched out each growing tip. A properly pinched plant is stimulated to grow on, and fairly soon there would inevitably be six side shoots where there had been only one main stem. The plant would then be pinched again. Within a few weeks there would be twenty-four to thirty-six side shoots growing vigorously. The plants could be pinched another time, so that eventually there were so many side shoots that the plant would carry over two hundred flowers!

Of course, each time the growing tips were pinched out, the time of flowering was delayed. It was all about delayed pleasure, holding off, waiting, knowing that when the moment came, the joy would be intense. Yet John had been unable to wait. He had pinched his special plants just three times. That meant, for a single-flowered variety, a wait of six weeks before the first blooms appeared. His new variety, his secret creation with the magic ingredient, could be expected to come into flower in August.

Beginning when he was a lad and could only grow a few plants in the back yard during the warm weather, John had crossed whatever variety he had to hand with any other he might beg from a friend (or later steal from Rochford's). A quick pinch of a plant as you passed it and you had a cutting which would take root in a small pot. His collection had grown to enormous proportions, and his mother had taken exception to the dazzling display in summer. During the winter, John buried them in clinker in the cellar with amazing success. Very few died. He knew how to strip two flowers on different plants to expose their sexual parts, how to prevent unwanted fertilization, how to place the pollen, keep the plant safe, collect the seed and make that seed germinate.

When old man Bulmer had given him a job at Capel,

John transferred his weedy cuttings and unnamed crosses to grander quarters and grew some respectable specimens that won praise from his boss, if not from his employer.

On this day, he could think of nothing else but his treasure, the seedling he was sure would produce an amazing display, a new variety.

He would call it 'Capel Bells'. 'Capel' because head gardeners quite often named new varieties of plants after the grand estates on which they worked, 'Bells' because fuchsia blooms hung down like bells, even those on the more upright varieties. 'Capel Bells'. He would take his cuttings with him when he headed for America. They would be his ticket to wealth and fame, his guarantee of work on the other side of the Atlantic.

'Ooh, innit grand!' Mabel cried, when they had passed through the turnstile at Chelsea. 'I never did see such a sight. Oh, John, I'm ever so pleased you brung me here. Look! There's tea rooms and everything. Oh, John, I'm ever so thirsty. Let's have a cup of tea first. We can look at plants any old time.'

The plants were past their best and the exhibitors, to a man, looked extremely tired. There were great crowds on the paths, however. The organizers reckoned that near enough a hundred and eighty thousand people had visited the gardens during the week, and ten thousand pounds had been taken at the gate. No wonder there was talk of holding another show on the grounds of the Chelsea Hospital next May, this time to be put on by the Royal Horticultural Society. Mabel and John saw every exhibit, she with pleasure at the brilliant sight and wonder that she had actually been able to visit so magnificent an event, he with secret pride and excitement. John had not seen anything to equal his 'Capel Bells'. Nothing at all could match his flowers – at least not the flowers he expected to see on his thirty plants come August. Feeling generous, he later walked his Mabel along the embankment, then took her to the Palace for a variety show. She clung to him in the train, her round face aglow with gratitude and love. John placed a kiss on her forehead, tipped his bowler hat forward and closed his eyes to dream of fuchsias on the long ride home.

Chapter Fifteen

The following day, Charlotte received a request for her presence from a Mrs Oswald Carradice who said she had heard about C. A. Blair, florist, from someone she had met at a party. Mrs Carradice would like to see Charlotte early the following week in order to discuss a dinner party she planned to give on June the twenty-ninth. 'We shall have recovered from Ascot,' she said, as if Charlotte would need such information. Mrs Carradice could not possibly discuss the floral arrangements on the fourth of the month, because that was the day before the Derby, and she would be busy arranging her clothes. Naturally, she would not be available on Derby day, nor on the day before the Oaks, which was the sixth, nor of course on the day of the Oaks itself. Wasn't it all too exciting? Mrs Carradice had the most delicious outfits to wear and everyone was being terribly kind, except her new mother-in-law, who was awfully old and stuffy and didn't understand the problems of a woman who had been married less than three months, she being so much older than Mrs Carradice. In fact, Mr Carradice was a few years older than she was, and she did so want to impress him by giving an absolutely wonderful first dinner party, and he had said to spare no expense.

Apparently, Mrs Carradice wasn't acquainted with Lady Smythe or Lady Briggs. Charlotte's reputation was intact in certain circles, so she hoped her business would not flounder. This commission must be sensational. Listening to the very young voice on the other end of the line, Charlotte began thinking of possible themes for the dinner. Racing was the obvious subject, perhaps a series of horseshoes arranged down the table with flowers in upturned riding hats . . .

Mrs Carradice's address was in Mayfair. The party was for twenty people. As the bride continued to talk rapidly, Charlotte's spirits rose. Perhaps the recent spate of burglaries could be put behind her. She would make a new start, produce something so magnificent for the Carradice party that every hostess in London would be determined to use her services.

Meanwhile, she had a party of her own to attend, a simple At Home, but one that exercised her mind considerably. On Friday, the thirty-first of May, Charlotte put on a pale green gown with a matching short coat that had a quantity of moulting fur on the cuffs, and had herself driven from Capel Manor to Theobalds Park to call on Lady Meux and the Admiral.

Passing through the gate of Temple Bar, the small carriage crunched along the gravel drive towards a huge house of old red bricks dressed in Portland stone. There was no symmetry to the house; rooms had been added on by successive owners in a manner that must have afforded ever more space connected by ever more corridors, causing increasing problems for the staff. The conservatory, with its curved roof, protruded in a rather ugly manner, but its vast size was impressive. To the right of the front door there was an oddly shaped room which was probably a perfect octagon when seen from inside. What could be the purpose of such a room, she wondered.

Mortified to find that she was the first person to arrive, she was led by a stony-faced butler through the handsome entrance lobby with its painted frieze in the style of ancient Egypt, through a sumptuous drawing-room directly behind the entrance hall and out through the french doors to the garden beyond. Still they walked, turning to the left, until they reached a formal garden where a fountain played in a large pool and one or two roses were already in bloom in the heavily manured geometric beds.

Here, wicker chairs with stylish Liberty print cushions had been arranged in a semi-circle. And here Lady Meux and the Admiral rose to greet her, graciously attempting to put her at her ease. Lady Meux, charming in a white lawn gown that swept the grass, spoke of her recent marriage to the Admiral, of her five daughters by the late Lord Chelsea, and of the newly built ballroom directly behind them. This, she said, was an essential addition to the house, for how could one marry off five young ladies if one hadn't a ballroom in which to entertain their friends?

Charlotte didn't know the answer to that question, but she could see the ballroom through more french doors. It was a magnificent room which could probably be decorated entirely from flowers grown in the Theobalds conservatory, the largest she had ever seen connected to a private home.

The Admiral was soon directing other visitors towards the conversational circle, and of course, Mr Bowles was among the guests, cheerful, amusing and extremely kind to a nervous young floral decorator. He even complimented her on her work for Mr Kitson at the International Exhibition.

Matthew arrived a few minutes later, having come downstairs from his rooms at Theobalds. Charlotte watched him walking towards her with gratitude; she had no idea what to say to anyone, and was embarrassed to find that her fur cuffs were distributing bleached fox hairs over the chairs and a few of her fellow guests. With his customary ease and grace, he greeted his host and hostess, had a pleasant word for every other person, before smoothly escorting her away from the small party in order to tour the green paths of the Italian rose garden.

As her hand lay in the crook of his arm, she remembered that she had every reason to be furious with him, but her temper had cooled and now she could not keep the warmth from her voice. 'I am most grateful to you for taking me away from the other guests. I have no conversation, as you well know.'

'I know nothing of the sort, but you did seem to be uncomfortable. I thought it best to give you a chance to relax before we have our tea. As you can see, everyone is wandering away. The grounds are famous and deserve to be appreciated.'

'This garden is boring. I much prefer Capel Manor. Here, the trees have all been artfully planted. All the lawns are mown to perfection and trimmed with not a blade of grass where it shouldn't be. Every flower knows its place, and I'm quite sure every rose will bloom on the day appointed for it. It's too perfect and too grand for my taste. However, I wish I could decorate an affair here. What a challenge that would be! Lady Meux has five daughters, but I suppose the head gardener will be charged with arranging all the flowers for any entertaining they do. The day I arrived at Capel Manor to discuss arrangements with your grandmother, I actually thought that this was the house I would be decorating. How fortunate that it wasn't! I was not experienced enough at that time to undertake such a large commission. And if I had come here, I would never have met—'

'*We* would never have met,' he finished for her. 'I don't care to dwell on such a horrible thought. Charlotte, will you forgive me? I don't want to quarrel with you. Can we be friends?'

'With the greatest pleasure. Let us never again talk of anything personal.'

He stopped, studied her face, then shrugged sadly. 'I will abide by your wishes, of course. I have a commission for you, but perhaps you would rather not do anything for me after—'

'This is business,' she said crisply.

'Yes, this is business. I spoke out of turn the other

day and have regretted it ever since. My confidence in your work is undiminished, I assure you. I am to give a dinner party for a few Japanese visitors and British businessmen. The Tokyo Nursery Company, as a matter of fact. I have been doing some translating for the company and find myself more involved than I had ever intended. The dinner is for sixteen men and is to be held at Rumpelmayer's restaurant on June the twenty-first.'

'Rumpelmayer's, the confectioners, on St James?'

'That is the one.'

'No,' said Charlotte. 'You must not entertain foreign visitors there when you own Capel Manor. It's not fitting. You must hold your party at Capel and I will provide the floral decoration. You can take them on a tour of the gardens before supper.'

'Charlotte,' he paused to choose his words carefully. 'This is to be a dinner party for businessmen, and no women are to be invited. I couldn't—'

'You mean, you couldn't invite me to join the gathering? Thank heavens for that! I wouldn't wish to attempt to make conversation with foreign gentlemen. I find it difficult enough to play at being a guest here. It's all settled then. I am to do the flowers on the twenty-first of June.'

'And you will send me a proper account of your charges?'

She looked at him askance. 'You really do think I'm mercenary, don't you?'

'Of course not. Your bill will be paid by Tokyo Nursery Company. Do your best to make the decorations outstanding.' As guests were walking down paths towards the narrow New River that cut its way through the grounds, Matthew murmured, 'Have you discovered the culprits?'

'There are none. No-one who works for me has taken part in any sort of wrongdoing. However, I have to admit you were right about Molly and Billy. They are to be married and will live with Vic.'

'Poor souls.'

'You are wrong about Florence and Jacko Boon, of course. It's absurd. Also, Vic has no interest in me whatsoever. I have had a number of cancellations, but I will survive, thank you very much. Only the other day, I received a commission from a Mrs Carradice in Mayfair. She will recommend me to others.'

'Mrs Oswald Carradice?'

'That was the name. Have you met the Carradices? Are they friends of yours? You must know everyone in London.'

'Hardly, but I do know Mr Carradice by sight. He is twenty years his wife's senior, married to please his mother who thinks he should produce an heir. He's a stickler, Charlotte. Everything must be absolutely correct. Try to avoid his presence. I have observed the way he speaks to women he believes to be his social inferiors, and I dislike his attitude excessively.'

'I shall be most careful. Thank you for the warning. By the way, I must tell you that you malign Arthur Brock when you accuse him of wishing to ingratiate himself with rich people in society. He has no such thought in mind.'

Matthew shook his head, laughing, appeared to be about to argue, then changed his mind. 'Your loyalty is equalled only by your determination not to delve into the motives of others. I don't know whether to compliment you or pity you.'

'Please don't pity me, whatever you do. Let's not discuss the subject any more. I'm sorry I spoke. You may believe whatever you choose. I will continue to think well of Arthur Brock.'

He saw her to her carriage, just half an hour after Charlotte had arrived. 'Have you personal calling cards?' whispered Matthew, as other departing guests drifted into the entrance hall.

'Yes, but—'

'Put two cards in the silver tray on the table.'

'Why?'

'One for Lady Meux. One for the Admiral. It is the proper thing to do.'

Reluctantly, she reached into her handbag and extracted some cards. 'They aren't as I would like.'

He took two from her, dropped them onto the silver salver unobtrusively and kept one for himself. It was not until they were standing on the steps of the house that he read her card with its misspelling of 'Covent' and its reference to her occupation. She saw the look of horror on his face. The Meuxs would laugh at her, and there was nothing Matthew could do to prevent it. How stupid of her to dream of a warm reconciliation. It would have been, she now saw, an impossible task to learn the rituals of the polite world, even with Matthew's help. With a sigh and a warm handshake, she bade him goodbye.

Brock was surprised and, being a superstitious man, convinced that he had received A Sign. Lady Smythe at Epsom, and alone! June the seventh was the day of one of England's classic races, the Oaks, and here was a rich, titled widow strolling across the grass without an escort. If he had thought about it at all, he would have expected her to be in the Royal Enclosure. Yet, here she was looking very grand and younger than her years. Turning her head slowly as she scanned the crowd, her eyes fell on him and she smiled slightly, clearly trying to remember where they had met. Arthur hurried towards her. He was meant to court her; his charm would win her heart.

'Lady Smythe! What a pleasure to see you here.' He lifted his hat, then settled it on his head to take the hand she extended.

'Mr . . .'

'Brock, your ladyship. The floral decorator, Miss Blair, is a friend of mine. Are you thinking of placing a . . .' He hesitated. Was it polite to say 'bet' to a lady?

Perhaps 'flutter' was a better word. What he actually managed to say was, 'Are you thinking of placing a fet?'

'I beg your pardon?'

'That is, a blutter? On the Oaks? I mean—'

'You know your trouble,' she laughed. 'You are too tense. I won't eat you. And not so much of the "your ladyship". I understand it's vulgar to mention a person's title too often. My husband told me that. Are you a tout?'

'Your ladyship, I am not a tout!' Her wry smile restored his sense of proportion and he laughed good-naturedly. 'However, I have been known to offer advice to special acquaintances. What do you fancy? I advise you to ignore the favourite.'

'Do you now? I was going to put my money on Tagalie. It won the Derby, so why not the Oaks? Which horse should I back?'

'Oh, Mr Prat's Mirska, without a doubt.'

She opened her handbag. 'In that case, suppose you nip off and put a hundred pounds on Mirska for me and twenty for yourself.' She handed him a hundred and twenty pounds.

In that instant, Arthur Brock's confidence disappeared. 'That is a great deal of money. Perhaps Mr Rothschild's Equitable would be a safer bet. I could back it each way.'

'Go on with you. I shan't eat you if this Mirska comes in last. Having a blutter is what it's all about, isn't it? Besides, a hundred pounds means little to me. Mind you come straight back! The truth is, it would be a pleasure to walk about on the arm of a handsome young man for a change. All my husband's acquaintances were so old!'

Brock was so delighted by such heady compliments that he nearly fell over his own feet in getting the bet placed in time. He duly put a hundred pounds to win for Lady Smythe and twenty for himself on Mirska at five to one. Then, because he could not resist, he put a five pound each-way bet on Equitable for himself. Filled with dread, he returned with the tickets, and they found a comfortable place for themselves close to the rails to watch the horses thunder past.

The race lasted just under three minutes, and Brock was certain he didn't draw breath during the entire time. Mirska won; Mr Rothschild's Equitable came second. Lady Smythe was loud and unrestrained in her joy, and Brock calculated his own winnings with quiet pleasure. He would be solvent for another month or two, provided he did not risk any more of his own money on unpredictable horse flesh for the remainder of the flat season.

They enjoyed the afternoon so much that Brock found himself returning to Town in her ladyship's motor, seated like a lord at the back while a uniformed driver patiently maintained his place in the queue of vehicles. Lady Smythe invited him to take her to dinner, and paid for the evening at Romano's by passing the cash to him before they arrived at the restaurant.

'So, who was the informant?' she asked when they had finished two bottles of champagne.

'I don't understand.'

'You must know that all the clients of your friend, Miss Blair, have been burgled following her visits to them. Somebody has been informing the criminals just where to look for jewels and valuable vases and silver. I don't blame the young woman, herself, but I do think she should take care whom she employs.'

Brock, who had just positioned his new monocle in his eye socket in order to read the bill, let it fall into his lap. 'What can you be saying? I knew nothing of this! You must be mistaken.'

'Well, she has lost many of her customers because of it. The silly girl should have written to her clients and denied any guilt. By saying nothing at all, she makes it look as if she has something to hide. She's clever with flowers, but something of a fool about getting on in the world.'

Brock stared at his companion, dumbfounded. 'But this is terrible. She's such a sweet girl. My old friend Vic Tavern fairly dotes on her. She must be distraught. You have not cancelled her, by any chance?'

'I have, but if you ask me nicely, I might reconsider. Brock, look at me. Tell me that you cannot hold anyone she employs responsible for theft.'

Brock stared very hard at Lady Smythe, but it was a difficult thing to do. The fact was, once suspicions were put into his mind, he could think of several people who might be responsible for dirty work. A lifetime spent uttering lies and half truths came to his rescue, and he managed to put up a strong case for Charlotte to have all Lady Smythe's floral commissions in the future.

'Well, I had proposed using her for a small dinner party in July. Send the girl to me next week and I will talk to her. If I am convinced of her innocence, I might be able to restore her reputation. I should enjoy taking up a floral decorator. I'm no longer terribly well connected, you know. Everyone received me when my husband was alive, but I don't get through too many front doors these days. You know, when the old boy asked me to marry him, I thought I would be in clover for the rest of my life. I was especially pleased about being a titled lady. Now I know that the important thing is that I've got enough money to live out my days in comfort. The trouble is, the people I used to know are a trifle intimidated by my title, and those with breeding don't wish to know me at all. I'm every bit as fond of the horses as the toffs are. Valerie, the previous Lady Meux, used to be very kind to me. We had a great deal in common, both of us having come from the stage and all. But she was really badly treated by the people close to her Hertfordshire estate. Most of them snubbed her, especially after Sir Henry died. I have spent a weekend or two at Theobalds Park. That's how I came to know the old dears who lived at Capel Manor. Val owned Volodyovski, you know. Poor dear, she died alone.'

Brock blinked. 'Volodyovski! We used to call it Bottleowhisky. Derby winner, 1901. But the owner was . . .' he closed his eyes, then opened them suddenly, 'owned by Mr Theobalds!'

'That's the name she raced her horses under. Her colours were red with a green sash, but they weren't often seen on the course. Mostly, she leased her horses. She left her fortune to Admiral Sir Hedworth Lambton, provided he changed his name to Meux. I know the Admiral. We nod when we meet at the races, but now that he's married to Lady Chelsea, as was, I don't expect to be invited to Theobalds again.'

'It's a small world.'

'It is when you like the horses. Oh, Brock, it's good to let my hair down, so to speak, and just be plain old Doris; but don't you ever take advantage of me. I make a fierce enemy.'

'I wouldn't cheat you, my lady. Not my sort of thing, I promise you. And not Charlotte's either. We must do this again soon. That is—'

'I've two tickets to the Royal Command Performance. It's at the Palace Theatre. Variety artists, for a change. I expect the King and Queen will really enjoy it. Would you like to escort me?'

'I should say I would!'

'July the first. We'll dine at my home before we go. Just the two of us. I was wondering who to take. Now it's all settled.'

Matthew was hot and very short tempered indeed by the time he reached the front door of Capel Manor. Normally he would have been at Epsom with friends without a care in the world, what with the money he had realized from the sale of some of his possessions now resting safely in the bank, and Buffy Morrison's promise of wealth to come in suburban development. Then, quite by chance, he met an old friend of his grandfather's being fitted for a pair of boots at Lobb's.

271

At first the talk had been about boots and shoes, old friends and new scandals, then Colonel Darlington had leaned close, given a grotesque wink and said something quite incomprehensible to Matthew.

'Received the dividend from Goldseekers, old boy. My word, eight per cent, and the company was only set up in the new year. Didn't see your name on the letterhead. Keeping quiet, eh? Your friends recognized the address, however. Capel Manor. I said to Sir Rupert – you know, he's a second cousin of mine – I said, "Rupert, old boy, if Matthew Warrender is behind this venture, it's sound as a dollar. Matthew wouldn't get mixed up in anything dicey, even if it's gold mining in Australia." ' The Colonel winked again, then turned his attention to his boots.

Matthew sat perfectly still until certain phrases trickled through his brain and began to make horrifying sense. Vic Tavern!

The Colonel turned to him again. 'Who is this C. A. Blair? All correspondence is addressed to Mr Popple Douse at Capel Manor, but the name C. A. Blair sounds familiar. Haven't you leased your property to someone with that surname?'

'It is quite a common name,' Matthew murmured. 'You know, I'm not feeling terribly well. I believe I will come to be fitted another day.'

The train journey had been short, crowded and uncomfortable. There were no cabs standing at Cheshunt station. Too impatient to wait until one turned up, Matthew had walked to Capel Manor, planning his attack on Charlotte with each step he took.

It was Rachel's misfortune to be the person opening the door to Matthew. 'Where is Miss Blair?' he demanded, and almost flung his hat and gloves at her.

Rachel, speechless in the face of his evident wrath, made no reply. The morning-room door opened and Charlotte came into the hall. Matthew could see Vic and Billy standing behind her. 'That will be all, my girl,' he said to the maid, then, 'No, bring me some lemonade. And knock loudly before you enter.'

He walked towards Charlotte without a greeting, noticing, even in his extremely angry state, that she looked stricken. 'I have just met an investor in Gold-seekers,' he began, as he closed the morning-room door. 'Is it possible you have been using my home as the registered office of a fraudulent gold-mining scheme?'

'Not fraudulent, Matthew,' said Charlotte quietly. 'Vic has assured me that it is perfectly honest.'

'Really! Perhaps you will then tell me the purpose of so much secrecy. Why did no-one suggest that I might care to purchase a few shares? Did no-one think I might wish to invest in so promising a scheme? Why has it never been mentioned? Are you part of this, Billy?'

'Me? No, my father wouldn't give me any shares. I'd have been glad of the chance, but—'

'Shut your face, Billy,' said his father. 'Look here, Warrender, suppose you and me step out into the library and I'll fill you in on all the details.' Vic took Matthew's arm and gently guided him out of the door and down the hall.

'Tell me the truth or I'll beat it out of you, Tavern. Is this company strictly legal?'

'Not strictly,' said Vic calmly.

'Does Charlotte know that?'

'Of course not! You don't suppose I'd tell her the truth, do you? It's not going to harm anyone what can't afford it, and I'll be setting the girl up for life. She won't need to spend the rest of her days working like a navvy.'

'No, she'll be picking oakum. I suppose it was you who informed your criminal friends where to look in the houses Charlotte had access to. You are a bounder, Vic Tavern.'

'None of that,' said Vic, showing some heat for the first time. 'I'm damned fond of that girl. I wouldn't do nothing to harm her. I may think her mother played

273

a trick on her, naming her after some north country woman what scribbled a bit, but—'

'You don't mean Charlotte Brontë?' asked Matthew, momentarily diverted. 'I have always considered it a beautiful name. A fine literary choice, and quite unexpected. What name did you think she should have been given, for heaven's sake?'

'Well, Victoria, I thought.'

And with that simple statement, everything fell into place for Matthew; the close association of the two, the shared toughness of attitude. There was even a certain similarity in the chins. 'She's your daughter, isn't she?'

'Yes, she is, but she don't know it. Now, do you see why I wouldn't harm her? How could I do that to my own flesh and blood?'

'You've been noticeably tight-fisted towards your son. I presume he is also your own flesh and blood. By the way, are they full brother and sister?'

'No, Billy's mother was a slut.'

'And Charlotte's mother,' said Matthew, calculating rapidly, 'must have been very much older than you.'

'Twenty odd years. I know it seems strange that a young lad of seventeen could fall in love with a woman so much older, but there's no accounting for the human heart, old chap. I loved that woman till the day she died. I won't let nothing bad happen to our daughter.'

'You're a fool, Victor Tavern. You have harmed Charlotte irreparably. This Goldseekers must be wound up. You must send back every investor's money. I understand Mr Douse is involved. Very well, he can find an excuse to return the money. No success. Company folding, that sort of thing.'

Vic was astounded. 'What are you asking of me? We just bloody well paid out an eight per cent dividend!'

'On what basis did you pay a dividend?'

'To get more investors, of course. Why else?'

Matthew ran shaking fingers through his hair. 'You will all go to prison. Charlotte will be ruined. And I

274

will be ruined, since many investors think the company has my blessing.'

'Well, it stands to reason, we ain't got enough money to buy back the shares, because we just give out the dividend.'

Matthew paced the floor for a minute or two while Vic leaned casually against the desk. 'Who else is involved?'

'Just Popple and Arthur Brock and me. We brought in Charlotte, because I wanted her to get rich. When I've enough to retire, I plan to give my business to Billy. He's a fool, but he ought to be able to manage a pawnshop in Covent Garden.'

'You must tell Charlotte that you are her father. You must not tell her that the scheme was dishonest. Just disengage as rapidly and quietly as you can. What with your having paid an eight per cent dividend, if investors have their capital returned, they can hardly claim to have been badly done by.'

'We ain't got the readies, I tell you.'

'Then you will just have to sell your business to raise the capital. Otherwise, I promise you, I will inform against you to the authorities.'

'If I sell my business, there won't be nothing for Billy.'

'Except a father who is on the right side of the law.'

Vic seemed unconcerned about his fraud. 'I've wanted to tell the child for years. Ever since her mother died. I'll go and do it right now. You take Billy out of the way.'

Matthew wanted to continue the discussion, but Vic parried every remark. He had made up his mind to tell Charlotte that he was her father. Nothing else was of interest to him at the moment. Matthew gave up in disgust and accompanied the older man back to the entrance hall.

Vic closeted himself with Charlotte; Billy sat on a straight chair by the fireplace in the hall and rested his elbows on his knees. Matthew tried to make himself comfortable, but could not stand still. Vic might have been his father-in-law! He had a sudden vision of himself introducing Vic to Buffy Morrison, but decided that the two men would probably take to one another. Lady Briggs was a different matter, but Matthew didn't particularly care what Lady Briggs thought. Nevertheless, he did not like the idea of being closely related to either Vic or Billy. Charlotte deserved better in the way of relatives.

They heard an angry buzz from Charlotte, her words spoken fiercely but too softly to be deciphered.

Suddenly, Vic bellowed. 'Damn it! Shut up for two minutes! I'm trying to tell you that I'm your father! Your ma and me loved each other. I'm your father, not that porter what—'

He got no further. There was a scream of horror from Charlotte. Matthew made a move towards the door, then thought better of it. Charlotte had dealt successfully with her brash father all her life, without knowing of their relationship. She must come to terms with the truth, and the best way forward was for her to continue talking to Vic. He turned, instead, to Billy.

'Did you know Charlotte was your half sister?'

'Yes,' said the young man, sadly. 'I was sort of in love with her when I was nineteen. My father had to tell me. I don't mind. I mean, she's very clever and beautiful.' He paused for a moment, listening to Charlotte's anguished wails, then said, 'I just wish, you know, that he loved me as much as he does her. I'm going to be a married man next week and there's a little one on the way. I mean . . .' He shook his head, unable to articulate the pain Vic had caused him.

Matthew walked over to the younger man and placed a friendly hand on his shoulder. 'If it's any consolation to you, your father formulated his Goldseekers scheme so that he could earn, that is, win some money for Charlotte and enough to enable him to retire. He had intended to give you his business. Now, of course, he will have to sell the business in order to repay the investors. It's hard but better than going to prison for fraud.'

'Is that true? If he sells the business, it could fetch anything up to six thousand pounds but—'

'What? You mean a pawnshop is worth that sort of money? I had no idea. Then there is no problem. There will be money left over to start another pawnshop.'

'Let me explain,' said Billy. 'You have to have a licence to practise as a pawnbroker. You've got to have good character and you've got to show you have the money to lend. We're like banks to poor people. They need us. Now, if he was to sell out and share the money, there wouldn't be enough for me to set up anything decent. A lot of capital goes into the business in order to make a fair return. Once the shop goes, there won't be nothing to turn to, no way of making a decent wage, no way of buying another shop. I ain't trained to nothing, you know. All I know is pawnbroking.'

Charlotte had stopped crying. The sound coming from the morning-room was considerably more friendly, but they were speaking too softly to be heard in the hall. Matthew thought about Vic and Charlotte and Goldseekers. And he thought about Buffy's brilliant scheme to make a fortune by building homes in the suburbs. He could not demand that Vic, Charlotte's father, sell his business to fund the return of the money to the investors, because Charlotte would not wish it and her half brother would suffer. Matthew would have to use some of his newly acquired wealth to set the family on the straight path to respectability. It was folly to sacrifice so much for a woman who had made it plain to him that she didn't love him, yet he could not contemplate any other action.

Ruefully, he considered his position. When he regained possession of Capel Manor, perhaps he could take in paying guests, or offer to introduce the socially aspiring to the socially superior for a fee. Was it only last Christmas that he returned from Hong Kong, determined to live the life of a gentleman, set up his stable, join a club and cultivate the acquaintance of the best people? Five months later, he was prepared to encumber his future to save the skin of an old rogue who should be behind bars. Brock, Tavern and Douse: so far as he knew, these were Charlotte's only close friends, and they were all scoundrels.

'My dad could be your father-in-law,' said Billy with amusement.

Matthew grimaced. 'A daunting idea, but I'm afraid Charlotte will not have me.'

'She's a fool. At least, sometimes I think she is. She's got a flame inside her, burning her up. I guess she is an artist, not with a paintbrush but with flowers. Artists aren't like the rest of us. They see things in a different way, and they can be a pain in the neck. Charlotte would work my poor Molly to death and never know she was doing it. Well, she works herself to the point of exhaustion. And I can't see the need for it. Sometimes I think she's mad, like the real artists. Didn't some geezer cut off his own ear one time?'

'Van Gogh. I believe I did hear something about it,' said Matthew. 'And shot himself about twenty years ago. His work was not known or appreciated in his own lifetime. Let us hope that Charlotte receives the recognition for her work that is her due. Talent is a stern master.' It occurred to him that Billy Tavern was more sensitive and more forgiving of the weaknesses of others than someone like Lady Briggs could ever be.

Matthew's future was once more extremely uncertain. Leading the life of a gentleman was no longer a possibility for him. Keeping the company of gentlemen would probably be impossible in future. He wondered why it had ever mattered to him so much. He would most certainly have to accept the position of translator for Tokyo Nursery Company and the small stipend the position paid.

Chapter Sixteen

'Come in, Miss Blair,' said Lady Smythe, showing Charlotte the way into a beautiful morning-room on the first floor of her home. The panelled walls had been painted white. There was very little furniture, all of it modern and plain.

'What a beautiful room, Lady Smythe! I didn't see this room the last time I was here.'

'You did, but I've completely redecorated it. I think my late husband would be horrified if he could see what I have had done to his oak panelling, but it is cheerful, isn't it? The furniture is by Charles Rennie Mackintosh, or someone very like him. It was all done for me by Liberty's. I am going to give you another chance, young miss, because our mutual friend, Arthur Brock, has great confidence in you. A dinner party for sixteen. What can you suggest?'

Charlotte took a seat and removed her notebook from her handbag with a flourish. 'I thought a pink dinner party might be attractive at this time of year. Pink roses, heaths and carnations. You could have dishes of pink bonbons on the table. I have recently bought some charming china cupids—'

'China cupids? Me?' laughed Lady Smythe.

'Yes, you see, one would be set before each place with a tiny scroll attached to its neck with pink ribbon. When your guests open the scroll, it turns out to be the menu. The table napkins should be folded into the twin boat style. I would place a small arrangement of pink flowers in one boat, and in the other a bundle of little bread sticks tied with pink ribbon. It could be charming.'

'Charming. But not for me, Miss Blair. I'm not the sort of person who gives pink dinner parties. Can you not find something more in keeping with my personality?'

Charlotte had worked out several possible schemes for Lady Smythe, but she could see that none of them would suffice. Lady Smythe was bold, vulgar and filled with a sense of fun. She was also apparently quite fond of Arthur Brock . . .

'Suppose we arrange a theme based on racing, starting at the entrance hall and going right through the reception rooms?'

'Hurrah! That's the style. What can you do?'

Charlotte flipped a few pages of her notebook until she arrived at the page on which she had written out her proposal for the Carradice dinner, and read from her notes. 'A series of flat horseshoes down the table. Yellow?'

'I like yellow, as you know. I shall make it my colour. Carry on.'

'Three horseshoes in the centre, their ends meeting. The "nails" in the horseshoes to be violets. Yellow wine glasses to continue the theme. A small china horse at each place and—'

'Oh, much better. I like it more and more.'

'Jockey caps,' said Charlotte, raiding the idea she had originally conceived for Mrs Carradice and wondering where she could buy sixteen. 'Each one upturned and filled with a selection of yellow flowers and greenery. The menu cards should be cut out in the shape of jockeys, with the menu printed on the back. And hurdles!'

'Hurdles? How? Tell me how.'

'Well, green arches, at all events. Eight inches tall and covered in greenery. We could have china horses riding through them. The same sort of china ones that accompany each place setting. Tall stands at either end of the table filled with yellow and purple flowers.'

'Splendid! You are a clever girl, Charlotte. May I call you Charlotte?'

'Of course.'

'Then,' said Lady Smythe, 'I am going to speak plainly to you. You must put this burglary affair behind you. It was probably no more than a coincidence, in any case. But never forget that gossip can be deadly to a fashionable enterprise. Now then, my girl, you dress in the most amazing manner I have ever seen.'

'I dress as I choose, but I haven't much time—'

'No, listen to the wisdom of an older woman. You try to dress conventionally, but fail. You are neither a complete eccentric nor a fashion plate. If you will take my advice, you will never attempt to be fashionable. You must place yourself firmly in the category of the eccentric. From this day forward, you must be *outré*. That means outrageous. It will do wonders for your business. Have you ever taken an interest in the theatre?'

'I was a child performer in pantomimes and my mother was—'

'Maud Blair, of course! I can see the resemblance. Good heavens, Charlotte, I knew her slightly. Character parts and walk-ons. Must have been a beauty in her youth. We were in a very poor production of *The Pirates of Penzance* in, let me see, '98. Well, you should know what I mean when I say you must dress in a theatrical way. Don't attempt to follow fashion. Forget about good taste. Let your imagination run riot. And as for your manner, stop trying to be pleasant and subservient. It doesn't suit you. You have a certain determined look that could be misconstrued as mulish. You can't change your nature, so flaunt it. You know your business, what you are about. I believe you are the most imaginative floral decorator in London. Act imperious. Take no nonsense. You are master of the situation. Let your customers understand that they are fortunate to have your services. Tell them what they should have as they won't know for themselves, then charge them an outrageous fee. If you will just listen to me, you will be rich and famous. I used the same tactics to catch my husband, and look at me now!'

Charlotte studied the happy woman in a georgette and lace morning wrap that must have cost as much as most men earned in a year, looked around the handsome room and decided that here was good advice. 'I'll do it, and thank you so much for taking the trouble to advise me. I can never behave like a member of the upper classes. Why should I try?'

'That's the spirit,' said Lady Smythe, and impulsively gave Charlotte a fierce hug. 'Now then. How much are the flowers for this dinner party going to cost me?'

'Two hundred and fifty pounds,' said Charlotte promptly.

Lady Smythe gasped, then laughed at having been caught out by her own advice. 'Wonderful. I can't wait to tell all my acquaintances how much I will be paying for superior flowers.'

Charlotte's business was expanding, but Molly's hours of work were shrinking, making it imperative that she train up other people. She took on two young women who had worked briefly for Carlton-White of New Bond Street. Alice and Letitia were experienced girls, capable of working quickly and efficiently. However, she knew they would not have left such a prestigious firm to work in Covent Garden if their work had met with approval. She drove them hard, therefore, and watched them closely. Her new style of flamboyant dress and extravagant manner seemed to impress them.

Her bold style was deceptive, however. Vic's revelation had wrested from her the last shred of her self-confidence. Only a totally new and different Charlotte could cope with the acquisition of a totally new and very different sort of father from the one she held in loving memory. There was, too, the painful business of reassessing her mother. This dear paragon and loving parent had apparently committed adultery with a man twenty-three years her junior. The discovery that she hadn't known the real Maud Blair at all stunned her. She couldn't think about it, didn't want to think about it. Her mother's affair was in the past and must be left there, undisturbed.

Meanwhile, Vic had to be dealt with. She had to decide how she felt about him and about Billy. These two men had not changed their attitude towards her at all since the day of the great revelation. Perhaps this was the wisest move. She should forget that Vic was her father, and continue to treat him as a friend.

On the other hand, Matthew's anger with Vic and the secret agreement that seemed to exist between the two men annoyed her. It was not right that Matthew should be on better terms with her father than she was. Neither of them would discuss Goldseekers, telling her not to worry about the sort of business that was the exclusive preserve of men. Exhausted by the struggle to keep her business afloat, and drained by the news of her parent's activities twenty-four years earlier, she was content to obey this instruction.

She didn't know anything about gold mining; she would put it from her mind and concentrate on winning new customers by doing something startling for the Carradices. Having given her racing ideas to Lady Smythe, she thought she would offer the pink dinner party to the sweet young bride. It would surely be appropriate.

The Carradice home proved to be a gloomy house filled with antique furniture. The atmosphere was Gothic, the dining-room a dungeon in dark oak, its windows shrouded in deep green velvet. This was hardly the place for a pretty pink dinner party.

'I'm afraid the dining-room smells of damp,' said Mrs Carradice, a plump young lady with a long upper lip and two protruding front teeth who could not have been more than eighteen years old. She was very pretty in a rabbity sort of way, although listening to her inane

283

chatter, Charlotte soon suspected that she was of less than average intelligence. Also, it soon became apparent that she was terrified of her new husband.

'Mrs Carradice, now that I have seen the dining-room, I feel that what is required is a dramatic scheme matching the dignity of the furniture,' said Charlotte, viewing the mahogany table and the twenty button-back chairs.

'Oh, yes, I do so agree. But you must surprise me, and after me, my guests. You must do something so incredibly clever that the whole of London will talk of nothing else. It is a magnificent table, isn't it? It's five feet wide and I have quite a lot of silver gilt that can be placed on it. Some of the pieces will take flowers, but then, that has been done so often over the years. My mother-in-law says the bowls should be filled with yellow roses and the epergne, which weighs tons, should be set in the middle. Isn't that the most boring thing you ever heard?'

'I don't arrange flowers in boring styles, Mrs Carradice.'

'Oh, I'm sure you don't!' exclaimed the girl, blushing unattractively. 'It's just – I don't know what to do for the best, to order my dinner parties as they have always been done, just to please my mother-in-law, or to do something different so that my husband will know I have a mind of my own.'

'Undoubtedly, you must prove to him that you have a mind of your own. Here is what I propose . . .'

Vic, Brock and Popple Douse sat in the library at Capel Manor, opening one hundred and twenty envelopes, most of which had the same sort of message: *How dare you offer to buy back my shares? Is this a plot to defraud me? I suspect you have struck gold and want all the profits for yourselves. Therefore, I will not sell at any price.*

'What are we to do now?' asked Vic, waving a letter from Colonel Darlington. 'This here letter threatens to expose us to his dear friend, Matthew Warrender, if we dare to demand the return of his shares. You know the trouble with that young man – he thinks he understands business, but he don't. One of these days I'll have to tell him the facts of life. Meanwhile, we must keep him sweet. We can't have him informing on us out of some damned fool sense of honour.'

Brock, hearing the crunch of footsteps on gravel, rose from his seat to look out of the window. 'It's Warrender! Walking up the drive, big as life and twice as dangerous. What's he doing here? And he's with some chap in striped trousers.'

Vic stood up with great speed. 'He mustn't find us. There's to be a party here at eight o'clock. Some businessmen from Japan, of all places. Charlotte told me he has use of the house tonight.'

Popple Douse swept the letters from the desk top into the open central drawer and closed it quickly. 'Well then, why did you ask us to come here today? Couldn't you have chosen some other time and place?'

'We had to see to the post, didn't we? Before his nibs found it. I wouldn't put it past him to open letters that weren't none of his business.'

'We're going to have to tell him some time,' said Brock reasonably.

'Yes, but not when Charlotte's in the house. We need time to think. Come on. He won't stay long. He's living at Theobalds Park and will return there to dress for dinner. Charlotte has forbidden anyone to enter the drawing-room or the dining-room. He'll have to leave shortly. Quick! Down into the cellar!'

They hurried furtively through the house, looking like the broker's men in a provincial pantomime, passed through the green baize door and opened the one leading to the cellar. Vic held a finger to his lips as a silent order to Rachel and Mrs Duck, then they all stumbled down the narrow cellar steps, unaware that there was no electric light below stairs.

'I'm sure my coat will be covered in whitewash,' whispered Douse. 'For I must lean against the wall to keep from falling. Oops! What was that hole?' A rattle of bottles told them that his hand had found its way into one of the many brick wine bins, designed to hold a dozen bottles of wine at waist height.

They travelled on, tripping over the clutter of generations, encountering unidentifiable smells, heading towards a dim light, the source of which always seemed to be one more turning away. At last, they were standing before a grate which rose up to ground level, beyond which were some steps. They were standing in the empty coal cellar.

The grate was unlocked, and Vic was about to suggest they make a run for it across the short area between the house and the walled garden, when a pair of bulbous boots appeared on the other side of the grate, attached to stout corduroy legs: the coal man.

'Back!' called Vic.

They retreated in disorder, blinded by the light flooding the entrance to the coal store. The grate opened; the first sack of coal was upended and heavy chunks plummeted to the basement floor. A cloud of fine black dust rose up and wafted its way towards the three men.

There was nothing they could do but continue moving back towards the cellar steps to avoid the danger of choking to death on coal dust. No-one could guess how many sacks of coal might be delivered to so large a house.

Matthew had a key to the front door of Capel, but he never used it. Rachel opened the door when he knocked, her cheeks bright flags. Poor girl, he had given her a fright by being so curt with her the last time they met. On this occasion, he smiled warmly.

'Hello, Rachel, this is my valet, Chalker, who will act as butler this evening.' Rachel's eyes grew rounder. 'I know Miss Blair doesn't want us to enter the drawing-room or the dining-room – at least, she doesn't want me to see these rooms. I assure you, I have no intention of spoiling her surprise. We simply want to check on the wines in the cellar, then Chalker will return at half past five.'

Rachel seemed to have some idea of blocking his way. Chalker, a taciturn Scot with a very short temper, was wearing his most formidable expression. Taking the girl by the shoulders, he firmly moved her aside, and the two men headed for the kitchen.

Matthew saw the cook whirl about to face them with a wooden spoon in her hand. 'Mrs Duck, I believe there is no electric light in the cellar, so we are going to need a candle. May I trouble you?'

Mrs Duck's expression was remarkably similar to Rachel's as she began to rummage for a candle, a holder and a match.

'This is Mr Chalker who will be acting as butler tonight. He will serve your food, together with a young man who is being lent to me by the Admiral.'

'Yes, sir,' said Mrs Duck, 'but do you need to inspect the cellar just now? Perhaps in an hour?'

'Now,' answered Matthew, keeping his temper. He directed Chalker to the small cellar door and led the way down the stairs.

Candlelight flickered over the whitewashed walls and threw a gruesome light on Vic, Popple Douse and Arthur Brock, looking like wild men with whitewash and coal dust liberally smeared across their faces and clothes as they stood in suspended animation by the first wine bin. Matthew was reminded of the occasions when his grandfather had taken him hunting at night. Deer and rabbits, frozen in the glare of their lamps, had worn the same doomed expression.

Vic, holding a bottle of claret by the neck, waved it to add emphasis to his words. 'Just picking out a bottle of something good to take back to town, old boy. I know you're having a dinner party here tonight, but it's Charlotte's wine, ain't it? I can take a bottle if I want to.'

Chalker began making mewling noises behind him as Matthew wrenched the bottle from Vic's hands. 'In the dark? The three of you were searching for a bottle of claret in the dark? Don't try my patience, Vic. That is my vintage claret, purchased for tonight's dinner and you're damned well shaking up the sediment.' Chalker gingerly removed the bottle from Matthew's grasp, but they both knew it was too late to save it. 'What the devil are you three doing here today? If I find that you have been up to your usual tricks—'

'Warrender, it is not as you think,' said Douse, making an effort to appear dignified, despite his soiled clothes. 'Although I admit we came down here to avoid seeing you. It was to spare Charlotte, you must understand. It is imperative that we speak with you, but today is hardly the ideal occasion.'

'I rather think it is. I find myself consumed with curiosity. You must relieve my doubts about your good intentions, if that is possible. Where is Charlotte?'

'In the drawing-room with a couple of her girls, Florence and two of your, that is, her gardeners,' said Brock. 'Since you are determined to interfere in what does not concern you, we can make it into the library, if we go quietly.'

'Chalker, stay here and check the wines. You will know what you want to serve. I leave it entirely in your hands. I believe I can now understand the strange behaviour of the Duck sisters. Perhaps you can use some of your famous charm to put them at their ease,' said Matthew.

'Yes, sir,' replied Chalker, who knew when sarcasm was being employed against him. 'If I might have the candle, sir?'

A minute or two later, the four men closed the library door very softly and settled themselves in the handsome panelled room.

'Now then,' said Vic in a voice barely above a whisper. 'We have received replies from one hundred and twenty of our investors. Four, who had only a few shares, have returned their certificates and want their money sent to them. We will do this, or rather Popple will. The remainder are up in arms, you might say. They believe we are trying to cheat them by demanding the return of their shares.'

'Don't try my patience!'

'I'm telling you the truth, Matthew. You're a cocky little toff what don't know nothing about human nature. If you did, you would understand why so many men are furious with us. Think about it. We give them a dividend. They think everything is going well. Then, for no real reason, we offer to buy them out. They think, "Aha, the directors was using our money to finance the search for gold, but now that it has been discovered they don't need our money any more and they want all the profits for themselves." Do you understand what I'm saying? They are suspicious. They think that if we was crooks, we wouldn't be giving them their money back, which, broadly speaking, is the truth. So they think there must be some other reason.'

Matthew chewed on his thumbnail, looking at each man in turn. He might know little about human nature, but he was adept at recognizing the truth when he heard it spoken. The investors, for reasons of greed, were refusing to have their investments saved. For a moment, he was tempted to leave these unknown gentlemen to their fates. That would not do, however, because the consequences of discovery continued to be catastrophic.

'In that case, we must hire a surveyor, purchase some land in Australia and search for gold. There is no alternative. What you are telling me is that investors cherish their dreams of great wealth above the certainty of keeping what they have entrusted to Goldseekers.'

'No one man has invested heavily,' said Brock. 'No-one of sense invests heavily in the chance of striking gold, but the idea appeals to the gambling instincts. I've often seen this sort of thing at the track. No person of sense bets heavily on a twenty-to-one horse, but people bet on these nags every day in the racing calendar.'

Brock's words were also the truth. Matthew recognized himself in the description of a gambler betting on a twenty-to-one horse. Buffy Morrison had held out to him the promise of wealth without effort in a field he knew nothing about. He was not a property developer, nor was Buffy. They had no logical reason for thinking the project would make them wealthy. Briefly, he considered the possibility of his friend's being as much a rogue as were Brock, Tavern and Douse, but soon dismissed the thought. Buffy, after all, was from a very good family.

'I have recently come into some money,' he told the three men. 'I think it will be more than enough to enable me to fund the search for gold. I will send a cable to a firm in Australia; I've a friend in Melbourne who can make enquiries. He will know who can do the work. We should have a man in the field within a month.'

'You would do that for us? But that's wonderful,' said Vic, louder than he had intended. 'Who knows? If we get hold of the right piece of land, we might really strike gold. We could all be rich.'

'Don't believe your own prospectus, Vic,' said Popple soberly. 'Leave that sort of dreaming to the fools who sent us their money.'

'By funding the search for gold,' Matthew added, 'I am buying myself onto the board. Remove Charlotte's name and replace it with mine. And don't offer any more shares!'

'In six months' time,' Popple said, 'when the surveying team has failed to find gold, we will declare the company bankrupt. Your money will be returned to you, Matthew, since you alone know the truth. We are, I suppose, grateful to you for setting us free from a possible brush with the law. We three will not have done too badly out of the venture: a modest profit in return for the effort, the risk to our good names and, of course, the anxiety which has been so injurious to our health.'

'I would rather not hear about any profits you expect to make,' said Matthew. 'Now, if you will excuse me, I must return to Theobalds Park and prepare for this evening. You, of course, will leave this house as soon as you have dealt with the post and cleaned yourselves up. I would hate to find you here at eight o'clock when my guests arrive.'

'An interesting conversation,' said Vic, when Matthew had left the room. 'Do you suppose he knows that there is no limit to liability if fraud is proved?'

Popple shook his head. 'I doubt if he understands about "limited liability" at all. I see your point. The good, the honest, Mr Warrender could conceivably lose Capel Manor as well as his reputation and his freedom by associating with us. We must do all in our power to prevent that happening, I suppose. The man means well.'

Matthew spent the next two hours considering what should be done and how quickly it was necessary to do it. At first he had been tempted to go directly to a post office and send off a shoal of cables. Common sense came to his rescue when he remembered the difference in time between Australia and England. He would send his cables as soon as the post offices opened in the morning. He would travel to one some distance from Capel Manor and Theobalds Park, as he had no wish to provoke gossip in the vicinity.

A short nap, intended to prepare him for a long evening of stressful entertaining, turned into a heavy sleep filled with dreams of being ostracized by every person he knew. Consequently, he was late arriving at Capel and had scarcely entered the hall, when he heard a string of carriages trundling up the drive. At that moment, Charlotte entered the hall to join him.

'Good evening, Matthew. How handsome you look!'

For several seconds, he found it impossible to respond. 'That is an . . . extraordinary gown, Charlotte.'

She held out her arms and turned slowly for his

admiration. 'Inspired by Mr Diaghalev's Russian Ballet. You know, the costumes were designed by a man named Bakst. Isn't it gorgeous? And no corsets, you see, just a pleated gown that hangs straight from beneath the bust. From now on, I am to be *outré*. That means—'

'I know what it means, thank you. I must admit it suits you, but—'

'Matthew,' she said earnestly. 'I can never be anyone but myself. We should not have suited, you see. I am a woman from Covent Garden, born into a theatrical family. I have to dress as I feel comfortable. I couldn't fit into polite society, even if I wanted to.'

'You are—' But there was no chance to finish the sentence. His guests had arrived. Chalker was at the door, ushering in the entire party.

'I shall stay just long enough to greet them,' whispered Charlotte. 'That's polite, isn't it?'

Fifteen men in evening dress crowded into the hall, half of them speaking loudly and employing exaggerated facial expressions to convey their meaning, half of them smiling politely, looking disorientated. As Matthew made the introductions all round, he presented Charlotte, noticing as he did so that she was receiving many admiring glances. There was considerable noise and confusion as he searched his brain for appropriate Japanese phrases, half the time finding only Mandarin ones available to him. She was a success in her bright green and blue gown, with her burnished, extravagantly arranged hair and enormous osprey feather on a jewelled band that circled her forehead. He saw, with some surprise, that every man was accepting her on her own terms, as a beautiful woman in a flattering gown. Not one of them was judging her by the standards of Lady Briggs and her set.

'I would like to present my card to the Japanese gentlemen, Matthew,' she said. 'Remember when we took tea at Theobalds Park? You told me that the presentation of calling cards is important to the Japanese.'

'Yes, of course.' Fortunately, he thought, most of the men present would not notice the error in the spelling of Covent Garden.

With grace, a deep bow and a shy smile, Charlotte presented her calling card to each of the Japanese men in turn, using both hands. With a little less ceremony, she then handed one to each of the Englishmen.

At the sight of the cards, Matthew felt slightly light-headed. The new, *outré*, Miss Blair had abandoned her flawed calling cards in favour of ones that did not come close to being acceptable to the *haut ton*. Each card was about four inches across and two deep, cut out in the shape of an upturned straw boater. The printed hat contained a profusion of violets. Admittedly, the hat and violets had been drawn to totally different scales, but the effect was strangely attractive. Her name, address and profession were printed on the reverse. The Japanese, in particular, were highly amused. The Englishmen, in gruff voices and expansive gestures, congratulated her on a charming conceit. She glowed with pleasure; he could have kissed her. A minute or two later, Charlotte retired to her room.

Matthew guided his guests straight through the house to the gardens, where Chalker served champagne and everyone was free for a short time to stroll around the grounds and enjoy the warm evening.

'Warrender,' said Mr Belper. 'Mr Notamura and I have been considering an important change to the company. We feel you would make a notable addition to our British board of directors. We would expect you to buy some shares, say five hundred pounds. What do you say?'

Matthew bowed slightly to Mr Notamura, aware of the great honour being conferred on him. Mr Belper was entirely correct in his assumption. Matthew did have something valuable to contribute to the British board: a knowledge of Eastern customs and languages. The European passion for all things Japanese had not diminished over the past twenty years, so the market for imported plants and objects was enormous. Tokyo Nursery Company needed Matthew Warrender, and Matthew needed to have an occupation that would make use of his talents. Unfortunately, he could not afford to invest in Buffy's scheme, pay for geological exploration in Australia and still have enough money in the funds to bring in a suitable income. Not, that is, if he also wanted to buy himself onto the board of Tokyo Nursery Company. For a moment or two, he allowed himself to be a trifle bitter, regretting the necessity of saving Charlotte's father from his own wickedness. The moment passed; he told the two men, first in English and then in Japanese, that he was deeply honoured, and could he please have a few days in which to think about it? They were content to give him the necessary time.

An hour spent drinking, talking and walking in the grounds greatly eased the atmosphere. By the time everyone was heading back to the house to dine, all the guests seemed to be having a wonderful time, whereas Matthew's head ached with the strain of translating so many conversations for so many people.

Chalker was waiting by the dining-room door and opened it with a flourish when everyone was assembled. There was a gasp of delight. Matthew looked at what Charlotte had produced and felt his chest swell with pride. Had any dining-room, whatever the size, looked so magnificent?

Hanging from the ceiling by their handles were over a dozen Japanese paper parasols filled to overflowing with white and orange flowers. Each parasol was suspended at a slight angle, as if about to spill its contents. In fact, so artfully had some of the flowers been arranged, they looked as if they had tumbled from the pleated paper and were suspended in time and space above the dining table. Into each parasol she had lowered a small electric bulb, its wire coming from the central rose, the central fitment having been removed. All wires were covered lavishly with ivy. Gentle light fell upon the table, filtered by the parasols. On the table were paper lanterns with candles inside, joined by trails of orchids. In honour of the occasion, Matthew had asked that various pieces of his Chinese and Japanese porcelain collection be placed on the table. The eighteen-inch-tall Boy with Outstretched Hand looked particularly amusing, for in that hand Charlotte had placed a perfect ball of yellow roses. Leading to the ball of roses was a step ladder fashioned from wire and covered entirely in lily of the valley. There were no flowers on the mantelpiece, but the overmantel reflected the floral glory of the room, including the orange and white arrangement above the dining-room door and the mirror that backed it. Fortunately, the windows had been thrown open on this balmy night, for the lilies of the valley emitted a heavy perfume that could have destroyed the taste of his carefully chosen wines.

Mr Notamura, seated on Matthew's right, leaned close to say in Japanese, 'Miss Blair is a genius. I have never seen anything like this. A perfect example of the English style of arranging flowers, unknown in Japan.'

Mr Belper, having no idea what his Japanese colleague had just said, spoke to Matthew at the earliest opportunity. 'Damned brilliant, Warrender. Miss Blair has captured the Japanese style of floral decoration exactly. You can see that our friends are deeply impressed by this compliment to their native style.'

Chapter Seventeen

As the dining-room was beneath her bedroom, Charlotte was disturbed by the thundering sound of masculine laughter for several hours. She had prepared for bed and was seated, reading, when she heard them leave the dining-room, at last. Now she imagined them walking the length of the entrance hall and entering the drawing-room. She had filled the fireplace and the embrasure on either side with several varieties of palms, brilliantly coloured crotons, luscious ferns and a few of John Green's fuchsias, although she found them messy and difficult to handle satisfactorily. In the morning, Matthew would be gone, but she hoped there would be a letter for her, some small message to say that he appreciated her efforts.

She had not been mistaken about his good manners. The note was waiting for her on the breakfast table. Florence, who had spent the night, came into the dining-room just as she was reading it.

'What have you there?' asked the girl, who was maddeningly bright in the morning, 'a billy doo? I daresay it's from Matthew. The flowers were wonderful, Charlotte. I think we all worked very well together. That Alice is a caution, although Letitia's a bit snooty. Did you know that her uncle is a baronet? I never thought I would meet a woman who worked when she didn't have to. Is it from Matthew? Do read it out.'

'It says, "Dear Charlotte, thank you for all your efforts on my behalf last night. The flowers in the dining-room were particularly successful. To win praise from the gentlemen of two nations is no mean feat. I was amused to see the use to which you put my Boy With Outstretched Hand. Please convey my congratulations to all your staff." '

'Oh, that's lovely,' said Florence. 'You must tell Alice and Letitia. I'll mention it to Mr Green and Ja . . . Mr Boon, if I should happen to meet them.'

Charlotte folded the letter carefully and slipped it into her skirt pocket. She had not read aloud the part at the end of the letter in which Matthew said he would always love her and wished that she could love a mere man as much as she loved flowers. This was an annoying interpretation of her character. Could it be possible that she loved flowers more than people? The truth was that she sought refuge among silent, uncritical blooms whenever mere men confused her.

And never had she longed for the reassuring company of a humble pansy or any other flower so much as she did when Billy Tavern arrived unexpectedly. Molly, he said, had not accompanied him because she was feeling unwell. However, she sent her warm regards, and had put the small bridal bouquet Charlotte had made for her register office wedding inside a glass dome.

'I think it's time you and me had a talk, Charlotte. Us being related and all,' he said when he had removed his cap, goggles and dust coat.

'Yes, of course. Shall we walk down to the grotto? We should be private there. It's too nice a day to stay indoors, don't you think? I love the garden at Capel Manor. Look, the roses are at their very best and . . . and so much is blooming today.'

They were walking down the lawn at a brisk pace. Billy grinned at his half sister, but made no comment, letting her babble on until they reached the Pulhamite grotto, when voices from within stopped even Charlotte's chatter.

'Jacko, don't!' came Florence's muffled voice.

Charlotte gave Billy a stunned look, then hurried

away, not prepared to confront yet another problem. They walked, this time in silence, until they reached the formal garden with its brilliant bedding scheme. She led him to a cast-iron bench beneath a honeysuckle arch and sat down as if exhausted.

'Matthew told me about Florence and Jacko Boon, but I preferred not to believe it.'

'Why are you afraid of the way people feel about each other?' he asked. 'Is it because you're an artist? I mean, don't artists like people?'

'I'm not really an artist, Billy. I am a floral decorator. Are you suggesting that I am not capable of loving mere men?'

Billy grinned, not the slow-top she had always believed him to be. 'Did Matthew say that to you? Well, why are you afraid of caring about people? It's a good feeling. When you love someone, chances are they will love you in return. If you love someone, you have somebody to worry about besides yourself. You know, I don't understand you at all. I think you must take after your ma.'

'And I think I have never fully understood you, Billy. You are a surprisingly sensitive person, and yes, I do take after my mother in many ways. She believed that a woman could protect herself from pain and disappointment if she kept her feelings, that is, if she kept her distance from people.'

'Especially men. I never could make her out, and when I was a boy, I was a little afraid of her. She was always very kind to me, of course. I've known about you being Dad's daughter for a year or two. And you know what I keep asking myself? How could that very proper old lady, your mother, find anything to love in my rough dad, who wasn't that old when they—'

'I try not to think about it.'

'I'm sure you do,' laughed Billy, 'but it has to be thought about, doesn't it? When Dad asks me why I had to fall in love with Molly, knowing that he wanted me to marry Florence, I just say to him, "What about you and Auntie Maud?" He's got no answer then. Sometimes he says something about the mysteries of the human heart. I like that. The mysteries of the human heart. You should marry Matthew.'

'Don't be absurd. He doesn't want to marry me.'

Billy shook his head. 'He says you won't have him.'

Charlotte sat up straight. 'He told you that? How dare he? That was none of your business.'

'I suppose not. I'm not clever like you are—'

'Please don't talk that way. I think you are much more intelligent than most people know.'

'Let me put it this way. It's not very pleasant living with Molly in my father's house. We need a little place, just a few rooms to ourselves. But there's nothing I can do about it. I must work for my dad, because I don't know where else I could earn so much money. He was going to retire, but your friend, Matthew, put a stop to that. Well, I suppose I am pleased he did, but it's an added complication. Now, if I was clever like you, I might be able to earn a decent living. Don't tell me I could work as a labourer. I'm determined Molly and the baby are going to live in comfort. It's too bad things worked out the way they did.'

Charlotte heard every word Billy said, but she was suddenly struck by the absence of nasturtiums in the south-west corner. They had been growing in profusion two days ago. She had demanded hundreds of them for the Japanese dinner party because they were almost the exact colour of the rising sun in the Japanese flag. Now, she knew which part of the garden had supplied them. The heliotrope was growing well. If she . . .

'Are you listening to me, Charlotte? Don't turn off your mind to what I am saying. It's important and it affects you.'

'I don't know why Matthew should have spoiled your plans. If it has anything to do with Goldseekers, I'm afraid I don't understand—'

'I won't let you turn your back on everything. You are, or were, a director of Goldseekers. You could have gone to prison if the investors had found out it was all a fraud.'

She put her hands over her ears. 'I don't want to hear about it. I have enough problems of my own. It is very difficult running a business. I am heavily committed. At first, none of my suppliers would give me credit, so I was unable to expand. But Lady Smythe told me to be imperious and eccentric. Now, I find that I have only to demand credit and it is granted. Hence, the commitments. I have bought many things – vases, ornaments and table runners – all sorts of things. I cannot worry about Goldseekers. I never wanted to be a part of it, anyway.'

'Matthew has ordered your name to be removed from the stationery and his own name put in its place. Do you understand what I'm saying?'

'Matthew did that?' She looked at Billy, wishing she didn't have to ask the next question. 'Does that mean Matthew could go to prison if the investors find out the business is fraudulent?'

'Possibly. He demanded that all the shares should be called in. He even guaranteed to buy back all of the investors' shares. It turned out that no investor wanted his money returned. Matthew is now going to see about employing surveyors to look for gold in Australia. That way, the enterprise will be legitimate. More or less. Do you understand?'

'Why has he taken such risks with his future for our sake?'

'You will have to look into your own heart for the answer to that question. Charlotte, you're my sister. I should be able to discuss my problems with you freely. I'm having trouble with Molly's family and it could affect . . . That is, I should be able to tell you—'

'Don't tell me! You have given me enough to think about. I can't concentrate on anything more.' She stood up and began walking quickly along the winding path. 'I am very upset, Billy. Matthew should not have interfered. If Vic and I ended in jail, it would serve us right. He shouldn't have done it.'

Billy cut across the closely shaved grass to catch up with her. 'He's not afraid of involving himself with other people. It was a thoughtful thing to do. He cares about us all, while you only care for yourself. You may be an artist, but you're damned selfish into the bargain!' These last words were shouted after her as she now ran towards the house. Billy collected his driving clothes and left Capel without speaking to his sister again.

The next day, Charlotte returned to Town. She had an appointment with a countess on Park Lane. The commission promised to be a very large one, and she needed to have a clear mind in order to devise a scheme worthy of her client.

On the advice of Lady Smythe, Charlotte never knocked at the tradesmen's entrance, no matter how grand the home she was visiting, so it was the tall, haughty butler who opened the front door to her. In spite of herself, she was intimidated. He instructed her to sit down in the hall, and she was given a full fifteen minutes in which to study the huge space she would be required to fill with flowers. The many-prismed chandelier hung on a thick chain all the way from the top floor; the staircase snaked around it, cantilevered into space. Black and white marble squares gave added drama to the entrance. The area to be filled was larger than any she had ever attempted. Situated in a dark corner, so overpowered by the size of the room that she hadn't noticed it at first, was an old sedan chair. Charlotte walked over to examine it closely. She had heard of this odd means of conveyance, but had never actually seen one. A relic of the eighteenth century, the sedan chair was quite simply a tall box with poles on either side. The passenger rode inside, carried along by two sweating men.

'Miss Blair?'

Charlotte started, then straightened the collar of beads around her neck, while resisting the temptation to adjust her turban. Such fussy actions suggested nervousness, and she wished to appear as calm as possible. 'Lady Fitzhampton? How do you do? I was just admiring your sedan chair. A delightful reminder of past times.'

'Yes,' said the countess. 'It has been in my husband's family for several generations. The drawing-room and the dining-room are on the first floor. Shall we?'

She indicated the curving staircase and led the way, an attractive woman in her early thirties. Mr Felton might retain the custom of the older generation. He might get all those commissions associated with the Royal Family, but C. A. Blair was fast becoming the floral decorator of choice for young ladies of quality.

On the way up to the reception rooms, Charlotte counted the stairs, calculating how long the swag would have to be, how many large arrangements on pedestals she would have to organize. The dining-room was very grand and quite chilling. The table could seat sixty persons, she was told, but there were to be only forty for dinner on the night in question.

Her knees felt weak. What on earth could she do to fill this room? 'Sedan chairs,' she said.

'Bring it upstairs, you mean? Have it here in the dining-room? But what for?'

'Sedan chairs,' repeated Charlotte, who had no other idea. 'On the dining table.'

'But it would be too large, surely. And it would scratch the wood beneath.'

Charlotte strode down the room, turned at the bottom and spoke with more authority than she felt. 'Small models of sedan chairs, echoing the one in the hall. Made of bamboo and covered with yellow flowers, whatever can be obtained in September. Probably chrysanthemums. The handles to be covered entirely in ivy or myrtle. There should be at least two of them, about two or three feet high. This table is so wide, conversation across it would be impossible, so why not have sedan chairs? And more sedan chairs in the ballroom. I shall decorate the one in the hall. Sedan chairs everywhere.'

The countess was frowning, trying to imagine her Georgian table bearing two or more miniature sedan chairs. 'A Georgian theme, do you mean? I . . . I think I like it.'

'The dominant colour would be yellow—'

'I have some vaseline wine glasses. They belonged to my grandmother.'

'Vaseline?' asked Charlotte, thrown into confusion.

'I'll just . . .' The countess, still not totally convinced of the beauty of Charlotte's scheme, went to a speaking tube beside the fireplace and called to someone to bring a selection of the vaseline wine glasses.

It transpired that vaseline was a rather nauseous shade of yellowy green, the colour, in fact, of the ointment. Charlotte grandly approved of the glasses, saying she would build her colour scheme around the vaseline, while secretly vowing never to be taken by surprise again. In future, she would bring Letitia with her. The girl travelled in circles scarcely less grand than the one in which the countess intended to make an impression.

Lady Fitzhampton, having placed a selection of her glasses on the table, began talking animatedly to her butler. His icy manner had melted. Models of sedan chairs? How amusing, my lady. Yes, that would be very dramatic. He would make sure Miss Blair and her staff had every assistance. The countess talked for a little longer, then pronounced herself pleased with the proposal. She made no enquiries about cost, but left Charlotte in the capable hands of the butler.

Now began the real work, the calculations of numbers of flowers, the schedule of work, the arranging of supplies. It would be necessary to lay out as much as five hundred pounds on flowers and foliage, vases and wages. The florist, Moyses Stevens, had a staff of thirty;

C. A. Blair must expand to ten people. That number would be needed to dress Lady Fitzhampton's house on the day of the party. She had recently taken possession of a small motor van, which had necessitated engaging a young man to drive it, and, as it turned out, considerable expense due to the frequent repairs. She was so deeply in debt that she sometimes day-dreamed about running away to some far-off land and never coming back.

She felt as if she were walking an endless tightrope. She mustn't look down, mustn't hesitate or doubt, must continue to find new commissions to pay the bills for past clients who had not yet paid her. It was a daunting prospect, with no end in sight. Sometimes she wondered why she carried on, but the thrill of seeing her ideas made real kept her at her work. Floral decorating was the breath of life to her. Matthew couldn't understand what drove her, and she would be hard put to express it in words. She knew, however, that she was too absorbed in her work ever to put herself out to solve the problems of others, as he was prepared to do.

Occasionally, since her conversation with Billy, she had been stricken with feelings that dangerously approached guilt. The pressures of work came to her rescue. At night, she was so tired that instant sleep prevented her from considering her predicament.

What remained of her peace of mind was shattered on the twenty-seventh of the month, two days before Mrs Carradice's dinner party, when she went to the market to buy roses for the table. She needed hundreds, six dozen of which must be in a deep shade of red.

'Where has your mind been lately, old girl?' asked her usual supplier. 'Don't you read the papers? There ain't a rose in the market that ain't already spoken for, nor will there be until after the Command Performance at the Palace Theatre.'

'You don't understand, Freddie,' she said patiently. 'I only want six dozen red roses and about a gross of other colours. Surely, you can let me have them today or tomorrow.'

He laughed roughly, making a joke about her to one of his assistants before explaining the situation. 'The Palace Theatre is to be decorated with roses for the Command Performance, which, if you don't know, is on July the first. They're using three million roses! Three million! Every rose in the country has been spoken for. There's none to be had.'

Charlotte gaped at the man, half a dozen thoughts jostling in her mind; she couldn't calculate how much money would have to be paid out in advance by the decorator. How could any firm stand the expense? Yet how magnificent to be called upon to decorate for the King and Queen! And how vexing that her scheme for Mrs Carradice would have to be altered.

Letitia and Alice accompanied her to the Carradice home. The bride was extremely nervous and would not leave them alone, preferring to watch their every move. Charlotte and her helpers went to work immediately, since the cloth had already been placed on the table. The three women began covering it with shallow troughs of damp silver sand. The containers were ugly, but they would not be seen. Over the troughs were placed small leaves of *Lycopodium* and other ferns, either lying on the cloth or with their stems anchored in the sand. Great hummocks of velvety moss were laid all over the table. Finally, six dozen bright red carnations on six- to ten-inch stems were inserted into water-filled test tubes pushed through the moss into the sand troughs where they were held upright. The effect was very dramatic, as if carnations were growing magically in a mossy vale. The entire cloth was covered, leaving just enough space for the dinner plates and cutlery. The wine glasses and other necessary condiment containers were placed on small platforms covered in green velvet.

Large floral balls, each one containing forty or fifty carnations, were suspended by red velvet bows in front of the windows. The work was taxing, but the women were very well organized and finished the table within two hours. The floral balls had, of course, been completed earlier.

'It is so beautiful!' exclaimed Mrs Carradice. 'I just can't wait until the party tonight. My gown exactly matches the flowers. It doesn't matter that you were not able to purchase roses. I think I quite prefer the carnations. My husband and I will see enough roses at the Command Performance, if what you tell me is true. But, can I be sure that the flowers won't wilt before this evening?'

Charlotte picked up a water-filled wine bottle with a glass squirter inserted into the top. 'The flowers will be quite all right. It is the moss that must concern us. Using this squirter, just spray the table once this afternoon and again, just before the guests sit down to dine.' She handed the squirter to the butler who nodded his head solemnly. Mrs Carradice was nervous about the moss, but said she placed her trust in Jennings.

Alice and Letitia had a number of vital tasks to perform the next morning. Molly was once again unwell, and Florence was not available, so Charlotte took Horace, the van driver, with her to the Carradice home to clear away the moss and ferns, and retrieve her sand-filled troughs. To her surprise, both Mr and Mrs Carradice joined her in the dining-room.

'So you're the fool who has ruined my table!' said Mr Carradice, as the butler stood stricken by the door and the forlorn bride sat down in a carving chair, sobbing loudly. 'Look what you have done! I won't pay your account, of that you can be sure. The water penetrated the cloth and the padding below. Stains! Look at them! The table will have to be stripped down and french polished.'

Mr Carradice was a tall, smartly dressed man of forty, with a full head of dark hair which was whitening at the temples. There was about him such an air of certainty and of pride that Charlotte began to tremble. The table had been cleared, revealing ugly marks, mostly outlines of the troughs.

'I arranged that table beautifully,' she said. 'It was sprayed too much after I left. I certainly am not responsible for the damage, sir.'

'Who sprayed the table?' demanded Mr Carradice. 'Jennings?'

'I did spray it once or twice, sir,' said the poor butler. 'Not wanting the moss to dry out, you see. But . . .' he looked towards his master's young wife.

She jumped to her feet in alarm. 'I didn't know Jennings had done it, Oswald. I sprayed the table three or four times. I wanted it to be beautiful to impress—'

'You little idiot! I don't need to impress anyone. I am a Carradice of the Ayrshire Carradices. My mother was right about you. You can't be trusted to perform the meanest of tasks. Have you no sense at all? Why did you not simply have the silver-gilt epergne filled with roses, as has always been done in the past?'

Mrs Carradice bent her head. The sight of the pretty little rabbit with her big brown eyes being reduced to such misery had a strange effect on Charlotte. 'How dare you speak so rudely to your wife in the presence of a servant and tradespeople? Have you no dignity? Poor Mrs Carradice wanted to impress *you*, not your guests. She is your bride and you should cherish her. I am disgusted at your behaviour and my bill is two hundred and fifty pounds. I have it with me.' She smoothed out the account and placed it on the damaged table. 'You are jolly lucky to have had my services. I am in great demand. Every young woman of consequence wants me to do her floral decorating. I daresay there were a great many compliments about the table last night.'

'Oh, yes,' said Mrs Carradice, while her husband stood transfixed by Charlotte's audacity.

'Horace,' called Charlotte. The boy was cowering by the door, his face a deep red. 'Pick up these troughs and take them out to the van. Payment by the end of the month, Mr Carradice, if you please.' She gathered up four of the troughs, checked that the moss and ferns had already been thrown away and marched from the dining-room with her head high. No-one called her back.

When they were seated in the van, Charlotte squeezed her eyes closed and took several deep breaths. 'I do not want to discuss what has just happened, Horace.'

'No, ma'am.'

'And I don't want to find it is being discussed with the others.'

'No, ma'am.'

There was a silence, heavy with shock. 'What on earth am I going to do now?' she asked rhetorically. 'Mr Carradice will never pay his bill.'

'I don't know,' replied Horace. 'If I was in your shoes, I'd just go out and hang myself.'

Hearing her high-pitched laughter, Horace turned his eyes from the road and smiled at her. But the laughter went on and on; the boy concentrated on his driving and began to wonder if he would have a job for very much longer.

A pyramid fuchsia wasn't like a standard fuchsia, not by a long chalk. If John Green had said it once, he had said it a dozen times to Mabel and her mother. You trained your standard over a period of years, growing the stem as tall as you wanted it, topping it off with a fine head of firm branches covered in blooms, or else growing a basket variety and training the head over a wire umbrella. After all danger of frost was past, you gave them over to Jacko to plant at the back of the border, or perhaps in the rose garden where they bloomed from late summer to the autumn.

Pyramids were different. It took a special variety to produce a decent pyramid, a strong bushy plant like 'Lye's Unique' with its white tube and sepals and its bright, orangey-salmon petals. A pyramid fuchsia could be coaxed over three years to grow seven to ten feet tall and so big around its base that a man's arms wouldn't encompass it. To move it out of doors, you had to put it on a trolley, and there was no question of planting it in the garden. Pyramids deserved a special position in the garden, or even in the conservatory if there was one. Pyramids deserved to be enjoyed, and the grower deserved to be appreciated.

Not every gardener knew the secret of growing this difficult shape. During the first year you kept the cultivar in a six-inch pot, and as each shoot grew it had to be gently tied upwards to a strong cane that had been slipped into the pot next to the central stem. During the first winter, growth had to be cut back to the first leaf joint and every leaf removed to give the plant a rest. Growing was started again in February when the plant was put into a larger pot with a taller, stronger cane. And once more every shoot had to be gently, oh so gently lest it snap, tied to the central cane with raffia. And now the plant was in a sixteen-inch pot. From May onwards the pyramid needed misting and feeding every day.

By the third year, a well-grown fuchsia, with foliage all the way down to the pot and all the way up to ten feet, would require one whole day's attention each week. And John had three pyramids.

As head gardener, he naturally had other responsibilities as well. He should be ensuring that the garden looked its best. He was, after all, paid to be head gardener, not a fuchsia grower. Normally, he would have relied on Jacko Boon to plan out the work and apportion jobs to the men, Jacko was in serious trouble. John, naturally, wished to help the man. Besides, if he could just get Jacko fixed up in reasonable employment elsewhere, he would be able to forget his own part in petty thieving and live the rest of his life with a clear conscience. He had vowed to himself never to manipulate the figures again, and he reckoned he had paid for his crime with hours of remorse and the fear of exposure.

Only the other day, he had told Jacko about a nursery that was up for sale in Cheshunt – an eighth of an acre of glass, with a snug two-bedroom cottage on the two-acre site. There was room to expand, and sweet peas were grown on an acre of the open land. With permission from John, Jacko had gone off to investigate. An hour later he had returned, looking gloomy.

'Sweet-pea seed is expensive,' said Jacko morosely, 'and the land has to be heavily manured. A lot of labour is needed. The season only lasts from April to the middle of July. When the stems begin to shorten, they ain't worth sending to market. Last year they fetched only half a crown for a dozen bunches at the height of the season. The old couple what own the place can't make a go of it.' —

'And what are they growing under glass?'

'Toms. I don't know nothing about growing tomatoes. Everything needs repairing. The house is falling down.'

'You'll just have to get Mr Douse to stump up more money.'

Jacko looked away, offering no answer.

'You have discussed this with Mr Douse, haven't you? He is happy for you to marry his daughter and he is going to set you up in business, isn't he?'

Jacko gave his friend a wry smile. 'Not exactly. Florence says he will do it, but I'm beginning to have my doubts.'

Jacko might have his doubts. For his part, John was certain that Mr Douse would not help his daughter to marry a gardener. It had all been a dream, some moonlight madness. Jacko would never marry Miss Florence Douse. He and John would continue to live at Capel Manor, sharing a disgraceful secret, until John was able to escape by emigrating. If the truth were known, Jacko was a fortunate man. John could certainly tell him that so-called wedded bliss was a delusion.

He finished watering all the pot fuchsias that had

not been planted in the grounds. He had a thousand of them. For some reason, he could not bring himself to destroy a single cutting, although there was never room for them all in the garden, nor were they wanted indoors. All must be fed, pinched, watered and shaded during the heat of the day. Very little time was left for anything else.

He took off his apron, changed his shoes and washed his hands vigorously under the tap in the glasshouse, then walked to the lodge for his dinner, praying that illness or disaster had prevented Mrs Wheems from coming to Capel for the midday meal. Soon, he told himself, he would see the last of her ugly face.

'Well, here he is at last,' said Mrs Wheems as he entered the kitchen. 'Got your hands washed? Here's Mabel standing over the stove for hours to make a nice steak and kidney pud and you come in late.'

'Only five minutes late,' he said. He hated kidney. Mabel knew he hated kidney and so did Mrs Wheems.

'And what has the great gardener done today?'

He glared at his mother-in-law. 'Nothing much. Just tending to a fuchsia seedling that I crossed last year which will probably make my fortune, that's all. It grows kind of lax but it's upright. Single flowers with light crimson sepals, all ribbed and whorled. That's the top bit of the flower that sort of wings back to reveal the corolla, the petals which are a pale mauve. But, and here's the important thing, every petal is edged with violet. I'm going to call it "Capel Bells".'

'If it's so wonderful, why didn't you name it after your wife?' asked Mrs Wheems, sitting back in her chair and staring at him through half closed eyes.

'Because I want to call it "Capel Bells". It was grown at Capel. I work at Capel. I want to call it "Capel Bells". Do you know what it's called when a petal has an edge of a different colour? A picotee, like picotee carnations. That's what "Capel Bells" has got. Kind of mauvy purple petals with a violet edge.'

'That's nice.' Mabel spooned a large helping of pudding onto his plate. He could see the little rubbery pieces of kidney glistening in dark gravy.

'A Take-a-pee, did you say?' cackled Mrs Wheems. 'Well, fancy that. Maybe you should name it Take-a-pee.'

'That's not funny. It's going to be a beautiful cultivar and it's got light green foliage with pale red stems and veins, and it's all mine. I found it and recognized it and I've got the plants coming on. They'll be blooming in a few weeks. Then you'll see.' With his fork, he slid the kidney to the edge of his plate and began eating the thick suet crust.

'Look at that, Mabel. Look how he gets rid of the kidney. If I was you, I wouldn't cook for him. He don't appreciate. Him and his Take-a-pee.'

Mable giggled. John threw down his fork. 'If you think I'm so awful, why did you marry me? Answer me that. Your old lady's here morning, noon and night. We're never alone. If you didn't want to leave home, why did you marry me? I'm sick to death of having her round here all the time. I make a good wage and you spend every penny.'

'You shouldn't talk that way,' said Mabel. 'You shouldn't talk like that. I married you because you asked me. If you didn't like my mother, why did you ask me to marry you?'

'I asked you, not her. Anyway, I'm sorry now I did. I've got a good job. Head gardener is a bloody good job. Joseph Paxton was a head gardener and he designed the Crystal Palace and became a Member of Parliament and got to be a millionaire. You can go a long way, being a head gardener, and I'd like to see a little appreciation.'

Mabel started to cry. 'I appreciate you.'

'You and your Take-a-pee,' snarled Mrs Wheems. 'You talk about them flowers as if they was your babies.'

'They *are* my babies.'

Mabel wailed, as her mother pounced on the words. 'You got another sort of baby coming into this family,

Mr Smarty-pants. A real one what needs a father with some sense.'

'Mabel!'

His wife's plain face crumpled and her entire body sagged into her chair. 'You don't love me. You don't want a baby,' she whined.

He had to admit, but only to himself, that this was true. How could he leave her now? How could he sail to America to begin a new life? For several seconds, he said nothing, fighting the sense of choking, of being trapped and gasping for air. A cup of tea was within reach, but he daren't stretch out an arm, daren't let these two women see his hand shake.

'That's wonderful. When is it due?'

Mabel opened her mouth to answer, but Mrs Wheems said, 'January.'

'I asked my wife a question and when I want an answer from you, I'll let you know. Now, shut your face and don't you never come into this house again until I invite you. You're a nosey old cow and I'm sick to death of looking at you. I'm off to America for sure. So there!'

'Well, I like that!' exclaimed Mrs Wheems, but to his absolute amazement, she rose from her chair as she said it, reached for her cardigan and headed for the door. 'If he harms one hair on your head, Mabel, you come home to your mother.'

The door slammed behind her. Mabel bent her head, racked with sobs. John, stunned by his unexpected victory, picked up his knife and fork and began to eat. Eventually, he even finished off the kidney pieces. He drank his tea and wiped his mouth with the back of his hand. Then, rising, he patted his wife on the head and left the house. He was beginning to feel a little better, a little less like he was choking. He was beginning to feel like a man who had bested his mother-in-law in a battle of words. Mabel wouldn't cry for long. She never did when there was no-one to watch. One time, he had sneaked back to the house and peeked through the kitchen window, angered to find her quite cheerfully washing the dishes and humming to herself, the way she did when she was happy. Since that day, Mabel's tears had no power to move him.

At this hour, the men would be eating their dinner in the bothy. He supposed the Duck sisters were also sitting down to their dinner. As for Miss Blair, she was in London. For another half an hour, the garden would belong entirely to John. He walked the narrow paths of the vegetable garden, past wigwams of beans and regiments of cabbages, feathered carrot tops and deep green borders of parsley, to reach his favourite part of the leisure grounds.

The richness of the formal garden, with its calceolarias and geraniums, its alyssums and lobelias and canna lilies gleaming in the hot sun, warmed his soul. For the first time in his life, he sat down in the shade of the honeysuckle arbour and laid one arm along the back of the wrought-iron bench. It was a beautiful garden. Even with his mind full of worry about Florence, Jacko had planted this part of the garden to perfection. There wasn't a weed in sight, not a fallen leaf nor a bloom past its best.

Capel Manor suited John. He decided not to leave home, after all. Not with the baby on the way. The lodge was comfortable, and he was proud that he was going to be a father. Today he had discovered a new strength. Whenever she got out of hand, he would threaten Mabel with his departure. Or, if the mood took him, he would demand that she emigrate with him to America. That would keep her in line and cut his mother-in-law down to size. He would be as much in charge of his home as of this garden. And in two or three weeks, when the sepals of 'Capel Bells' burst open to reveal a thin line of darker colour edging each petal, he would find reasons to be happy and content with his lot.

Chapter Eighteen

Saturday, July the sixth, was the day of the Jubilee at Haileybury School. Matthew had every intention of attending. For this reason, he had taken advantage of the Admiral's hospitality and arrived at Theobalds Park late on Friday night.

His valet was due to arrive the following morning, but Matthew had shaved and dressed himself by the time the morose Scot arrived with a cablegram that had been delivered to his London address. It was from Australia.

Land purchase in area of great activity. Geologist hopeful. Gold tellurides. Sylvanite. Further report soon.

'Chalker, I must go over to Capel Manor at once. See if you can get someone from the stable to drive me in the fly. I'm sure the Admiral won't object.'

Chalker left the room and Matthew sat down on his bed to read the startling news again. The message was necessarily brief, the language technical. Nevertheless, the magic word *gold* lit up the small buff sheet. He could not believe the good fortune of three rogues who didn't deserve to escape so easily from a mess of their own making. Once more, he read the fifteen words, impatient to be at Capel, to see Charlotte's face when he told her the great news. Perhaps Vic would also be spending the weekend. Matthew would be able to point out that virtue could be rewarded. If the men had gone about their project honestly, they might now be very wealthy.

Vic was staying at Capel Manor, together with Popple

Douse and Florence. Matthew found them and Charlotte seated in the shade of a chestnut tree on the front lawn, and jumped from the fly to join them before the horse had come to a halt. They all rose to greet him, sensing that his undignified behaviour signalled either great good news or a catastrophe.

'Well, I'll be damned,' said Vic when Matthew had finished reading the cable to them all. 'What do you think of that? We struck gold! Let me see that cable. I just can't hardly take it all in. We struck gold. It was there all along. Nobody was going to be cheated. You were too hard on us, Matthew.'

'I must remind you that you would have cheated your customers if I had not stepped in. You see, it is possible to run a successful business honestly.'

Charlotte had said nothing when he announced the good news. Matthew saw her turn away and walk off towards the low ditch, the ha-ha, that kept the horse from trespassing onto the south lawn. He moved away from Vic and the Douses and caught up with her.

'Aren't you pleased with my news?'

She turned and he saw the tears standing in her eyes. 'So relieved. I was afraid you would be imprisoned for my . . . my father's crime. It has been a great strain.'

'You look terrible.'

She managed a wry smile. 'I must get away from everyone. Shall we walk in the formal garden? I don't visit the rose garden at the moment. The roses went over so quickly in the heat. And now it will be weeks before we have a second flush.'

'I would be delighted to walk in the formal garden. I am to attend the Jubilee at Haileybury School this afternoon. Would you care to come with me?'

Charlotte waved to Vic and the Douses, indicating that she and Matthew would be going off alone, but they scarcely noticed, being occupied in a loud discussion of the gold find.

'Thirty people are coming for an *al fresco* supper this

316

evening,' she said. 'Local growers. The Rochfords and the Pauls, the Pelhams and the Butterfields and Mr and Mrs Kitson, of course. Perhaps you could join us when you return from Haileybury. I must stay here to see to the arrangements.'

'I would be delighted to join you. Have you made some exotic floral arrangements for the house as you did for my Japanese guests?'

She shook her head. 'I didn't do it for the Japanese. I did it for you. Today there will just be some simple low arrangements for the tables out of doors. Billy told me that you guaranteed the return of the investors' money. Is that true?'

'Yes, but it was not needed. I intend to go into a business venture with a friend of mine, Buffy Morrison. Now that my money will no longer be needed to prevent the police from knocking on the door, I shall invest some of it with Tokyo Nursery Company. I have been retained as an adviser, but they have also invited me onto the board of directors.'

'How wonderful! But you purchased my shares in Goldseekers.'

Matthew laughed. 'It seems that no money actually changed hands for your shares. Popple Douse is a genius when it comes to juggling sums on paper. Nothing, happily, is required of me beyond paying for the exploration in Australia. I shall soon be reimbursed for that, I dare say. All's well that ends well.'

They reached the formal garden, having walked most of the way in thoughtful but friendly silence. Charlotte went immediately to the wrought-iron bench which was shaded from the hot July sun by the scrambling honeysuckle. She sat down, rubbed the back of her neck and closed her eyes. 'My head aches.'

Matthew slid his arm along the back of the seat and laid a hand gently on Charlotte's shoulder. 'My dear, what is wrong? I hate to see you looking so sad.'

Her eyes opened. She looked at him in surprise.

'Does it show? I have been at great pains to give the impression of being a happy, successful business woman. I am in such a mess, Matthew. I am heavily in debt.' He started to speak, but she held up her hand. 'I don't want your money. I would be quite well off if my customers would just pay me on time. I have to admit that there have been a few disasters. The Carradices, for one. Their mahogany dining table was ruined.'

'Yes, so I heard. But I will tell you a little secret. Oswald Carradice was very taken with you. He is exceedingly wealthy and will pay your account. I strongly advise you to keep your distance from him, however. He found you almost as attractive as I do.'

'He did? He said that? I thought he might sue me for insolence.'

'Happily, English law doesn't recognize such an offence. Have there been other—'

'Oh, yes! I did a dining-room with a lavender theme. Heliotrope, lavender and masses of lily of the valley. It was a wet night. The windows were closed and the perfume became oppressive. Two of the ladies had to leave the room before the pudding, and the client's husband said I had totally destroyed the taste of his fine wines.'

'Have they refused to pay?'

'No, but they will not recommend me.'

'My dear,' he said gently. 'These are surely the fortunes of commercial life. Every business has its little catastrophes. Tokyo Nursery also has problems of this sort. We are doing some work on the Japanese garden at Fanhams Hall in Ware. Things have gone wrong, I assure you, but all will be well in the end.'

'My worst moment,' she said, her voice faltering, 'was when I was asked to arrange some heavy branches in a huge Ming vase. To steady the branches, I poured in some sand and gravel. I just tipped it in all at once. The vase cracked.'

'My God,' said Matthew, able to sympathize fully with the owner.

Charlotte bent her head and covered her face with her hands. Matthew was deeply moved. He didn't know exactly how it happened, but she was suddenly in his arms, her head on his shoulder. Their knees were pressed together as they twisted on the bench in an awkward embrace.

'Don't cry,' he murmured, stroking the nape of her neck, and after a moment or two she was still. A small, work-worn hand crept up to caress his cheek. Quickly, he turned to kiss the palm, her temple, her lips. She responded, clinging to him, returning his kisses with passion.

'You can't say you don't love me, Charlotte. I know you do.'

'Yes I do but let's not talk about the past.'

'I want you to marry me. I have a respectable post with the nursery company. You love Capel as much as I do. We can manage somehow. Say you'll be my wife.'

She lifted her head. 'I was wrong to say no before. Stupid. Afraid to allow myself the luxury of loving, afraid of being hurt. Of course I'll marry you. Don't speak, my darling. Just kiss me.'

He kissed her again, long and hard. 'So you see, there will be no more of this distressing business of hoping to please the likes of Oswald Carradice. As my wife, you need never work again. You would be willing to give up your flower arranging business for me, wouldn't you?'

The joy that had so recently brightened her face, disappeared in an instant. Why must people talk so much? she wondered. It always led to pain. 'Why do I have to choose? How can I decide to give up the work I love? If you loved me, you wouldn't ask it.'

'I love you more than anyone or anything on earth. I want you to love me the same way. How can you place my needs second? As chatelaine of this house, you will be fully occupied. Of course, you must use your skills to decorate our own home, to entertain our guests. You will, I presume, wish to have children. Would you want to be for ever running off to the homes of others to ensure the success of their dinner parties while your own children cry for you? Why can't you love me more than you love flowers?'

She stood up, took a few deep breaths and wiped the tears of anger from her cheeks. 'You just don't understand, do you? I am pleased for you in your appointment to the board of a proper business. However, knowing you as I do, I am certain that you would willingly give up the work in order to sit about the house all day smoking a pipe—'

'I no longer smoke—'

'Reading the newspapers and chatting with your fashionable friends. But I have a calling. I'm driven to arrange flowers. You have my permission to laugh at me, since it is inconceivable that you would understand.'

He stood up, too, eager to continue the quarrel in the hope that plain speaking would lead to a greater understanding. He had faith in his powers of persuasion, but before he could marshal his thoughts to make a telling point, Rachel came trotting into the formal garden with his manservant from Theobalds at her heels.

'What is it, Rachel?'

'A message from Theobalds, Mr Warrender. It seems Mr Bowles has a visitor. What's her name?' Rachel turned to Chalker.

'Miss Gertrude Jekyll, sir. She's visiting him. They want to come here to Capel Manor in about twenty minutes to see your garden.'

'Good God, what an honour!' He turned to Charlotte, his eyebrows raised in silent enquiry.

'Of course they must come. Telephone Mr Bowles, Matthew,' said Charlotte. 'I must run upstairs and change my gown.'

'Bowles has no telephone. Have you come in the fly, old chap? Good. Ride over to Myddleton House and say that I will be delighted to take them on a tour of the grounds.'

'Miss Blair,' said Rachel, 'we got all them people coming tonight. My sister and me can't get up a decent afternoon tea for visitors. We just ain't got the time.'

'I'll help you,' said Charlotte.

'No, you won't,' snapped Matthew. 'You will get changed. This house is understaffed indoors, while outside there are too many people doing too little. Where is Mrs Horn? She will help, and Mrs Green must be called into service temporarily.'

'Oh, Lordy,' said Rachel. 'There's going to be fun and games in the kitchen today!' She went off at the trot, followed by Chalker.

Dangler Stritch bent to his work in the vegetable garden, revelling in the heat of the sun on his back. Monday would see the beginning of the summer pruning of wall fruit. He didn't trust anyone to attend to the peaches and nectarines. The leaves had to be turned back around each fruit so that it could ripen properly, a delicate job that gave him much pleasure.

There wasn't a weed to be found among the vegetables and fruit. You saved yourself a lot of work by stirring the soil frequently, keeping the weeds from taking hold. He had cut a vast quantity of asparagus for the house on this important Saturday. There would be none for the next three weeks, and what there was might not be very tasty. After midsummer's day, you shouldn't cut asparagus.

He had made sure that a crop of Dutch Long Pod beans had been sown the day before. This morning, they had pricked out the latest spring crop of broccoli, capsicums and cabbage.

The paths, which ran north to south and east to west, were packed hard, had a gentle slope to either side so that rain water would run off them, and were covered evenly in gravel. Dangler knew he was a first-rate kitchen gardener, despite the disaster with the grapes.

He could bring on the early salads under lights or in cold frames. He was master of the hot bed, that tricky heap of horse manure that had to be managed just so, lest the early heat should cook the roots, or else seedlings, transplanted too late, failed to grow away. It was his pride that there were potatoes, cabbages and cauliflowers all the year round. As for the cordoned fruit, it was acknowledged by Mr Green himself that he was a genius with the pruning knife. In addition to the cordons, Dangler was in the process of training four pyramid pear trees. Mr Green might pride himself on his pyramid fuchsias, but Dangler reckoned it took just as much skill to train a pear tree into a pyramid. The soil in the walled garden was in prime nick, if he did say so himself. Double digging, plenty of horse manure and careful crop rotation had seen to that.

His young days had been spent on a farm in West Hertfordshire. Dangler had been thirteen when he was apprenticed to Mr Hobday; he had found the early years sheer hell. When it came time to plant out the seedlings in the fields, the old man used to stand at the far end of the row with an alarm clock. Seven minutes was all you had to prick out cabbage plants that had reached the two-leaved stage. You handled each plant as little as possible, holding it by one leaf, gently but safely, put it into one side of the hole you had dibbed, pressed soil up against it and moved on, never straightening your back until you reached the end of the row. And God help you if it took more than seven minutes. Those were hard days that Dangler now looked back on with a degree of pride.

Commercial growers, whether they were farmers or in the glasshouse trade, had to make every second count. There was no time to exercise one's finer talents. It was get up in the morning, work full out until dinner time, fall into bed at night, only to start the whole thing over again the next day.

Dangler was very happy at Capel Manor. He had a room to himself in the bothy, a head gardener who never made any demands on him, and time to prepare each day's vegetable order for the big house with care.

He'd pack the basket for Mrs Duck with all the skill of an artist preparing a composition to paint. Often, he would walk up to the kitchen himself and discuss with the cook what was at its best that day. The only pity was, there was usually no-one living in the big house to appreciate what Dangler produced.

This day was different, of course. There was to be quite a dinner party. *Al fresco*, they called it. Cold meats of all sorts, prime salads and six or seven different puddings to delight the guests. There were few strawberries left, and those that remained were past their best, but Mrs Duck had hit upon a way of using them that should please the palate.

Dangler liked to see a neat but attractive edge to the paths. None of your low box hedging for him. Better to have mint, carefully controlled in sunken troughs, parsley and scented geranium, borage and other herbs along the edge. He was huddled down, trimming the spearmint edging, half hidden by the cold frames, when he became aware of a party standing at the west doorway. Startled, he looked up to see Miss Blair and Mr Warrender with Mr Bowles and an elderly lady with a black hat on the top of her white hair. He realized with an excited thump of his heart that he recognized the lady who was speaking.

'Yes, Mr Warrender, you must have to deal with that middle class of gardener, a man of narrow mental training, in all probability. Now you, sir, as a boy at public school, undoubtedly had any petty or personal nonsense knocked out of you at an early age. You have been in the great world, widening your ideas and experience. You have, I am sure, cultivated your taste in literature and the fine arts. I daresay if you employ a narrow-minded gardener who believes that he already knows everything important about gardening – and to his mind, that will be the technical part – so he will imagine his crude ideas about the arrangement of flowers are as good as yours.'

'They probably are, Miss Jekyll.'

'He will object to your criticism, will fail to see

that he can only reach to a dead-level of dullness, compared with what you might produce. In your fully justified criticisms, his small-minded vanity will only see a distrust of his own ability. You must take charge of this garden.'

'I fear I am totally unsuited to the task, but I would value any suggestions of yours, ma'am,' said Mr Warrender. Dangler thought he could detect a scarcely controlled anger in Miss Blair's nervous fidgeting. She looked very put out, and turned her back at one point.

'This area would make an excellent pleasure garden,' said Miss Jekyll.

She was a famous lady gardener whose books and articles on the subject were well known to Dangler.

'The vegetables could be moved elsewhere, but there would be no need to move the wall fruit. I would suggest removing the present utilitarian paths in favour of stone ones coming from the four corners, converging at the centre with a sundial or armillary. And pergolas, of course, wisteria-covered to provide a cool walk on a hot summer day such as this. Or you might grow grapes. The beds should contain a mixture of roses and delphiniums, yuccas and hydrangeas, choosing your colours carefully to create a striking effect. You must have some carnations, not those huge things that florists are over-fond of, but the old gilliflower. Put in low plants like *Alchemilla mollis* close to the path and allow them to encroach to soften the line. You will need grey-leaved foliage, that's most important. Oh, yes, if I were you, Mr Warrender, I should set about moving the vegetable garden as soon as is practical.'

The party turned away at the invitation of Miss Blair who said that tea was ready on the south lawn. Dangler sat back on his heels and thought about what he had heard. Could it be that Mr Warrender knew all about the designing of a garden just from having been to a public school? It seemed unlikely. However, Dangler was prepared to believe that Mr Green was a man incapable of finer feelings for the grounds. The head gardener thought about nothing but fuchsias, cared about nothing but fuchsias, to the detriment of the gardens. Often Dangler would lie on his bed in the evening, thinking about how he would manage Capel's grounds if he were in charge. Nevertheless, Miss Jekyll's comments were hurtful. Hadn't she seen him? Had she not cared who heard her words? Then he remembered that the great lady gardener was nearly blind, which would explain her speaking so disparagingly of the staff at a time when one of them was in a position to overhear. Then again, he wondered why she had failed to mention that a lady like herself, who had not been to one of the famous public schools, was considered to have finer taste in garden design than almost any man alive.

As they gathered for tea, Matthew explained to Florence and Popple Douse and Vic that Miss Jekyll was a notable authority on the subject of gardening, that she had written several books on the subject, that she often designed the gardens for houses built by the architect, Edwin Lutyens. Charlotte could have told him that to praise the lady so highly would only serve to make the Douses and Vic speechless with awe. What could Vic Tavern find to say to a great lady gardener? Nothing, so he kept his mouth shut. Florence stared in astonishment at Miss Jekyll for several seconds, then concentrated on her own hands whose slender fingers and well manicured nails seemed to please her. Popple Douse managed to say that it was a fine day and that he enjoyed a stroll around Capel Manor's gardens, but then his conversation ran out.

Matthew, Mr Bowles and Miss Jekyll didn't seem to notice. They talked animatedly, directing a kind question or innocuous remark to each of the others in turn. However, Miss Jekyll spoke more earnestly to Charlotte, whom she knew to be a floral decorator, saying that she approved of greenery and flowers laid directly on the cloth. 'I like light wreathes of foliage, preferably something with pinnate leaves. I disagree with Mr Felton. Coloured table runners can be quite attractive, but everything must be simple, in good taste. I cannot stress that strongly enough. Top quality china, the best silver. A range of glass vases has been made to my suggestions. Have you heard of Munstead glass?'

'I use Munstead vases, Miss Jekyll. Funnel-shaped glassware doesn't hold enough water to keep flowers alive for more than a few hours. Munstead glass vases are ideal.'

'Where table decorations are concerned, every hostess is a slave of fashion, but styles change continually, and I suppose it is your duty, Miss Blair, to give customers what they crave.'

This was patently true, and Charlotte could not disagree, although she was still annoyed by Miss Jekyll's ridiculous praise of public school boys.

'Women like ourselves are capable of fashioning taste, are we not?' said Charlotte, then thought that her remark sounded absurdly conceited. 'In our different spheres, I mean. You are . . . but I am only . . . that is—'

'Quite correct, Miss Blair,' said Matthew, coming to her rescue. 'Miss Jekyll has had enormous influence on the style of gardening in this country. While you have turned the heads of all young hostesses who wish to be à la mode.'

'You have an enviable reputation, Miss Blair,' added Miss Jekyll, and went on, ignoring Charlotte's blushes, 'I hear you spoken of everywhere. Daring and original, and willing to try something new. A true artist is always experimenting.'

Charlotte resisted the temptation to test the heat of her cheeks with her hands. 'Experimenting, but not always successfully.'

'But of course you can't always be successful. An artist working in any medium must fail in order to go forward. You're a clever girl.' Miss Jekyll patted her hand.

After that, Charlotte was quite reconciled to the great lady. Perhaps it was true, after all, that something besides confidence and exquisite manners were taught in the better educational establishments.

'Why, there's Mr Brock!' cried Florence, jumping up from her seat and walking off down the drive to meet him. He was on foot, having evidently arrived by train and walked from the station. He looked hot and, Charlotte thought, put-out to find so many people seated on the south lawn.

Miss Jekyll and Mr Bowles stayed for a few minutes after Arthur Brock arrived, then called for their carriage and made a graceful departure.

'Arthur,' said Charlotte, 'there is some very good news which Matthew will tell you. I haven't the time to hear it all again. My guests will be arriving in an hour and I haven't had the chance to prepare any decorations.'

'Hold on, old girl,' said Brock. 'Before you go, I have some news for you. I would have told you yesterday morning, but instead of coming yourself, you sent one of your girls to clear away the wilted flowers at Lady Smythe's.'

'Yes, that was Letitia. Was everything all right?'

'Top hole. That's just the point. Lady Smythe took it into her head to invite Admiral and Lady Meux when we came upon them at the races. One couple had dropped out, you see. I was surprised when they accepted at such short notice. Well, racing types, you know. We were quite a party, I can tell you. No-one spoke about anything but horses for the first three quarters of an hour. Then, the talk was all about you. Lady Meux proposes to write to you, but I think it's safe to say that she will want you to decorate her entire house and terrace for a function she's having in September. I believe they have a prime conservatory.'

'About the size and shape of a railway terminal,' said Matthew, drily. 'There should be a wealth of plant material for you to choose from, Charlotte, and thirty gardeners to offer you every assistance.'

Charlotte was too overwhelmed to speak for a second or two. This was the commission she had been striving for: a grand country house, a titled family of impeccable reputation, the chance to show the greatest people in the land what she could do. And they had not chosen the Feltons or Moyses Stevens. They had chosen C. A. Blair. Smiling, she turned to Matthew.

He made a slight, ironic bow. 'Congratulations. Everything you ever wanted.'

Her sense of triumph evaporated in an instant and she looked away. 'That is wonderful news, Arthur. I look forward to hearing from Lady Meux. Will you excuse me? I think I will have to make do with a few flowering plants in pots. There is no time to arrange anything else.'

She walked away, hearing Vic making quite a drama out of telling Brock about the cable from Australia. It was a moment or two before she realized that Matthew was following her.

'I will help you in any way I can before returning to Theobalds to change. I presume you do still wish me to stay for the party this evening. It's too late, now, to attend Haileybury's Jubilee.'

'I want you to stay more than ever. I want you to meet the real aristocracy, the commercial growers of the Lea Valley and beyond, men who have achieved something worthwhile and brought beauty into all our lives with their magnificent plants.'

He grimaced. 'The evening is to be a lesson to me in the virtues of hard work, I presume. Let me remind you that I am soon to be a member of the gardening trade. As a director of a nursery company, I believe I will qualify on that score.' Seeing John Green walking towards the house with a potted fuchsia in his hand, Matthew called out. 'I say, Mr Green! Will you come over here to lend some assistance to Miss Blair?'

The buffet was to take place on the north lawn, handy

for the back door and the kitchen. Four round tables had been set up on the lawn, each one covered with a dazzling damask cloth. About twelve feet of long narrow tables had been laid end to end, and a handsome silver coffee urn was holding the white cloth down at one end. The effect was blinding, the tables bleak in their nakedness.

'What have you in pots that I can use to decorate this area and the table?' asked Charlotte when John Green had reached their side.

His face lit up with pleasure. 'Fuchsias. I can give you a first rate display of fuchsias.'

'That will be excellent,' said Matthew. 'Miss Blair is pressed for time and must get changed for the party. That looks a splendid specimen you have in your hands.'

'Yes, sir,' said John. 'A new cultivar of my own. I call it "Capel Bells".'

Charlotte snatched the terracotta pot from John's hands. 'I don't want fuchsias, Matthew. Especially not in the open air close to the food. I'll show you why.' With considerable force, she set the pot down on the corner of the long table. Half a dozen blooms fell onto the cloth. John made a strangled noise in his throat, indicative of great pain, but he was ignored.

'Good Lord,' said Matthew. 'Do all fuchsias shed their blooms so readily?' He lifted the pot and crashed it down again. Another four blooms joined those already on the table. 'I suppose a strong breeze would carry away a few more.'

'Yes, and right into the food, more than likely.'

'Please,' croaked John. 'That's a new variety. Me own. I've called it—'

'Really, Charlotte, it doesn't matter,' said Matthew. 'Let the man arrange a display of his fuchsias. God knows it costs you enough to maintain all these plants. They shed their blooms, but there seem to be enough left on the plant. Mr Green, I want to see a really impressive display here. Make sure that the staff have room to reach the back of the serving tables and that the guests can walk freely along the front of it, but make it *impressive*, do you understand? Prove that you are worth the money being paid to you. Charlotte, go now or you will not have time to dress. I must return to Theobalds to change my clothes, but I will be as quick as I can. Where's that man of mine?'

Mabel Green had squeezed herself into a black blouse and skirt, pinned on a lace collar and tied a white apron around her waist. With a starched white cap set low on her forehead, she felt the perfect fool. Her mother, who had also been encouraged to help out, looked quite attractive in her uniform, and both women were discovering the pleasure of watching a noisy party without the necessity of making conversation. There was no need to pretend interest in the stories of others or even to be polite. The best part of this warm summer evening was listening to the private conversations of the guests. No-one seemed to notice she was within earshot. It was as good as a play.

The spread was mouth-watering: cold ham and chicken, galantines and salads, two whole salmons and, awaiting their turn to shine, half a dozen different puddings staying cool in the larder. That Jacko Boon was dressed up in a striped waistcoat and helping to serve, and Mrs Horn was in the kitchen with Mrs Duck. Mr Warrender's man, Chalker, was being very superior as he saw to it that every man and woman had a full glass of champagne. Miss Douse looked ever so pretty in a gown of white lawn with lashings of lace. For some reason, she was being very rude to Jacko and he was being very cheeky to Miss Douse. Mabel didn't approve of staff getting onto such intimate terms with the guests. As for Miss Blair, everybody knew she had strange taste in clothes. The full skirt of her blue and green gown stopped a few inches above her ankles, and Mabel could see full pantaloons drawn in at her shoe tops! Mabel was not too surprised, but she did

330

hate to see the better sorts failing to maintain their dignity.

'I hear you have a motor car, Mr Warrender,' said Mr Rochford as they stood next to the buffet table. 'We still send our plants to market by wagon. We've sixteen fine Shires and, although we now send four thousand tons by rail, the horse-drawn vans take our plants to market. The drivers mount the box and promptly fall asleep, you know. The horses walk sixteen miles to market without a single hand on the reins, one following the other. And they arrive at half past two in the morning.'

'I didn't know horses were that clever,' said Charlotte.

'Occasionally,' laughed Mr Rochford, 'some young wag – though not one of our employees – will guide the lead horse down a side street and the rest will inevitably follow. Then there is the devil to pay. Ours are not the only vans on the road at that hour. Every nurseryman in the Valley sends his produce in the same way.'

'How many acres do you have?' asked Mr Warrender.

'The family has eighty-six acres under glass.'

Mr Warrender whistled softly. 'The Rochford family must be the most important employers of labour in the whole Valley.'

'That is true, and the whole of Cheshunt turned out to show appreciation of that fact when my father died. His funeral was on the seventeenth of October, 1901. He was not an old man, but he left us a sound business. On that day, the streets were almost empty and every blind was drawn. The *cortège* left Turnford Hall at two o'clock, after about three hundred people had viewed the body. There were six mourning coaches, at least a dozen private coaches and almost five hundred people, from the various family businesses, walking behind the *cortège*. We went along Cheshunt Wash and Cheshunt Street, round by Turner's Hill and up College Road, and everywhere the streets were lined with people. I believe my father's funeral proved what the horticultural trade has done for this area. I was very proud.'

'A funeral fit for a king, Mr Rochford,' said Miss Blair. 'I would rather entertain the peerage of the nursery trade here tonight than dine with the King and Queen.'

'And I hear you may join the fraternity,' said Mr Rochford, turning to Mr Warrender. 'Tokyo Nursery? A fine company. Any time Rochfords can do business with your firm, just telephone me.'

'Magnificent display of fuchsias!' called Mr Butterfield.

Mabel's bosom expanded by an inch or two as everyone began to talk about John's fuchsias. He hadn't attempted to do anything artistic like Miss Blair would have done, just brought over some tiered staging which he set up against the wall of the house and filled the shelves with three long rows of fuchsias. One of his fuchsia pyramids had been wheeled over with great effort on every man's part. It stood by the buffet table, making it difficult for the staff to serve the guests, which made Miss Blair very cross.

'Finest pyramid fuchsia I've seen outside Lye's own,' said someone else.

Then a man – Mabel thought it was Mr Paul – picked up a plant from the buffet table. 'Good Lord! This fuchsia is a picotee.'

'A new variety,' said Miss Blair. 'Our head gardener calls it "Capel Bells".' Then Miss Blair came over to her and whispered, 'Go and fetch your husband, Mrs Green. I think our guests would like to congratulate him on his achievement.'

Mabel gave her startled mother a triumphant smile and hurried off to find John. Mum shouldn't have said that about 'take a pee'. That was rude and unkind. Mum could be very coarse at times, and she didn't like John. Mabel wished now that she hadn't laughed at her mother's joke. All those nursery men and their wives were talking about John's plants, and they really seemed to value his work. She hadn't realized John was good for anything, what with her mother always taking him down a peg. In future, Mabel decided, Mum would have to show a little respect.

She fetched John who was, of course, in the fuchsia house, and they jog trotted back to the party where he received lavish praise. Mabel was pleased as punch, especially when John happened to pass her mother and Mum reached out and patted him on the back. Mabel thought John was going to go into a dead faint with surprise, but he held up well. Then Mr Warrender called him aside and they talked very softly for quite a time. Matthew and Mr Kitson each held a pot of 'Capel Bells'. 'My head gardener is very proud of this plant,' said Matthew. 'He thinks this little thing will make his fortune and my own, but I rather fear that Fuchsias are *passé.*'

Mr Kitson studied the plant closely. 'Well, that's true and yet it isn't. When you say fuchsias are out of fashion, you're talking about the smart people, the people in the know. I daresay you won't find a standard fuchsia in Miss Jekyll's garden, nor at Myddleton House. Mr Bowles prefers his rarities. On the other hand, your common man, your man who is buying or renting a house in the suburbs, doesn't know about fashion, doesn't care what the smart set think. He wants what he always dreamed of having, and that includes gardens that look like miniatures of public parks. He's not interested in woodland gardens, for the simple reason that he hasn't got the land. He wants a bright display, a splash of colour and everything neat as a pin. Fuchsias are popular if you know where to market them. You've got the makings of a nursery right here at Capel Manor.' Kitson raised a hand, afraid that he offended. 'Not that you would want to bother yourself with a commercial concern.'

'Oh, I don't know,' said Matthew casually. 'It might be amusing, if it were profitable.'

'There's a nurseryman selling up in Roydon. Wants to get rid of his stock for twenty quid. Rooted cuttings and bigger plants of all the old faithfuls. Fuchsias are a bit like weeds. Cuttings strike very well. You can increase your numbers very easily. Finding new varieties is the trick, and training them into desirable shapes. Your man knows all about that. He's been damned clever with his pyramids.'

Charlotte was tired but happier than she had been in many weeks. The party had been a success. She had carved a niche for herself in the milieu of her choice. Miss Charlotte Blair, the well known floral decorator. More importantly, she had successfully kept away from Matthew all evening. He wanted to talk to her, probably to argue with her, but she was most anxious not to get into a discussion with him. Talking about how she felt was painful, something to be avoided at all costs. Recently, so many thoughts and emotions had been churning inside her head that she wished only for sleep as a means of escaping from the pain, although sleep often eluded her. Matthew had left Capel Manor with a curt goodbye, but Vic was not so easily dealt with.

She had taken refuge from her guests in the morning-room, sitting in the largest and softest of the armchairs, had slipped off her shoes and drawn her feet up under her. A light bulb overhead cast an unflattering light through the green fringe of the ceiling fitment. She was at her most vulnerable when Vic came into the room.

'I want a word with you, my girl.'

'Vic, I am very tired. I was just about to go to bed and—'

'I want to talk now, dammit. I'm your dad and you could show me a bit of respect. By the way, I don't wish to see my daughter wearing obscene frocks like the one you got on.'

She uncurled her feet and stood up. Vic was so tall, she made a point of never arguing with him from a sitting position. 'Obscene? That's ridiculous. There is nothing obscene about this gown. I'm over twenty-one and will wear what I choose. My style of dress singles me out from the common herd. People notice me. I've been very successful with these tactics, thank you very much.'

'No, you ain't. Billy's been keeping an eye on your business, and I know you are in dead trouble. Didn't nobody never tell you that you can be too successful? The more business you take on, the more money you've got to lay out in advance. You've stretched yourself at the bank, and your posh customers ain't going to pay you for months. You'll be bankrupt before you collect from the half of them.'

'You set Billy to spy on me? How dare you? I run my own affairs. I don't need your advice or anybody else's.'

'You little fool. I'm your dad. I'm not nobody. I've given you everything you ever wanted since the day you were born, and all you could ever do was put your arms around that porter and call him dada. Don't you recognize a father's love when you see it?'

At Vic's reminder of their relationship, the anger and sense of betrayal she had tried to contain for weeks could be held in no longer. Every grievance came tumbling out, shouted at the top of her voice.

'My father! Ha! You seduced my mother who was no better than a slut. To think she used to give me moral advice! I loved my dada. Can you understand that? I really loved him in a way I can never love you. And you've destroyed my memories of him. Poor wretched man, to be so deceived by the woman he loved.' She put her hands to her head. 'I wish I had never found out the truth. What good has it done me?'

She stopped speaking, glared at his sad face. 'And while I'm about it, please tell me why you are so cruel to Billy. You've never appreciated him. Yet you chase after me, offering me money. Don't you think he has feelings? I hate you! You are disgusting, vulgar and over-bearing. I never want to see you again.'

Her anger spent, she fell back into her chair, but not for long. The tears that rolled down his cheeks brought her out of her seat, to wipe his face with shaking fingers.

'Oh, Vic, I didn't mean it. Forgive me. I was so shocked when I found out the truth. I didn't know what to make of it all—'

Suddenly, he pulled her to him in a clumsy embrace. 'We did wrong, your mum and me, but you came out of the wrong we did. How can I be sorry?' Charlotte's face was driven into the smooth alpaca of his evening jacket. She pushed against his chest, embarrassed by this show of affection. 'I've thought about it, God knows I have,' he said. 'I wanted you to know, but I didn't want anybody thinking you was a bastard like Billy, so I kept quiet. It was Warrender what told me to tell you, and I'm grateful to him. Now, at least you know you ain't alone in this world.'

'Vic, please—'

'Billy's mum wasn't like yours, the stupid slut. It was a strange thing between your mother and me, her being so much older, but I never truly loved another woman, although heaven knows I tried. Charlotte, I want you to love me just a little. I wouldn't do you no harm, and I'll never tell a living soul, except Popple and Arthur. What you say about Billy makes me think. It's sisterly, you taking an interest in the boy. Maybe I have been hard on him. I didn't want him to turn out like his old lady, you see. You was always so clever and hard working.'

An enormous feeling of pity overwhelmed her and she sagged against him, wishing she could get away without hurting him further. Misinterpreting her movement, he clutched her closer, swaying with her, whispering words of comfort to them both. 'There, there, my little daughter. Let it all out. Things ain't going well between you and Matthew, are they? I can tell. I swear I notice every time you so much as frown. Let's you and me get off on the right foot for a change. I tell you what. I ain't retiring from my business. What in God's name would I do with myself? Supposing I give Billy some money and he comes into the floral decorating business with you?

He could manage the business side. I reckon I've trained him well. You like him, don't you? And that there Molly don't want to be at home all day. Says she's bored. I tried to tell her she don't need to work, but I reckon she's as mad on flowers as you are.'

Charlotte moved away and sat down in the chair, exhausted by the rush of painful feelings, but experiencing a strong sense of release. Something approaching a peaceful state of mind was creeping upon her for the first time in weeks. Vic had been the rock on which she and her mother had built their lives. Why had she not seen what there was between them? She was beginning to understand the emotion that had gripped her parents. Love was powerful and painful, she knew that now. In time, perhaps, she could forgive her mother for having failed to live a perfect life, for having given way to ordinary, human needs.

The memory of the man she had regarded as her father was growing fuzzy in her mind. He had been quiet, unassuming and totally in her mother's power. Charlotte had trouble recalling his face after all these years. Although her supposed father was long dead, she had gained a vibrant, flesh-and-blood one who loved, cajoled and scolded her whenever the mood took him. Looked at another way, she had lost two friends, who might have deserted her at any time, and exchanged them for two relatives who would for ever be both a burden and a support. For the rest of her life, she would have to consider their feelings and their wishes. Was this a good thing or not?

'I do love you, Vic. I'm sorry I said all those terrible things. I lost control and I hate that. It's true that I am very fond of Billy. He's clever and sensitive, and I do need someone to handle the business side. I love arranging flowers, having new ideas, meeting the clients. That's the part that fascinates me, not the bookkeeping. Billy would help me enormously, and I have missed Molly's clever fingers. As for Matthew, he doesn't understand me and I don't wish to try to explain to him why I cannot give up arranging flowers. He doesn't understand the importance of honest toil. I can't respect him.'

'That, my girl, is because you're like your mother and you set standards for everybody. A bloke must be like this, mustn't do that, must say so-and-so, mustn't say x, y and z. She was a harsh judge of manhood, I can tell you. And what's more, she was wrong nine times out of ten. I ain't saying you shouldn't revere her memory, but while you remember her with love, spare a little time to show some charity towards the human race. We're all mere mortals, after all. You included. You're not perfect. Matthew is worth a dozen of any man I've met. He cares about everyone, including me, although he admires me even less than you do. He's kind and he's got himself a good position. Did you ever think about that? Those Japanese nursery people don't want him just because he talks with a plum in his mouth. He's clever with other people's languages. I don't understand you.' He shook his head. 'You don't half remind me of your mother. All laced up, I used to call it, although any man with half an eye see you ain't wearing your stays in that get up.'

Charlotte didn't want to hear any more. She was so sleepy, so desperate to undress and slip between the sheets that she merely nodded as she placed a swift, absent-minded kiss on his cheek and left the room. Being part of a family was an exhausting business.

Matthew walked to Capel Manor from Theobalds the following morning, and went directly to the fuchsia house. The house was now largely empty; a few baskets hung from the centre of the span, a few plants in pots stood on the staging. John had been watering the paths, and turned off the hose when he saw that he was not alone.

'Mr Green, I would like to have a word with you privately. Shall we go into the office, where are we least likely to be disturbed?'

'Here, I suppose.' John wiped the palms of his hands down the sides of his trousers. 'Is there something wrong? Perhaps . . . I thought—'

'Not to worry, old chap. There's nothing wrong.' Matthew moved smartly when water dripped from a hanging basket onto his head, then laughed at his own foolishness as he folded his arms, trying to put his listener at ease. 'I have never really paid much attention to fuchsias. Pretty things, aren't they? Very colourful. I'm looking forward to seeing them in bloom, but it's too early in the year, I expect. How is it that "Capel Bells" is in bloom now?'

John, amazed and delighted to have some interest shown in his babies, rushed into a confusing explanation of 'stopping', the art of delaying the blooming of fuchsias, and the equally tricky business of getting them to bloom earlier than normal. Without pause, he spoke for fifteen minutes and during the whole of that time Matthew continued to smile and to make little noises of understanding or approval. It was a heady experience, the first time John had ever been allowed to say all that he wanted to say.

'Hold on there, old man,' laughed Matthew at length. 'I can't take in all this technical information at once. You are certainly a knowledgeable and dedicated fuchsia grower, which is just what I had hoped for. For some time, I have been trying to think of ways to defray some of the costs of running Capel Manor. And do you know, I believe you have done it for me. I would like to put up, say, half an acre of glass at the northern end of the property, cut a road from the gates directly to that part of the estate and put you in charge of a fuchsia nursery. The beauty of "Capel Bells" notwithstanding, I believe our success lies in producing well grown standards, fans, and other shapes. I have been advised here by Mr Kitson, who tells me you are very clever at such things. Also, I can buy up the stock of a Roydon grower who is going out of business.'

'Grow fuchsias?' gasped John. 'You actually want me to grow fuchsias? All the time?'

'Yes, but for the moment I do not intend to increase the staff. The growing would be very much your responsibility. My time is fully occupied with Tokyo Nurseries. This is to be a side-line, a profitable one, I hope. I say, you're not going to faint, are you? It's very hot in here.'

John, overcome by joy, not heat, thought that he might very well pass away, and grasped the staging to stop himself from doing anything so foolish. 'Maybe we better go outdoors,' he murmured. 'I got lots of plants to show you.'

Chapter Nineteen

'We could have met at my club,' said Buffy Morrison, drawing in his knees as Chalker offered him a whisky. 'Your *pied à terre* is the smallest I have ever come across. How the devil do you manage?'

Matthew lifted his own glass from the silver tray and nodded dismissal to Chalker. He intended to speak plainly to Buffy, and hoped that if they kept their voices low Chalker would not be able to hear every word in the adjoining kitchen.

'I wanted to talk to you about the development of suburban property. Have you purchased the land?' asked Matthew, knowing that he hadn't.

'Give me time, old boy. I must get a few more investors. This is to be a very large project. Already land close to the underground stations is being snapped up. I'm negotiating with some very important people. You'd stare if I told you their names, but I'm sworn to secrecy. We'll be building superior properties. By the way, when can you let me have a cheque? I don't wish to press you, but . . .'

Matthew set his glass on the side table and stood up. There was not much room to walk around, due to the excessive amount of space taken up by his oriental collection. 'There won't be a cheque. I invited you here so that I could tell you in private. I'm sorry to let down an old friend, but I have other plans.'

'It's that floral decorator, isn't it? Whatever you do, don't marry the girl. You'll live to regret it.'

'I have no intention of marrying the girl. Where on earth did you hear about her? There has been a spot of bother, and nothing further will happen on that score.'

'Her family, I dare say,' said Buffy knowingly. 'What does her father do?'

Matthew laughed harshly. 'That is just the sort of thing you would think of. Mr Blair has been dead for many years.' He thought he had sidestepped the question very neatly.

'Yes, but what did he do before he turned up his toes?'

'Mr Blair was an actor, as was Miss Blair's mother.'

'Blair,' mused Buffy. 'I don't recall the name, and I'm very fond of the theatre.'

'It doesn't matter,' said Matthew irritably, wondering why he felt compelled to talk about Charlotte to Buffy. 'I wanted her to sell her business. She has been very successful, but I thought she should retire. She disagreed.'

'Couldn't have a wife in trade,' nodded Buffy, full of sympathy.

'That is not an obstacle, Buffy. I can't invest in your scheme, because I intend to grow fuchsias commercially. I've met a few members of the horticultural trade, and you would be surprised how charming and well-informed they are. And wealthy, of course. Naturally, there are expenses connected with starting up a new business. I will need all of my capital.'

'I'll be damned. Going into trade yourself. I heard you were a director of some Japanese nursery. It's all beneath your touch, old boy. Very strange thing to do.'

'I find that I don't care whether it's beneath my touch or not. If Lady Briggs chooses to cut me, I shall know I have made the right choice. I'm hoping to find my place among the aristocracy of the glasshouse industry. Gentlemen all, they will accept me when I meet their exacting criteria.'

'I'm beginning to worry about you. Much better come into business with me. You don't know a damned thing about growing flowers.'

With a menacing smile, Matthew sat down on the arm of an easy chair and bent forward so that his face was but a few inches from Buffy's. '*I'm* beginning to worry about *you*, old chap. I know more about growing fuchsias than I do about property development. And you don't know anything about building houses. In fact, the word is that you have no money of your own, and no past experience as a businessman. I think my money will be safer in fuchsias.'

'If you knew as much about business as you think you do, you would know that any scheme requires confidence. Now, all I am trying to do is build a little confidence. I will be able to build houses as soon as enough people believe I can. Anyway, you're going into business to raise an old-fashioned plant. Who wants fuchsias?'

'Some people do. You know what their flowers look like, don't you? A little tube and four petals that flare out? Well, they aren't petals, they're sepals. They look like petals, I grant you, but those of us in the know refer to them as sepals. The little skirt of petals which really are what they appear to be, may well be of a different colour, can be single, double or semi-double.'

'You've read this up in a book.'

'No, I have it first hand. Fuchsias are easily reproduced from pieces of stem cut from the plant and stuck into a pot. You can increase the number of blooms on any plant by pinching out the ends of the little branches at the proper time. Blooms increase on a mathematical progression. Damned clever little things. My head gardener knows all about them. Initially, I'm putting up half an acre of glass at the far end of my grounds, arranging a new drive that will enable the carters to come and go without passing the house, and I shall be moving the vegetables out of my walled garden so that I can have a pleasure garden based on the suggestions of Miss Gertrude Jekyll.' Matthew was prepared to explain who Miss Jekyll was, but Buffy surprised him by saying that the great lady had often visited his parents' home.

'Miss Jekyll, eh? You've got the gardening bug for sure. My mater talks of little else. I should be bored to tears every time I go down to Surrey, if I ever listened to what she has to say. Matthew, don't desert me in my time of need. I have to have some name I can flash about when I'm looking for other investors.'

'Don't flash mine. In fact, find some other source of income. Much better to find yourself a rich wife. Visit Lady Briggs and ask for her help. She never refuses an indigent gentleman, so long as he is presentable and has engaging manners. A man of your charm should fill her heart with joy. I think I can already safely congratulate you on your coming nuptials. She never fails.'

'I'm not interested in taking a wife at the moment. The idea of marrying money is repugnant to me, if you must know. I don't want some rich woman reminding me every minute of the day that I am indebted to her. You think my scheme is suspect, don't you? You think I'm a damned criminal.'

'No, but I think you would like to be a damned criminal. Seriously, Buffy, don't get mixed up in something you don't understand. I would hate to see you in a suit with arrows on it.'

Buffy could not help laughing. 'You are wrong about me, but I'm still your friend. You can't insult me, you know. I think your plan to grow fuchsias can't succeed. If I can't build houses, I'll do something else. You'll see. One day I will be a rich man, respected by one and all. And I won't have to go into trade to do it.'

They parted several minutes later on the best of terms. Matthew thought his old friend bore an amazing similarity to Charlotte's father. No wonder he had always been tolerant of Vic. He was clearly drawn to charming rogues!

Popple Douse removed his handkerchief from his pocket and wiped his face. The August day was extremely hot, making life difficult for portly gentlemen to endure stiff collars and sixteen-ounce suiting. Popple always wore spats and a waistcoat when in Town, and temperatures in the eighties could not make him deviate from the style of dress he felt appropriate. He therefore trudged along two sides of Hanover Square in search of Warrender's lodgings, feeling increasingly exhausted. He had walked from the little Goldseekers office he and his friends had rented on Oxford Street as a safe retreat from the world, and was just thinking of abandoning his plan to call upon the young man when he read the number of the red brick building before him, and realized he had reached his destination.

Matthew welcomed him inside, but expressed his surprise. 'I might so easily have been in Kingsway at the nursery, my dear friend. Your journey could have been wasted. Do sit down. Chalker, prepare something refreshing for us, will you?'

When Chalker had returned to the kitchen, Matthew bent over his guest and studied the blotchy complexion. 'The windows are open, Mr Douse, but I think you should remove your jacket and loosen your tie. You are overheated. Here, allow me to help you.'

'Very kind,' murmured Douse. It took the two of them a full minute to get the heavy jacket off, since the older man hadn't the strength to stand up or to give much assistance.

'Lemonade,' said Chalker, returning to the sitting-room with a tray. 'I thought alcohol would be inappropriate at this hour and in this heat, sir.'

'Lemonade?' said Popple. 'Oh, well, I suppose it is for the best.'

Matthew looked on anxiously as his guest drained the glass. 'Feeling better,' gasped Popple. 'Had to speak to you. Don't know why. That is, didn't know anyone else to turn to. Her mother's dead, you know. Florence was only fourteen. A very unfortunate age for a girl to lose her mother. I've failed. Can't say I haven't. Up to every prank you can think of. Hoped she'd grow out of her naughtiness. Hoped you might take an interest in the girl. I don't suppose—?' Matthew shook his head. 'In the soup now. Don't know where to turn, Warrender. I need your advice. No, dammit, I need your *help*. He works for you, after all.'

'Jacko Boon,' said Matthew helpfully.

'You knew? You knew about it and you said nothing? Why didn't you warn me?'

'It was not my business to do so, Mr Douse. Florence is a very attractive young woman and will have many admirers before she settles down.' He frowned. 'She hasn't run off with him, has she?'

'No, but she threatens to do so. She tells me they plan to marry. She will live in the bothy at Capel Manor, unless I purchase a nursery for him. He fancies growing orchids, she says, or perhaps roses. I am to reward the man for robbing me of my daughter!'

'Ah, then I believe she is in no danger. He can be bought off. I'm sure you have enough money to meet this man's price. A hundred pounds? Perhaps, if he is determined, a hundred and fifty.'

'My life's savings,' said Popple, rubbing the inner corners of his eyes. 'Of course, when we actually strike gold, I will be in a much stronger position.'

'Let's see. Today is the twenty-third of August. The cable from Australia arrived on the day of the Haileybury Jubilee. I remember the date perfectly well. It was the sixth of July. I don't know how long these things take, but I would say that by the beginning of September we should know something positive. Surely there is no hurry in completing this business with Jacko Boon?'

'I don't know. She's headstrong. Pressing me every day to speak to this man. Will you come with me when I do? As a witness. I mean, he is a gardener on your estate. I want to make sure he sticks to our bargain, especially if I have to go to a hundred and fifty pounds. I never thought . . . I mean to say, I imagined you could just have a word with him and warn him off. Don't you think that would work?'

'Your daughter would . . .' Matthew hesitated, stumped for a polite way of saying that Florence was a spoiled young woman who must know that she was in a strong bargaining position. Otherwise, she would have continued to dally with her gardener in secret.

'I shall be tied up for the next few days. Suppose we meet on . . .' They both consulted their pocket diaries. 'On the twenty-sixth. That is a Monday. Most important, you see, because Miss Blair will be in Town. I should not care to have her involved in any way. Technically, Jacko Boon works for her, as she pays his wages. I have no claim on Capel Manor, and visit it only as a guest. Of course, she has given me written permission to put up a fuchsia house. We could drive along the new road I have had cut, going directly to the glasshouses. That way, no-one at the Manor will know we are on the premises. I think I really would prefer it that way.'

Popple Douse struggled to rise from the chair, feeling half naked without his coat. With shaking fingers, he readjusted his tie, tugged his waistcoat into place and slipped his arms into the sleeves of the jacket now being held for him by Matthew.

'Awfully grateful, my dear sir. I only wish there were some way that I could repay your kindness in this matter. I'm confident of a successful outcome, now that you are involved.'

'The only thing you can do for me,' replied Matthew casually, 'is to refrain from selling any more stock in Goldseekers.'

'Of course I won't. Dear me, Warrender, do you think I'm a fool? We want all the shares for ourselves, now that gold is about to be discovered. Three more former investors have asked us to take back their stock at the original selling price. Tavern and Brock and I have been quick to comply. Don't worry your head on that score.'

'Thank you. I shall meet you at Capel Manor at two o'clock on the twenty-sixth of August. May I suggest that we gather in the grotto, for privacy, that you send no advance warning to Boon, and that under no circumstances should you inform Miss Douse of our plans. We must hope to have the matter settled to our satisfaction before she hears of it.'

The day was oppressive. Even within the dark, moist depths of Charlotte's shop, the heat made everyone irritable. Billy had been talking at length about fixed costs and the large payroll, about the advisability or otherwise of selling the van and employing carters when necessary. He acknowledged the advertising value of having a van with the name C. A. Blair on it, while wondering if the cost was justified. He had congratulated himself on obtaining a thousand pounds' worth of cheques from customers for work done during the previous quarter, suggested a substantial amount of insurance in case of breakages or other damage, and worried at length about the state of Molly's health in the heat. Charlotte had come to love her brother very much in the past six weeks, but she had serious doubts about enduring his company all the way out to Theobalds Park, where she was due to meet Lady Meux at half past twelve.

'I'll fetch the car and meet you in front of the shop in five minutes,' he said, laying down his pen. Billy had undergone a remarkable change in recent weeks. His dedication to the business was commendable, but it gave her the feeling that C. A. Blair belonged less to her than before. Charlotte could not decide if this was an advantage or not. It was true that she had been struggling recently to hit upon new and daring ideas for her customers, and the strain was telling on her. Billy's active presence lessened her burden considerably. He always had a sympathetic ear to hear her complaints when customers became irritating. On the other hand, his ideas about expenditure sometimes differed considerably from her own. At such times, she found it annoying to have to accommodate some other point of view, even though she had to acknowledge that she was no longer in debt because of his efforts.

'Thirty days hath September,' she murmured when she was alone, 'April, June and November . . . so July has thirty-one days. This is the twenty-sixth of August. He has not spoken to me since July the sixth. Fifty-one days! Can it be fifty-one days that, except for one business letter, Matthew has made no attempt to contact me? He doesn't love me, for if he did he would not have been able to stay away for so long.'

Whenever a break in her work left her a moment for reflection, she asked herself what to do. Should she write to him? Telephone? Ask Vic to intercede on her behalf? Invariably, she did nothing, since fear of rejection rendered her incapable of action. Regret at having refused to marry him alternated with a sense of resentment that he should have demanded such an enormous sacrifice as the price of the marriage. She didn't know what she wanted in the future, one minute believing herself justified in refusing to give up her work, the next convinced that Matthew was right to ask her to sell up.

A horn sounded. Charlotte gathered up her drawings and list of suggestions for Theobalds, as well as the sketch pad that nowadays accompanied her everywhere, and hurried out to Billy's car.

He held the door open for her and saw that her skirt was well tucked in before closing it. 'Have you got everything? Shall I walk around the estate with you? What's that great pad you're carrying?'

'I have everything, Billy. I would like to have you accompany us, provided that you offer no suggestions.'

'Ask for a thousand pounds.'

'I haven't done any calculations yet!'

'I know,' he said. 'But I have noticed that when you charge two hundred and fifty pounds, your client later boasts that she paid three hundred. As a result, your next client feels cheated if you don't overcharge *her*.'

'I never overcharge. They pay for my creative imagination and my reputation. Such things are worth whatever
people think they are worth. I understand Lady Meux
wants the entire house to be filled with flowers. I think
the sum is more likely to be fifteen hundred pounds. We
will need an enormous team to arrange it all in such a
short time, for we can hardly start before four o'clock
in the morning, and the guests will begin to arrive at half
past twelve. I just wish that I could think of something
outré.'

'Ootray?'

'Different, outrageous. Lady Meux seems to have
heard of every previous commission I have had. I can't
repeat what I have done for others.'

'What is that big pad of paper?'

'A sketch pad. Not for my work. As a means of
relaxation, I have taken to drawing in my spare time. I
wish I knew how to use water colours. Matthew knows,
but I can hardly ask him for advice.'

'And what do you draw? Flowers, I suppose.'

She flipped up the cover of the pad and held it up so
that he could glance at her latest drawing. 'Sometimes,
but not always. Recognize this man?'

'That's me!' he cried, delightedly. 'Well, I'll be a
monkey's uncle. That's good, you know, except that
you've made me very handsome. Will you show it to
Molly?'

She turned the page. 'How about this one?'

'Matthew. I like it. Who else have you done?'

She turned the page again, holding up the pad in
such a way that his vision was momentarily obstructed.

'Watch out! Here, let me draw up to the kerb. I
want to look at this carefully. I don't like this one,
Charlotte. You have drawn yourself looking almost
demented.'

'I drew what I saw in the looking-glass.'

'I believe you, my dear, but I hate to look at it. Why

don't you write to the man or send for him? You know you love him.'

'He wants me to give up the business, to stop arranging flowers. I can't do that.'

Billy pulled out into the traffic. 'I admit that was stupid and insensitive of him. Artists aren't like the rest of us. I would have thought a clever bloke like Matthew would know better. Shall I have a word with him?'

'No thank you,' she said crisply.

'Where did you go on August Bank Holiday? Molly and Dad and I had a great time in Southend. We would have been happy to have you with us.'

Charlotte sighed. 'I preferred to go somewhere quiet. I have been so busy lately that I needed time to myself. As a matter of fact, I took the train to Cambridge. I had never been there before. The botanical garden is wonderful. You must visit it some time, because I'm sure Molly would enjoy it.'

'Botanical. That's plants again. Can't you get away from flowers for a single day?'

'It seems not. However, I have taken to making careful drawings of them. That's relaxing. In my work, I always have to find new ideas, which is the real strain. I have been visiting museums and art galleries, hoping for inspiration. Matthew once said . . . oh, never mind.'

'What do you make of these new glasshouses that are going up at Capel Manor? I presume Matthew had to ask your permission before he could start building.'

'He wrote to me and I naturally agreed. In a little more than six months, I will have to leave Capel Manor. How could I refuse him permission to build?'

'Where will you go? You're going to miss that house.'

'Billy, if you don't mind, I believe I'll take a rest to prepare myself for the interview with Lady Meux. I didn't sleep very well last night.' She slipped down in the seat and closed her eyes. As she had hoped, Billy didn't ask any more questions about her future.

'We're nearly there,' he said suddenly. To her surprise, Charlotte realized that she had slept all the way from London.

'We'll be there in another minute or two.' He turned a corner with a screech of tyres. 'I just want you to know that Molly's family have all emigrated to Australia. I paid for them to go. Or rather, Dad did.'

'That's nice.' She smiled at the gate-keeper who waved them through.

'So there won't be any more trouble from that direction.'

'What trouble?'

'You know. Burglaries at the homes of your clients. Molly's twin brothers need a strong hand. Australia should suit them.'

'Molly's brothers? They robbed my clients? Oh, Billy.'

'Yes, and they're only fifteen years old. I said to my father-in-law that I would inform on them unless the whole family emigrated, and I didn't really care where they went. Mr O'Rourke was pretty stroppy, and Molly cried a lot. However, it turned out that Mrs O'Rourke was on my side. I think she might have preferred to leave the twins here and get as far away from them as possible, but I wasn't having that. I bought the tickets to Australia and gave them fifty quid to get started. Molly was fit to be tied, but I cooled her off, saying we would go out to visit them one day.'

The motor was eating up the yards as they travelled the long drive. There was not much time for Charlotte to digest this startling piece of news. 'Are you telling me that my own dear Molly, your wife, informed them what to steal and where it might be found? Molly?'

'Well, here we are,' said Billy cheerfully. 'Terrifying place, isn't it? It looks like a whole street of houses pushed together, higgledy-piggledy. She had to do it. I didn't know anything about it until after we were married. And I couldn't inform on them, could I? A man doesn't do that to family. Anyway, it's all over. I tried to tell you that day in the garden, but you didn't want to listen to my problems.'

'And I don't want to listen now. I must concentrate, Billy. I must put this out of my mind.'

Billy smiled wryly. 'I thought you would.'

Lady Meux was very gracious, but in a hurry. Setting a blistering pace, she took them on a tour of the rooms to be decorated: sitting-rooms, drawing-rooms, a ballroom, and the Italian garden next to which was to be a huge marquee.

'The party has grown into something quite different from what I originally intended,' she said when they were all seated by the fountain. 'The weather is very close, isn't it? I think it's going to rain. How dreadful if it rains on the seventeenth of September. This is to be a celebration of our marriage and a party to introduce my five daughters to the neighbourhood, although of course we have lived on the grounds for years. The guests will not be – how shall I put it – they will not be select. Neighbours, tradesmen of the better sort, the glasshouse fraternity. Three hundred people, in short. Now, can you give me an idea of what your decorations will cost?'

Charlotte took a deep breath, failed to find the courage to ask for fifteen hundred pounds, and murmured as casually as possible, 'A thousand pounds.'

Lady Meux also took a deep breath. 'When the Admiral inherited Theobalds Park, he sold off the effects of the previous Lady Meux by auction. The sum realized was just ten thousand pounds. Egyptian antiquities. Fine paintings and other objects. Silver, some of it quite old. And no more than ten times what you propose to charge, Miss Blair.'

'I know, but I should imagine that what was sold was of little practical value in establishing a position. This garden party will be the talk of East Hertfordshire and beyond for many years. Three hundred people, Lady Meux. What food could you possibly serve that would astound your guests and cause them to remember the afternoon with awe? Nothing. And you must not ply them with drink until they fall down, although I grant you that would be memorable. No, the party will stand or fall by what I provide. And, for a thousand pounds, I will not fail you.'

Lady Meux smiled. 'I had heard you were outrageous. I'll do it. Now then, how do you propose to astound me?'

Chalker drove the small car safely, but with the air of a man at war with the combustion engine. He turned to the right inside Capel's gates, crunching over the new cinder drive, which ran parallel to the New River canal, before eventually curving to the left where the new glasshouse sparkled in the brilliant light.

Matthew longed for a cold drink. His mouth was full of dust and he was extremely hot beneath his goggles, hat and dust coat. However, it was three minutes past two and he didn't wish to keep Douse waiting. Some amazing information had been given to him minutes before he intended to leave the office. Naturally, he had to stay a few minutes longer to ask questions, to think about the consequences, and to come to some difficult decisions. All of this made him late in starting. Chalker had done an admirable job of making up lost time, but Matthew did not relish the thought of the return journey with his valet at the wheel.

'I shall put up the roof of the car, sir,' said Chalker. 'I believe it's going to rain.'

Throwing off his driving clothes, Matthew hurried away. He saw Jacko Boon talking to one of the gardeners, and signalled with one hand that Jacko should meet him in the grotto. He reached it first, in time to discover that the ferns, so recently planted, had been allowed to die, and that Popple Douse was there before him.

'He's on his way,' said Matthew, shaking hands. 'Are you well? It's another hot day, but I fear this one will end in rain.'

'Damned close.' Douse wiped his face, then saw Jacko enter the grotto and put away his handkerchief.

'Will you begin, Mr Douse?' asked Matthew, then, seeing the distressed expression on Douse's face, turned to Jacko. 'Perhaps I should state the case.'

'Is it about Miss Florence?' asked Jacko. 'Shouldn't she be here with us?'

'Certainly not!' Popple Douse found a crumbling edge of what was probably intended to be a small pool and perched on it.

'Mr Douse is willing to give you the money to purchase a nursery, Boon. You are a lucky man. Naturally, you will not wish to take up a business anywhere near Capel Manor. Surrey or Kent would do very well, I think. Mr Douse proposes to give you a hundred pounds.'

'You're buying me off, is that it? You're going to pay me to abandon my Florence?'

'A hundred and twenty-five,' said Douse. Matthew frowned at him, trying to convey that it was too soon to raise the offer. Unfortunately, the older man was too perturbed to notice a signal.

'Miss Florence and I love each other. You think I'm not good enough for her, sir, and you would be right. Only thing is, no man is good enough for her. I don't know how you could ask me to give up the woman I love, sort of thing.'

'A hundred and fifty, and that's my last offer.'

Matthew bit his lip, turned away from the old man and tried to put himself into Boon's shoes. No amount of money would have made him give up Charlotte. True love had no price. On the other hand, a hundred and fifty pounds was an enormous sum to a man like Jacko Boon. The gardener must have known that there was no chance of her father agreeing to the marriage, and Florence was under age. A little more discussion and a few carefully chosen phrases, designed to make Boon see the difficulties if he didn't accept the money, should do the trick. Always providing that Douse, usually a brilliant businessman, didn't allow his heart to rule his head.

Billy drew up to the front door of Capel Manor and waited until Charlotte had got out before making a five-point turn in the drive to park the car in the stables. Florence saw her from the hall window and dashed to open the door before Charlotte had a chance to ring the bell.

'Florence, what are you doing here?'

'I had to come. I followed my father, as a matter of fact. He never saw me. I've been very clever, but probably too late. I must talk to you.'

'I must have a quick wash. I'm filthy. I've been to Theobalds Park to discuss my commission. Come up to my room. Whatever is the matter, Florence? You're in a terrible state. It's not . . . the police are not involved, are they?'

'No, no.' Florence sat down on the edge of the bed and watched Charlotte remove her hat and begin to unpin her hair. 'Oh, leave your hair alone. There's no time for that. Popple is here to see Jacko, and I'm sure it will end badly. You must help me. I love him, Charlotte. I must have him. He knows how to control me.'

'Nonsense. He's totally wrong for you. I have been thinking for some time that I will have to give him notice. Really, Florence, you must find someone more suitable. Anyway, you are too young. Why not—'

Florence stamped her foot, confirming Charlotte's opinion of her as a spoiled child. 'You are a selfish beast, Charlotte Blair. I hate you. Everybody knows you think of no-one but yourself. Just because you are incapable of loving anyone but Charlotte Blair and . . . and daisies, doesn't mean that others were born without hearts. Why can't you save my beloved for me?'

'I wouldn't know how to go about it. Anyway, if I

am the terrible person you say I am, why should you want me to interfere?'

'Because Popple will listen to you, because the three of us can, together, persuade him that marrying Jacko is the right thing for me. Because you lost your own man and should want to see another woman find happiness. That's why.'

As Florence was speaking, Charlotte turned around to face her. 'Is that what you think? I am not envious, I assure you. I wouldn't want to spend my life cooking and cleaning for a man who will never earn enough to keep a woman in comfort. Heaven knows you aren't talented enough to work and help out. How on earth do you think the two of you would manage, living in the bothy? You're not meant for such a life, my girl.'

'Popple could buy us a nursery. Jacko was talking about one for sale close to here that grows sweet peas and tomatoes. A hundred and fifty pounds would see us on our way. We could make a go of it and I would work ever so hard. Charlotte, I beg of you, help me!'

'I am not heartless. Where is your father? I will do what I can. If you are poor, overworked and miserable for the rest of your life, it will serve you right for insulting me.'

'Yes, yes, I am a terrible, rude, naughty, spoiled girl. But if you didn't have iced water in your veins, you would know what it is to love a man. I saw my father heading down towards the pond. Jacko and I often meet in the grotto. Perhaps that's where they are.'

Jacko Boon offered no great challenge to Matthew's skill as a negotiator. It was obvious within seconds that the man intended to take the money. With admirable forethought, Popple had actually withdrawn a hundred and fifty pounds from the bank and was in the act of counting it out into Jacko's palm when they heard Florence call. The effect on Jacko was amazing. The gardener actually looked frightened. He pushed the money back into Popple's hand and looked around for a means of escape. As luck would have it, he chose the very passageway through which Florence and Charlotte stormed.

'What are you doing here?' asked Charlotte of Matthew. 'I might have known you would be involved in destroying a woman's happiness.'

'I might ask you the same question. This is a matter for the Douses and Jacko Boon. But it so happens that I was asked to give my assistance.'

'And I was asked by Florence to see that a great miscarriage of justice does not take place today. She loves him. That should be sufficient. It's wrong to frighten away a man simply because he is too poor to stand up to wealthier bullies.'

'No, no, don't blame him, Charlotte,' said Popple, rather pathetically. 'Matthew was merely acting as my agent. This man does not wish to marry you, Florence, so you may dry your tears and thank heaven you found out in time.'

'Is that true, Jacko?' asked Florence, clutching Jacko's arm. 'Don't you love your little girl? How could you do that?'

'No,' muttered Jacko. 'I didn't say . . . I was just . . . your father wants to buy me a nursery and—'

'Stand up for what you believe in,' said Charlotte fiercely.

'He believes in taking the money and moving away,' answered Matthew.

Florence flung her arms around Jacko's neck, nearly bringing him down in the process. 'I knew you would get my father to buy us a nursery. Oh, my darling, you are so clever. Popple, you gave me quite a fright.'

'Get off me, Florence,' said Jacko in embarrassment.

Florence immediately released her love, saying to her father, 'Do you see how I obey him? Whatever Jacko asks me to do, I will. He knows how to control me, which is more than you ever did, my dear father. We will be happy, I promise you, and everything will turn out all right.'

Matthew took a pace backwards, the better to observe this little tableau. Jacko Boon had just expressed his intention of moving to Cornwall to grow daffodils. He had been doing some investigating, he said, and found that a hundred and fifty pounds would set him up nicely, with money in the bank to carry him over the loss-making years. He had said he would be gone from Capel within the hour. Now, the poor devil looked like a quivering hare caught in a trap.

'We shall buy that nursery you were talking about, dearest,' said Florence. 'Where they grow sweet peas. I love sweet peas.'

'They don't fetch much in the market—' began Jacko forlornly. He turned to Popple Douse helplessly.

'Florence, if this is the man you want, then I cannot stop you. Are you sure? Are you both sure?' asked Popple, a defeated man.

'Of course we are, aren't we, Jacko?' She tugged his arm, intending to drag him from the cool shade of the grotto, then had another thought. 'Have you given him the money, Popple? We could go straight away over to the nursery. There's no time to lose.'

Like a man living in a nightmare, Popple handed over the whole of the one hundred and fifty pounds, this time counting it into Florence's hand.

Jacko looked equally miserable as she put it into her handbag. 'Come along, Florence, we'd best get out of here.'

Florence waved to Charlotte, Popple and Matthew. 'See how I obey him? I'm coming, my dear. Just tell your little girl what you want her to do.'

There was silence in the grotto, broken only by a distant rumble of thunder. 'Do you really think they will be happy?' asked Matthew of Charlotte. 'Are you proud of your part in this charade?'

'I had no part to play in the end. Florence knows

her own mind, which is a wonderful thing. It will give me pleasure to see one woman happily settled in life. It seems an unlikely match, but I can think of others that would not prosper so well. Try to look on the bright side, Mr Douse. Your daughter will not give you any more anxiety, although she may cost you some more money. Before his brains were addled by Florence, Jacko was adequate as a leisure gardener. He is not as clever as he thinks, however, and may find he's not up to the task of being his own employer. But,' she laughed, 'I was forgetting about Florence. She will keep him in hand. Life on a nursery may well develop another side of her character.'

No-one believed this. They walked in silence, accompanied by ever louder thunder, until they reached the back door of the house.

'Won't you help yourself to refreshment, Mr Douse?' said Charlotte wearily. 'The whisky is in the drawing-room. I believe you know where. Or ring for Rachel. She will bring you whatever you wish. I am very tired. I believe I will just lie down for half an hour. I have been given a great deal to think about today.'

Chapter Twenty

Charlotte reached her bedroom and slammed the door behind her. The windows were open, the muslin curtains hung limply in the still air. She pressed her fingers to her temples; the heat was oppressive. Far off, distant lightning lit the underside of low black clouds, and a full minute later thunder rumbled menacingly.

'I must concentrate,' she murmured under her breath. 'I must think about what I am going to do at Theobalds. All of the plant material must be brought here to Capel forty-eight hours before the day. That means placing my order in the market two weeks in advance. How many people will I need to employ to decorate twelve rooms, a large marquee, the entrance to the house and the short set of steps at the back? There will be sixty people for lunch, before the less important people arrive, but I forgot to ask how the tables would be arranged. How could I have been so unprofessional? I need a theme!'

She walked over to her dressing table, picked up a comb and put it down, opened the jewellery box and closed it, then studied the photograph of her mother that she had slipped into a silver frame belonging to Capel. She picked up the frame, slid off its blue velvet back and removed the picture of Matthew which she had hidden behind that of her mother.

How handsome he was! Today, he was wearing the same light tweed jacket and matching double-breasted waistcoat, the same white trousers in which he had been photographed. The high forehead and deep-set, intense eyes were the same in real life as pictured, but the photograph failed entirely to convey his humour and kindness. There could be no way of telling from the picture that the voice was a pleasant tenor, gentle and amused most of the time, capable of conveying great emotion when its owner chose to show his displeasure.

He had no right to try to buy off Jacko. He interfered only because he assumed that a poor man can be lured away from the woman he loves by an offer of money. Whatever Florence's faults, she is prepared to fight for her man and win. How I admire her! She knows Jacko is weak, but she is willing to put up with his failings.

She sat down on the bed to unbutton her shoes and slip them off, then lay back on the coverlet. *But I must not think of Matthew. I must think of Admiral and Lady Meux and of five handsome daughters. What is the matter with me? I used not to be able to think about people at all, preferring to concentrate on my work. Now, I can't bring my mind to the problems of Theobalds Park. Think, Charlotte, think!*

Her eyes closed and she saw, not Lady Meux but Matthew, his face alight with love for her at the moment when he asked her to marry him. She felt again the soaring pleasure of his kisses, heard him ask her to give up flower arranging, to be the – what had he called it? – the chatelaine of Capel Manor. She had failed to take the opportunity of happiness offered to her, failed even to attempt to make him see her point of view. As a result, Matthew had embraced fuchsias. They were his new love, the all-absorbing hobby that shut out thoughts of marriage and children. She wished him well in his business venture. He was realistic, at least, knowing that it would take time to build up stocks, knowing that he would have to attend to the bookkeeping side of the business, while John Green concentrated on growing the plants. Charlotte could certainly inform Matthew – if he showed any inclination to speak to her – that he would be obliged to employ another head gardener, as

Mr Green was no longer interested in managing the grounds of Capel.

But she must think about Lady Meux! She dared not dwell on the complexity of what lay before her, or her capacity to do the job, or the penalties of failure. Theobalds Park was enormous. The scale of the decorations required was larger than anything she had ever attempted before. A year ago, she would not have been in a position to accept the commission. Today, she had not only accepted, but, in a moment of insane bravado, guaranteed that Lady Meux's guests would be astounded.

'Matthew!' whispered Billy, sticking his head round the morning-room door as Charlotte went upstairs to her bedroom. 'I've taken in that great box which Chalker delivered.'

'Oh, good.' Matthew joined him in the morning-room. 'It is for Charlotte, a present from Tokyo Nursery. It contains ten yards of artificial wisteria vine and flowers. It's a very good imitation. Felton used similar artificial material when he decorated Claridges. She will need something extravagant for Theobalds Park. I believe Lady Meux is hoping to impress the entire county!'

'Charlotte has given her an estimate of a thousand pounds,' said Billy with satisfaction. 'She used to calculate the cost of the flowers and treble it to find her fee, but now that she's all the rage, she quadruples the flower cost. Lady Meux accepted. I knew she would.'

'A thousand pounds! She must be doing very well.'

'Yes,' said Billy triumphantly, 'especially now that I am taking a hand in managing the business. You should have seen me collecting the bad debts.'

'I'm quite sure I would not have enjoyed it.'

'The turnover for the last twelve months was ten thousand pounds. She needs working capital. You can't tell women about such things. She thought she was in debt, but she wasn't really. I soon put the bookkeeping in order.'

'Well!' said Matthew, attempting to hide his chagrin. 'The Tavern family seems to have the gift of making vast sums of money. I wish I had the knack. Let me see, she charges four times the value of the flowers, so of the ten thousand pounds turnover, two thousand five hundred is profit.'

'No, no,' scoffed Billy. 'By simply charging four times the cost of the flowers, she is failing to calculate her true costs, as I have told her a dozen times. There's wastage, overheads like heat and light and the telephone, there's wages and running her van. I'm trying to teach her about these things, but all Charlotte wants to think about is the artistic side. She's been too busy doing the flowers for rich customers, to keep the books in a proper state. I keep telling her, no matter how clever you are, nor how good your product, if you want to be successful, you've got to attend to the finances. Nevertheless, she made four hundred pounds for herself last year. I expect you would be happy to make so much money.'

Matthew sucked in his breath, determined not to admit the truth of Billy's words. He had been extremely pleased to accept a director's fee of one hundred and fifty pounds. He would also realize something from his share of the profits, but Charlotte would probably sneer at such an income. As for the fuchsia nursery, he knew that it might not make a profit for several years. He would have to be content in the knowledge that John Green would earn his wages, while the rest of the gardening staff kept the gardens in trim.

He turned away and went to stare out of the window, giving Billy a view of his back. 'No wonder she didn't want to give up her business.'

'I'm ashamed of you, Matthew. You should never have suggested such a thing. Charlotte is an artist, and you know better than I do that artists are different from the rest of us. There will never be another man in her life. She loves you and needs you to look after her while she gives her talent free rein.

Can't you see that you could help her to develop her talent?'

Matthew turned. 'My dear chap, you are her brother and entitled to be biased, but Charlotte is a technician, a craftswoman, if you like. A true artist is a different animal altogether. Charlotte hasn't . . . what have you there?'

'Her sketch-pad. Come over here and look at these drawings. There's me wearing my bowler, and there's you in evening dress and here, this one is the way she sees herself. Look at this drawing and then tell me she's a happy woman. And while you're about it, I dare you to tell me she isn't an artist.'

Matthew almost snatched the pad from Billy's hands and took it over to the window, the better to study the pencil drawings. Her line was strong and sure, her modelling very well executed. These could be early sketches for paintings, although he knew she had no idea of the techniques of working with oils. That familiar frisson of excitement, the tightening of his scalp, told him that he was looking at the work of a great talent. Of course she was an artist, confusing her admirers by working in an unconventional medium. He had been mistaken once again, prejudiced. Conventional wisdom had it that a true artist arranged flowers merely as a prelude to painting them. One admired the painting, rather than the way the flowers had been combined. Why had he not appreciated before that flower arranging could be raised to an art form, could be as exhilarating to view as any type of sculpture or carving or pottery? The only difference lay in the transience of the medium. The poor flower decorator saw her creations die within hours and had to find new inspiration, new ideas almost daily in order to provide fleeting thrills for people who were not worthy of an artist's talents.

Billy shook his head as he studied her self-portrait. 'She's been feeling very depressed just lately. She could do something drastic.'

Matthew grimaced, dropping the pad casually onto the plush-covered table. 'In that case, you will have to look after her, for it is none of my business. Charlotte has made it plain that I have no place in her life, and I am now content to have it so.'

'You never wanted to marry into our family. We're not good enough for you.'

'That's not true. I admit that at first the idea of being related to your father was a little daunting, but I have long since changed my mind.'

'Well, you can just change it back again. It was my Molly's twin brothers who burgled those houses.'

'Charlotte's clients?'

'Yes, and I've sent the whole blooming family to Australia.'

Matthew rubbed his chin, taking in this information. 'I presume Charlotte knows this.'

'I told her today. She said she didn't want to hear any more about it.'

'How very typical of her. Please believe that your news does not change my attitude towards you and Molly at all. You know, I was never comfortable in the company I used to keep. You may find that hard to believe, but it is true. My values have changed. I am extremely proud of my association with Tokyo Nursery Company, and wake up each morning amazed to find myself gainfully employed. To win the respect of a man like Tom Rochford is now my goal. Of course,' he added sarcastically, 'I could never hope to earn the sort of money that seems to come easily to every member of the Tavern family. The three of you have a gift that I find more mysterious than the gift that made Rembrandt great.'

Billy grinned at the compliment and slapped the older man on the shoulder. 'For God's sake, marry Charlotte.'

'I cannot. She has rebuffed me in the most brutal manner. Your sister is incapable of deep feeling and—'

'That's not true!'

'Oh, but it is. I think the blame rests with her mother.'

Billy clawed his hair, very agitated. 'You're quite clever, aren't you? You really see how people's minds work.'

Matthew shrugged. 'It's a dark gift, I assure you: my only talent. There's no fortune to be made from it. As for Charlotte, if she continues to run from close involvement with other people, she will end her days as a very lonely woman.'

'You may be right. When I told her about the O'Rourkes, she didn't say a thing. I wanted to tell her how it happened, but she's got a way of not thinking about unpleasant things. I just hope she doesn't hate Molly for ever.'

'Explain it to me. I promise you I will listen carefully. I'm afraid Charlotte has developed a way of dealing with worrying problems. She simply denies that they exist. She gets on with living which, in its way, is very commendable. Now, tell me how your sweet wife came to aid her brothers in burglary.'

'You see, she used to go home and brag about everything she saw in the posh houses she visited. Those two young scalliwags was into the first house she told them about within forty-eight hours. When Molly found out, she was demented! Then, she saw that the money was making life a little easier for her mother. Well, she has had a terrible time. So Molly took to telling the boys exactly where they could find a few choice items. You see, she thought they're rich folks, they won't mind what they lose, and they're probably insured. She never realized it might harm Charlotte. Why, she thinks the world of my half-sister.'

'I do understand, Billy. Thank God you have managed to get them abroad.'

'Now,' said Billy sadly, 'aren't you glad Charlotte wouldn't have you? We are a bad lot. Your type wouldn't want to be tied to us.'

Matthew shook his head emphatically. 'I have been lucky to escape from marriage to a cold woman. Molly's actions have nothing to do with it. Enough. I will not discuss this further.'

Florence and Jacko walked to the stables in silence. The swish of her white duck skirt against her petticoats had an angry rasp. Jacko felt like a schoolboy caught in the act of stealing an apple.

'You there,' said Florence to the crock boy whose misfortune it was to be in the stable courtyard. 'Harness the horse to the fly. We have an appointment.'

'Florence, you can't order the staff around and I can't leave the premises.'

'Of course you can. Give the boy a hand. The weather is threatening and the fly has no protection. We must be going. Where is this nursery?'

'A couple of miles east and north, close to Rochford's nurseries, but I can't leave Capel Manor in the middle of the day—'

'Why can't you find something nearer to Capel Manor?'

'There's nothing for sale closer, that's why. There's lots of glass out that way.'

'Oh, Jacko, don't vex me. Get into the fly. There's no time to lose.'

He shrugged his shoulders apologetically to the boy as he climbed into Mr Warrender's two-wheeled carriage. Ominously for their future life together, Florence took the reins. Jacko wondered if he would ever again be allowed to drive a vehicle or control the direction of his life.

'I want you to know I will never forgive you, Jacko,' she said, passing through the gateway with an inch to spare on the left side. 'Don't try to deceive me. You were going to take the money and run away, probably without a word of apology.'

'If you can't forgive me, then we'd best part now.

You won't want to marry a man what was prepared to be bought off.'

'*Who* was prepared to be bought off, not *what* was,' corrected Florence. 'You're going to have to mind your language. I don't intend to spend my life apologizing for your ignorance, and especially not when we are rich and entertain people like the Rochfords and Mr Bowles.'

'Florence,' he moaned. 'Be reasonable. I ain't . . . I mean I'm not never going to be rich like them . . . those men.'

'Why did you even think of abandoning me? Tell me the reason. I must know.'

'They was both so determined, Mr Warrender and Mr Douse. You're under age, you know. Your old . . . your father said as how I wasn't good enough for you, and it's true, I'm not. I love you as I've never loved another woman, so help me God. I want to marry you, although I couldn't tell you why, to save my life. But they convinced me they knew what was best for you.'

'They don't. I'll ignore Matthew Warrender's involvement in my betrayal, but I shall never forgive my father. He's going to pay handsomely for his interference.'

'He already has. Admit it, my dear. A hundred and fifty pounds is a handsome wedding present.'

'It will do for a start, but he needn't think he can get off so lightly.'

Jacko could think of nothing to say. He did love his Florence, and excitement was building in him as he thought about the decaying nursery they were about to visit. He used to think he was a good gardener, and thought he knew the extent of his talents, but things had not been going right lately. The failure with the orchids had shaken his confidence. In spite of everything, he thought he could make the sweet pea nursery pay, and how could he have possibly started up in the nursery trade without the use of someone's money? True, Mr Douse had been prepared to give him the money for *not* marrying Florence, but Jacko was shrewd enough to know that his sweet-looking little love would be a tremendous asset.

'There's the drive ahead on the left. Slow down, for God's sake, woman!' said Jacko and lunged for the reins. There was a short tussle which he won and they drove onto the property in some style, his dented masculine pride almost restored.

'Is this it?' cried Florence, looking around in dismay. The house was of red brick and had a yellow painted door. There were several roof tiles missing, and cardboard had replaced three window-panes. The glasshouse looked sound enough, but weeds grew everywhere and the deep brown wooden barn sagged several degrees to the east. 'Is that the house I am supposed to set up home in? The land is so low-lying, I imagine it floods every winter.'

He helped her down. The elderly couple who had been struggling to make a success of the nursery had seen the fly from their window and now came out of their front door as quickly as their old legs would take them.

The negotiations were short and brutal, conducted entirely by Florence. She was once again the innocent young daughter of a well-to-do man, the sort of young woman who obeyed her future husband's every command.

'Charming,' she said of the house when shown round. 'But my affianced husband, Mr Boon, is head gardener of a large estate in Hertfordshire. We will have to spend a great deal of money to bring this property up to a decent standard. I am accustomed to the best of everything. Mr Boon, therefore, and my father who is a partner in this venture, will not go above ninety pounds.'

Mr and Mrs Watson protested with great vigour that their frailty obliged them to leave the land in order to live with their daughter in Chelmsford, but that the nursery was well worth the asking price. When Florence, with a great show of having lost the argument, raised her offer to a hundred and ten pounds, they leapt at the opportunity to sell at a price forty pounds below the value they had set on their property.

Jacko had no sympathy for them. The poor were his own sort and he judged them harshly for having failed to thrive, assuming stupidity and laziness. The two couples had just agreed to complete all formalities with the greatest speed when the wind rose suddenly, black clouds raced across the sky and dumped gallons of water on their heads.

'Hurry, into the house!' cried Florence. 'You two men must see to the horse!'

Mr Watson went immediately to the horse and began to lead it into the barn, but Jacko made no move, staring at Florence as the wind and rain buffeted him. 'No more, Florence. I am a free man and I intend to stay that way. I'll not let any woman lead me by the nose.'

'You must both come inside!' cried Mrs Watson and turned towards the house to follow her own advice.

Florence ignored her as she met Jacko's eyes. 'I love you, Jacko. You can't blame me for being hurt by your treachery. I've fought to give you what you want. You are an ambitious man and I admire that, but I must be able to rely on your steadfastness.'

'Do you want to help me work this nursery? Can you do what's needed? It's a hard life. Your hands will be dirty and your back will ache. Can you do it, Florence?'

'I should have thought you could see by the way I work for Charlotte that I am not afraid of hard work. Or perhaps you think being assistant to a floral decorator is easy.'

Mr Watson returned from the barn. 'Mr Boon, we must all go inside. This is a real storm. Your lady's gown will be ruined.'

'Well?' said Jacko.

Florence smiled suddenly, a radiant smile that told Jacko more than words could express. He stepped towards her and, mindful of Mr Watson's presence, limited himself to caressing her cheek. 'Best get inside, my love. It's going to be some time before I can afford to buy you another dress.'

Charlotte didn't lie on the bed long, being too restless to remain in one place for more than a minute. She was pacing the floor when hailstones as big as marbles began to fall. *Matthew's fuchsias!* All the pots had been brought outside several days ago and were shaded from the blistering sun.

Hailstones rattled against the window-panes as she reached the dressing table to tidy her hair. Down below, she saw Dangler Stritch in what used to be the kitchen garden. The new garden was taking shape under his guidance: brick pillars were going up to support the cross beams of the pergolas. The hailstones had three men and a boy dashing about to protect their hard work.

She rooted in the wardrobe for an old pair of shoes, put them on with nervous fingers and dashed from the room, shouting for Billy to lend a hand. There was no answering shout, but Matthew's jacket and waistcoat had been laid across a chair in the hall. She ran through the house and out of the back door, seeing Billy with Matthew about to disappear from view. They were headed towards the northern-most corner of the property, where the fuchsia house would be enduring a pounding from the hail.

Dangler had hoped to finish laying the bricks on the sixth pillar of the pergola before the rains came, but he had misjudged the weather badly. No-one could have predicted that the ground would be white with hailstones within seconds.

'Get some tarpaulin over this damp cement!' he called to Squabby Horn and Bertie Cox. 'You there, Nat, start moving the chrysanths into the house. No! Never mind! Stay with your dad. I'll do it. The hailstones may start breaking glass.'

He had been working in his shirtsleeves and saw his

jacket hanging on the handle of a garden fork. Snatching it up on his way, he ran to the long house which rested against the back wall. Before he could reach the first heavy pot of yellow chrysanthemums, the hail stopped, only to be followed by sheets of rain. The potted flowers were taking a terrible beating, as would be those planted in the pleasure grounds. There was a bed of bright red dahlias he particularly liked, but nothing could be done to save them.

Nat Horn, who was not quite eleven years old, immediately ran to help his father to cover the board where a heap of wet cement was rapidly turning to soup.

'Jacko's gone out somewhere with Miss Douse!' shouted Bertie Cox. 'We'll have to manage without him.'

We have done all summer, thought Dangler. There was the wicker garden furniture to move. He had brought it out onto the cool north lawn behind the house less than an hour ago. The cushions had turned to sodden lumps of wet feathers by the time he reached them. Snatching up a dozen in his arms, he ran towards the kitchen door, where Rachel was waiting to relieve him of the weight.

Returning to the walled garden, he ran his eye over the houses looking for broken glass, while pausing to catch his breath. No broken panes. But the wall fruit was taking a pounding. Some of it could be picked immediately and put into the dark fruit house to ripen. Working carefully but with great speed, he began to relieve the gnarled branches of their burden, scooping up fallen fruit from the mud below and placing each piece on a sieve that chanced to have been left close by.

Nobbie, the crock boy, ran to assist him, so he handed over the task to the youth. 'Squabby, we'd best run down to the new vegetable garden. It ain't got no protection from the elements and it'll be washed away in another half an hour.' Squabby, busy moving pots to the safety of the glasshouse, nodded his head, and the two

373

men left the walled garden and made their way through the formal grounds, past drooping calceolarias, broken spikes of canna, and geranium blooms lying forlornly on the ground.

Dangler had no breath to speak, nor would he have put his thoughts at this moment into words, but resentment was building within him. He loved this garden, had taken over from the fuchsia-absorbed John Green, had covered up the laziness of the love-stricken Jacko, had planned the later bedding schemes and had supervised the rebuilding of both the walled garden and the new vegetable garden. For the past two months, he had crawled into bed each night at nine o'clock, intending to read the weekly editions of *The Gardener's Chronicle* to keep up with all the latest techniques. And every night for the past two months, he had fallen asleep before half past nine. He was damned if he was going to continue to do the work of three men while still living in the discomfort of the bothy. John Green could not expect to continue to be head gardener as well as managing the fuchsia nursery, and that meant he would have to vacate the lodge. Dangler reckoned he deserved the superior accommodation and the larger salary that went with responsibility for the grounds. Mr Warrender could build a new house on the grounds for Mr and Mrs Green, if he was of a mind to.

'Oh, my God!' said Squabby when they reached the newly ploughed, partially planted kitchen garden. It had taken the ploughman four hours to turn over half an acre into six miles of neat seven-by-three inch furrows, and the men had spent a full week breaking down the clods and digging in sufficient horse manure to enrich the light soil. Dangler had drawn up a plan, discovered that no-one was prepared to comment on his scheme, and had gone ahead to lay out the kitchen garden as he saw fit. The paths had been marked out and consolidated, but there was too much work to be done on a thirty acre estate for rapid progress in the kitchen garden.

He and Squabby arrived at the site to find the manure heap, which yesterday had been pungently steaming, today turned to a murky slurry, the goodness being washed onto the paths. A good vegetable garden provided a succession of vegetables for the table, which was why the removal of the kitchen garden to another site in the middle of the summer was such a headache. Now was the time to sow certain crops for autumn, winter and spring. They had sown 'Early Horn' carrots for the spring, now washed away. American cress was well under way, until the rains carried the tiny seedlings on to the path. Cauliflowers, that staple of the kitchen, were planted on the twentieth, only to be washed away on the twenty-sixth. And the cos lettuces! 'Green Paris' and 'Hammersmith Hardy Green Cabbage', now gone. Dangler felt tears of frustration prick his eyes. Wasted. Good work, aching backs, attention to the details of the best gardening habits, all for nothing.

'I think some of the cold frames are damaged,' said Squabby. 'Do you want me to save what I can?'

'I don't think we need bother. I've a feeling this rain isn't going to let up in the next hour or two. This is no short violent storm. We're in for a deluge. We'll be lucky not to have the entire garden washed away. Let's go over to the fuchsia house and see if we can help Mr Green.'

Charlotte's high-necked white blouse was pasted to her skin by the time she reached the fuchsia house, and her skirt and petticoats were a damp tangle, the bottom twelve inches soaking wet. Matthew and Billy were attempting to manhandle the last of the fuchsia pyramids onto a small two-wheeled trolley of the sort her father had used in the market. She couldn't imagine how many pounds such enormous plants weighed.

There were still hundreds of pots of fuchsias standing outside on cinder staging, protected by muslin canopies which were now sagging with water. For the past week, the weather had been well into the eighties, too hot for the plants, even though the house had been heavily shaded and all the ventilators opened.

Without a word to anyone, she fell in beside the men and, taking a pot in each hand, walked into the house. Each one was snatched from her hands by John Green, who seemed on the point of bursting into tears. He muttered under his breath, placing the pots in an order known only to himself and crooning to the plants as if they were human.

'My poor babies! I've got a thousand plants and most of them is outside. I wanted to give them a little fresh air. I couldn't plant them all and I've been taking cuttings all summer. Oh, they're all going to be ruined!'

They were joined after about twenty minutes by Squabby Horn and Dangler Stritch. The two healthy men urged Charlotte to rest, and she had no choice but to obey. Her breath was coming in rasping gasps and her back ached each time she attempted to bend for another pot.

'Go back to the house, Charlotte,' said Matthew, coming into the steaming glasshouse. 'There is no point in your continuing to help when we five men can finish the task in a few more minutes.'

'I want to talk to you,' she said.

'Later, when you have had a chance to change your clothes.'

'Now.'

He sighed. 'I must help to get the plants indoors. This fuchsia nursery is my commercial enterprise. I admit that I won't be able to charge a thousand pounds for one commission. Nevertheless, the project is important to me.'

'Now,' she repeated, glaring at him.

Matthew ran his hands through his hair, slicking back the wet locks so that they no longer dripped rainwater into his eyes. It was a futile gesture. 'Very well, let's go.'

The rain was falling as powerfully as it had in the beginning, stinging their faces, standing in puddles on the grass so that they churned up the lawn with each step they took. Charlotte was too breathless to speak, but with a touch on his arm, she led the way to the shelter of the grotto. No grass grew within its depths, but the rain had entered in torrents, turning the ground into a quagmire. The heels of her shoes sank in immediately, making it hard for her to walk or even stand with dignity.

'I want to marry you,' she said harshly. 'But I also want to continue arranging flowers. I don't care what you think my position at Capel should be, I intend to continue with my work, just as I intend to marry you.'

'Wait until you are asked,' he said, with equal roughness.

'No. You have had your turn. Now, it is my turn to ask. I will not run away from my heart any longer. I want to talk. I intend to argue with you until I make you see that my work is important to me. You must understand that, much as I love my work, I love you more. Will you marry me?'

'You are very demanding, madam. Have you been taking lessons from Florence Douse?'

'I have. She fights for what she wants.'

'The man isn't worth it.'

'No,' she admitted, 'I don't believe he is, but you are worth fighting for. Will you marry me on my terms?'

'May I speak?'

'You may say "yes" or "no".'

'It's more complicated than that.'

She gasped, clutching her stomach. 'Are you refusing me?'

'I have been asked by Tokyo Nursery to travel to the Far East. They want me to leave in the middle of September. The sea journey takes twenty-nine days to Hong Kong, but I will naturally wish to spend several months on the Islands and also in mainland China and Japan. I expect to be away for six months.'

She sensed that he was challenging her to give in, to say that she would abandon her business and travel with him, if he would just marry her. His expression was expectant, although he had folded his arms across his chest in a forbidding manner.

'An exciting journey,' she whispered.

'Not for me. I have been there before.'

'But you will return one day.'

'Probably.'

She might swallow her pride and beg to go with him, but he was quite likely to rebuff her. So much for his undying love. There was no future for them together. How could she exchange the certainty of a successful and satisfying business and the independence that a handsome income gave to a woman, for the precarious position of a man's chattel?

'I see,' she said finally. 'Then I must wish you *bon voyage*. You may be home just in time to reclaim Capel Manor.'

'If I should be . . . delayed, please feel free to live here until I return.'

There was nothing more to say. A gentle breeze, funnelled through the grotto's narrow passageway, struck her wet clothing with force and made her shiver. Not wishing to touch him, not even to shake hands, she nodded solemnly and left the grotto. The rain was falling as forcefully as before, but now that she was thoroughly chilled, she could not endure it. Breaking into a run, she made it back to the house and the sanctuary of her bedroom in five minutes.

Chapter Twenty-One

The next day, being Tuesday, found Charlotte back at
Covent Garden. Several new commissions had arrived on
her desk within the past twenty-four hours. Molly, looking haggard, said she had booked an appointment for half
past two for Charlotte to visit Countess Framlingham.
There was to be a twenty-first birthday party for a
hundred guests in Park Lane.

The rain, which had not let up since the previous
afternoon, spread itself across the window-panes in a
solid sheet and surged under the front door to create a
dangerous puddle on the shop floor. The market, now
in its closing stages, was awash, the drains blocked by
cabbage leaves and flower stalks. Wretched stall holders
were gathering their wares, preparing to leave, looking
like saturated rats.

The doorbell clanged and Molly pushed herself away
from the workbench, but Billy came into the work-room
before she had taken two paces.

'Oh, you're soaked,' she said, as he took off his
cap.

'Never mind that. There's trouble. It's Dad.'

'What's wrong?' asked Charlotte. 'Is he ill?'

'Nicked.'

'My God. Goldseekers!'

'No.' He wiped his face with a handkerchief. 'It's all
my fault. The police came this morning and searched the
shop. They found the tiara and arrested him for receiving
stolen goods.'

'But you said the tiara was paste,' cried Charlotte. 'Why is it so important?'

'The police say only some of the stones were paste. I went round to see Grimsdyke, but the old geezer was dead. He lied to me. He could have taken it off my hands and then there wouldn't be all this trouble.'

'Mr Tavern will need a lawyer,' said Molly calmly. 'What about Mr Douse?'

'Him? I telephoned him. He doesn't want to get involved, says he was in trouble with the law some years back and they will remember him. A fine friend he turned out to be. Then I tried Arthur Brock, but he—'

Molly reached for her umbrella. 'We must get Mr Warrender. There's no-one else.'

Charlotte closed her eyes for a moment, remembering the important appointment with Lady Framlingham. She wished Billy had never accepted the tiara, and was annoyed that Vic had not shown some foresight in disposing of the stolen property. Yet she knew that on this occasion she could not turn away and think about something else. In fact, to her surprise, she resented the suggestion that Billy should turn to Matthew for help.

'You will not send for Matthew. I will go down to the police station and see what I can do.'

'You!' scoffed Billy.

'There's no need for that, Charlotte,' added Molly. 'You don't want to be going to police stations. You're not used to it. I've had more experience.'

'He's my father.'

Billy clapped his hands. 'How nice of you to remember! Nevertheless, I will send a message to Matthew.' He turned to Molly. 'Don't cry, old dear. I'll just have to tell them it was me what bought the tiara. Dad will look after you while I'm inside. Try to be brave.'

Not unnaturally, these words failed entirely to console his bride. Charlotte, a straw hat perched at an angle on her hair, removed her apron and shrugged into her mackintosh. 'Molly, you are not going anywhere. You look worn out. Letitia, telephone Lady Framlingham and make some excuse. I will visit her tomorrow, if possible. If she wishes to cancel, that is just too bad.'

The police station was not far away, and was crowded with half a dozen very wet men, women and children, all of whom were complaining loudly. When Billy and Charlotte were able to struggle through the crowd and enquire after Vic, they were told he was being questioned in a room down the corridor. Before anyone could prevent her, Charlotte ran towards the interview rooms with Billy right behind her.

'Papa!' she called. 'It's your daughter, Charlotte. Where are you?'

Several doors opened. Voices were raised, but Vic's shouted instructions – to go home where she belonged – helped her to locate him.

'Go home, miss,' said a large detective. 'This is no place for a young lady like you.'

'Papa,' she repeated and hurried to Vic's side. He had been seated, but stood up in time to receive her in his arms.

'Get out of here,' he whispered. 'First time you've ever admitted in public that I'm your father, and it has to be in the nick.'

'Oh, sir,' she said to the sceptical detective. 'How awful that my father should be here in this shameful place, just because he bought a paste tiara for my coming wedding.'

Vic squeezed his daughter tightly, as if by so doing he could shut her up. 'Get Matthew,' he murmured over her shoulder to his son. 'I need a shyster.'

Unnoticed by Charlotte, Billy left the room. She clung to her father, while turning so that she could rest soulful eyes on the detective. For his part, the detective was looking rather bored, probably because such scenes had been played out for his benefit on many occasions.

'Does my father have a criminal record, sir?'

'I've no idea, miss. We're looking into that. He's well known to the bobbies.'

'Yes, but all pawnbrokers are well known to the police. It is an occupation fraught with danger.'

'Fraught?' muttered Vic.

'Dishonest people will attempt to sell their stolen goods to pawnbrokers, who must be vigilant at all times. The tiara was clearly paste, but my dear father thought it would look attractive with my bridal gown.'

The detective picked his teeth. 'How much did you pay for it, Tavern?'

'A fiver, Mr Connolly. I swear it.'

Charlotte buried her face in Vic's jacket, lest the detective see by her expression that this was a lie of breath-taking audacity. Then she had a cunning thought and lifted her head to engage the eyes of the law.

'Isn't it true that dishonest pawnbrokers make every effort to pass on the stolen goods they have bought as quickly as possible? Why would my father have kept this piece if he thought it was illegally come by?'

'A matter worth considering, miss, but I have to tell you that I meet rank stupidity every working day of my life. I've seen amazing mistakes made by the most experienced villains. So, while you may have a point, it doesn't mean that your father is innocent of the charge. He should have recognized immediately that the man who sold the tiara would not normally have such a thing in his possession.'

'Well, sir,' said Vic. 'I can tell you that the most amazing people come to me for a few quid when the chips are down. Toffs don't want to go to any of the posh brokers up the West End, for fear of being recognized by someone. Of having their possessions put in the window to be seen by friends or family. No, no. There was nothing naughty about this transaction.'

The detective, faced with passionate denials of wrongdoing from a well-dressed man and his pretty, plainly respectable daughter, was beginning to feel unsure of his ground. He said he would have two cups of tea sent in to them, then left the room to consult with others.

'I didn't expect to see you here,' said Vic, sitting down opposite her at the table.

'I never thought I would be in such a place. Vic, you are my father and I couldn't turn away. I just couldn't.'

'You've done well, but Billy's gone for Matthew. This is men's business. Go back to the shop. I don't like to see you here.'

She thought of Lady Framlingham. It would still be possible to keep the appointment. She hated this place. The ghosts of villains and victims seemed to live in the fabric of the walls. The interview room smelled of grief. 'I'm not going anywhere. You wouldn't go away and leave *me* here, would you?'

The door opened and Matthew entered, closely followed by a middle-aged man wearing a top hat, frock coat and spats. His neatly rolled umbrella dripped gently onto the old wooden floor. Before anyone could speak, the detective and Billy crowded into the room.

'Mr Warrender, is this young lady your affianced?' asked the detective, attempting to watch everyone's face at once. He strongly suspected that he was being manipulated, but the absolute composure of Matthew and the lawyer intimidated him.

Matthew sucked in his breath, but smiled almost immediately. 'Yes, Miss Blair, that is, Miss Tavern, is to be my wife.'

Charlotte's eyes, pleading for understanding, met his and held. How good it was to see him! 'My dear, please tell the detective that my father bought this paste tiara as a present for me, to be worn on our wedding day. And tell him that dear Papa paid only five pounds for it.'

Matthew licked his lips, a man unaccustomed to lying to authority, as he struggled to find an acceptable form of words. 'I clearly understood that my . . . my future father-in-law is an expert at valuing such items and that he believed it to be paste. I understand that there are a few real gems in it, but they could easily have been missed.'

'What of the insurance?' said the lawyer, whom no-one had bothered to introduce. 'I, myself, am suspicious of this tiara. It is my suggestion that the legitimate owners sold several, indeed most, of the diamonds and replaced them with paste, meanwhile claiming the full amount from the insurance company when it was reportedly stolen. Is that correct?'

'Well, it seems—' began Mr Connolly.

'—and what better way to carry out this despicable fraud than by selling it to an unsuspecting pawnbroker far away from the owner's home? It never ceases to amaze me what so-called respectable people will get up to. Nor, I might add, what trouble these bounders cause the ordinary decent working man and woman.'

Within five minutes, the entire party was on its way back to King Street. The evidence was conflicting. The police had more urgent business, and Vic was on the best of terms with the constables on his patch.

The solicitor, Mr Fotherington-Ferman, declined a warm invitation to join his clients for lunch, warned Matthew that he reckoned he had fully repaid any debt he might have owed to the late Mr Gryce, and departed. Everyone else crowded into Charlotte's work-room, where they were joined within a few minutes by Popple Douse and Arthur Brock, both with elaborate reasons for having failed to visit the police station.

'Ah, ha!' Vic greeted the two men triumphantly. 'You see before you a happy man. Not only my son, but also my daughter and her future husband came to my rescue.'

'Vic,' said Charlotte, avoiding Matthew's steady gaze. 'There is something I must explain. You see, I thought that—'

'You must be very proud,' said Matthew, ignoring

her. 'Charlotte clearly played a vital part in your release. There was no need for Billy or me or my pompous friend to assist you.'

'She's a Tavern, all right,' said Vic. 'What her mother would have thought, I dare not consider.'

'Vic, I must explain why I—'

'What Charlotte wishes to explain to you is that we will be leaving you for a few months.' Matthew was leaning against the wall and had not taken his eyes from Charlotte for several minutes. 'In September, we will be travelling to the Far East, and expect to be away for six months.'

'Splendid! You may be sure that Billy will manage the business very successfully. He would have made a Gawd-awful mess of running a pawnshop, but he's just the ticket for a florist's. When Molly's dropped the babe, she can design the arrangements.'

'Just a minute!' said Charlotte, but no-one was listening.

'Our departure will have to wait until after the affair at Theobalds Park,' continued Matthew, 'but then I'm sure the staff can manage for a short time. When we return, Charlotte will once again be in charge of the designs. Meanwhile, she needs a period of rest to refresh her creative imagination and give herself a chance to gain inspiration from other cultures. She will be an even greater success when she returns, I'm sure.'

'I wish someone would consult me. After all, I am the one—'

'In addition,' said Matthew above the laughter, 'I intend to see to it that she hones her talent for drawing. I will teach her all I know about painting with water colours. I know the techniques. The talent is entirely her own.'

It was all becoming too much to bear. She longed for solitude, for a chance to think things through. Also, she wondered if Lady Framlingham had agreed to see her the next day; but she was given no time to think. Billy crossed the room to lift her in a bear hug and wish her well.

There was a clamour of voices, kisses, pats on the back and a great deal of broad humour. During it all, Matthew, smiling wryly, remained with his shoulders against the wall.

For a moment or two, she was dismayed by the public celebration, then like one who jumps into a cold sea, the shock wore off, leaving her feeling both warm and elated. She approached Matthew, took his face in her hands and kissed him on the lips.

A roar went up and Matthew's face coloured slightly, then he wrapped his arms around her. 'My Charlotte!' he said, laughing. 'My own dear, loving, warm-hearted bride.'

The winter curtains had been hung at Theobalds Park, the muslin ones washed and put away until the following summer. Yet, on this Saturday, the seventeenth of September, the sun shone brightly and the thermometer was steadily rising. Temperatures in the low seventies were predicted. The rains, which had brought sudden devastation to all the gardens in the neighbourhood, had flooded Norfolk, where seven inches fell in twelve hours. The gardeners of Theobalds had worked steadily to repair the lawns, dig up and replace all damaged bedding plants and bring all the miles of paths to such a pitch of excellence, that they wouldn't allow members of the Meux family to walk on them until this great day.

It was three o'clock, and the first of the afternoon guests were arriving to mingle with the sixty who had been privileged to take luncheon with the Admiral and Lady Meux in the great dining-room.

Matthew had returned only that morning from a week at Tatton Park in Cheshire, overseeing the refurbishment of the Japanese garden. Since he was a good friend of the Meux family, he and his wife had been invited to take luncheon in the room which Charlotte had so recently spent an hour decorating. They dined at the second table, the one laid with solid silver rather than the one set with gold plate, but they had for company Lady Smythe and Arthur Brock. The Navy was well represented at the top table, the officers looking splendid, and very impressed by the décor.

Charlotte and her staff had made a dozen floral galleons which sailed down the cloth, with smaller ones for the second table. The main table also held a rectangular fish tank with dozens of beautiful tropical fish swimming in it. The menus were pink bivalve shells opening just enough to contain the menu card. Seaweed decorated the cloths. It smelled a little fishy, but aroused much favourable comment. A huge basket of imported pink roses filled the bay, and above it hung a moss ball into which her staff had stuck four hundred pink carnations. It was customary at large affairs to crisscross the room with garlands of greenery. Charlotte had used a variation: delicate loops all along the walls at picture-rail height, consisting entirely of pink roses.

The curious hexagonal room, lit by a lantern skylight, turned out to be a gun-room. It was open to the guests, so Charlotte hung thirty feet of imitation wisteria, made in Yokohama, Japan, around the high ceiling, where it looked both spectacular and real.

The entrance hall had a magnificent painted ceiling, a design in turquoise and terracotta that was vaguely Egyptian. Charlotte filled the niches with large vases of flowers, and the curving staircase carried a sumptuous garland. The hall was turned into a winter garden, with almost a hundred palms of every variety placed in groups. Guests who were feeling particularly giddy with delight could sit down on the piles of bright cushions placed under the fronds.

The Queen Anne bedroom at the top of the stairs had been set aside for the use of the ladies, and here Charlotte let her imagination run riot. The most outstanding feature of the decorations, and the one which caused Lady Smythe to gasp in admiration, was a 'beaded' curtain between the bedroom and the adjoining dressing-room made entirely of stephanotis blooms threaded on to long cords. Each time it was touched, a rich scent filled the room. Posies of dried flowers, supplied by Parents of Regent Street, were a longer lasting reminder of this great day.

The lounge, which had been turned into a sweet-smelling bower, was directly behind the entrance hall; guests had to walk its length in order to descend the few steps to the east lawn. To direct them through the room, Charlotte had arranged ropes of myrtle threaded through wooden posts.

As they strolled across the lawn towards the great marquee, Charlotte looked at her husband and smiled. 'I do hope you like the way I have decorated the marquee. It's been done especially for you.'

'Of course I will like the way you have arranged the flowers! How disgraceful that I had to leave my bride for an entire week, so soon after our marriage. However, I think I might well have been neglected in recent days.'

She shook her head. 'I would have put you to work.'

Their wedding, intended to be a quiet affair in a Covent Garden register office, had not been without incident. Matthew discovered that he had a Gryce cousin. Or rather, the cousin discovered Matthew and so had to be invited.

Neither the bride nor the groom had been accustomed in recent years to considering the wishes of their families, so they were stung when the cousin objected to Matthew's choice of a bride, while Billy objected to Charlotte's choice of Florence as a witness, who was invited to sign the register. Molly was the sister-in-law, he said. She could write her name perfectly well, so why had she not been asked to put her signature in the great book? Vic said Billy should also have been asked to sign. Who the hell was Buffy Morrison, for God's sake?

Vowing never to be critical of relatives, themselves, Charlotte and Matthew broke this vow almost immediately when Molly sobbed loudly throughout the ceremony, because her family had emigrated to Australia, and Vic, drunk even before the wedding, explained the interesting details of Charlotte's parentage to Buffy. On the whole, however, Mr and Mrs Matthew Warrender had decided that they were quite pleased to have families to whom they could turn in times of trouble.

Charlotte saw Florence and Jacko Boon walking across the lawn. Florence looked magnificent, wearing her favourite white lawn gown and large straw bonnet. She seemed the perfect lady of leisure, but she had been at work since before dawn, helping Charlotte and the rest of the staff to put up the decorations, and incidentally earning herself a much appreciated ten shilling note.

'Oh, Mrs Warrender, everything looks beautiful,' said Jacko, who could not yet bring himself to address his wife's best friend by her first name. 'Florence has been showing me her contribution. Perhaps next year you will consider using our sweet peas for some of your clients.'

'Most definitely,' laughed Charlotte. 'The King loves sweet peas, so I predict they will become a very popular flower.'

After the two couples had exchanged greetings, Matthew excused himself and hurried over to the sunken Italian garden where he had seen Arthur Brock, Popple Douse and Vic in solemn conversation.

'Vic, I should not have handed you that cablegram today of all days. Like you, I am deeply disappointed that gold was not found in Australia, after all. You will have to write to the investors, Douse, and tell them the scheme has failed. How fortunate that you didn't tell them a few months ago that there was any chance of mining a fortune.'

'Don't you worry about that, Matthew,' replied Vic

magnanimously. 'You and Charlotte will be off to-morrow and must not worry about anything. Billy has the business well in hand, and I will keep an eye on the fuchsia nursery, although you will be back in this country before the first orders arrive. We're not too disappointed, are we, men?'

'Not at all,' said Douse.

'Never counted on it,' added Brock.

The three men watched Matthew as he walked back to Charlotte, now chatting to Billy and Molly. Silently, Popple offered round his cigar case. Silently, they lit up and puffed with great concentration for a few seconds.

'Billy is going to cost me a fortune,' said Vic. 'I have to invest in C. A. Blair now that both my children are involved in it. And I'm building Billy and Molly a house in Enfield town. Billy's got to live as grand as Charlotte, or almost. I will not play favourites.'

Arthur Brock tapped cigar ash onto the lawn. 'My expenses are rising daily. Lady Smythe don't care to exchange a title for plain Mrs Brock, and I can't say I blame her. But I must maintain a position these days. Russell Square is not a good address, she tells me. She would like me to move closer to her.'

Popple nodding knowingly. 'Florence has never forgiven me for trying to buy off Jacko. She's costing me a fortune. Improvements in the house. An extra span of glass. A couple of labourers. She's determined to be as successful as the Rochfords, would you believe?'

'I'm delighted that the gold field turned out to be a dream,' said Vic. 'There's no skill in making money from the sweat of some strange man's brow half a world away. Now that my son-in-law is going to be in the Far East for six months, we can carry on where we left off.'

Popple agreed. 'I will write to the investors, telling them that our project has failed and Goldseekers has gone into liquidation. We will offer them shares in our new venture in exchange for a further investment. How fortunate that I ignored instructions, and told each of them they were on the point of finding gold. They should all be eager to try again.'

'A new business scheme would suit me very well,' said Brock.

'We are business men,' added Popple. 'We know how to make money and, if I may say so, we can do it very much better without Matthew Warrender's squeamishness curbing our activities.'

Vic chuckled as he puffed on his cigar. 'I can't wait to take the bastards for a few thousand quid.'

'Shall we go into the marquee?' asked Charlotte when they were once more alone. 'I have been so eager for you to see what I've done. You can admire my work and . . .' She frowned. 'At least, I hope you will admire it.'

'Have a little confidence. Of course, I will admire it. But what can you have done that is so new and daring? I came today only to see the marquee, I assure you. This party is yours, a triumph for you. It doesn't matter that Lady Meux may think she is the hostess.'

At the entrance to the marquee stood a perfectly still footman and a maid. Matthew was completely taken in, but close inspection showed them to be composed almost entirely of chrysanthemum blooms. Imitating a Japanese festival tradition described by Matthew, Charlotte had obtained two department-store mannequins and, leaving their faces and hands untouched and exposed, she had mossed and wired both figures, then clothed them in chrysanthemums of suitable colours to represent powdered hair, a footman's livery and the mob cap and apron of an eighteenth century maid. Thousands of blooms had been used, many of them supplied by the Theobalds gardening staff, who also helped in the construction. Matthew gasped at the sight of them, but there were more shocks to come.

The marquee had been turned into a Temple of the Fuchsia. The ceiling and sides had been draped in mauve, pink and purple silks. A rosy glow fell on the white-clothed tables, which each bore a half standard of 'Capel Bells'.

At the far end of the marquee, fuchsias were banked from ground to ceiling, a dazzling profusion of different leaf colours, as well as different blooms. As the eye adjusted to the dim light, so the bank of fuchsias took on the appearance of a mountain scene. Varieties like Meteor, with foliage of dark red, represented mountains, deeper greens were the valleys, while the meadow in the foreground was apple-green Cloth of Gold. What appeared to be an apple orchard could be glimpsed in the distance, but the 'apple blossoms' were actually the near-white blooms of Countess of Aberdeen.

Nearer at hand was a three-foot-wide stream, actually a lead-lined trough set into the ground, that threaded its way between the tables throughout the entire marquee. Here and there, steep, curved bridges made it possible for guests to reach their tables.

The marquee was filling up rapidly, the guests eager to tell each other how unexpectedly beautiful was this display of fuchsias. Charlotte led Matthew to the table at the front reserved for the Meux family, where they were presently joined by the Admiral and Lady Meux.

The arrival of the hosts was the signal for the lights to go on. First a moon appeared, peeping over a fuchsia mountain, then it rose higher. Hidden lights changed the tableau. A waterfall became visible. Suddenly there was a gasp of delight. A small boat had appeared on the upper right side of the tableau, sailing gently to the left of the display, where it turned to continue its journey downwards to the right. A final turn and it sailed smoothly onto the stream set into the ground. By the time the first boat reached ground level to tour the tables, there were twenty more on their way. Each boat carried sails of 'Capel Bells', as well as real bells which were set tinkling by the movement of the flowing water, and dishes of oil in which wicks burned brightly. Very quickly, the marquee was alight with sailing boats, winking like glow worms, announcing their arrival by a burgeoning chorus of bells. And still they came, a hundred of them afloat before the first was lifted by unseen hands and taken to the top of the tableau to start its downward journey once again. The dazzled guests rose to fill the tent with thunderous applause, and Charlotte blinked back her tears. Matthew had no words to express his feelings, but he squeezed her hand and offered his handkerchief.

'For years to come,' said Lady Meux ruefully, 'this will be known as the day of the Warrender party at Theobalds Park.'

After tea, Charlotte and Matthew left the marquee and headed for the great house, accepting the congratulations of friends and acquaintances on the way. They crossed the lawns in silence. Matthew had exhausted his vocabulary of superlatives. Charlotte was beginning to succumb to a feeling of blissful fatigue.

An honour guard of 'Capel Bells' grown in pots as standard trees marched up each side of the steps to the lounge. As they prepared to re-enter the house by the back door, a soft breeze shook the trees. Showers of pink and mauve blooms swirled to the ground, joining many dozens already fallen. Guest had trampled them under foot like crushed grapes, staining the stairs purple and red. She had never liked fuchsias, believing them to be old-fashioned flowers which held their heads like weeping women. How wrong she had been! They were beautiful, delicate yet vibrant, blooming so lavishly that one could feel drunk just looking upon such a generous display of elegance.

Seeing John Green's proud standards, and suffering from a severe lack of sleep, she suddenly fancied she could hear 'Capel Bells' tolling for her future.

The words of the old nursery rhyme came back to her and she modified them slightly. 'You will live well, say the bells of Ca-pell.'

Matthew laughed. 'You're a much better artist than a poet.' Then he had a go at versifying. 'Arrange every flower you see, but I suggest you leave the rhyming to me.'

THE END

PARSON HARDING'S DAUGHTER
by Caroline Harvey

The Reverend Henry Harding, parson to the excellent living of Stoke Abbas, was a handsome and prepossessing man. Unfortunately fate had seen fit to bless him with a family of extremely plain and unprepossessing children. Caroline was the least offensively plain according to Lady Lennox, but the entire Lennox family also admitted that Caroline was the most insignificant person in the county of Dorset.

Caroline, already twenty-six, was bullied by her elder sister, was nervous in company, and had no prospects at all. She had one golden memory, of an admirer when she was eighteen, but John Gates, nephew of the Lennox family, had gone to India and forgotten her. Or so she thought.

When Lady Lennox summoned her and said that Johnny Gates had sent a proposal of marriage, Caroline at first declined. She suspected that somehow Lady Lennox – for reasons of her own – had contrived and pressured her erstwhile suitor into proposing. But within a few short weeks tragedy had overtaken Caroline. The little contentment and security she had known vanished from her life and left her no option but to accept Lady Lennox's offer.

In the October of 1776, Caroline Harding set sail for India, to a new life, and a man she had not seen for eight years.

Caroline Harvey is the pseudonym of the award-winning writer Joanna Trollope.

0 552 14299 9

MARIANA
by Susanna Kearsley

As soon as Julia Beckett saw Greywethers, a handsome sixteenth-century farmhouse in a small Wiltshire village, she had a strange feeling that she was destined to live in it one day. But when, many years later, it became her home, she found that the house's turbulent past began to intrude upon the present.

While becoming friendly with the residents of the village, including Geoffrey de Mornay, the handsome young squire, Iain, a local farmer, and Vivien, the village pub landlady, Julia found herself being transported back in time as Mariana, who lived at Greywethers during the great plague of 1665. She experienced, as Mariana, all the terrors and hardships of that grim time, and the dangers of the Civil War's aftermath, as well as falling in love with Richard de Mornay, the forebear of the present squire. As her present-day relationships prospered, Julia increasingly felt that her other life as Mariana was threatening to overwhelm her. She found that she had to play out the ancient drama and exorcise the past before she could find love and happiness in the present.

Mariana is the second winner of the Catherine Cookson Prize which was set up in 1992 to celebrate the achievement of Dame Catherine Cookson.

0 552 14262 X

THE SUGAR PAVILION
by Rosalind Laker

1793 – and Sophie Delcourt, the enchanting talented daughter of a Parisian confectioner, finds herself forced to flee from revolutionary France with a four-year-old aristocrat in her charge.

Bereft and abandoned in the Sussex countryside, she is saved by the intriguing Tom Foxhill, art collector to the Prince of Wales, and a man with whom Sophie is to form a passionate bond which even her love for another man cannot sever.

Settling in Regency Brighton, she does not at first realise that threats of vengeance have followed her from France. As she strives to build her own confectionery business – which eventually carries her to the glorious Sugar Pavilion of the Prince Regent himself – her life becomes more exciting, dangerous and challenging than she had ever expected.

0 552 14045 7

THE HUNGRY TIDE
by Valerie Wood

In the slums of Hull, at the turn of the eighteenth century, lived Will and Maria Foster, constantly fighting a war against poverty, disease, and crime. Will was a whaler, wedded to the sea, and when tragedy struck, crippling him for life, it was John Rayner, nephew of the owner of the whaling fleet, who was to rescue the family. Will had saved the boy's life on an arctic voyage and they were offered work and a home on the headlands of Holderness, on the estate owned by the wealthy Rayner family. And there, Will's third child was born – Sarah, a bright and beautiful girl who was to prove the strength of the family.

As John Rayner, heir to the family lands and ships, watched Sarah grow into a serene and lovely woman, he became increasingly aware of his love for her, a love that was hopeless, for the gulf of wealth and social standing between them made marriage impossible.

Against the background of the sea, the wide skies of Holderness, and the frightening crumbling of the land that meant so much to them, their love story was played out to its final climax.

The Hungry Tide is the first winner of the Catherine Cookson Prize which was set up in 1992 to celebrate the achievement of Dame Catherine Cookson.

0 552 14118 6

THE LAND OF NIGHTINGALES
by Sally Stewart

1919 – when Phoebe Maynard – after her mother had died – found the old journal in the attic it reminded her of several things – of her early childhood growing up in Spain, of her father's distress whenever she spoke of that country, and of her mother's long years of fretful ill-health once they had returned to their Oxfordshire manor house. Phoebe, and her sister, Lydia, had never understood why the 'land of nightingales' was such an emotive subject within the family, but when their father died it suddenly became clear. His will revealed that Phoebe and Lydia had a Spanish half-brother – Juan Rodriguez.

It seemed that Juan was as shocked as they were by his foreign connections and was determined to have nothing to do with his English relatives – but the blood-tie was there.

As Phoebe and Lydia finally found a happiness of their own in England, the past constantly intruded on their tranquil lives. It was when young Holly, Phoebe's orphaned niece-by-marriage, came onto the scene that the two worlds met and exploded into an emotional turmoil that was to be made even more violent as Holly and Juan found themselves caught up in the turbulence of the Spanish Civil War.

'A marvellous panoramic book . . . I feel very impressed indeed' *Susan Sallis*

0 552 14296 4

A SELECTED LIST OF FINE NOVELS
AVAILABLE FROM CORGI BOOKS

THE PRICES SHOWN BELOW WERE CORRECT AT THE TIME OF GOING TO PRESS. HOWEVER TRANSWORLD PUBLISHERS RESERVE THE RIGHT TO SHOW NEW RETAIL PRICES ON COVERS WHICH MAY DIFFER FROM THOSE PREVIOUSLY ADVERTISED IN THE TEXT OR ELSEWHERE.

☐ 14036 8	MAGGIE MAY	*Lyn Andrews*	£4.99
☐ 14058 9	MIST OVER THE MERSEY	*Lyn Andrews*	£4.99
☐ 13992 0	LIGHT ME THE MOON	*Angela Arney*	£4.99
☐ 14044 9	STARLIGHT	*Louise Brindley*	£4.99
☐ 13952 1	A DURABLE FIRE	*Brenda Clarke*	£4.99
☐ 13255 1	GARDEN OF LIES	*Eileen Goudge*	£5.99
☐ 13688 3	THE OYSTER CATCHERS	*Iris Gower*	£4.99
☐ 13687 5	HONEY'S FARM	*Iris Gower*	£4.99
☐ 13977 7	SPINNING JENNY	*Ruth Hamilton*	£4.99
☐ 14139 9	THE SEPTEMBER STARLINGS	*Ruth Hamilton*	£4.99
☐ 13872 X	LEGACY OF LOVE	*Caroline Harvey*	£4.99
☐ 14299 9	PARSON HARDING'S DAUGHTER	*Caroline Harvey*	£4.99
☐ 14138 0	PROUD HARVEST	*Janet Haslam*	£4.99
☐ 14262 X	MARIANA	*Susanna Kearsley*	£4.99
☐ 14045 7	THE SUGAR PAVILION	*Rosalind Laker*	£5.99
☐ 13910 6	BLUEBIRDS	*Margaret Mayhew*	£4.99
☐ 13904 1	VOICES OF SUMMER	*Diane Pearson*	£4.99
☐ 10375 6	CSARDAS	*Diane Pearson*	£5.99
☐ 13987 4	ZADRUGA	*Margaret Pemberton*	£4.99
☐ 13636 0	CARA'S LAND	*Elvi Rhodes*	£4.99
☐ 13870 3	THE RAINBOW THROUGH THE RAIN	*Elvi Rhodes*	£4.99
☐ 13934 3	DAUGHTERS OF THE MOON	*Susan Sallis*	£4.99
☐ 14162 3	SWEETER THAN WINE	*Susan Sallis*	£4.99
☐ 14154 2	A FAMILY AFFAIR	*Mary Jane Staples*	£4.99
☐ 14230 1	MISSING PERSON	*Mary Jane Staples*	£4.99
☐ 13746 4	MIXED BLESSINGS	*Danielle Steel*	£4.99
☐ 13526 7	VANISHED	*Danielle Steel*	£4.99
☐ 14296 4	THE LAND OF NIGHTINGALES	*Sally Stewart*	£4.99
☐ 14118 6	THE HUNGRY TIDE	*Valerie Wood*	£4.99
☐ 14263 8	ANNIE	*Valerie Wood*	£4.99